OFFICER INVOLVED

A Kingman & Reed Novel

To Ryan,
Go-kart legend and
my media center
buddy

OFFICER INVOLVED

Bill Zah— (signature)

BILL ZAHREN

Mill City Press, Minneapolis

Mill City Press, Inc.
322 First Avenue N, 5th floor
Minneapolis, MN 55401
612.455.2293
www.millcitypublishing.com

ISBN-13: 978-1-63413-772-0
LCCN: 2015914303

Cover Design by Lois Stanfield
Typeset by Colleen Rollins

Printed in the United States of America

For Rhonda, Jena and Haley ... and the people of Siouxland.

CHAPTER 1

Newspaper reporter Tom Kingman let go of the window sill with his left hand and twisted around. He was looking for a way off the lawn mower that he was standing on that didn't involve breaking one or both ankles. While the goal of the pirouette was graceful stealth, it had the opposite outcome. The mower graduated from wobbling under his weight to rolling as the energy from Tom's body moving off axis caused the laws of physics, gravity and Murphy to send him screaming past the point of no return. In a flash the mower skittered ten feet along the house toward a group of old-school trash cans in front of the detached garage as Tom became airborne.

Three, two, one … impact. The mower crashed into the aluminum trash cans with a bang that was nearly as loud as the gunshot Tom had just witnessed. He landed on his left side and back, the impact whipping his head back against the concrete, implanting a few pebbles in his scalp. "*FUCK*," flashed through Tom's brain, if not across his lips, and then for a second everything went as snowy as a local TV station at 3 a.m.

Blinking away the mental static, Tom rolled gingerly onto his back. "Son-of-a-bitch," Tom coughed, barely aware of the sound of running footsteps crossing the porch.

"Hold it."

Tom arched his neck and saw the hole of a gun barrel three feet above his head. It's amazing how large nine millimeters look when they're drilled into the end of a semiautomatic pistol.

"Easy," Tom said, still struggling to catch his breath. He stretched his open hands out like a tall, thin, journalistic crucifix and tried to look non-threatening.

"Who the hell are you and what the hell are you doing?" a member of Sioux City's finest Tom recognized as officer Bryan Van Grunner barked into Tom's face. He and Van Grunner had crossed paths before and he was definitely not on Tom's Christmas card list, truncated as it might be.

The best approach with Van Grunner was full-on smart ass. Luckily, he was fluent in the language.

"What the hell do you think I was doing, Bryan? Washing the windows?" Tom coughed again. He ran a body systems check, detecting only bruises. He hoped the subsiding shock of the fall wouldn't be replaced by the pain of a broken bone. "Can I give you a tip, Bry? Never stand on a lawn mower. It may seem like a good idea when you need a boost to see two cops kill someone inside a house, but the devil is in the details."

"Jesus, it's the press." Van Grunner finally recognized Tom as a reporter for the *Sentinel-Leader,* which had been keeping the residents of Sioux City, Iowa, informed since God knows what year. Tom supposed it was 18-something. He wasn't real strong on his local history.

Van Grunner holstered his gun. "Get up. Shut up. Don't say anything and don't hear anything until the lieutenant gets here."

"Or you'll do what? Work me over with your baton like you so kindly offered to work over Joyce in there?" Tom said. Van Grunner grabbed Tom's outstretched left hand and pulled roughly, causing Tom to growl in pain.

"Fuck you, news boy."

Tom ripped his hand out of Van Grunner's and rolled slowly

onto his side. He checked that his notebook was in his back pocket and cellphone, miraculously still in one piece, was in the front. He pushed himself up onto all fours. "News boy?" Tom chuckled just before Van Grunner's foot thudded into his ribs. Tom coughed and slumped back to the pavement.

A second cop, a muscular black man, stepped between Tom and Van Grunner and gave Van Grunner the universal "take it easy" gesture.

"You better get your buddy here under control, Officer ... um," Tom said. His failure to recognize the black cop probably meant he was new to the force.

"Powers," the cop said.

"You're not printing any of this unless you want me to visit your house at 4 a.m.," Van Grunner said.

Tom gingerly plucked a small rock out of his scalp and held it up to show Van Grunner, whose expression didn't change. "I just took that out of my head," he said, again showing the pebble to both Van Grunner and Powers. "Nothing? No? Tough driveway."

Tom sat up as he tossed the pebble aside. "Well, that sure is a tempting offer, Officer Van Grunner, just make sure and give me a heads up that you're coming over so I can have some Jell-o shots ready. We'll sit and swap stories about the *bitches*. But I think for right now I'm going to roll up a newspaper and jam it up your ass." Van Grunner looked on the verge of pouncing when Lieutenant Harry Benning's car screeched up. Benning was out of the car almost before it had stopped moving.

Go a few more rounds with Van Grunner or talk to Harry Benning? Tom wondered as he watched Benning march up the driveway. *Toss-up. Getting pummeled by Van Grunner would probably be less painful.*

"Don't these people ever sweep their driveways?" Tom dug another pebble out of his scalp and showed it to Van Grunner,

Powers and then Benning, as if the addition of the third person to the audience would make the gag funnier. It didn't. Tom scanned the low-rent neighborhood and answered himself: "Stupid question."

Benning joined the group. Powers held his ground between Tom and Van Grunner.

"Lieutenant," Tom said with a nod, now gingerly inspecting a bloody tear in the elbow of his white shirt. Tom could hear other officers attending to the woman inside the house. He had been introduced to Joyce, albeit indirectly, just a few minutes earlier, before gunfire broke out in the living room. Also still in the house was a man named Chuck, another of Tom's new acquaintances. Chuck was currently exercising his right to remain silent, primarily due to the two nine millimeter holes in his chest.

Joyce screamed "they just shot him in cold blood" over and over. Benning ignored her and launched into a series of questions that centered on "What the hell is *he* doing here?" before huddling with Powers and Van Grunner just out of Tom's earshot. Van Grunner seemed to be doing most of the talking within the huddle and Benning did most of the glancing back toward Tom.

"Hey, I'm okay, guys. No need for medical attention. Talk amongst yourselves," Tom said, continuing his physical systems check by bending and straightening his elbow.

"Why are you here, Mr. Kingman?" Benning asked as they broke huddle.

"I heard the domestic disturbance call and wanted to watch your boys in action," Tom said, his shoulder starting to stiffen. The scrape on his left arm had stopped oozing blood, but only after leaving a five-inch trail down his shirtsleeve. "I saw the mower. I used to stand on them all the time as a kid. Got me up to where I could see the boys in blue. Helluva show. I really hope I'm not bleeding too loudly over here for you guys."

"I think you'll live," Benning sneered. "You know, what you

did was stupid, and probably illegal."

"Let's ask Chuck if he wants to hit me with trespassing charges," Tom said.

"You're a funny guy. So funny, I think I need to share your wit with the people down at headquarters." Benning reached down and gripped Tom's sore left shoulder hard, making him grimace.

"Yeah, let's go talk, Lieutenant. Let's talk about, say, I don't know, maybe your officer kicking me in the ribs or his kind comments to the victim's wife, girlfriend, whatever after he *capped* her significant other. Or maybe his thoughtful offer to show her his night stick. She had to be tempted by that one. Let's form small groups and discuss those topics. Hey, any chance I could get a beer down at police HQ? Don't pretend that you don't have some brews down there."

"We'll get into what you *thought* you observed, but downtown while the sergeants and crime scene boys work this place over," Benning said.

He led Tom down the front walk, with Van Grunner following close behind. "I hope you guys got some craft beer," said Tom, who really could have used a beer right then. "Big brewery stuff makes me puke."

Tom turned his head just in time to see a five-year-old Ford Escape emblazoned with the KMJR TV station call letters come to a stop across the street. You're not going to have shots fired and police calling for backup in Sioux City without the local TV stations getting wind of it. Tom actually admired the local TV reporters. Well, "admired" was a bit strong. Maybe "marveled at." Ripping down nine bucks an hour and they *still* sleep with their scanners. What really made the TV station people erect was a good, old-fashioned Iowa blizzard. During the chaos of a blizzard the Iowa weather people were like George C. Scott as Patton looking over the carnage of a battlefield: "I love it. God help me I do love it so. I love it more than my life."

Second to a great blizzard—preferably one that left highway ditches festooned with marooned cars—TV loved a good shooting. Local television reporter Larry Kelso was Johnny on the spot tonight and intercepted Tom and the police about halfway down the walk.

"Wow, Tom, you got here fast," Kelso said. He was a reporter so fresh from college Tom doubted he had returned his cap and gown yet. Kelso had hired on just six months ago for the lucrative $21,000-a-year plan with KMJR. Pretty bright on-air presentation, but, fortunately enough in this case, he could be a bit slow to catch on.

"Larry. Glad you could find the address. Thank God for GPS, huh?" Tom moved his arm to hide the torn and bloody sleeve.

Time and a half for Larry. That's about twelve dollars an hour. That's like hitting the lotto at KMJR. Good demo reel stuff for the kid, too.

Tom dashed off a prayer of thanks that Kelso was not shrewd enough to have his camera rolling. Tom had a pleasant face, somewhere between cute and handsome, but he thought it a bit too long for television. He wore his dark brown hair very short, mostly because that meant less maintenance. Overall, though, Tom didn't think he had a good look for TV, and he definitely did not have the look to be on TV tonight.

In the scene-of-the-crime excitement, Kelso didn't seem to realize the police near Tom were escorting him, not merely going the same direction. Benning stopped long enough to tell Kelso someone would have a statement in about thirty minutes and then continued on toward the car. He stopped a few feet in front of Tom to make sure he followed.

"Were you riding with the cops tonight or what?" Larry asked, making an admirable attempt at being perceptive. Perhaps Tom had underestimated Kelso. With Kelso's looks and even some small potential, he would probably leave for a bigger market in under a year.

"It was crazy, Larry. I was just attending the local NRA club meeting down here, hanging with the homeys, when *boom*, someone started firing at this plush locale. I decided that maybe I should check on it, same as you."

"Who got shot?" Larry asked, oblivious of Tom's attempted wit. By now Tom had brushed past Kelso and was doing his best to act as if he hadn't heard while keeping his bloody elbow out of view. Kelso kept glancing between Tom and the front door of the house. Just then a television crew from rival KZVN screeched up, distracting Kelso for the second Tom needed to disappear through the crowd of gawkers assembling on the lawn.

Minutes later, Tom was seated behind the Plexiglas barrier in a police car for the fifteen-block ride to police headquarters. They'd given him a gauze pad to swab up the blood on his arm before roughly seating him in the rear. Tom guessed the pad was more out of consideration for the upholstery than concern for his injuries. Tom briefly thought about letting himself bleed all over the cracked vinyl, but instead checked his watch—9:49 p.m.—closed his eyes and let his head tip back onto the seat. He savored even five minutes rest ahead of what he knew came next.

CHAPTER 2

It took five minutes to get to the parking lot behind police headquarters—it takes five minutes to get most anywhere in Sioux City— and Benning made Tom sit and swelter in the car for an extra few minutes while talking with a patrol cop. Once the show of dominance was over, Benning escorted Tom through the station's rear entrance, allowing them to avoid the brightly lit front lobby and any curious looks from the records clerks, many of whom Tom knew well.

Up on the second floor, Benning led the way into a small interrogation room. It was more like a bland office conference room than the stereotypical interview room of TV drama fame: a table and three chairs, one on one side of the table and two on the other. At the end of the table sat a digital clock, which Tom suspected was actually a sophisticated recording device.

"Sit." Benning stabbed a thick finger at the single chair and abruptly left, pulling the door closed. Tom had just begun to wonder if the door was locked when it opened and a female emergency medical technician walked in with a medical kit. As she examined Tom's head and elbow, he snuck glances at her tight, blue uniform pants, complete with ten or more pockets. "Just want to check you over," she said, the light glinting off her "GROVER" name tag as she donned rubber gloves.

"If you lube up your finger, I'd like a nice dinner first," Tom said, coaxing a small chuckle out of Grover. "Don't let them force you to use your medical skills to get information out of prisoners. Say no to the dark side of medicine. I'm a reporter. We can blow the lid on their medical perversion. Just say the word."

Grover gave Tom a quick smile but said nothing while examining his head and arm. She wiped both with a moist pad that stung. She had Tom roll up his sleeve and then put a large self-adhesive bandage on his arm.

"Your head and elbow are just scraped. I cleaned both. You don't need a bandage for your head, but you're going to have a knot up there. Take it easy when you wash your hair or you could get it bleeding again. Change the bandage on your arm when you get home." A tiny smile flickered across her face. "Sorry, no lubed fingers today. Maybe another time."

"Thanks. Look forward to it," Tom said, rolling his shirtsleeve back down and pulling a business card out of his pocket and handing it to Grover. She glanced quickly around the room, raised an eyebrow and pocketed Tom's card. Grover gathered up her trash, stripped off her gloves, and left without another word.

The ventilation fans abruptly and noisily came to life, pumping out cool air. Tom responded by flapping the back of his sweat-soaked shirt away from his skin to aid the cool-down process.

His maneuvering under the overhead vent reminded him that there was a small camera hidden somewhere behind the grill capturing interrogations. He knew from the angle of the resulting videotape that the camera was in there, somewhere, even though it now seemed very well camouflaged.

Benning and the other five or six cops in the building that time of night were probably in another room, watching him on a monitor, talking about what they wanted to do. Tom resisted the urge to wave at the unseen camera—or maybe flip it off—and reminded himself not to pick his nose or adjust his crotch. He decided to keep his knowledge of the camera to himself. Having the session recorded could turn out to be an advantage if he handled it right. The bigger question was how long Tom would let himself be delayed at the station without starting to raise some hell about it.

After about ten minutes the door opened again and Lieutenant Benning strode in.

"Mr. Kingman." Benning started off with exaggerated formality followed by an exaggerated pause. "Thank you for agreeing to join us tonight."

The video is definitely rolling. Let the record show Mr. Kingman is here of his own free will.

"This business on West Jarred has us all a bit shaken," Benning continued. "Very unpleasant. Which, of course, we want to clear up as soon as possible. This won't take long if we can all come to some agreements."

Agreements. That, Tom knew, would be the thrust of this conversation/interrogation.

Tom cocked his left wrist and pushed up his sleeve: 10:29 p.m. He flashed to the scene in *The Wizard of Oz* where Dorothy was terrorized by the Wicked Witch's draining hourglass.

Where are those flying monkeys when you need them?

Benning jolted him back to the present: "Well, Tom—is it okay if I call you Tom?—you've landed yourself smack in the middle of something here. Now, you can appreciate the department's situation. We've got an officer-involved shooting, which means a number of concerned citizens would love to jump on that as an excuse to storm down here and march around with banners making a scene for the TV cameras, accusing us of everything from killing children to being the second gunman on the grassy knoll."

A JFK assassination reference. How old does Benning think I am?

"Maybe Officer Van Grunner lost his head. He was in shock from shooting a man in self-defense. You can understand that. You were probably in shock at the time as well. We need you to not overreact."

"Overreact?" Tom let out a chuckle that he hoped irritated Benning. "Here, Harry—can I call you Harry?—why don't you just get down on all fours right here so I try for a forty-yard field goal with your ribs. Then we'll see if *you* 'overreact.'"

"Officer Van Grunner had just shot a man, for Christ sakes," Benning said. "I'm sure you'd have been cool and calm after that."

"Maybe not, but I wouldn't have threatened the dead guy's live-in, waved around my baton and then assaulted a witness. You'll call it sensationalizing the story, but I call it including all the facts. So, if you don't mind, I think I'll just saunter back to the paper and let my buddies down there know why you all just carried Chuck out in a body bag and dispatched the professional cleaning crews to 219 West Jarred Street. I've got a deadline."

As Tom began to stand, Benning grabbed him by the left arm. It was painful confirmation of Tom's theory that Benning wouldn't let him go so easily. Not that Benning had a lot of juice here. Tom knew the only legal way Benning could prevent him from leaving was to arrest him as a material witness, which would require Benning to read Tom his Miranda rights—the right to remain silent, the right to speak to an attorney and so on. After that, all Tom had to do was look into the camera and say, "I would like to speak with my attorney, please"—clearly and "for the record" as they say in court—"and I refuse to answer any more questions until he arrives." If they wanted to get rough, Tom would answer every question with "attorney," littering the video with requests for legal counsel. Their supposedly secret video system would become documentation of rights denial. Tom would do it, and more importantly he hoped Benning knew Tom would do it, so they could dispense with all the bullshit and make Tom's life a lot easier.

"Look, this isn't just another traffic accident. It's time for you to think more about the public good than about selling papers."

Tom leaned back and ran his hands through his hair. He casually checked his arm bandage. "Geez, Lieutenant. Maybe you'd like to come down to the office and write this one yourself. I can see it now: 'There was a report of shots fired somewhere on the west side last night, but don't worry. Even though they shot someone, the police are handling it in their usual professional style with your best interests at heart. Take our word for it. And, if you don't, we'll beat you with our batons.' "

Benning leaned close to Tom.

"Listen, you little vulture," Benning hissed—*that'll look good on the video in court*—"that smart-ass mouth of yours is going to get you in trouble someday. Maybe you'd like to spend a night in jail as a material witness. I can arrange that very easily."

"Material witness?" Tom let his head roll back as he scoffed at the ceiling. "I love that, Harry. But that may not be the best plan when it comes to keeping this whole thing low profile. I'd love to watch you tell a judge why you thought someone who has shown up for work every single day for the last six years and who came down here *voluntarily*, turned into such a flight risk that you had to arrest him, especially when there's no gunman at large or any sort of urgency for me to talk to you."

"Or, wait a minute," Tom said, his face contorted into mock surprise. "Do you think that might bring *more* attention to the case? Maybe every news organization in the upper Midwest would meet me on the steps of the jail at 9:05 tomorrow morning when the paper makes my bail wondering what the hell is going on. Right now it's just me and the TV geeks, but if you want to make a bigger story out of it …" He held his wrists out as if waiting to be cuffed.

Benning leaned back, as if to adopt body language that conveyed cool and control. Tom wasn't buying the posture or the material witness threat.

"Okay, let's cut the shit," Benning said—*if the gloves aren't off, they're definitely unlaced*—"just tell me what you saw tonight."

Tom closed his eyes and flashed back two and a half hours.

CHAPTER 3

Tom dropped into a squat at the front corner of an unkempt old house on West Jarred, one of Sioux City's most ramshackle neighborhoods. He peered around the side of the house just in time to see two cops—one black and one white—warily approaching the front porch that spanned the width of the structure. He could hear the couple inside screaming at each other. "Domestic bliss," Tom had murmured to himself.

Just five minutes before that, Tom had been driving home from a long day at the *Sentinel-Leader*, the major newspaper in Sioux City, which is great as far as it goes, and as far as it goes was a metro population of about 100,000. The *Sentinel-Leader* was not even the biggest newspaper fish in the little pond of Iowa. That dubious honor went to the mighty *Des Moines Journal* in Iowa's capital city with a metro population of nearly 500,000.

Tom's skill-taxing assignment that day had been a story on a heat wave that had seemingly started in March. Tom had written one story for every one of the 1,000 beads of sweat that were making him the walking embodiment of his uncle's bizarre phrase for extreme heat: "underwear soaker." Typical for Iowa, the weather had gone from slush on the streets to roasted, brown grass almost overnight. Now it was mid-June and Iowa had sweltered under its combination of heat and humidity for the last two weeks, leaving a string of broken high temperatures records in its wake. Somehow he had found new ways to relate the old news: 1) It's hot and 2) It's going to stay hot. Long periods of heat and drought were big news to Iowa, where agriculture pumps seventy-two billion dollars a year into the state's economy and supports one out of every six jobs. Still, there were only so many ways you could say "farmers are screwed" in print.

On his way home from a story covering the dangers of the heat to construction workers—for the twelfth time in his career—and smarting over the Puritan editors' veto of the quote he'd gotten from an asphalt worker, "It's just a hot bitch," Tom's police scanner had picked up a domestic disturbance with "possible weapons."

A couple of turns, some driving with his lights out and a hunched-over shuffle had brought him and his soaked underwear flush against the house just as the police approached. "What the hell? Probably nothing," Tom said, mocking himself in a barely audible voice and attempting to imitate the line from Bruce Willis in *Die Hard*. "Come out to the coast, we'll get together, have a few laughs..."

Squatting by the porch, brushing off flecks of peeling paint, Tom mulled the fact that if he hadn't diverted from his commute home, right now he would have been in his house, showered, lying on the bed with the air conditioner going full blast and a glass of microbrew beer in his hand. But nooooo. Mr. Hot Shit reporter had decided to take a look.

The two officers drew their weapons at the front door.

We got Doc Holiday and Wyatt Earp going in the front.

Tom considered shuffling back out to a safe distance to wait for gunfire. But, what the hell, he'd come this far.

Still crouching, Tom looked down his side of the house.

Whaddya know? Open windows in the 'hood during a heat wave. I couldn't be more shocked if I woke up with my head sewed to the carpet.

The rarity of functioning air conditioning in this neighborhood meant everyone lived with the windows wide open, simultaneously sweating their asses off and sharing their TV viewing and conversations with the general public. Tom used the growing volume of words you'd never find in a family newspaper as an audio bread crumb trail that led him to the best window for seeing the action.

Had to be the living room, Tom thought, drawing on his memory of similar houses he'd been in for one story or another. People always fight and kill each other in the living room in these neighborhoods, if not out on the lawn. Not in the bedroom. Not in the kitchen. Not in the backyard and never upstairs. In the living room or front lawn. Tom once went to a front-yard stabbing that started with an argument over a leather coat and a twelve-pack. Tom couldn't decide if he was more appalled that the argument was over a twelve-pack of *Bud Light* or that someone had died. Probably the death, but dying over Bud Light struck him as a very shitty way to go.

A "motherfucker," "cocksucker"—*old school!*—and a couple of "stupid whores" assured Tom he was at the right window. But even after he raised himself to his full five feet, eleven inches, the windowsill remained just above his head. Hearing is not as good as seeing. That's when Tom spotted an old lawn mower about twenty feet away.

A ten-second survey confirmed the mower was all he had to work with, so he rolled it under the window and stepped on top of the engine, feeling it sag, but not collapse, under his 165 pounds. The mower boosted him just high enough to view the entire room through the torn window screen. Thanks to the indoor lights and the window screen, Tom felt virtually invisible to anyone in the living room.

He clearly saw a white man, about 6' 4", surprisingly gaunt, with thick, greasy black hair flowing to the base of his neck. He wore a sweat-stained, wife-beater undershirt, dirty jeans and black boots. A woman cowered on the couch before him.

"Are you ready to listen to me now, bitch?" the man growled. "Then wipe that shitty look off your ugly face and get *up*." The woman drew her knees up to her chest. She wore blue cut-off shorts and a white men's tank top similar to her beau's (his and hers wife beaters!), dirty blonde hair with dark roots, and no makeup, her eyes puffy from crying. Her legs showed a few bruises. Her feet were dirty, Tom surmised from a day without shoes.

The room was filthy, littered with trash and beer cans. Old, frayed furniture sagged in front of a new-looking TV. Tom saw dark spots on the headrest and arms of an aging recliner, and the room's paint was peeling in one corner, near the ceiling.

Crappy furniture, new TV, landfill cleaning standards. Pretty standard décor for the neighborhood.

The woman came out of her cower long enough to fire a verbal salvo. "You bastard, Chuck. Get away from me."

"Chuck" took a step toward her, causing a beer can to flop over and gurgle its last few ounces out onto the carpet. Natural Light beer. Tom was repulsed.

She grabbed a lamp from an end table, sending framed photographs clattering to the floor. "I'm gonna call the cops," she said, yanking the lamp hard enough to pop its plug from the wall and holding it up as a feeble weapon.

"Go ahead and call them, Joyce," Chuck responded, turning his back on the woman and running both hands through his hair. Tom could see Chuck's unshaven face twitch just as he felt the mower beneath him wobble. He was about to glance down when Chuck spun around and leaped on Joyce, his knees astride her bare legs. She dropped the lamp in shock, its bulb breaking with a soft pop. Chuck's left hand grabbed Joyce's right arm as she raised it to strike him, and then he countered with his own savage blow, opening a small cut on Joyce's face that sent a bloody smear across her mouth.

Geez. What are Doc and Wyatt on the porch waiting for? The body bags?

Chuck again leaned slightly right to reach into the end table's drawer while still straddling Joyce. Tom focused on Chuck's hand, coming slowly out of the drawer.

Gun.

Tom was suddenly extremely interested in the thickness of the exterior walls of this circa 1923 house.

"What you think of this, Joycie?" Chuck said, running the side of a snub-nosed .38 revolver across her bloody cheek. Joyce's eyes flared, following the barrel of the gun as Chuck slid the weapon from her left cheek, across her lips and to the right. Blood seeping from her two facial cuts smeared across the gun barrel.

Knock knock knock: "POLICE, open up."

Thank God; donut break on the porch is finally over.

"Did you call them, bitch?" Chuck snarled, jerking his head from the door back to Joyce. She didn't respond, her gaze making a continuous circuit between Chuck's face, the gun and the door.

Dude, someone a block over could have called them, as much noise as you're making.

"Just calm down, let us in and we'll talk this over," the cop voice yelled. Tom knew a lot of cops, but he couldn't quite place this voice.

Stay alert. Don't blink. Don't get distracted. Things will happen fast. Focus and remember. And don't puke or pass out.

"Go away, cop," Chuck barked, having rolled off of Joyce and putting one finger over his lips as he looked at her. "We don't need any of your help."

"Can't do that, sir. We got a call and have to check it out. If you cooperate, this should only take a few minutes."

"You whore," Chuck said in a low growl. "You did call them." Chuck turned to face Joyce and took a slow step back. His elbow started bending, bringing the small dark gun up toward Joyce's chest.

"He's got a gun!" Tom yelled, louder than he thought possible.

Chuck jumped in surprise and spun toward the window, causing Kingman to start to duck. In mid-turn, the door exploded inward leaving a trail of wood splinters from the broken lock. Chuck staggered back as if buffeted by the door's explosion until he was close enough to the window for Tom to smell him. Tom raised back up to full height just as two hands, each gripping a dark pistol, protruded just inside the doorframe. Chuck turned toward the door and fired in one motion, unleashing a roar that battered Tom's face.

Chuck's bullet cracked the plaster just to the left of the front door as both cops fired almost simultaneously. Tom ducked for cover as Chuck's body pitched back slightly and his hands flew up, sending the still-smoking .38 tumbling end-over-end toward the floor where it thunked onto the carpet.

Tom was back at the window just as Chuck's body and his gun hit the floor. Chuck landed a couple feet in front of the window, giving Tom a good view of his dirty undershirt blossoming with crimson. Two shots, center mass. Sgt. Hartman from *Full Metal Jacket* barged into Tom's head: *"Outstanding, Private Pyle."*

Holy shit.

Nervous tremors danced across Tom's chest as he reminded himself: *don't hurl.* The cops were through the door now, guns first, with the black cop slowly moving toward Chuck while the white cop focused on Joyce. Joyce's face contorted into a cry, which Tom expected to start low and quickly escalate into a wail.

"He's dead," the black officer crouching over Chuck said, his fingers checking for a pulse.

Blood from Joyce's facial wounds trickled down her cheek and onto her shirt. "You killed him, you filthy pigs," she said toward the white cop. Joyce's wails escalated into dog-being-run-over territory as she dove onto Chuck's body, their bloodstains mixing. As the white officer stepped closer to the window to try and separate Joyce from the corpse, Tom recognized him as patrolman Bryan Van Grunner.

"You stupid bitch," Van Grunner hissed. "He took a shot at us." The sobbing woman didn't seem to hear him.

Van Grunner broke off his efforts to separate the love birds and squeezed the button on the small, triangular radio microphone attached between his shirt collar and shoulder as he turned his head toward it.

"Dispatch? This is D-1," Van Grunner said, his voice amplified by the walkie-talkie clipped to the other cop's belt, causing the black cop to reflexively crank down the volume.

"D-1," the dispatcher answered.

Van Grunner released the radio button and turned to the woman. "Hey, quit your screaming. I'm trying to call dispatch." He returned to his radio. "We need an ambulance at 219 West Jarred. We've got shots fired and a suspect down. Powers and I are fine, the scene is secure. Will need an ambulance for a female subject who has minor injuries and is hysterical. We'll need crime scene and you better send Lt. Benning up here."

Van Grunner's call ended any fleeting thoughts Tom had of an exclusive story. As soon as Van Grunner said "suspect down," Tom knew the TV reporters would be on their way, alerted by their police scanners. Tom hoped someone on the *Sentinel-Leader* staff had heard Van Grunner's call as well. The media mob would soon be on the front lawn, looking groggy and unkempt, ready to ask, "How do you feel?" and similarly probing questions. Tom's editors would probably want a weather "tie-in." Maybe the heat drove Chuck to it. It was all Tom could do not to bang his head against the house at the thought of it.

But God, what a story—the specter of a weather tie-in notwithstanding— Tom thought, struggling to calm his raging pulse and de-escalate his breathing. Shootings like this were rare in Sioux City, Iowa.

Joyce turned abruptly toward the second officer, her face streaked with a pink concoction of blood and tears. "You stupid cocksuckers"—*old school!*—"I'm going to tell everyone you shot him and beat me. I'm going to sue the fuck out of you both. I'll call the goddamn *Enquirer*. I'll be all over every TV station until you bastards rot in hell."

"Who will believe some drugged-out skank like you?" Van Grunner said, pulling his police baton out of its holder.

'Sue the fuck out of you' and 'drugged-out skank.' Gotta remember those tasty quotes. This story just keeps getting better.

"Van Grunner," Powers said slowly, "what the hell are you doing?"

"Thinking about beating this silly bitch senseless," Van Grunner answered sharply.

"Come on, Bryan," Powers said, grabbing Van Grunner's arm. "Don't get all freaky on me." The shriek of approaching sirens jerked Tom's attention from the two cops inside to the street outside where he saw lights coming on inside the surrounding houses. His instant plan was to get back to the paper, write a rough draft, and then go down to police headquarters to do his civic duty as a witness to the shooting.

Maybe the proper thing to do was to identify himself at the scene and immediately give a complete statement to the police. But he was a reporter, and this was a monster story for this town, so the proper thing to do wasn't going to be what actually happened. And at no point was he going to get scooped by the minimum-wage TV geeks in this town. No. Drive to the paper, write something up, file it, print it, lock it in a drawer and have a very cold IPA and then go to the police station—after the presses ran. Thinking of that cold beer, Tom decided to dismount the lawnmower, which he did, but not as gracefully as he would have liked.

CHAPTER 4

Back in the police interview room, Tom concluded his story from the point he windmilled off the mower, including graphic detail about getting kicked in the ribs, and paused for effect, again savoring the air-conditioning.

"What do you know about the suspect?" Benning asked.

"The dead guy, or the cop who shot him?"

Benning gave an exasperated sigh. "You know, this would take a lot less time if you'd lose the smart ass act."

Tom led with his best "good point" smirk and said, "Nothing. I never saw him before in my life. All I know is that he was slapping the woman in the room pretty good, threatening her with a gun, and was definitely on something. Either that or he had twenty-three cups of Starbucks in him. He weighed about fifty pounds, had some wild, paranoid eyes, and kept making quirky, jerky spasmodic movements. I'd guess meth head, given that the poor white folks usually go for the home-brewed methamphetamine."

Tom fixed his gaze on Benning, who returned it in silence. Methamphetamine, commonly known as "crank" or "meth," had swept the Midwest in the last few years. Sioux City's unique position at the point Iowa, South Dakota, and Nebraska touched and on a major north-south Interstate made it the "Meth Capital of the Country," according to stories in Tom's own paper, which accounted for Tom's above-average knowledge of the drug.

Most of the meth addicts Tom had interviewed appeared apathetic, gaunt and sickly, seemingly on the edge of falling asleep. Usually some incident—a car accident, an arrest, domestic abuse—got them into treatment. Doctors told him the odds of relapsing were high during the months of cravings, irritability, nightmares and depression that lined the road to recovery.

"So, you saw the officers fire at the victim?" Benning asked.

"I heard the roar of the shots, saw their guns buck, and saw Chuck sprout a couple new orifices and hit the floor right in front of me."

"And you definitely saw the victim shoot at the officers first?"

"Yep, he popped off the first shot. It hit the wall just left of the door. I'm sure your boys have already dug the slug out."

Benning leaned back a bit. "Why would someone who had two cops pointing their weapons at him, with no cover, decide to fire?"

"Who knows? He probably thought your guys were coming in firing, or was so pissed off he just took a shot. How do I know what goes through the head of a tweaker? Crank makes you paranoid and crazy, you know that. A guy gets all wired up on that stuff and there's no telling what he'll do if you bust down his door. Or maybe he was just suicidal."

Or desperate. But about what?

Tom's face went blank as he mulled the afterthought.

Benning: "So, if you had been one of the officers, you would have fired?"

"Oh yeah. If I thought he was even considering firing at me, I would have blazed away at him big-time. Full magazine," Tom said, matching Benning's distance from the table and enjoying his own ability to cooperate on at least this point. His adversarial role with the police was necessary, but it was also taxing. He wanted the cops to catch the bad guys, just got sick of their "we'll let you know what to write" crap. Tom had learned to use a sarcastic mask to regulate his natural impulse to please.

"Your boys were more than provoked," Tom said. "They yelled through the door for him to surrender, but he started waving around a gun and was going to take a shot at the woman. That's when I yelled, 'He's got a gun.' I thought Powers and Van Grunner ought to get in there before he popped Joyce. Not sure if they heard me or not. It was an involuntary response."

Benning gave a grunt that was halfway between amusement and disgust.

"So you concur that the woman's life was in danger?" Benning didn't wait for a response. "Well, we're all very pleased that our officers' ultimate actions and reactions suited you, Mr. Kingman. I don't think there will be much trouble with that end of the investigation. After all, we've got the victim's gun, the bullet near the door, a witness to rebut the woman's claims—and thank you very much for that. I'm sure our victim will have a rap sheet longer than an Iowa winter. Did you hear what the woman said after the shooting?"

"Yeah, I heard her, and she's crazy. It pains me to back you guys up on this one, especially with such a sweetheart like Van Grunner involved, but the shooting was justified. The stuff after, that's a different story, but the shooting was justified."

"We'll need your written statement, of course," Benning said.

"It would be the highlight of my writing career. Now that we're all acquainted, Lieutenant, what did you say the victim's name was? Chuck, ah, what was it again?"

"Pollard," Benning said. "But I'm only giving you that because we gave it to your colleagues at the scene half an hour ago. I'll do the questioning here, if you don't mind."

"And what a nice job you've been doing so far." Tom sighed. He let his head loll back for a moment as he collected himself. He had been up since 7 a.m. and fatigue was gnawing at his restraint.

Stay cool. Don't get him pissy now. Pollard ... rings a drug-related bell. Hope somebody from the paper got to the scene. I should have called in the copy from the car. Time to get going...

"So, if there's nothing else, I'm going to have to insist I get down to the paper," Tom said as he stood up. "I'll call you later to see what else you can tell me."

"And just what, may I ask, do you propose to put in your little article?" Benning said, leaning forward, causing his leather gun belt to audibly chafe.

At last, Tom thought, the real issue—what gets printed in my "little" article. To the SCPD, his articles were always going to be "little," as in insignificant, a cute, mediocre trifle worthy only of chuckles and ridicule.

Tom looked at his watch again. Almost 11 p.m. and ninety minutes from the last deadline of the day. He could always get something out on the *Sentinel-Leader's* website, but he hated that thing. Everyone kept telling Tom that print was dying, but he was still philosophically against letting your own web site scoop the printed version.

He decided he had time to play things out a bit more with Benning and lowered himself into the molded plastic chair, trying to blink the dryness out of his eyes. He looked at Benning, still leaning over the table with his hands on his knees underneath it. Despite his resolve to stay cool, Tom was really getting tired of the "Mickey Mouse" as his father would say. *No offense, Mr. Disney.* Tom imagined the joy he'd feel from grabbing Benning's blue tie and yanking it down, causing Benning's head to spank the table. The image goaded an involuntary chortle out of Tom.

"I thought I'd start with what I saw," Tom said, the sentence rolling out of his amused snort. "You know, busting down doors, shooting a woman-beater in the chest, having the woman freak out, Van Grunner threatening to use his stick on the woman—got a tasty quote from him in that area—me getting kicked, that kind of—air quotes—*sensational* stuff."

"Are you going to name the officers *and* talk about Van Grunner's *alleged* actions after the shooting?"

"Seems kind of pivotal for my *alleged* story."

"You can't do that."

Bile gurgled in Tom's lower throat. "Hold the phone, Harry. Let me just get this down. 'The First Amendment has been suspended' or maybe 'Harry Benning hired as *Sentinel-Leader* managing editor.'"

"Your precious First Amendment does not give you the right to get those officers killed," Benning said, his voice rising with the color in his face. "This whole incident could be gang related. You know how they operate. They'll send a few boys to Van Grunner's and Powers' houses tonight to rape their wives and kill their kids. You want that on your head because you wanted to sell papers? I sure wouldn't."

Again with the "selling papers" bit.

Although his rational brain dismissed Benning's graphic scenario, Tom's emotional brain paused. Contrary to the asshole façade, Tom didn't want to get anyone killed.

"Are you saying that the names of the officers are going to be kept secret?" Tom asked. "Two officers kill someone in the line of duty and you think that's none of the public's business? My publisher will explode if I 'forget' the identities. I'll have little publisher bits all over me as I walk to the unemployment line. Besides, the public provides the authority and money for what you do. You're saying they don't need to know about some little traffic-ticket sized trouble like this?"

"Oh, we'll release the names," Benning said, "but only Thursday, *after* we've taken some precautions to make sure no one can harm anyone in the officers' families over this. We need some time, is all. Give us a day."

Tom shook his head. "Thursday? That's two editions away for us—the Wednesday paper will hit the streets at around 1 a.m.

That's about two hours from now. And it will hit with whatever we have now, which is a lot. If you hold the names until Thursday, that means we don't have them until Friday morning's edition."

Benning stared blankly.

"Let me explain how this works, Lieutenant. You release the name at noon Thursday—because you and I both know you can't go much longer than that without risking the appearance of a cover-up—and the TV geeks put it on the air Thursday night and we have it in the paper Friday."

We could put it up on the paper's website the same day, but screw the website.

Tom paused to see if any of this was registering with Benning. Benning only crossed his arms and leaned back.

"That puts us a day behind the electronic media when we really had the names a day before them," Tom continued. "Hell, I was an *eyewitness*. Van Grunner introduced himself and it's going to be easy for me to figure out Powers' first name. We only have about five black officers in the department. So you see my problem."

"No, I don't see your *problem*," Benning said.

"It's very simple." Tom struggled to control his voice. "My boss goes to a restaurant called Billy's every morning for breakfast. He gets *really* pissed off if one of his breakfast cronies saw something on the TV news and then says to him, 'I didn't see anything about it in the paper.' Then he comes and yells at me about it."

Tom leaned forward, pausing to regain himself. *Let's try sympathetic/honest. What the hell?* "Look, I sympathize with Van Grunner and Powers. I really do. I was there and they did what they had to do, but this stuff just seems like it's part of being a cop."

Benning grew more agitated as Tom's statement continued.

"This is not normal '*part of being a cop*' as you put it," Benning snarled, "not that some newspaper reporter would know what the hell being a cop is all about. Some people passionately hate us because we arrest them or say mean things about their rapist children. I tell you, every time you go out the door you never know what's going to happen. We're armed to the teeth, wear ten pounds of body armor and we're still at a disadvantage."

Tom snorted. "Come on, Benning. This is Sioux City, Iowa, not L.A. It's not 1956 out there anymore, but it's also a long way from Iraq. Hell, this is the first time in thirty years a cop in this town shot someone. We both know there are some gangsters running around Sioux City, but calling this Little South Central is a stretch. I appreciate you being cautious, but let's not get paranoid. Better get your 'precautions' for those two guys in place because their names are coming out tomorrow."

Tom pre-empted Benning's protests by moving quickly to a topic he knew was even more sensitive. "And then we have the whole issue of Van Grunner's corpse-side manner."

CHAPTER 5

A few rooms down, a group of blue uniforms huddled around a TV monitor, sipping from Styrofoam coffee cups and watching the hidden camera video. Bryan Van Grunner spoke into a wall phone on the other side of the large room.

"Yeah, it's done," Van Grunner said, turning toward the wall and lowering his voice to a near whisper. "He made it easy for us. What? Powers was there. Oh, and a newspaper reporter, name of Tom Kingman." Van Grunner glanced back at the group as an excited buzz filled the ear piece.

"Calm down. He was watching through a side window when we busted in. He'll help us prove the woman is full of shit when she says we shot Pollard in cold blood. I don't know; he saw it all so I suppose he'll want to put it in the paper. Don't worry, it was a good shoot. He has no clue. Look, I've got to go."

Van Grunner hung up the phone softly and glanced back at the members of the group still intent on the monitor. A few of them looked over at him.

"That was my girlfriend. She's freaking out," Van Grunner said. "I told her to take a Valium and go back to bed."

Powers had gone home to his wife after finishing his preliminary interview. Van Grunner had no interest in leaving the department until he heard what Tom had to say, and so far he hadn't liked what he heard. Tom had turned out to be more resilient to Benning's pressure than Van Grunner anticipated. Of course that doddering idiot Benning was going too easy on him.

"That little piss ant is going to give us up in print," Van Grunner, his hurling SCPD coffee cup causing a ceramic explosion in the coffee center's sink. "The little bastard just wants to sell papers and be famous." The shattered cup and Van Grunner's growing volume had the attention of the entire room. "I'll get home and find my house burned down and my girlfriend shot. She's already packing up to go stay with her mom."

Cops in the room murmured support, but at the same time edged farther away from Van Grunner. He had already given a preliminary statement to officers from Internal Affairs. On a force the size of Sioux City's, the I.A. officer doubled as the records lieutenant. Every department has a few bad apples, but by and large, even Tom would concede that the SCPD was 95% regular people trying hard to do a tough job. The questions had been pretty soft and Van Grunner recited the incident in the monotone vocabulary of an official report: "We proceeded into the residence and confronted the armed party … ."

The sound of the door opening spun everyone's head around.

+++

Even at 11:10 p.m., Assistant Woodbury County Attorney Hillary Reed looked chic. This evening's ensemble featured khaki slacks, imported loafers, and a well-made, smooth dark blouse. Her only jewelry was a small gold chain with a cross around her neck and black-banded watch on her wrist. Hillary's neat exterior masked a turbulent mental state. From the moment she'd gotten the initial call with some sketchy details from police headquarters, Hillary had known she faced one of the biggest decisions of her career.

When she'd heard Tom Kingman had witnessed the shooting, Hillary had quickly thumbed through the copy of the *Iowa Code of Professional Responsibility for Lawyers* she kept in her study.

Among the most important of its canons was *Rule 32.3.6, Trial Publicity:* "A lawyer participating in or associated with the investigation of a criminal matter shall not make or participate in making an extrajudicial statement that a reasonable person would expect to be disseminated by means of public communications . . . ." In other words, don't say anything to reporters about criminal cases.

The code listed exceptions to the rule, things like discussing information already in the public record, commenting on the general scope of the investigation, or using the media to request assistance from the public or alert them to any dangers. The officer-involved shooting threatened an 18-month-long investigation, and Hillary's hopes rested on one exception to 32.3.6. She had formed her action plan while driving to the station. Her next dozen sentences would make it impossible to turn back.

"Miz Reed," Van Grunner said, "you've got to help us shut this Kingman guy up."

"I've been briefed on what happened," Hillary responded, turning toward the group. She demonstrated the same rigid emotional control that served her so well in the courtroom. "Sounds like we've got a justified shooting here. We just have to keep things from getting crazy in public."

Time to drop a name, let them know she's not making this up on her own.

"I called County Attorney Dick Anderson on the way over, and we agree that rather than try to block the publicity, we need to manage it." Hillary waited for the response. She didn't seem surprised by Van Grunner's sneer.

"Are you insane?" Van Grunner took a step toward Hillary. "We have to grill that little puke Kingman until he promises not to print anything, or throw him in some goddamn closet somewhere.

God knows what he'll write. He'll probably get it wrong, then he'll put our pictures in the paper along with everything he and his vulture friends can find out about us and then say I beat that lying bitch, Joyce. It's easy to see your tight little ass isn't in the sling here."

Hillary deflected the sentence with a two-second stare. Van Grunner's tirade reminded her of how much she loved to get men like him on the witness stand. Hillary enjoyed watching them swagger up to the stand, confident that they could parry the thrust of a mere woman's examination. But Hillary knew how to blend their underestimation of women with their misconceptions of lawyers and the judicial system to make them look more foolish. For example, she would sometimes goad such witnesses into answering her question with a question, knowing that it would earn the witness a scolding from the judge. If she was really living right, the witness would then argue with the judge. Nothing pisses judges off more. Once she had the macho witnesses flustered, Hillary got out of the way and watched them self-destruct.

Because Van Grunner sometimes testified for her prosecution, however, she also had to find ways to keep him in one piece on the stand, a more formidable task than destroying him. So she had to toss him softball questions, stroke his ego subtly, hold his hand and walk him methodically through the examination.

Hillary also knew of Bryan Van Grunner's reputation for collecting female conquests like boys collect sports cards. He had all the physical tools· tall and blond with a muscular, athletic build buffed by frequent workouts. His wide shoulders and back tapered to a firm rear. Van Grunner also always seemed to have money to lavish on his latest female trophy, and Hillary had a few clues as to why.

If Hillary had any doubts about her course for the night, her mental montage of Bryan Van Grunner drove them away.

"Officer Van Grunner, what do you suggest we do? Arrest Tom

Kingman? For what? A judge would keep him in jail for about eight hours and once he got out every news organization in the country would be waiting to interview him. All that does is make a local, manageable story—cops shoot a wife abuser in self defense, which nobody cares about—into a regional, uncontrollable story: cops arrest a reporter to suppress a news story. That is ill advised, to say the least." Hillary scanned the other faces for support, finding some.

"The focus of the story," she went on, sensing allies in the room and pressing her point, "will quickly become, 'If everything was so proper, why jail a reporter who witnessed the shooting?' While we try to think of that answer, we'll have a dozen civil rights groups marching outside within a week. No, we're going to be smart with this and keep it local."

She stepped toward Van Grunner, who held his ground. "You should have kept your talk professional and your hands off your night stick, officer. And kicking a witness goes beyond foolish into reckless, maybe criminal."

Be careful, Hillary's brain flashed. Don't say too much.

"Sorry, princess, I had just shot a man and saved this woman's life and she starts screaming lies about us. I lost my head. Even you might have lost your private school calm if you had pulled the trigger."

Hillary looked at Van Grunner for several seconds and then turned away. In that moment, she fully committed to her plan.

Back to business. "Yes, the public will buy 'heat of the moment,' for your post-shooting actions, but they won't buy it for locking up a reporter. We have a strategy on controlling this incident. I need to talk to Lieutenant Benning. Please don't talk to the press if they call. Just refer all questions to the County Attorney's office."

Van Grunner let out a groan and started to protest, but Hillary shot him a not-up-for-discussion glance as she disappeared out the door. A few strides later, she knocked on the interview room door, causing the loud voices inside to stop abruptly. As Benning came out into the hall, Hillary and Tom held eye contact for a few seconds until the door closed. Hillary surprised herself by thinking Tom looked much better in person than on the video monitor down the hall.

"What is it? I'm trying to convince Mr. Kingman not to plaster this all over tomorrow's paper."

"How long have you been at it?" Hillary asked.

"I don't know. Forty-five minutes or so," Benning said, glancing at his watch.

"You're doing fine, but Tom is either too smart or too stubborn to buy the 'lives at stake' argument. I think we're going to have to make it worth his while if we want to get him to hold off on certain details, at least for a few days."

Hillary outlined an edited version of her plan for Benning. "We're going to have to give Tom something in order to manage this story," Hillary said. "I can convince him to keep some aspects out of the paper if we feed him some harmless inside information, like what we found at the scene, maybe some of Pollard's background. He'll feel like an insider and get on the team. You know how these reporters are. They secretly just want to be cops."

Hillary didn't really believe her last sentence, but it had the desired impact on Benning.

"Do you think he'll go for it?" Benning asked, adjusting his weight from one leg to the other.

"He'll go for it, especially since we're offering him something no one else has."

"And your boss has approved this?"

"Yes."

Benning shrugged and then stepped away from the door so Hillary could enter. "Hello, Tom," Hillary said as she walked in, flashing a smile that caught Tom flatfooted.

"Hillary Reed. I finally get a break, although it's tough luck for you being on call tonight," Tom said. Hillary felt lucky as well, since being on call put her in a position to work something out with Tom.

Hillary sat down and studied the familiar face across the table. She hoped she could play this right and that Tom's fatigue and his desire to get the hell out of police headquarters would work to her advantage.

Hillary and Tom often talked during his daily visits to the County Attorney's office. They knew each other well enough to exchange pleasantries during chance meetings at the supermarket, but it never went beyond cordial. The Woodbury County Attorney, a sweaty man named Dick Anderson, did nothing to dissuade Tom and Hillary's professional familiarity. At times, Anderson asked Hillary to make sure Tom knew about a successful prosecution or staff accomplishment in hopes of getting some favorable publicity. Tom and Hillary usually recognized Anderson's clumsy manipulations, but Tom played along when it seemed plausibly in the public interest. Helping Anderson publicize a Prosecutor of the Year award or some similar news flash built a reserve of good will Tom could later draw upon.

Hillary liked and trusted Tom. At first Hillary thought his personality an ingratiating ruse. But years after they had first met, Hillary now found Tom's attitude refreshing, especially for a man. And he was reasonably attractive, which didn't hurt anything. A bit too thin, perhaps—his clothes always seemed a little too big on him and he could use some fashion help. He wore the same thing a lot. Too conservative too often. But Tom's longish, narrow face with perpetual five-o'clock shadow, quick smile and short, brown hair struck her as honest, interesting and even attractive.

Hillary appreciated Tom's talent for giving a complete account of the court news, including the prosecution's side of the case. That accurate, public airing of the prosecution's points headed off many of the complaints that a one-sided or inaccurate story could create.

It also helped publicize that the police *were* putting criminals away. Without the stories of justice being served to counter the crime stories in the news, Hillary feared the public would see prosecutors as inept, lazy or incompetent in the face of escalating crime. Getting good publicity was benefit enough to make it worth tipping Tom in ways that still stayed within sight of Hillary's personal and professional code of ethics.

+++

So far, the mutual trust and respect between Tom and Hillary remained unspoken. That was about to change now that Tom had the ability to unwittingly ruin more than a year of Hillary's work. Only a fluke of on-call fate had put Hillary in position to salvage the situation.

Tom had always thought Hillary attractive in a thinking man's sort of way, but as she sat across from him in that moment, she seemed to light up the sterile room.

"I was just minding my own business," Tom said, noticing the tiny flecks of brown in her green eyes. "Going home after work, when I happened to see a couple cars outside a house on West Jarred. I should have just gone on driving home and caught up to it the next day. But no, I have to stop, get out, sweat my ass off, climb up on a stupid lawnmower and watch two of Sioux City's finest shoot some taxpayer in the chest. Then Van Grunner comes unhinged, I get kicked in the ribs and win a deluxe, all-expenses-paid police car ride to these fine accommodations, where I have spent an hour with Lieutenant Happy out there."

Hillary smiled. "Come with me."

Tom looked surprised for a second and then quickly got to his feet, thankful for any reason to move out of the white cell. They went to another conference room two doors down, this one featuring an active coffeepot. Hillary poured herself a cup and fished a bottle of water out of the mini-fridge for Tom as he ran some water over his hands at a sink near the coffee. He sluiced his face, trying not to get water on his shirt. As he grabbed a paper towel from the wall-mounted dispenser, he looked himself over in the mirror above the sink.

Tom had always been a bit uncomfortable with his body, which he thought was too skinny and generally unimpressive to either sex. His race horse metabolism forced him to eat just to keep weight on, much to the disgust of his weight-conscious friends. The face in the mirror didn't show much evidence of the lawn-mower tumble or his growing fatigue, but he'd looked better. His cheap JCPenney shirt was shot. Maybe he could write it off.

"No cameras. No recording," Hillary said, as Tom joined her at the table and accepted his bottle of water. Hillary sipped her coffee, looked at Tom for several seconds and then inhaled deeply.

"This is all between you and me," Hillary said, her voice lowered. "Very off the record." She paused until Tom gave an acknowledging nod. "I've been working with the state police for eighteen months. Only Dick Anderson, a few people in Des Moines, and I know what I am about to tell you."

CHAPTER 6

Hillary let her last sentence drift through the room for a few seconds. Tom felt her gaze probing his eyes. He'd seen that look before, most often from people about to say something they didn't know if they should, but wanted to anyway. Normally, he'd try to make himself look friendly and caring, but he knew such affectations would be counterproductive with Hillary. "I understand and agree," he said.

"We suspect Van Grunner is part of what could be a group of officers involved in criminal activity," Hillary said. "We're not sure what, but we've been watching him and quietly investigating for some time. It has to do with assaulting citizens and probably drugs. There have been rumors of confiscated drugs never finding their way to the evidence room. Van Grunner sometimes leaves his patrol area and drives across town, supposedly to get lunch, but conveniently losing contact with dispatch for a little too long."

Tom sat back in his chair, not sure how to react.

Hillary's eyes swept Tom's face and then continued. "So far everyone on the force thinks we're putting together some huge case against a meth distribution ring in Sioux City. Only a few people know that the investigation includes looking into a possible connection inside the department. We've kept that covert because we know Van Grunner will sever ties with the operation if he smells any investigation. If you print everything you saw tonight, there will be a public uproar and Van Grunner's contacts outside the department might think he's too hot and just cut and run, ruining eighteen months of work. I've just told Benning I'm going to try to get you to omit certain details from your story by feeding you a few choice tidbits and appealing to your innate desire to be a cop. I'm afraid Lieutenant Benning doesn't think reporters are very bright."

"And you do?"

"I think you're too smart to fall for Benning's 'be a team player' and 'lives are at stake' pitches. And I'm always going to be honest with you. I might not be able to tell you everything you want to know, but I've never deceived you, and I think you've always been straight with me. I appreciate that, Tom. We have to trust each other. You trust me for the big story later, and I trust you not to screw up my investigation now."

Tom sat forward in his chair, sliding both arms onto the table top and reaching for his water. Hillary laid her hand on Tom's left forearm so lightly Tom couldn't decide if he could really feel her touch through his shirt.

"Benning probably has already told Van Grunner what I told him. If nothing gets reported, we think Van Grunner will assume you caved. Knowing him, he'll think I slept with you to keep you quiet. Frankly, I don't care what he thinks as long as he doesn't say anything to his criminal colleagues. That would be admitting a mistake or a weakness, and I can't imagine him doing either."

Hillary lowered her head and then looked up, catching Tom's gaze. Tom involuntarily zoomed in on her fine auburn hair cut just above shoulder length, parted off center and swept mostly to the right side of her face. He'd looked at Hillary many times but realized he had never *really* looked at her. Hillary's face was heart-shaped and, like the rest of her body, had a whisper of softness to it. Her flawless ivory skin was accented by very light make-up. Tom couldn't quite get her scent over the room's odor of industrial cleaners and old coffee.

Tom had long ago decided that Hillary looked more "pretty" than "sexy," although he suspected she was quite capable of cranking up the sexuality whenever she wanted. The police station's surreal environment, his fatigue, Hillary's role as rescuer and confidante made Tom aware of an allure beneath her professional exterior. She had a sort of inviting warmth about her, a striking, independent, intelligent woman.

Tom stared at Hillary's hand on his arm, surprised at all these personal thoughts.

Must be the fatigue.

"Let's hear your deal," Tom said.

"Here's what we can do for you," Hillary said, withdrawing her hand. "I'm prepared to give you certain information on the victim, Chuck Pollard. And, I promise you'll be in the front row with an exclusive when we bust Van Grunner and whomever he works with. In return, you omit some of what he did immediately after the shooting."

"Jesus, do you know what you're asking?" Tom said. "I mean, this isn't looking the other way on an officer who says 'fuck you' to an old lady. He threatened Joyce and assaulted me."

"We'll get him, and soon. I just need more time," Hillary said. "This guy knows how to operate inside the department. He's kissed all the right asses, laughed at all the right people's bad jokes and played poker with all the right commanders to make him the department's golden boy. We need solid evidence to nail him and his buddies, whether they're inside or outside the department."

"Well just FYI, he's also mental, Hill. He's going to go off on someone someday and this place could go up like Baltimore or Ferguson. And we both know that your investigation may last another year and come up with nothing. What if he snaps and kills someone before then? What am I going to say, 'Oh yeah, I knew he was crazy, but I just forgot to include that in my story'?"

"He's not going to kill anyone. Besides, my ass will be in the sling right next to yours."

Tom sighed and let his head roll back. He studied the ceiling for a minute while his get-the-story-now zeal wrestled his desire to help Hillary. He knew she would keep her word on an exclusive when Van Grunner went down. What he didn't know was if the day Van Grunner tumbled would ever come. He imagined a TV report about how he had the goods on a bad cop but held it at the request of an "alluring assistant district attorney."

"Do you know what you're asking me to sit on?" Tom said, repeating himself on purpose.

"Yes, I do, and I wouldn't ask if this wasn't legit. You know me, Tom. I'm always square with you. We respect each other. You print what happened tonight and our investigation into Van Grunner is dead."

"Who, exactly, does 'our' refer to?" Tom asked.

"I can't tell you that."

Tom stared at his water bottle for twenty seconds, letting the silence settle around him. The deal was like passing up a sure thing to bet on a thirty-to-one shot. Then again, a cop threatening a victim's wife and kicking a reporter was hardly on par with high-profile cop crime like Baltimore and North Charleston. He looked again into Hillary's eyes and had a feeling. It was very unusual for a prosecutor to lead an investigation. He knew that some state cop somewhere was running the show. Still, Tom knew enough about Hillary to know she would stalk Van Grunner as long as it took. Not only had she made it clear she viewed law-breakers equally, whether they wore a badge or not, but she had to relish the chance to bust a chauvinist bastard like Van Grunner.

Take the deal.

"Okay, here's what I can do for you, Hillary," Tom said, feeling the electricity of a long-shot bet. "I'm willing to temporarily forget a few things, but I want your word I'm in early and alone when you bust Van Grunner. This goes beyond knowing when he'll make his initial court appearance. I want to be there when he's arrested. I want to be within five feet when they put the cuffs on him."

Tom paused. Hillary looked down at her coffee cup.

"You realize if you don't nail Van Grunner and I hold this stuff and people find out, I'm screwed as a reporter," Tom said. "I'll be labeled a prosecution lackey or cop sympathizer. Either is lethal. But before that even happened, I'd resign. It's time to find that ethics book of yours and look for loopholes. If I'm going to risk my career on this venture, you're going to have to put up a chunk of yours. Now, besides being in on the actual arrest and then having as much access as you can legally muster afterwards, what do I get for Wednesday's paper?"

"You get some stuff on the victim and some stuff the TV stations won't have. In all of this, you quote anonymous sources or I'll steer you to some existing documents. I guarantee the information will be right on."

Tom had already decided to roll the dice with Hillary Reed. No more haggling.

"Do we have a deal, Tom?"

"Yeah, I'm in it up to my notebook. But I want out of here, now. I don't want Benning trying to keep me here for seven hours of interview just so I miss deadline."

"Agreed," Hillary said.

"Good. Now let's hear what you have to tell me."

"Not here," Hillary said. "I'll give you a ride back to your car and we can talk on the way so you can make that deadline."

The two of them stepped into the hall, nearly hitting Benning. "We have an agreement, Lieutenant," Hillary said. "No photos of the officers involved until Thursday. But they will be identified in tomorrow's paper, so I suggest you take whatever precautions you need before then."

Tom could see Benning verge on protesting the deal that

gave up the identities of his officers. He had already decided to stonewall the TV stations and refuse to release the names until Thursday, even if they were in the Wednesday paper.

"We wouldn't want to prevent Tom and the other media vultures from cashing in on crime and violence," Benning said and then turned to stride down the hallway, tossing his final sentence back over his shoulder just as he rounded a corner. "I still think we should arrest him and throw him in with all those wonderful citizens he's so rabid to protect."

CHAPTER 7

Hillary led him to a pristine white 2002 Chevrolet parked in front of the station. "Old-school Camaro?" Tom said. "I haven't seen an antique like this since college. Did it come with an eight-track?"

"Yeah, yeah, I've heard them all," Hillary said, unlocking the doors. "I bought it from my brother who had trouble making the payments and just hung on to it. Get in."

The two settled into the leather seats in a spotless interior. "What I'm going to tell you is fact, but you didn't hear it from me, okay?" Hillary said.

"Yeah, we never met," Tom said with a sigh, turning his head back toward the passenger side window as Hillary started the car and drove away from the police station. Tom pulled the notebook from his back pocket and found a pen.

"Chuck Pollard was a major methamphetamine dealer for this area. Things have improved a lot, but Iowa is still a big center for meth. Your own paper has done many stories about that. Pollard has been a sort of traffic control man for some local gangs, organizing the movement of raw materials and finished product in and out of Sioux City. He's got a tight organization, but we've never had enough on him to bust him for anything much more than possession of small quantities of marijuana. He did get caught with a few ounces of meth some time back and did three years at Anamosa for it. He got out and went right back to coordinating shipments in and out of the area. You can find his priors at the courthouse."

"Anamosa" was shorthand for the state prison located in Anamosa, Iowa. "That explains his happy attitude at the house," Tom said. "Can you take me to the paper? I don't have time to go back to my car right now."

"No problem," Hillary said, changing her turn signal to reflect the new course. "Pollard may have sampled his own merchandise. We think it's cooked on some farm just outside town. The sheriff's department is looking for it. We think we know the area but can't narrow it down to which farm building, let alone get enough for a warrant. You can make the stuff virtually in a closet, so it's tough to nail the house. You can write we're testing his body for the presence of drugs, because we are. And, we've found a stash at the house. You can probably throw that in the article as well. It will be public record in a few days when we get around to filing the return of the search warrant. You could have observed us finding it. Two kilograms of meth in a crawl space in the basement."

Tom finished writing "2 kilos meth, crawl space" in his notes and turned to watch Hillary's eyes study the road ahead. On one hand, he appreciated her generosity with information. On the other, he bridled at her directing his story with "put this in" and "leave that out."

But he kept quiet. Journalism 101: Know when to talk and when not to. Journalism 102: A source doesn't ever have to know how much you already know.

Besides, Tom wouldn't have learned about the drug stash if Hillary hadn't told him. Either someone had briefed Hillary, or she had already been to the crime scene. Impressive. But, he would check with some friends in the crime lab just to make sure Hillary wasn't yanking him a little on some of the details.

"Two kilos? Geez. That's four-and-a-half pounds. So Chuck is the subject of an ongoing investigation?" Tom asked. He felt compelled to at least make a show of trying to get something out of her in light of the severe spoon feeding.

"He is, but if you print that then they'll know the leak is inside the department and that's too close. Isn't it enough to say he was arrested before and that we found meth in the house? That alone, along with your eyewitness account, will put you miles in front of the TV people. Check with Denise and she'll probably tell you that Chuck was high as a kite."

Denise Marcheck, the Woodbury County Medical Examiner, would be pulling on the rubber gloves and firing up the skull saw in the morning. Tom scrawled "call Denise" in his notes.

"That's about all I can tell you tonight, but we've agreed there will be more. Here," Hillary said, handing Tom a card. "My cell number is on the back. Please don't let anyone else see that, and please only call me on my cell about this case. If it's an emergency and you have to call the office, use the direct line. It comes right to my desk. No receptionist."

Tom produced one of his cards and scribbled his cell number on the back. "Call the cell. I'm away from the office a lot lately, hanging out with my new friends at the police department or consulting orthopedic surgeons and rib rehab specialists."

A smile briefly shouldered its way through Hillary's stoic expression only to vanish as quickly as it came.

Tom pulled his phone out of his front pocket and turned it on. A banner on the touch screen indicated he'd missed three calls. "I turned it off on the way to the police station," he said to a quizzical-looking Hillary. "Nothing ruder than having your phone ring while being interrogated by the Gestapo." He speed-dialed the *Sentinel-Leader*. The familiar voice of fellow reporter Skip Ensley answered.

"Skip!" Tom said with exaggerated exuberance. "What's happening, baby? Some kind of shooting or what?"

"Very funny, Tom. Where the hell are you? I got my butt pulled

into work by Papa Bear at 10 p.m. and I've been calling you all
night. I think it's strange enough that a sixty-eight-year-old sleeps
with a scanner next to his bed, but when he starts calling me
because he can't reach you to run down his scanner calls, I've got
a major problem."

"Skip, between you and me, you could use a little exercise.
Running down scanner calls might be just the ticket."

"Funny. Oh, you're a riot, Tom. My wife was so mad the covers
were smoking when I left home. If you're going to be wonderboy
down here at least you can keep the Bear informed where you are
or answer your damn phone."

"Sorry, Geoffrey," Tom said, using Skip's proper first name and
glancing at Hillary. She did a good job of pretending not to listen.
"Get kind of surly when you have to handle actual news, don't you?
I'm inbound right now. I was kind of busy at the scene to be chat-
ting with you on the phone. I've got stuff going on. Irons in every
fire. Mr. Sioux City After Dark."

"Yeah, we heard you were there, Mr. Big Stuff," Ensley said.
"Kelso told me he saw you. Then you disappeared on him. By the
time I got to the scene, the cops had hustled all the witnesses off. I
saw your car. It's a wonder they didn't tow it."

"First of all, my car is legally parked and fully insured, so if I'm
lucky someone will steal it or set it on fire. Second, as for witnesses
to the shooting, you can interview one right there at the paper,
because I saw it all. From door kick to gunshot, I had the front-
row view."

Hillary stiffened in her seat.

"No way," Ensley said.

Tom braced his undamaged elbow against the car door as
Hillary took a corner aggressively. He glanced at the door lock to
make sure it was down.

This woman drives like Danica Patrick.

"Oh yeah. I was front and center, standing on a friggin'

lawnmower outside the window. Nearly killed myself." Tom gently felt the back of his head where an angry knot had grown. "Got some tasty details that will cause the TV people to spew their Cheerios all over their kitchen walls when they read them tomorrow."

"Well, get your butt in here, Wonderboy. Presses run in an hour. I have what I know written. You can just throw your stuff into my story. Bear is going to have a woody for a week when he hears this. About all I got was the official crap, and a woman who says she was in the house during the shooting. She's telling everyone it wasn't justified."

"That would be Joyce." Tom snorted. "She's high. I saw it all. Chuck took a shot at the cops. They had no choice. Hey, got to go. I'll be there in a second."

Tom punched the "end" button and stowed his phone. He shot Hillary a glance, then immediately had a sexual thought that caught him off guard. Maybe their roles as co-conspirators in this story nudged Tom's appreciation of Hillary up a few notches. Then again, maybe it was the stress talking.

As they wheeled into the *Sentinel-Leader*'s parking lot, Tom's mind was already on his story, working the first paragraph over and over.

"Thanks," Tom said, getting out of her car. "Don't worry about my end of the deal. I'm sure we'll be talking again soon."

"I hope so." she said.

Tom slammed the door and held up his hand in a wave as Hillary's car sped away.

'Hope so.' What did that mean?

CHAPTER 8

By the time she had cleared the *Sentinel-Leader*'s parking lot, Hillary was well into re-examining her ethical position. She would argue that she'd met the threshold of an exception to Rule 32.3.6 dealing with pre-trial publicity. Based on her professional relationship with Tom Kingman and his promise not to publish, she had told him nothing much beyond public record that "a reasonable person would expect to be disseminated by means of public communications." Hillary trusted Tom to live up to his off-the-record agreement. If he did that, her more sensitive comments would stay out of the paper and thereby preserve her adherence—albeit with a little stretching—to the code of professional responsibility.

Perhaps she exaggerated, but for a woman who relied so much on living up to ethical standards, Hillary felt like the course of her career now depended on Tom keeping his word.

+++

Tom felt a familiar high as he walked toward the building. He always felt that way when he faced a big story and was fueled with the raw information he needed and go for liftoff at his keyboard. Even while typing, Tom's brain would lope far out in front of his fingers, like a dog bounding out in front of a plodding hunter. Now and then the dog would pause to look back and circle around to some other thoughts, until the hunter caught up, sending the dog bounding far ahead of him again.

With deadline about fifty minutes away, Tom would have time for three, maybe four passes over Skip's story. If he did it well, and he usually did, most of the 90,000 subscribers would read his words as urgently as he wrote them, which was what Tom lived for.

The *Sentinel-Leader* building was a large, one-story brick structure, essentially a huge rectangle with an ornamental facade. Built in the late 1970s, it now had several antennas and satellite dishes lining its roof, some of them merely artifacts testifying to previous generations of telecommunications.

Tom swiped his security key card through the lock on the employees' entrance and walked in, the security system silently noting the time as 11:37 p.m. The building contained a relatively tiny staff which, at this time of night, was concerned with the mechanics of transferring computer-designed page layouts back to the gigantic printing press that filled the back half of the building.

There were two other people in the building who weren't normally there so late. In the middle of the large, open newsroom, Geoffrey "Skip" Ensley sat hunched over his keyboard wearing a T-shirt emblazoned "Echosmith," a band that had played Sioux City's Hard Rock Hotel last year. He also wore jeans and loafers with no socks, his hair still in the full glory of bed head.

Skip was a short man with a barrel chest, a bit older than Tom. He had a round face and black hair going prematurely gray around the edges. His hair framed a low forehead. People who met him often guessed truck driver or mechanic rather than reporter. Skip had a quick wit and passion for up-and-coming or semi-obscure bands and hard-core board games. In six years of working together, Tom had never seen Skip panic or lose his cool. Even in victory, as Tom danced around the room Skip maintained his stoic discipline, limiting his outward celebration to a wide grin.

The only other person in this part of the building was Abraham Benjamin Pennington. Bear—even his wife called him Bear—sat in a large office between the front door and the employees' side entrance. Windows lined the office, allowing the Bear to see and be seen from both the front counter and the newsroom. His nickname came from decades of roaring at anyone who dared to violate his sense of duty to the First Amendment, something he clutched to his beating heart like Holy Scripture.

Tom had seen the Bear in action many times, often in clashes with a mayor or local business leaders who either weren't warned about him or chose to ignore the warning. Many mayors, fresh from an election victory with an imaginary mandate from the thirty percent of citizens who bothered to vote, took at least one run at Bear, thinking they could cow him into "getting on the team" and trading the media's role of watchdog for that of lap dog. The Chamber of Commerce—Bear called them the Sunshine Squad—was a recurring foe. Eventually, they all learned Bear had one team: his.

While local politicians relied on their perceived popularity with the voters, business leaders in Sioux City tried to use their advertising dollars to pressure the media into being a kinder version of the Fourth Estate. Every reporter on the *Sentinel-Leader* staff had heard "Print that and we'll pull our advertising" at least once. It was the same, more or less, at every paper Tom knew of.

Bear, however, never once backed down in the face of such threats, including one from the president of a multi-state grocery chain. His stock answer: "Piss on them. Where they gonna go for the kind of audience we deliver? TV? Not in this town. Blogs?"—derisive snort—"They'll be back." And then he would personally call the offended business's competitors and tell them that now was the perfect time for them to advertise, what with the competition boycotting the *S-L*.

The attitude made the *S-L* staff extraordinarily loyal to Bear.

Tom had turned down offers and inquiries from papers in Des Moines, Chicago, St. Louis, and Minneapolis. Working in Des Moines, a town that thought Sioux City was in South Dakota, wouldn't have felt right, and Tom was allergic to traffic, so that helped rule out other suitors at well. Mostly Tom felt lucky to work for such an endangered species: a publisher who bled ink and made decisions based on something more than numbers on a spreadsheet.

A bank of television monitors mounted to the wall lined one corner of the newsroom. They showed soundless infomercials and late-night talk shows for an audience of empty chairs in the newsroom. The local TV stations had larger screens, with a few smaller screens orbiting the main monitors. When Tom arrived at the newspaper almost exactly two hours after the shooting, Bear sat hunkered over a large legal reference book on his desk—that was his idea of leisure reading. Tom gave Bear a wave as he headed over to his desk facing Skip's.

"Golden boy has returned," Skip said, turning down the police scanner on his desk as it intercepted a dispatcher sending an ambulance to the edge of town for an auto accident. "Mr. Eyewitness. I'd love to see Kelso's face tomorrow morning. You look like you were mugged, by the way."

"I feel like it too, and thanks for noticing. But this story keeps getting better, Skip," Tom said, throwing his notebook on the desk along with his car keys. He filled Skip in on his visit to police headquarters.

"Bear is going to shit his pants." Skip leaned forward. "He'll want you to print a word-for-word transcript as a sidebar. He'll be so happy he may ask you to move in with him."

"I've also got a source who leaked me some stuff that will make Bear explode into little publisher shrapnel," Tom said, taking a seat and calling up a blank document template on his computer. "The source wants me to keep bits of what I saw to myself for now, and in return I get some advance info on the case. Super confidentially, I made a deal, which I'm not sure Bear will like, but after I tell him what's in it for us, I think he'll support it."

Actually, Tom knew that, given their history and his loyalty, Bear would support him no matter what. The big question was how happy Bear would be about it. Tom, like almost everyone at the *Sentinel-Leader*, had sustained the berating and lectures that came when Bear judged them guilty of dereliction of journalistic duty.

"Is the source connected?" Skip asked.

"Connected? Oh yeah. This is some big stuff, so hot I can't even tell you who my source is, not yet at least. Of course I'll have to tell Bear, but this source is definitely connected."

"Did you say Powers and Van Grunner did the shooting?"

"Yeah, they plugged this guy Chuck Pollard like a bad hair weave. Pretty good shooting for a pair of cops."

Skip and Tom had been working together too long for Skip to buy Tom's "no-big-deal" bravado, but still he admired Tom's calm. "I would have yakked up a lung right on the spot," Skip said.

"Pretty intense," Tom said quietly, his wired expression giving way briefly to seriousness. He quickly readjusted his jocular mask. "I was outside watching through the window when the shooting started. As much as I wouldn't mind seeing Van Grunner swing, it was self-defense. They had no choice. Let me get started here and then we'll talk about what you've got from the scene."

When Tom was ready, he would reveal some of his own feelings about watching someone die, but it would be a while before he was ready. Tom could compartmentalize his feelings like no one else, keeping them tucked away until he could vent them in a controlled way, often added by craft beer, snooty Bourbon or single-malt scotch, or all three.

He rolled into attack position in front of his computer and began formatting the page, a ritual he'd repeated to the point of instinct.

By Tom Kingman
Sentinel-Leader Staff Writer

Two Sioux City police officers shot and killed a man Tuesday
night while responding to a domestic disturbance in the city's old
warehouse district.

From there, Tom raced through the story, habitually hitting
"control-S" on his keyboard to save it on his computer every few
paragraphs. After finishing the first draft, Tom found Skip's story
on the *S-L* computer network and scanned it. Ten minutes later, he
had combined the two into a longer article plus a sidebar.

He saved the stories and asked Skip to take a look. He appreciated Skip's refraining from quizzing him on the story details
and respecting his writing zone. Bear had continued to read his
book without much apparent concern. Tom would bring him up
to speed once the story was safely filed before deadline. Bear had
ordered the presses delayed for thirty minutes to give them more
time to work the story.

While Skip edited the story—he was a better pure writer than
anyone Tom knew, including himself—he went to brief Bear,
knocking once on the door frame as he walked through the open
door to Bear's office. "What're ya reading, Bear?" Tom asked, feeling the post-deadline freedom to take a bit of a circular route to
the hot topic.

"It's a collection of Supreme Court rulings that deal with freedom of expression over the last five years, plus commentary," Bear
said. His puritanical regard for the First Amendment would have
struck someone meeting Bear for the first time as quaint, amusing,
even compulsive. "We need to keep up on the latest law just to keep
the lawyers on their toes."

"You don't need any books to keep people on their toes, Bear,"

Tom said, taking the high-backed leather seat in front of Bear's desk. Tom suspected Bear liked the high backs because they made people feel trapped and therefore vulnerable.

Order ruled the Bear Cage. Bear or his assistant for two decades, Eileen, meticulously filed everything—whether it was digital or paper—and kept Bear's oak desk well polished. Legal books lined one wall and a few framed historic *Sentinel-Leader* newspaper pages dominated another. A collection of seven small TV monitors peered out from the wall behind Bear's desk. An internet news ticker service scrolled across the bottom of Bear's computer screen.

Might as well just plunge in head first.

"I was there," Tom said. "I saw the entire shooting through the side window of 219 West Jarred. A drug dealer named Chuck Pollard took a shot at two Sioux City cops—Bryan Van Grunner and a rookie, Neal Powers—and they cut him down with two shots to the chest. Each cop hit him once."

"Excellent." Bear rose from his chair. "Well done. This will really stick in the craw of those chain papers and blow the hapless TV stations out of the water—again. So it was a justified shooting?"

"Yeah, it was justified." Tom ran through his eyewitness account again.

"Lucky for them they didn't screw it up. It would have meant another story that set Chief Banks off. Poor baby. He already hates us. That doesn't bother me, of course, because I'm not that fond of him, either. The man is so friggin' paranoid right now. It's nice not to have to listen to him jabber on about how the *S-L* is against him and trying to disgrace his department and blah, blah, blah. Instead of screaming about us, he should pull his head out of his butt and fix his department."

"There's more," Tom said. "After they shot the guy, the woman inside started screaming at Powers and Van Grunner, going on about how they shot him in cold blood and a lot of other crap.

Well, Van Grunner lost it for a minute and pulled out his baton. He was talking, at least, like he was going to rap the woman in the head, but then I fell off the lawnmower."

"Lawnmower?" Bear said, resuming his seat without breaking eye contact with Tom.

"I was standing on it outside the window. It was the only thing I could find to boost me up high enough to see what was going on. Made quite a noise when I fell off. Next thing I know, Van Grunner was standing over me with his gun in my face. We exchanged pleasantries, and he kicked me in the ribs."

"You've got to be shitting me," Bear growled, thumping his fist on the desk. "Those bastards. Get Skip in here —"

"Hang on, there's still more. They asked me to come down to headquarters and talk to them. I decided to go along with it in case they continued to be stupid and leak more details. Unfortunately, Lieutenant Benning took over once we got downtown. He's not exactly Mr. Sunshine, but he made it past the sixth grade, unlike Van Grunner. I got nothing off Benning but pressure to keep the names of the officers and Van Grunner's post-shooting actions quiet."

"Typical. What are they going to do, build a fortress around the cops' houses? I know you didn't go for this garbage."

"No way. But after I'd spent some time with Lieutenant Warmth, they sent in Hillary Reed, who is a bit harder to say no to."

Careful.

"You didn't start thinking with your dick, did you? You know we've got a responsibility to the American people here to tell what we know. I mean —"

"No sir, I did not cave in, and I kept my dick out of it."

Mostly.

Bear chuckled. "Glad to hear reason prevailed."

Tom recapped his deal with Hillary, carefully watching Bear's face for any adverse reaction.

Finally, Bear said, "Hell, Tom, that's what they always say. 'You'll screw up our investigation.' I heard that when I was a beat reporter hacking out stories on a manual typewriter."

"Not Hillary Reed," Tom said. "She always plays it straight with me. When she says she's close to having something on Van Grunner, I trust her. Plus, the last thing I want is to screw something up so Van Grunner walks. I know I'm playing around with my reputation and career here, but I'm giving up the detail now to get the huge story of a bad cop later."

"What do we get from Reed to look the other way on Van Grunner tonight?" Bear said.

"Leaks from the county attorney's office and a chance to be there when they unravel this whole Van Grunner thing."

"I just don't want to lie to our readers," Bear said, disappointment leaking into his words. "And I don't want this to come out later and make us look like we were covering for the jerk-off cops. You are really putting a lot on the line for both of us on this one."

"Look, if you have trouble with this, we can call Hillary and you can talk to her," Tom said. "I trust her not to use us, Bear. And I'm not thinking with my crotch. My instincts told me to make the deal, and they've never let me down yet. She'll make it worth our while in the long run."

"Worth *our* while or worth *your* while?" Bear said. "I don't like my reporters being too cozy with the other side."

Am I?

"Come on," Tom said, fighting the sting of Bear's real or imagined insinuation. "Who are you talking to here? Some college intern? I need to know I have your total confidence. If I don't, put someone else on it right now. I'll understand."

I won't, actually. I'll start looking for a new gig. But let's not go nuclear when we don't have to.

Bear paused. "Calm down. You and I both know I trust your judgment and you have my full support. We've just got to be careful. A lot of papers and magazines have been screwing up lately. Remember that Cincinnati paper had to issue a front-page apology and pay some corporation ten million dollars because they published when they didn't have everything solid? The story was probably true, but it wasn't solid, leaving them open for attack. Columnists and reporters get caught making up sources and quotes ..."

Nip this in the bud...

"It's solid. Sorry if I got a little testy there. Been a long day."

Bear grinned and snorted. "Forget about it. Watching a man die will put anyone on edge."

Please, not one of your unending Vietnam stories ...

"I'll ask Skip to send you a draft in a minute," Tom said, rising to leave, "and I'll keep you posted."

"Good work as usual, Tom," Bear said, pulling his book back in front of him.

"Thanks, Bear. I'm going to need some time on this one. I may not be around much, or at all, in the next week or two. I'll work with Skip on our daily coverage and probably file stuff from my laptop and email you updates."

"Take all the time you need. If it's too sensitive, give me a call," Bear said, tapping the law book he had been reading. "Paper trails screw a lot of people."

Well my shit's in the fire now. Hope you're not playing me, Hillary.

CHAPTER 3

Back in the newsroom, Tom walked directly to Skip's desk. "You get it done?"

"Yeah. Great stuff, Tom. Just a few typos, a little tweaking and some tightening. The copy editors and Bear have it now so we should make deadline."

"I appreciate the Skip magic," said Tom, who could be relied upon to have at least one or two typos in anything he wrote. "Let's get something to drink."

Tom and Skip walked into a smaller adjoining room lined with a coffee maker and vending machines. Both grabbed coffee, Skip filling his prized University of Minnesota mug, and sat at a table. The break room featured a faded 1980s motif of rare ugliness. Few members of the public ever saw the break room; instead they were shuttled into a more modern conference room used for interviews and staff meetings. The break room looked fine to Bear. Employees seemed to agree since they knew money saved on redecorating would be used for salaries and high-tech news-gathering tools.

Tom took his favorite spot in an easy chair while Ensley flopped onto the couch and put his feet on a worn coffee table. Tom felt himself sinking into the chair as he answered all of Skip's questions. Tom and Skip had built a professional intimacy while collaborating on many long-term projects. Often, Tom would disappear for days while Skip worked the same story from the newsroom. During those times, Tom remained tethered to Skip by phone, text, and email.

For Skip, the relationship meant that he could focus on his first love—writing—and let Tom run all over town, stand on lawnmowers, and go face-to-face with police. Their collaboration also allowed Skip to go home at regular hours and see his wife and children, which he happily acknowledged meant more to him than his job. The *S-L* had all the technology that allowed remote access, dramatically reducing the need to be physically present in the newsroom.

While Skip was tied down by some husband and fatherly duties, Tom enjoyed his freedom to roam. Skip was a family man, but Tom was all about the job. Tom didn't even keep a pet at home for fear that it would inhibit his nomadic abilities. Sure, Tom sometimes envied Skip during those nights in crappy motels, sleeping in the back of his car, or even at home, alone. Maybe he was getting older, but the high of the byline seemed to be a little less dazzling each time.

Tom and Skip often shared bylines and always shared any prizes that resulted from their projects. The two took Bear out to dinner to celebrate any journalism awards or honors—where the "snooty beer" and scotch flowed—and there had been quite a few. Both knew Bear's focus on news afforded them the luxury of producing award-winning work.

Skip's gift was for writing, Tom's for reporting. Apart they were great; together they were brilliant. Both men knew it and were thankful for it, although they'd never said it out loud.

Tom got back to his desk from the break room just as his phone started ringing.

Hillary?

Nothing showed up on the Caller ID. He answered with his customary one word: "Kingman."

"Are you the reporter who saw that shooting tonight?" a female voice said.

"Depends," Tom responded, glancing at his watch: 12:45 a.m.

Who could know that so soon after the shooting? Does TV have something up on the web by now? One of the neighbors?

"Who is this?" Tom said as he called up the TV news websites. Nothing.

"A friend," the woman said. "I have some information you might be interested in."

"Who are you?" Tom said.

"Somebody who knows things, lots of things. Why don't you come visit me and see for yourself?"

Tom hated anonymous calls. Anonymity usually disguised ignorance, malice, greed, jealousy or all of the above. And yet, sometimes anonymous sources offered a grain of sand that grew into a pearl. Problem: it takes from one to twenty years for a grain of sand to become a pearl. Apparently oysters don't operate on a deadline.

"If I come see you, what will we talk about?" Tom asked.

"I have a lot of, ah, *associates* who did business with Chuck Pollard, the man who got shot. He provided them with certain pharmacological services. He had a thriving business around here, as I'm sure you know. Some of my acquaintances are a little distressed about what happened tonight. They tell me that there's some interesting timing involved."

The woman said she was staying at the Regal Hotel, a historic, fourteen-story structure that lived up to its name, which was a holdover from a hotel from Sioux City's days as a raucous riverboat town in 18-something. If this woman was crazy, at least she had good taste and apparently some money. Tom decided to agree more because the caller was confirming Hillary's rundown of Pollard than because of her taste in hotels. The swanky surroundings would be reassuring, at least better than meeting at, say, lot twenty-one of the Budget Park mobile home court, a.k.a Zip Gun Land.

"Sure, I can come down to the Regal."

"What time is it now, quarter to one? Be at the Regal at 1:30 tonight. Room eleven fifteen," the woman said. "Call from the lobby before you come up."

"Okay, the Regal at 1:30," Tom said, recording the time and room number in his notebook. "I don't want to seem ungrateful, but why are you calling me?"

"Let's say seeing what I have to tell you in the paper would not ruin my day. Be here at 1:30." The woman hung up.

Tom moved to a large but seldom-used coat closet, pulled the door open, stripped off his torn shirt and pulled a fresh one off a hanger he kept in there for just such occasions. The many times he managed to spill on himself during work had originally motivated him to stash clean shirts in the closet, but ... happy accidents. Once freshly buttoned and tucked, Tom and Skip left the building together. Skip headed home and Tom caught a ride back to his car on West Jarred from one of the delivery truck drivers who had arrived early.

It took ten minutes for him to drive from Pollard's house to the Regal and another few to park and get to the lobby phone. Room 1115 answered on the second ring.

"This is Tom Kingman," he said.

"Hi, Tom," said the smooth feminine voice. It seemed much clearer on the house phone. "Give me five minutes and then come up to my room." She hung up without waiting for a reply.

The Regal's lobby offered dark paneling, polished antique furniture and expensive carpets in homage to the 18-something name. Tom expected an elder statesman or riverboat captain wearing a smoking jacket and puffing on a pipe to come around the corner any second. It was almost over-the-top "historical," but it still seemed to work. The staff had done a nice job of mixing in just enough contemporary touches to elevate it from "museum" to "timelessly elegant."

He found a seat among the antiques and glanced at his watch: 1:28 a.m. He'd wait until at least 1:40 before going to the elevator. It was his turn to act breathy and casual. He didn't quite know what to expect, meeting a strange woman in a hotel room, but charging up to the room early seemed to send the wrong signal.

At 1:41, Tom stood before the door marked "1115." He studied the ornate numbers and listened for sounds coming from inside. Nothing. Perhaps some low music, but that could have been from an adjacent room.

Here we go.

He raised his hand and knocked softly. The door opened about four inches and a woman peered out.

"Mr. Kingman?" the woman said, unsmiling, her perfume advancing from the shadows into the dim hall.

"I'm Tom Kingman."

"ID?" she asked.

ID? What am I, a cop?

"Ah, sure," he said, fumbling for a moment before presenting the woman with his driver's license and press credential. She looked at both, smiled and handed them back through the door.

"Let's just say I'd like to be assured that you are who you say you are," the woman said, opening the door more widely. "Please, come in."

He entered a two-room suite. Quite nicely decorated, Tom thought, with colorful carpets and finely upholstered furniture. An antique-looking desk filled one corner. The bathroom, with its Jacuzzi tub for two, was directly to his right.

Ah, THAT kind of room.

Tom glanced into the bathroom. No signs of life. The bedroom door stood open, revealing the end of a four poster bed, a table with a phone and phone book slightly askew on top of it.

Tom returned his gaze to the main room, getting a good, full-length look at the woman for the first time as she turned—he sensed on purpose—in front of him.

Her midnight blue wrap dress stopped several inches above the knee, revealing toned legs covered with shimmering, sheer, and second-skin nylon. The sleeveless dress caressed her upper body firmly, plunging down to expose a few inches of cleavage. A magnificent back rose above her taut rear.

The woman slowly completed her turn and looked at Tom, who hoped his face didn't register the pirouette's sensual impact.

"Thank you for coming, Mr. Kingman, or can I just call you Tom?" the woman said. Fine facial bones, short, perfect, brown hair and inviting lips matched the arousal firepower of the rest of the body. "Can I offer you some champagne?"

"No, thank you," Tom said, being hit again by the woman's evocative scent. "Tom will be fine, Miss—?"

"Just call me Brenda. I'd prefer to keep my real name out of this. You understand."

Tom gave his best nod-and-shrug combination.

Brenda's movement caused her skirt to ride up and dared Tom to look at the flashes of thigh as she moved. Tom focused on Brenda's face, willing himself not to look at those firm legs. He had always been a leg man, and if she sat down, Tom thought his eyes would leap from their sockets in defiance.

"Please, make yourself comfortable," Brenda said, gesturing toward a grouping of furniture in front of a gas-fueled fireplace. Tom could see the definition of Brenda's shoulder muscles where they flowed into a firm upper arm. Her muscles rippled subtly over her shoulder blade.

Aerobics and probably weight training too. Slightly muscular women with great legs … my kryptonite.

Tom had met his last girlfriend, Joan, in the gym, instantly mesmerized by her sculpted calves and defined shoulders. Tom thought of Joan in a sports bra as "poor man's Viagra."

As Tom advanced toward the couch in front of the fireplace, Brenda slowly leaned against the end of the sofa, her hemline gaping open. Stay on target, Tom's brain screamed at his eyes. He managed to look relentlessly at Brenda's face. She moved from the arm of the sofa to a chair situated at a 90-degree angle to Tom's seat on the couch. An end table served as the elbow of the "L" created by the sofa-and-chair arrangement. Brenda and Tom could have easily touched feet and her amazing thighs were two feet from Tom's right hand, which had quickly joined his eyes in conspiracy to mutiny.

She's good.

Tom's mind was not so enfeebled by lust that he didn't recognize the well-orchestrated erotic barrage.

Very good.

When Brenda glanced over to find her drink on the end table, Tom's eyes bounded to Brenda's upper leg. He was almost powerless to stop them.

"You called me, Brenda," Tom said, not taking his eyes off the stocking tops peeking from under Brenda's skirt.

That explains the hot-weather nylon. Judas H. Priest on a palomino.

"I'd love to hear what you have to say."

"I'm from Omaha and I travel to Sioux City maybe once a week on business. One of my, ah, business associates knows all about Mr. Pollard. He was not surprised that Mr. Pollard died earlier tonight."

"Why wasn't this associate of yours surprised?" Tom said, managing to rein in his mutinous eyes and return them to Brenda's face. "I certainly was."

Brenda smiled. "Yes, you were there, weren't you? Very fortunate for certain people to have you there. What a great eyewitness—a newspaper reporter. And one with your reputation. You may not recognize it, but you're a very powerful man, Tom." She uncrossed her legs with a hiss of nylon, leaned forward to expose a bit more cleavage, and then re-crossed her legs. "I find powerful men very exciting."

INCOMING.

Tom was no physical trophy, yet Brenda's body language was coming on to him in a series of emphatic, one-syllable commands.

Why the white-hot treatment? Remember what Bear said about thinking with your dick ...

Despite his rational defense, Brenda's escalating sexual fire had driven Tom's heart into his throat. She kept her leg movements artificially slow, giving Tom a one-second look at the garters and stockings. He could not prevent himself from imagining the wispy panty that went with Brenda's ensemble, if indeed there were any undergarments at all.

Get a grip on yourself.

"Just what kind of business are you in?" Tom said, battling to control both his voice and the interview.

"I think you know, Mr. Kingman," she said, leaning forward and dropping her shoulders just enough to display all but the nipples of both breasts.

"I perform certain *services*"—she smiled approval of her euphemism—"for some members of the business community. I entertain a few of them in this hotel every week. It's quite lucrative as well as very satisfying work, for both me and my clients."

Tom nodded. He'd heard of high class prostitutes who regularly traveled to Sioux City from Omaha, rented a room for a couple of days and entertained the more discriminating clients. They were sex trade contractors, freelancers, if you will. There wasn't enough demand for such services to establish a Sioux City-based *business* but enough to spur the occasional trip up from Omaha.

Most of the prostitutes in Sioux City were drug-dependent women who plied their trade in a certain area of downtown. Tom had covered prostitute roundups several times, even ridden along with police during one sting.

Clients from higher social standing—doctors, lawyers, CEOs—preferred to make discreet arrangements with women like Brenda for private, more leisurely encounters. The rise of the internet and smartphones had made scheduling even more convenient for everyone involved.

Tom still couldn't figure why Brenda was giving him the full-frontal come-on. She surely couldn't hope to get her fee—which Tom estimated at $750 or more—from a newspaper reporter.

Brenda ran her hand over the top of her crossed thigh while taking a sip of champagne. She smiled as she saw Tom's eyes jerk down to watch her delicate gold chain bracelet dance across the nylon, throwing sparks of reflected light as it went. "Chuck Pollard was supposed to die and now he's dead. My acquaintances say the person who got that job done sits very high on the social ladder here. He's a prominent member of the Chamber of Commerce, respected, has a lovely wife and big house, and donates to charities. Never a hint of scandal. He's also the man to see if you're into methamphetamine."

"And who might that be, Brenda?" Tom asked.

Brenda bore in like a sexual fighter with an opponent on the ropes, uncrossing and recrossing her legs.

"His name? Sorry, Tom. I don't think I can go that far. Although I wouldn't mind going quite a distance with you." She took another sip of her champagne, letting her tongue slowly chase a stray drop around her lips.

"You'll have to come up with a name on your own. Just remember, Pollard isn't the top of the organization chart by any means. I think if you check into his history a bit you might find something interesting."

"Why tell me all this?" Tom said, shifting his weight and wishing he could cover his lap with his notebook.

Just tell me a little more before I have to run for my life …

"Let's say I wouldn't mind seeing the top of Pollard's organization knocked off the chart," she said, staring at Tom's erection as she talked.

"I have some time before my next appointment," Brenda said as she rose from her seat, took a step over, edged up her skirt and sat down on Tom's lap, her legs straddling his. The idea of preventing the move flashed through Tom's brain, but his body rejected the idea.

She lowered her mouth to his ear, letting her subtle scent tease him again. "Why don't you do what you've wanted to do since you walked in? No charge. Maybe get a little more information out of me."

She kissed him hard while pulling his hand onto her upper thigh.

Holy fuck.

Tom's control of his voluntary muscles ebbed by the second. His hand grew a will of its own, rubbing Brenda's upper leg, sliding over the strap of her garter and onto her warm, naked skin. The sensations tore at the door restraining Tom's animal side.

Brenda eased her mouth off Tom's as she covered his hand with her own and urged it higher up her leg.

She stood up, giving Tom a lusty gaze, and untied her dress at the side, allowing it to fall open. Brenda slid both hands up over her naked breasts and back down slowly, letting out a thermonuclear purr.

Mayday. Mayday. Mayday. I am taking fire. Repeat. I am taking fire.

Tom's mind filled with an image of Brenda, wearing only her shoes and stockings. His mouth went dry. His pounding pulse made his head ache. His face started sweating and the muscles in the back of his neck contracted to the point of snapping.

"I, ah, we can't do this."

Brenda's lusty look returned. She knelt to the left of Tom's left leg, sliding her hands up Tom's thighs and lowering her mouth to within inches of his crotch.

"From here it looks like we can," Brenda said, raising an eyebrow slightly. She expertly undid his belt and had his pants unbuttoned and fly unzipped before Tom could mount a defense. If Brenda succeeded in taking him into her mouth, Tom knew even the pretense of resistance would crumble. Every molecule of his animal brain screamed out for Brenda's body as visions of torrid sex with Joan flashed through his brain. His rational mind fought ever more desperately, forced into a corner by howling desire. Tom saw the image of Brenda poised over his crotch reflected in the fireplace doors. The carnal Tom hungered for Brenda's breasts and mouth.

No way. NO WAY. This is some kind of wrong. Don't be a fucking idiot. This is a set-up or something. GET THE FUCK OUT.

"Brenda, no," Tom said, grabbing her hand. "I can't do this. We have to stop."

Brenda responded by running her free hand down Tom's chest and abdomen and over his underwear-constrained erection. Tom's rational brain turned and ran.

A loud rap at the door broke the pornographic moment.

CHAPTER 10

The knock at the door caused Brenda's head to jerk up, the smoldering look draining quickly from her eyes. She sat upright and quickly got her dress back in place.

"Who is it?" Brenda called, looking at Tom.

"It's me," came the cryptic response.

"Be there in a minute." Brenda winked at Tom, who was just coming out of his erotic coma. "He's early," she whispered playfully into Tom's ear. "If he finds you here, he'll kill you."

Hearing "he'll kill you" was like plunging a white-hot piece of metal into an ice bucket. Tom bounced to his feet and pulled his pants up, frantically tucking in his shirt. Brenda smiled at Tom as she moved toward the door.

I'm so glad she's amused by this. Shit shit shit shit. Now what? Balcony? And squat out there for a few hours while Brenda entertains her guest?

The route from the balcony to the door went right through the sofa area. And God help him if the visitor went out on the balcony for a post-coital smoke. Tom imagined himself flapping like a bird for all eleven floors of the descent.

"The bathroom," Brenda whispered.

From white hot to ice cold inside two minutes. Hmmm.

Tom crossed to the bathroom, his belt still dangling open,

trying to move silently. Brenda was right behind. "Just about ready," she yelled at the door as Tom was about halfway to the hiding place.

Tom plunged into the dark bathroom, ramming his hip on the sink. *Son of a bitch!* Brenda reached in and grabbed the door handle.

Before pulling it shut, she slipped her free hand around the back of Tom's neck and sharply pulled him into a kiss. Brenda held the kiss for a second, quickly probing Tom's mouth with her tongue before pulling back.

"Next time, I hope," she whispered as she closed the bathroom door softly. Tom lurched back in reaction to her release. He drove off the last lingering sensations of Brenda's kiss. His erection had long since made a hasty exit, and fear, not lust, now motivated his pounding heart.

What the hell is happening to this town? Just this morning I was writing about how the weather was roasting all the corn in the fields, now I got dead meth dealers and a hooker coming on to me. WTF?

Tom held his ear close to the bathroom door and prayed that Brenda's client wouldn't need to take a piss before getting down to business. He went over possible ways to confront the visitor if he did enter. The shower curtain could provide precious little cover. There were no obvious weapons. Throwing hotel shampoo didn't seem like an effective tactic.

Tom heard Brenda's muffled voice.

"Come in," she said. "I was just getting dressed for you. You're early."

"I got my business taken care of," a man's voice answered. Tom decided to risk gently pressing his ear against the door. "I remembered you said you didn't have any other appointments tonight so I thought I'd come early."

"Sorry you had to wait in the hall. Hope you like this." Tom imagined Brenda showing the man her dress—or something. "I've got the champagne chilling over by the sofa. Why don't you make yourself comfortable?"

"Why don't I?" the man said, and Tom heard what he thought were kisses. "You have a talent for making me comfortable, Stephanie. Very comfortable."

Stephanie? At least I know her professional name—one of them, anyway.

"Come over to the couch and I'll start providing you with some comfort then," Stephanie said, her voice husky.

Brenda/Stephanie must have an on-off switch. Sure worked on you, asshole.

He wanted to get a look at the client, but he had to wait until they had moved farther into the room. He knew even cracking the door with the man standing virtually on top of it would ruin Tom's day, and probably his body.

After the voices had faded, Tom opened the door enough to look through with one eye. He could see a tan-haired man wearing a white dress shirt sitting on the sofa where Tom and Brenda had gotten acquainted. The man's head was rolled back and Tom could just make out a band of leather around his left shoulder.

Perfect, a shoulder holster. What kind of 'business man' wears a shoulder holster even in today's concealed carry permit craze? Is this guy a cop?

Tom focused on the man again, looking for anything that might identify him. Suddenly Stephanie's head popped up from the other side of the couch. She licked her lips before giving the man an aggressive kiss. "Comfortable?" Stephanie said slyly. The man said something and Stephanie slid slowly down in front of the man, out of Tom's sight.

If you're waiting for a diversion, they don't get much better than what Stephanie is doing for Mr. Shoulder Holster.

Tom slowly eased the bathroom door open far enough to slip out. He paused to make sure the visitor was still occupied. From his new angle, he could see Stephanie still actively administering to the man's needs. Tom took a step to the door to the hall and reached for the knob, only to find it chained.

Shit.

Tom's head whipped around to get another look at the couch. From his new angle, Tom could see Stephanie on her knees in front of the man, her head bobbing up and down as the man groaned. Tom froze, transfixed by the raw sex as Stephanie came up for air. A flower arrangement on an end table blocked Tom's view of the man's face.

Stephanie saw Tom and her eyes widened. She gave him a brief smile before returning her gaze to her writhing client.

"Don't stop now," the man said, as he pushed her head back down toward her task. Stephanie smiled at Tom again and stared at him while she resumed servicing her client.

The scene fascinated, excited and repulsed him all at once. After a second or two, a small shudder broke Tom's pornographic trance. His face flushed, as if he'd been caught watching an X-rated movie.

Why the hell did she put the chain on the door?

Tom slowly grasped the top of the chain. He couldn't afford to look back to the couch for fear that the chain might rattle. Slowly—it seemed to take five minutes—Tom moved the chain the length of the slide, his ears concentrating for any slight scrape from the maneuver. Finally, the head of the chain slid free. Tom gently stretched the chain out against the doorstop and released it slowly. Another glance showed Stephanie still on the job. The client was grunting and groaning, oblivious. Tom nearly vomited when the client interrupted Stephanie by pulling her head up in front of his face.

"Is something wrong?" the man said, the soft sexual tone lessening with each successive word. Tom half expected to hear gunfire in the quarter second it took him to get the door open enough to slip out. "Is someone at the door?"

I'm dead. I'm a little dead reporter who just watched a hooker give his murderer a blow job.

If the man had not had to struggle to get out of his half-reclining position in order to turn, Tom's death visions might have come true. But his effort to get up gave Tom time and audio cover to open the room door, step through and ease it shut as quickly as he thought he could.

CHAPTER 11

He was alive—but in no-man's land. Room eleven fifteen was about halfway between the elevator and the stairs. Getting caught in the hall standing in front of the elevator would seem more natural than getting caught running for the stairs.

Then again, he preferred not getting caught at all. Tom sprinted for the stairway door some fifty feet away, counting down doors as he passed. Five, four, three, two—he heard a doorknob behind him start to turn.

One.

He reached the stairwell door, slapped the handi-capped-friendly door lever and slammed shoulder first into the door, stumbling over the entryway and falling onto the stairway landing. Tom grabbed desperately for the door as it started to arc to close. A slam would sound like a rifle shot breaking the quiet of the corridor.

Tom's right shoulder hit the floor just as he flashed his left hand into the jamb a second before the door closed on his fingers.

FUCK.

Pain radiated through his hand and into his shoulder. He saw flashing lights and growled out loud.

"Son of a bitch."

Tom pulled himself toward the door, grabbed the handle with

his undamaged hand, and retracted his squashed fingers before quietly shutting the door. He slumped toward the stairway, shaking his throbbing hand as he stumbled down the stairs to the tenth floor, crashing out of the stairwell into the hall. Finding the hallway empty, he sank to his knees and let out a litany of whispered profanity, kneading his bad hand with his good. A quick series of finger flexes and clenched fists told him that everything seemed to be working and that there were no obvious fractures. The swelling, however, had already started.

Not wanting to attract attention, he got to his feet and headed for the elevator, still flexing and shaking his hand. The elevator was empty, thank goodness. Tom scanned the compartment's ceiling for cameras as the door closed. Nothing obvious. He returned to shaking the pain out of his wounded hand. He needed ice soon to keep the swelling manageable.

The elevator descended non-stop to the lobby and opened its door to a glassy-eyed couple, the woman partially wrapped around the man.

Drunk.

The couple barely noticed Tom as they hurried by him into the elevator, selecting a button and then embracing in a passionate kiss, the woman wrapping a leg around the man as the doors closed.

Apparently everyone's getting some tonight.

Tom nodded happily at the front desk attendant as he walked out into the cool night air, brain buzzing over the identity of Stephanie's client and hand throbbing with a reminder of his narrow escape. He hadn't gotten a look at the man's face. All he knew was that he was white and probably a businessman, judging by the nicely trimmed hair and well-starched white shirt. Make that an *armed* businessman. That narrowed it down. Not many businessmen packed heat on their way to get laid. That seemed to fit the definition of "overdressed." He scanned the cars in front of the Regal, looking for something familiar, something that said "gun-toting CEO." The man would have to be pretty brazen to park right up front when stopping at the Regal for a quick tryst with a prostitute. Still, it took a certain amount of arrogance just to hire a prostitute at all.

The cars shimmered under the Regal's parking lot lights, each one alive with a halo of swarming insects. The lot offered domestic cars of various quality and ages. A Lexus in the corner was a promising candidate, but Tom dismissed it when he saw the Missouri license plates. He took one last look around and then headed for the back lot where his car waited.

He glanced over his shoulder as he rounded the corner, catching sight of an immaculate red car parked along the fence. It stood out like a thoroughbred among draft horses.

He veered off toward the car, trying to appear nonchalant enough to communicate casual curiosity to anyone watching. The red car was a BMW, unusual but not exactly rare in Sioux City. He glanced inside without getting too close. He could see only a briefcase on the back floorboard. Not such a good idea, leaving a case like that in plain sight, Tom thought. A quick smash and grab and someone could have the case and be down the alley. He backed away and studied the license plate: Iowa MRQ 215. Tom repeated the numbers over and over, trying to lock them in memory until he got someplace where he could write them down. He turned and walked toward his own car, glancing up at the hotel as he went.

+++

When Stephanie pulled her guest into the bedroom she already had her dress undone. Barry Garrett took it from there, roughly pulling Stephanie's dress off her shoulders and letting it fall around her perfect ankles.

Forty minutes later, Stephanie sat in bed, wearing only shoes, stockings and a bemused look. Garrett walked slowly around the bed, tucking in his shirt and reaching for the shoulder holster he had managed to drape carefully across a nearby chair even in his frenzy to get undressed. The sex had been frantic, with Stephanie's exquisite legs and come-fuck-me heels spurring Garrett like a bucking bronco until one final plunge finished her ride. Garrett loved it when she kept her shoes and stockings on. It was his "thing." For Garrett, it gave Stephanie a tawdry edge that helped him to spectacular ejaculations. Stephanie preferred her sex a bit more leisurely, but she'd also managed an orgasm right before Garrett erupted. That was about a fifty-fifty occurrence, sadly. Still, she got paid per orgasm from her client, not herself. Plus Barry Garrett wasn't used to waiting for anyone, in bed or at work. He was the top dog at the dominant trucking firm in Iowa. If you could load it on a truck, Garrett's fleet of 200 could take it anywhere in the U.S.

Twenty-three years ago, Garrett had driven his first truck by himself, concentrating on transporting the region's agricultural bounty. Sioux City had always been a transportation hub, first via the Missouri River that flows through the city and forms Iowa's western border, then by railroad, and lately thanks to Interstate 29, which rolls through downtown Sioux City, parallel to the Missouri River. From the bluffs that overlook the river in Sioux City, you could still see the big three—river, railroad, and highway.

Garrett had endured those tough times and fought through them, steadily adding trucks and employees. Now his empire, Blade-Garrett Worldwide, moved everything, from retail merchandise to coal, chickens, hogs, corn, whatever. A subsidiary of his company even moved people and their possessions from house to house. He had offices in Minneapolis, Omaha, Sioux Falls and Des Moines and was thinking about going into Kansas City.

His ability to read people was key to Garrett's economic stardom. He sensed from the first meeting who would make it big and who wouldn't and found himself accurate about eighty-five percent of the time. He learned to trust this instinct and allied himself with whoever his gut said would succeed. He kept Blade-Garrett on the lookout for startup operations with promise. By extending generous credit terms to a struggling business early on, he found that a relatively small investment often came back a thousand-fold as that fledgling business prospered, making him a very rich man. It was almost like an in-kind form of venture capitalism.

Garrett concentrated his personal skills on maintaining a warm relationship with his few biggest customers, often shuttling around the Midwest in his private Learjet to stroke clients in person. The plane remained crouched and ready at a moment's notice in its hangar at Sioux Gateway Airport on the southern edge of town. And if they needed extra special personal stroking, he could always call on the services of Stephanie and her network of professional associates.

Putting on his suit coat, Garrett stopped to peer out the hotel window just in time to see another Blade-Garrett truck go past on nearby Interstate 29. "Thanks for letting me leave and come back like this," he said as if he were talking to a dentist.

"My pleasure," Stephanie said, slipping off her shoes and covering her lower body with the bed sheet. She had had enough of the slutty whore role she played for Garrett. It was time to get out of costume and character for a while. "That call you got earlier really seemed to rattle you. I thought you might need my services again." She recalled that before his cellphone rang around 11 p.m., Garrett was charging toward her as usual, his lance ready for battle. After the call, not even her expertise could return him to better than half-staff. Luckily for her, Garrett's inflated sense of manhood forced him to confide the source of his temporary disability. He had promised to return at around 2:30 to finish the appointment.

Garrett had been Stephanie's client for three years. She met him through a colleague. It hadn't been difficult to reel in Garrett, who immediately showed all the signs of someone with a lot of money and even more desire for a sexual adventure, provided that adventure made him look like a stallion. She used her repertoire of moves to determine that he liked breasts, so she took pains to present hers in some pleasing way. She could always tell what part of a woman turned a man on. His eyes gave him away. Leg men look at a woman's knees as she approaches. A breast man's eyes drop like rocks from a woman's face to her tits, like two marbles pulled by gravity down her cleavage, and then spend the rest of the night bouncing back and forth like ocular ping pong balls.

Tom Kingman had disappointed her. She expected a reporter, a professional observer, to be more disciplined. He'd taken her first leg offering. She knew he was a leg man long before Tom confirmed it by groping her thigh and garter.

Even though she had become a bit numb to it all, Stephanie liked a square jaw and an adventurous bedside manner. But what really turned her on was a man who saw to her needs before gratifying himself. Perhaps the rarity of such men made them more exciting, especially in Stephanie's profession, and she rewarded them with intense, unembellished orgasms. Too often, though, her clients saw her as little more than a receptacle for their semen.

Still, Garrett wasn't unattractive. He was about five foot eight and reasonably fit for a forty-four-year-old. His light brown hair was always cropped short and expertly styled. He wrapped himself in the uniform of a high-rolling executive: $1,000 suits and $500 shoes, expensive watches and golden Super Bowl-sized rings. He countered the hated "trucker" stereotype with liberal doses of Armani.

He checked his Rolex, a gift from a grateful client. The red BMW in the parking lot was a company car. Barry Garrett had done his time behind the wheel of a big rig and hadn't driven one himself for a decade. He would never go back.

"Won't your wife miss you tonight?" Stephanie asked, sweeping the sheet off her legs, sitting up on the edge of the bed and letting her nyloned toes graze the carpet. She leaned slightly forward, enjoying the flex of her triceps as she pushed down on the edge of the bed and gave Garrett a good look at her breasts. She finished her show with a slow walk over to the closet and donning of a short silk robe. She tied it loosely, making sure an ample amount of cleavage remained exposed. Always leave them wanting more.

"I doubt Missy cares where I am," Garrett said, his mouth turning hard. "She spent the day in Omaha with her cackling brood of friends. I'm sure I'll be amazed at how much she spent. Sometimes I think she's going for a record."

Missy and Barry Garrett had been married more than twenty years. She was disarmingly thin, thanks largely to power aerobics four or five times a week at the most expensive club in town. If that didn't keep the pounds off, Missy just marched into the bathroom and vomited up any high-calorie transgressions.

Missy liked the fact that other men and women often complimented her on her thin five foot six, thirty-eight-year-old body, even if it required the occasional bathroom purge.

"She's sick, Barry," Stephanie said. "She looks like a frail child. And the way you talk, she spends more time in the bathroom every day than a sixteen-year-old on prom night."

"She likes to be thin," Garrett said, shrugging it off. He had stopped caring much about Missy's health sometime in the late 1990s. "It makes her think the other women envy her. She's always interested in having other women envy her, be it physically or financially. Guess she got sick of being called a trucker girl."

So whether via Armani or hurling into the toilet, both Missy and Barry were out to shake the "trucker" label, Stephanie thought. When not obsessing over the extra pound or two, Missy spent her days flitting from some social event to the latest fashionable charity cause. Among her largest challenges was deciding which of her fellow idle wives to have lunch with and where to dine. Sioux City wasn't exactly back woods, but neither was it a national hot spot for fine restaurants, especially since Missy had mastered the spoiled rich wife art of finding something to sneer at in most everything. Still, she did know which restaurant's bathrooms offered the most privacy for her purging, so the local eatery scene had at least one plus.

When Sioux City failed to amuse her, Missy and her girlfriends would drive her white Jaguar south to Omaha or Kansas City or north to Sioux Falls or Minneapolis for a shopping spree, often lasting days at a time. When even that became boring the Blade-Garrett company jet was always fueled and standing by.

"Missy looks good with me in public and at church. She gives me the appearance of stability that's great for business." He stopped at the door, holding the knob. "And she gives me some sex every six weeks or so. Nothing on your level, Stephanie. Nobody's that good."

Stephanie and Missy did have one thing in common: their ability to stoke Barry's desires at will. Missy even joked with her girlfriends that she could make Barry hard with a certain look or low enough neckline. Missy liked her sex athletic—might as well burn some fat while she was at it—with frenzied desire carrying the action forward.

"Does Missy know about us?" Stephanie asked, standing with Garrett at the door.

"She's not stupid," he said. "I have my side interests and she has hers."

He adjusted his tie. "Do you feel threatened, Stephanie? Don't flatter yourself. Remember, this is business. We have a mutually beneficial arrangement. I pay you well and you treat me well."

He reached into his inside coat pocket, pulled out an envelope, and handed it to Stephanie. "This should bring our account current," he said.

She nodded slightly and opened the door, being careful to stay behind it.

"When will you be in town next?" he asked.

"Friday."

"Seven o'clock?"

"Fine. Text me before you come up."

Garrett left without another word.

+++

Barry Garrett discovered his gift for logistics and fleet management during a four-year hitch in the United States Army. After discharge, he and Missy had worked long hours, scrimped and saved until they had two trucks, then four, then a fleet. While he still made plenty of money off moving tons of grain around, a decade earlier he had discovered another cash crop: methamphetamine, which was manufactured, not grown. The ingredients read more like drain cleaner than drug: hydrochloric acid, red phosphorus, acetone, mercuric chloride, thorium dioxide, benzene. Good old American innovation came up with multiple ways to make crank, which could be brewed almost anywhere, provided you had the recipe and ingredients.

As the U.S. tried to control meth ingredients, Mexican meth cookers became a cheaper source of supply. With some special alterations, Garrett's trucks could store a little extra on their trips all over the country. The clandestine payloads of raw ingredients or finished goods had transformed Garrett into the shadowy leader of a distribution network that stretched from Minneapolis to Kansas City. He operated from Sioux City, in part because he could keep a lower profile here, and there were fewer important people to be wired into to protect himself. Also, even though he dealt drugs, Garrett allowed himself the sentimentality of liking his home area. People just didn't ask so many questions about a hometown boy. Besides, lots of jobs depended on Barry Garrett staying happy and not moving his business to Omaha or anyplace else. Civic leaders were very motivated to keep Garrett happy.

And who would suspect Barry Garrett of being involved with drugs? He had a thriving business and wonderful wife. Nice house. He made regular, generous contributions to charities and his church. And his covert business had been getting better and better. While that meant more customers for Garrett, it also got the attention of competitors, Southwestern drug kings who were starting to move north and east. Garrett's piece of the action in Omaha and Minneapolis had already been cut into by the new competition. Recently, his operatives had heard rumblings around Sioux City of a new source of cheaper, higher-quality crank from dealers who shipped the drug up from Omaha on Interstate 29, known locally as the "Meth Pipeline."

And, like any competitor, the new drug dealers had come to town trying to lure away the most talented employees of the old-line meth lords. Chuck Pollard, treated as a functionary by Garrett, appreciated the attention from the Southwestern visitors and jumped ship.

As Garrett drove north through town, past the Catholic high school and a nearby Army recruiting station, he thought about how for the last five years he had treated Chuck Pollard well and provided him a living, even though he managed to drink and gamble away most of the money. Everything changed when the rival dealers from the Southwest came muscling into town.

Garrett couldn't ignore the betrayal. Van Grunner, for all his huge, red-necked stupidity, had pulled it off well. Pollard taking a shot at them had been fortuitous. The whole affair had gone even better than Garrett had scripted. The general public would continue in its average existence, buying the cop story of reluctant self-defense, while Garrett was rid of the traitor. He counted on the police instinct to close ranks around a brother officer, ensuring a halfhearted investigation.

But what he hadn't counted on was Tom Kingman. A newspaper reporter, for Christ sakes, who stumbled onto the scene and witnessed the killing. The news about Tom at the scene was enough to make Garrett go limp with Stephanie. No easy feat. But Van Grunner's telephoned assurances made everything sound okay. Just as long as the reporter wasn't too bright—a safe bet in this town—and Van Grunner didn't screw it up by thinking or talking too much—not such a good bet—things might just turn out.

Still, the situation called for some insurance.

CHAPTER 12

About the time Garrett and Stephanie were conducting their business, Tom lowered himself into his car behind the Regal, pulled out a small notebook and scrawled down the BMW's plate number. He looked again at his damaged left hand and reviewed the image of Stephanie's sly smile above his crotch. He convinced himself he had been reeling from physical exhaustion and the mental shock of witnessing a shooting, making him easy prey for such an experienced seducer.

Bow chica bow bow.

Tom laughed at his thought, shook off the visions and pulled his phone from his pants pocket. After a moment of amazement that the phone hadn't been broken or lost during the night's acrobatics, he found Hillary's card still in his breast pocket and dialed the phone. It was after 2 a.m. "Hillary is going to be pissed," Tom said, looking at his watch and checking himself in the rearview mirror. "But she said to call her at night."

An answer on the second ring surprised him.

"Hillary? Were you up? Sorry to call so late. This is Tom Kingman."

"I was up. Couldn't sleep. Just reviewing some paperwork."

"I'm in my car. Something strange just happened. Can we meet? I know it's very late, but I think it's important."

"Sure. Come over to my house," she said, and rattled off the address. "Gray house. Look for the *antique* Camaro in the driveway. I'll turn the front light on and put on the coffee."

"I'm not far from there. Ten minutes."

As Tom's car, an early 2000s Ford Taurus with an intermittently working air conditioner and a heater that smelled like a smoldering bonfire, wheezed out of the parking lot, he considered how much of the night's events he would share with Hillary. Describing a woman yanking down your pants and then going for your underwear like Japanese carp after popcorn wasn't exactly an accepted topic of professional conversation. Tom wanted to be professional, cool and detached in front of Hillary. Smooth, quippy and unflappable. James Bond-level ambivalence about everything.

Bond, Tom Bond.

He snorted.

Hillary's house, an older, snug-looking two-bedroom, matched its occupant: nothing out of place, decorated tastefully, the gray house accented perfectly in dark trim. There were enough shrubs and flowers to adorn the front lawn but not overpower it.

He spotted Hillary's Camaro and decided not to park along the front curb in case a random cop came by and recognized his car or ran the license plate for whatever reason. There was nothing illegal about the visit, but Tom preferred to minimize the department's clue as to their arrangement. To be safe, he pulled around the corner onto Twenty-third Street and parallel parked along the curb, between two cars. The Taurus blended right in.

She came to the door in a baggy sweatshirt and jeans. It was a sharp contrast to Stephanie's shock-and-awe presentation, but Tom found Hillary's casual attire only enhanced her natural beauty. Perhaps it had to do with the fact that people always seem more confident and at ease on their home turf, one of the reasons Tom always preferred to interview people at their homes. Tom had never seen Hillary this way before and found it mildly intoxicating.

Then again, it could be the exhaustion talking.

"Thanks for letting me come over," Tom said as Hillary let him in. "I'm glad you were still up."

"I'll be up early and late for the next month, the way this is going." Hillary closed the door and joined Tom in the center of the room. "Look, we're still off the record here, aren't we?"

Tom was used to having people talk to him in guarded, vague, overly careful ways. He had heard "are we off the record?" hundreds of times, but it mildly surprised him coming from Hillary, especially after their discussion in her car. Tom sighed. "Yeah, off the record. Just consider this more of a social call if that makes it easier."

The two made their way to the living room, which Tom found decorated with contemporary colors and leather furniture with family photos sprinkled throughout. A big, antique-looking cross hung on one wall. A table next to what had to be a reading chair was stacked with a Bible and some daily devotionals.

Behold the Christian prosecutor.

Tom plopped down on the sofa, habitually using his left hand to control his landing, causing his damaged fingers to be bent in painful directions. His throat contracted in a growl.

The sound caused Hillary to stop in mid-descent to her chair and stare at him.

"Sorry. I smashed the shit out of my hand tonight." Tom regretted the vulgarity as soon as it left his mouth.

"Let me have a look," Hillary said softly. Tom couldn't tell if that was a request or an order, so he nodded and extended his swollen hand, which she took lightly by the wrist.

"Looks painful," she said, her touch again impossibly light. "You might have some purple fingers tomorrow. Let me get some ice."

"Thanks." Tom retracted his hand as Hillary brushed by him on her way to the kitchen. He refused to show pain. James Bond never grimaced over some bruised fingers. He hated looking needy or pitiful, but he suspected he fit both descriptions.

Hillary returned a minute later with a plastic bag of ice wrapped in a kitchen towel. "This should help."

"Thank you." This time Tom looked directly into Hillary's green eyes.

"You're welcome" she said. Her face was pleasantly full, accented by a button nose, her smile quick and radiant.

I could get used to the off-duty Hillary.

"This is just part of Tom's big adventure tonight," he said, holding up his left hand briefly before gingerly placing it back on the towel-covered ice. "I got a call at work about two hours after the shooting. It was a woman who wouldn't tell me her name. She knew I had witnessed everything on West Jarred."

"It didn't take her long to get that bit of information, did it?" Hillary said, sitting with her legs crossed, her feet tucked under her knees. "Did you go see her?"

Tom now considered Hillary an acquaintance, maybe on the way to friendship, but telling her about nearly getting oral sex from a prostitute, well, that wasn't something he was going to rush into.

"Did I ever see her. I saw a *lot* of her."

Surprise flashed across Hillary's face, replaced by a shadow of a smile. She leaned back in her chair and uncrossed her legs, lightly landing a white-socked foot on the floor. The image of Hillary's naked foot and leg danced through Tom's head.

What's gotten into me? My brain is like a random porn scene generator.

"Perhaps we should have a chaperone if we're going to talk about it," Hillary said, arching her eyebrows.

Everybody's a comedian tonight ...

"She invited me to her room at the Regal," Tom said, encouraged by Hillary's lack of embarrassment to plow forward with his story.

"Very cozy."

"Cozy in a black-widow kind of way. She said her name was Brenda, but I heard her called Stephanie later. She said she lives in Omaha and makes several 'business' trips to Sioux City every month. Let's just say her business is quite an ancient one."

"She's a hooker." Hillary's word cut like cold, surgical steel through Tom's verbal pirouettes. "We know about a few women who come to Sioux City from Omaha to entertain in some of the local motels for a night or two. We've tried to sting them, but they have an established clientele and never take on new customers without great references. Besides, their clients are doctors, lawyers, CEOs—men with money. Hard to get people enthusiastic about taking away the rich boys' toys in this 'victimless crime' when there are poor crank users to bust."

"Well, Brenda, or Stephanie, or whoever she really is, hinted that the shooting on West Jarred was some kind of setup. She confirmed Pollard's involvement in the local drug network, but said he was an underling and he apparently pissed someone off badly enough to get on his list. Brenda suggested, and quite strongly, that I check Pollard's past for some interesting reading."

"Did this Brenda say who wanted Pollard dead and why? Or anything about the leader of this network?" Hillary asked.

"Only that the head of the organization is a mover and shaker in Sioux City. A country club, chamber luminary of some kind. It was all very cryptic."

"Did you get anything else from her?" The eyebrow arch returned.

Tom lifted the ice from his fingers and shifted positions on the couch. "She volunteered a few things free of charge. I told her I wasn't in the market."

"She *offered*?"

"Oh yeah."

"What, *exactly*, did she offer?" Tom couldn't decide if he

was aroused or shocked by the lascivious edge in Hillary's voice. Probably a little of both.

"Let's just say she chose some things from her professional menu and offered them in a very demonstrative way."

That's all you're getting, Ms. Reed, unless you got some scotch or a subpoena in your hand.

"And you turned her down?" Disbelief knifed through her voice.

"I tried to turn her down," Tom corrected.

"Tried?"

"Hey, nothing happened," Tom said, unsure why he was suddenly defensive. "She *was* very insistent. A very hard sell." It was Tom's turn to arch both eyebrows to drive home the double meaning. "I'll admit I was to a point where saying no would have been a major miracle, but one of her regular clients came knocking at the door in the midst of her generous offer. Talk about killing the mood. I had to hide in the damn bathroom."

Hillary let out a small laugh. "So you're hopping into the bathroom, hard as a rock, trying to get your pants up."

Hey, did she really say 'hard as a rock'?

"Look, I said nothing happened. I'm glad you find this so funny. The guy she let in was wearing a suit and a shoulder holster, which often comes with a gun when used as a male fashion accessory."

Hillary's chuckle ended abruptly and she sat up a bit. "A gun? Didn't you find out who the man was?"

"I was kind of busy not getting shot," Tom said. "Interviewing someone while he's in the middle of oral sex is never a good plan."

Hillary wrinkled her forehead slightly.

Tom realized the adrenaline rush from his encounter with Stephanie had drained away, leaving him even more exhausted, and that his fingers had started throbbing.

"Sorry." he rubbed his face with his good hand. "I couldn't see his face. These near-death experiences kind of make a guy ragged around the edges."

Hillary nodded. "So what happened to your hand?" she said with a look toward the ice bag.

"I smashed it in the stairway door after I managed to sneak out of the bathroom and into the hotel hallway. I was trying to grab the door so it wouldn't slam and attract Mr. Armed Client."

"Did he see you?"

"I don't think so, based mostly on me not being dead right now. Stephanie seemed to think the whole thing was quite amusing. If the guy'd found me, he probably would've saved his second ammo magazine for her. But she was having a good old time."

Hillary shrugged. "My night can't top that—I kept all my clothes on."

"Let the record show all my clothes were *technically* on my body at all times."

"So noted," Hillary said. "I did get a call from Chief Banks tonight."

"Tonight?" Tom said, arching an eyebrow. "Kind of late, or early, for him, isn't it?"

"First officer-involved shooting in this town in years gets everybody *up*." Hillary chased "up" with a smile.

Gonna be a while before I hear the end of this.

"What a sweetheart, Chief Banks is," Hillary continued, "melts a girl's heart. The smoke hasn't even cleared on West Jarred and he's already pressuring me to wrap up the shooting investigation quickly. He even mentioned that having you as a witness was a big bonus for us."

"I'm all warm and fuzzy to be of service to the SCPD," Tom said. "Does he know about your investigation of Van Grunner?"

"No."

"Is he a subject of your investigation?"

"He might be. Nobody in the department knows because we

don't know who, if anyone, is involved with Van Grunner." Hillary shifted her weight slightly. "Banks doesn't see why this can't be wrapped up by Monday."

"And you exploded," Tom said.

"I made my position clear," Hillary said, using her formal court voice. "I told him five days was a bit hurried, what with witnesses to formally interview—don't worry, I'll be gentle—backgrounds to check, and on and on all without the urgency caused by suspects on the run. Proceeding that quickly could have the dangerous appearance of a cover up." She dropped out of her formal court tone and continued. "But he wants to be able to have a big press conference on Monday to release at least the early findings before the protesters can descend in earnest. That means I have to have an inch-thick document stating our preliminary conclusions ready for you media people by then."

"Those vulturous media bastards," Tom said with mock outrage. "I would have thought you could make Monday no sweat—until Stephanie showed up."

"Yeah. She doesn't know you and I are, ah, sharing information, does she?"

"Give me some credit," Tom said.

"Easy, Tom. It's just that in my profession I deal with a lot of men whose IQ's go down as their penises harden up."

Did she just say penis?

Tom felt himself flush mildly. Tonight was turning into a full-on exploration of *Hillary Reed: After Hours*. At least she didn't say "dick" or some other slang word for it. That would have cracked if not burst his Hillary Reed bubble. Still, she didn't seem timid about talking about the male erectile functions.

"Sounds like we need to find out who this Brenda-Stephanie person is," Hillary continued. "It would also be nice to identify the client who interrupted your tryst. He might have some connection to this drug network she talked about."

"Tryst, what tryst? Nothing happened. I swear."

"A prostitute?" Hillary said shaking her head. "You were ready to go with a prostitute?"

Tom looked down at the floor. "Ready to go is an overstatement."

Okay, maybe it wasn't.

"Look, Hillary, she's obviously very good at getting what she wants from men. Of course, my rational brain recognized having sex with a prostitute—which for the record I did not—as a bad move. But from the second I arrived she launched a full, frontal assault with all her tools aimed at a section of me located somewhat south of the rational brain. She's good; she's very, very good. And I'm exhausted."

"Why do men always see women as a chest, vagina, butt and pair of legs?" Hillary asked. "I wish I could meet a man who didn't immediately start looking me over like a side of beef."

Uh-oh … this is getting out of hand quickly …

Tom regretted letting his eyes dance over her breasts and legs when she walked into the police interview room four hours earlier. "I've seen women do the same thing," Tom said. "How do you think Van Grunner gets dates?"

Tom tried to dial down his defensive tone. "Men are just very visual creatures. It's been that way for a million years. When it comes to women, the visual stimulus comes from the areas you so comprehensively listed there. Women seem to react more to emotional stuff and are less swayed by visual images."

"Oh really? You sound like you've been reading up on this. Did you also read that many women hate to be called emotional? It's so overused; it's gone from descriptive to derisive. 'Now, don't get all emotional, honey.' Men seem to think 'emotional' means 'weepy.' And I am *not* weepy."

Does the word 'emotional' make you emotional, Hillary?

Tom shook off the idea of vocalizing his thought as a needless provocation and instead held up his undamaged hand to head off

Hillary's response. "Let's just pretend I said women react to 'intellectual or mental' stimulation instead of 'emotional,' okay? And I *have* been reading up. I used to read my sister's teen magazines all the time. It was mostly for the underwear ads, but still."

Humor, the great defuser... I hope.

Tom and Hillary exchanged slight look of truce before he continued. Tom might have been going for the Tom Bond image, but Hillary certainly wasn't a Bond girl who started stripping at the merest come-hither glance from 007.

"With some men," Tom said, "looking at the hot spots is almost instinctive. If we were total animals—and some of us are, I'll admit—we'd jump whoever was available and in heat, like some lion taking a lioness or something. But many of us at least try to control our response to the visual stimulus, even if we can't control looking. Sometimes, as with my debacle tonight, we don't do as well controlling ourselves."

"I wish men *would* control looking," Hillary said. Tom wondered if she was using "men" to refer primarily to "Tom Kingman." "It would be nice not to have to wear frumpy clothing, avoid makeup and put my hair up in a bun in order to be sure a man I'm dealing with is motivated by my intellectual abilities rather than by 'visual stimulus.'"

How did we even get on this topic?

He felt growing friendship, not sexual desire for Hillary, who wasn't afraid to present her viewpoint on this very personal, philosophical topic. Perhaps that made him reluctant to shut down such an unlikely topic of conversation at close to 3 a.m.

"Women react to visual stimulus too," Hillary said, also passing up the chance to end the personal discussion. Tom saw her eyes drift from his face to one bicep, across his chest to the other, and then down his abdomen to his crotch. During the whole eye movement, she wore an appreciative, coy look.

She had just given him the once-over, one with a Stephanie-level sexual edge. He hung halfway between shock and appreciation.

While Tom's brain stumbled, Hillary kept talking. "But most of us want more than physical satisfaction from a man. We want men who don't just see a pair of legs, an ass and a set of tits." Hillary flashed him a you-heard-me-right exaggerated eyebrow arch. "We want someone who will hang in there with us when the water heater blows or the kids get mono or we gain ten pounds from chocolate-intensive stress therapy."

She rubbed her hand up and down her jeans and then tucked it between her crossed legs at the knee.

"I'm not sure why I'm telling you this, but ever since high school, I've been ogled by men, and it gets a little old. Pretty girls attracted pretty boys, who thought the way to care *for* a woman was to take care *of* her. I learned that the very hard way. People still try to steer pretty girls toward pretty occupations, like wife, mother, school teacher, nurse—all good professions, don't misunderstand—but why limit someone just because that person was born with a vagina?"

Tom imagined Hillary as an eight-year-old. He didn't need her yearbook photographs to know she had always been one of the naturally pretty girls. Maybe not the prettiest, but one of the group. Tom wondered what during those yearbook years caused the tinge of bitterness he now heard in her voice.

"You're from around here, aren't you?" Tom said, in an awkward attempt to divert the conversation to less emotional ground.

"Born and raised in a little town called Lake Park in the northwest corner of the state, by Lake Okoboji in Dickinson County." Lake Okoboji was one of several large lakes in Northwest Iowa called the "Iowa Great Lakes." Many affluent people from Sioux City, Omaha, even Des Moines had summer homes at "the lakes." Lakefront homes could go for well over a million dollars, big cash for Iowa, and definitely large money for second homes. Tom had made occasional weekend runs to Okoboji, where bars and entertainment ranged from high-class to dollar beer night dives with carpets so repeatedly saturated with beer they would likely burn for days if ever ignited.

A pretty, small-town girl, Tom thought, his eyes meeting hers again, who saw the male response to her looks as a handicap. He imagined the analytical Hillary Reed questioning every opportunity that came up during her life, wondering if she could thank her butt or her brain for the good fortune.

"And you?" Hillary asked.

"I was born in South Dakota but grew up in Council Bluffs."

"Counciltucky!" Hillary said, invoking the much-hated nickname for southwest Iowa's largest town.

"No more Counciltucky. We got casino money now. New library. We got a Google data center."

Tom's mind buzzed. He would have enjoyed spending a few hours with Hillary discussing the philosophy of sexual attraction, beauty and their little inner children, but he was suddenly aware again of his own exhaustion.

"Well, Miss Lake Park, I was thinking: either I rummage through the digital criminal files online and at the courthouse, not one hundred percent sure I'm seeing everything or ...." He glanced at Hillary, who smiled broadly.

"Or you could find someone who has full access to the network," Hillary finished, increasing the wattage of her smile.

"You wouldn't know anyone like that, would you, Ms. Reed?"

Hillary held both hands up and rolled her eyes in exhaustion, real or exaggerated. "Okay, okay I can have something by tomorrow night, but I'll only search what's public record for you."

"Tomorrow night. Great." Tom paused, considering the leap he was about to take. Sometime during their discussion of non-sexual gender relations, of all subjects, Tom experienced substantial growth in his personal interest in Hillary.

"Since you were so kind to invite me here, maybe you could

come to my house for dinner tomorrow—or I guess technically later today—and go over what you find."

His nervous glance landed on a noncommittal look from Hillary. Pretty sure they both knew a line was being straddled, if not crossed. She didn't look thrilled, but she didn't look repulsed either.

Looks like she's running the pros and cons ...

A refusal would have actually been okay with Tom, because it would have at least established a boundary he could work with during this "relationship."

"Unless you'd rather meet here or someplace else," Tom injected, offering Hillary an escape route. "I'm very flexible."

Hillary flashed a small smile.

Those flash-bang smiles are like stun grenades.

"I can come over," she said fiddling slightly with her sweatshirt. "Probably better than being seen having dinner in public. You know how tiny this town is. What time?"

"Well, since we're both apparently going to be up all hours, we might as well get together around nine." He gave her the address.

"Sounds great," she said jotting it down as he rose to leave. Her eyes went immediately to Tom's crotch and then back to his face.

"You totally did that on purpose," Tom said.

"How do you like it?" She smiled.

I hope that's a rhetorical question because, ah, I did like it ...

For someone who didn't like being inspected, Hillary could make a man feel like a side of beef when she wanted to, and Tom kind of wanted her to make him feel that way right now. He handed her back her towel and ice pack, making sure to position his hand so it would make contact with hers when she accepted the offering.

"Thanks," Tom said. "My hand feels much better. Nine ibuprofens and some scotch and it'll be fine. Should be back to normal in a couple of days."

"I'm glad," Hillary said, not moving to break their hand

contact. "I'll see you tomorrow. I should be here after about six tomorrow night if you need to call. You have the number."

Tom patted his rear pocket. "Right here," he said, followed immediately by a blush when he realized he had just drawn her attention to his ass.

"Thanks for sharing those records. It will save a lot of time."

"Let's just hope we find something," Hillary said, her eyes lingering on his back pocket. Tom turned and stepped out into the night. As he went through the doorway, he cast a backward glance in time to catch Hillary taking one last long look at Tom's pockets and smiling ever so slightly.

CHAPTER 13

It took only ten minutes for Tom to get home, but then it took only ten minutes at the most to go anywhere in Sioux City, especially at 3 a.m. Tom lived in an unfashionable neighborhood halfway between downtown and the outer ring of houses in Sioux City. It was a simple, white, two-bedroom house typical of towns across Iowa.

He lived sparsely. No pets. Not much food in the refrigerator. He had the expected forty-something-inch TV in his living room. Down in the unfinished basement were some weights that Tom lifted whenever ambition and free time intersected, which wasn't that often.

More frequent exercise came from walking his next-door neighbor's golden retriever, Chester, a few times a week. It usually took Chester about five blocks to get over the raw thrill of walking, which manifested itself in dragging Tom by the leash. After that, Chester danced along, feet lightly kissing the sidewalk, nose sniffing the air. It didn't take long for Tom to realize Chester had a fantastic ability to attract women. Most everyone they met wanted to pet the dog, who obliged by quickly sitting, tilting his head back and pulling off what Tom swore was the golden retriever version of a smile. The animal seemingly could pour on the cuteness whenever he wanted. Some of these encounters with twenty-something lovelies had actually led to dates. Who's a good boy?

No doubt Chester's owner, Bud Caldwell, an energetic eighty-two-year-old, had seen Tom arrive. He took up station in his front room and watched with the vigilance of an embassy Marine guard. Caldwell stood about five feet six inches and was mildly plump. His ebony skin puckered into wrinkles around his eyes and across the back of his hands. White, cropped hair capped his head like snow on a mountain.

Caldwell and Chester still ventured around the block a few times, but at an eighty-two-year-old pace. Chester seemed to have a Bud gear and sauntered in perfect stride with the older man, saving his workout speed for Tom, who had befriended Caldwell and Chester soon after Tom moved into the neighborhood six years ago. After Caldwell admitted that he could no longer give Chester the well-paced, long walks the dog enjoyed, Tom had volunteered.

Tom parked at the top of the drive in front of his detached garage. His house was neat, partly due to lack of use. He entered through the back door, threw his keys in the usual spot on the counter and surveyed the domestic landscape.

I'd say medium clean ... Mom would say medium filthy. Potato, patahto ..

Tom had trouble with the idea of vacuuming a carpet that looked clean already and dusting furniture that was rarely used. It didn't seem to be a very efficient use of his time.

Most of his life centered on the *Sentinel-Leader*. He walked through the bachelor-sparse living room into a spare bedroom/office overseen silently by framed historical newspapers, sayings from famous journalists captured in lead letters once used to print papers, and photographs from stories he'd covered as well as those of some *Sentinel-Leader* coworkers. He flopped into his office chair and nodded silently at framed photographs of his parents who still lived in Council Bluffs. They had adopted Tom when he was a week old. There were also photos of his brother and two sisters—years out of date now.

After a quick check of his email inbox on his laptop, he walked toward his bedroom, stripping and dropping his clothes as he went. Naked by the time he got to the bed, Tom reminded himself to call his parents the next day, toppled into bed, pulled up the sheet, rolled over and passed out.

+++

The clock said 8:46 a.m. as a garbage truck slammed down the just-emptied dumpster in back of a convenience store on the other side of the block. Tom's eyes popped open upon dumpster landing. He rolled his head to look out the open window, feeling the heat already billowing in. His pillow was damp with sweat. He found himself fully exposed, the sheet kicked aside. He glanced again at the window and scurried to the side of the bed where he could sit with his back to it.

What a striking sight for the neighbors.

Tom staggered to his dresser, raked out and put on some clean underwear and a pair of jeans and went for the front door, stopping briefly to fling his clothes from last night into the general direction of the hamper in his room. He retrieved the Wednesday morning *Sentinel-Leader* from the front step and plopped heavily onto the couch. It took a lot to get him to put paper before coffee, but such was the gravity of the situation. Tom and Skip's stories about the shooting dominated the upper half of the paper, the prime real estate known as "above the fold." He rarely read his own stories in newsprint, but he did skim this one. He liked it, an accomplishment since he was his own harshest critic.

Tom mentally determined where he would have inserted bits about Van Grunner threatening the woman or punting Tom's ribs, if he hadn't made the deal with Hillary. He allowed himself to replay some of the police headquarters and late-night conversations with

Hillary, searching his memory for any feeling of deception or insincerity. Now that the story was printed, it was too late for second thoughts. A deal was a deal.

Skip had polished the stories and added official comments and witness quotes. Joyce, who turned out to be Pollard's common-law wife, protested in print, modifying her story to say Chuck was trying to surrender when brutally murdered by police.

She's whack. Angling for fifteen minutes of fame or a settlement from the city.

A police spokesman countered with the allegation that Pollard fired first and said they had dug a slug out of the wall by the door. The spokesman promised an investigation but had full confidence that it was a justified, self-defense shooting. Tom looked forward to today's version of Joyce's ever-evolving story and anticipated some public challenges to his account of the shooting. Those challenges would probably hit print today. Surely someone would accuse him of being a police sympathizer and co-conspirator. Nothing new, of course, but unpleasant nonetheless. At least they had corroborating evidence, including Chuck's fired gun, gunshot residue on Chuck's hand and the bullet in the side of the door.

It did bother him—actually, "chagrin" was a better term than "bother"—that a department that had regularly been hostile to "negative" media coverage now saw him as a star witness. The *Sentinel-Leader* had never failed to cover police charities, good deeds and heroism, but still the "negative spin" accusation persisted.

What do you think of my negative ass now, boys?

+++

More than two hours earlier, Police Chief Jimmy Banks had greeted his paperboy on the front step. The boy arrived before 6 a.m. most days, but today Banks paced off the kid's fifteen minute tardiness. The local morning television news shows hadn't deviated much from official statements. They also included some sound-bite accusations from Pollard's wife and hints that some Sioux Cityans thought their police were a bit too quick on the trigger. Nothing Banks hadn't expected and not exactly a march-and-loot situation.

The *Sentinel-Leader*, however, was a different story. Banks knew all about Bear Pennington's emphasis on digging. But Banks didn't feel obliged to make it easy, just because the part-time fools at the legislature declared something public record; some things best remained private. If all else failed, Iowa law allowed police to shield information in the name of protecting "ongoing investigations," and Banks's definition of "ongoing" was broader than a Midwestern corn field.

"Good morning, Bobby," Banks said, startling his sleepy paperboy.

"Good morning Chief. Big story today."

"Don't believe everything you read in the papers, son," Banks said as he took the paper.

"No, sir," Bobby said with an indifferent look.

Banks's first grunt of reaction came on the front steps, causing Bobby to turn and make sure everything was okay. Banks read as he stepped back inside. Despite his initial grunts, he didn't consider the story too damaging. No photos of the officers. Tom had lived up to his word, at least on that much. He'd have to read the stories to see if Hillary had persuaded him to look the other way on Van Grunner's indiscreet yet understandable actions after the shooting. Benning had seemed confident when he'd briefed Banks about Hillary's plan, but Banks had been burned by reporters before.

Banks spent the next thirty minutes studying the paper, carefully reading each of the four stories on the shooting. The large main story gave the basics of what happened, including Joyce Common Law's ludicrous claims of a cold-blooded killing. A second, eyewitness story by Tom confirmed police accounts of self-defense and countered Joyce's ravings.

"Sources close to the investigation confirmed that Pollard had a history of drug arrests and that police suspected he organized deliveries of methamphetamine into and out of Sioux City for a larger drug ring," Banks read from the largest story.

"What the hell did that stupid bitch Reed tell him?" Banks asked out loud, although he was alone with his half-eaten breakfast cereal. "It's a wonder she didn't give him pictures, maybe some video of one of our raids on a suspected meth lab outside of town."

+++

Twenty blocks north, the sentence about Pollard being connected to a larger meth distribution ring almost made Barry Garrett spew coffee all over his breakfast nook. Garrett had two big concerns: First, a hint of his operation was in the paper. That could lead to a public frenzy demanding the police do something about it, which could be bad for business. Second, the story also hinted that the police knew a bit more than Garrett realized. So his sources inside the police department were shit on this story. Not knowing what the opposition knew was also bad for business. He scooped up the phone and dialed Banks's home number. The chief got it on the second ring. "Jimmy, this is Barry Garrett, what the hell is this shit about drugs in the paper today?"

"Relax, Barry," Banks said. "Tom Kingman got lucky. It was a fluke. A known drug dealer got shot. That never ruins my day. We'll have a talk with his publisher and make it clear that this kind of information sets our investigation back and could get people killed. They'll come around."

"I sure hope so," Garrett said. "I've got some leads on some new start-up businesses that might come to town. This is just the kind of thing that could scare them off, costing the city economic development and me personally a buttload of money. I sold these people on Sioux City being a quiet, low-crime place that still had what they needed to thrive as a business and attract employees looking for a good place to raise families. This shit in the paper is screwing it up for us all."

"We're working hard on it," Banks said. "Just a domestic disturbance that got out of hand. It'll fade away in a day or two. Kingman witnessed a lot so he kind of had us by the short hairs. We'll shut him down from here on. There's just no story there."

Garrett was glad to hear Banks's "domestic disturbance gone wrong" line of thinking.

"So if it's a domestic gone bad, what's this shit in the paper about a drug distribution ring? The guy your boys whacked ... Pollard? ... he was part of something bigger?" Garrett asked.

"Seems so, but I can't say anything else. The state people made it clear that if much about this got out, they would crucify someone for it. Besides, it's mainly their show anyway."

State police. Shit. Des Moines sticking its goddamn nose in Garrett's business again. They never gave a shit about Sioux City unless it was to bust some meth users. The only consolation was that half the people in Iowa's capital thought Sioux City was in South Dakota, and the other half couldn't give a shit what happened in "Sewer City." Thoughts of a hick police chief like Jimmy Banks or some state Department of Criminal Investigation agent infiltrating his operation enraged Garrett. His years of getting close to Banks were supposed to guard against any surprises. He cursed himself for not detecting the "ongoing investigation" Banks just confirmed.

"Well, you just get to Reed and Anderson and tell them that this case, and the resulting press, are already breaking deals for me," Garrett said. Sioux City officials would piss their collective pants if they thought something would ruin a rare chance to bring business to town. "And get down to the paper and make them see that civic duty is a bit more of a priority than selling papers, unless they have jobs for about 100 of my people who will get laid off because we sound like the Meth Capital of the World."

"Already on my calendar, Barry," Banks said. Garrett thought he heard Banks take a slurp of coffee. "We'll have this wrapped up inside a week. Guarantee it." Garrett spent a few more minutes stressing his points to Banks, who always needed the remedial reinforcement, before hanging up and unleashing a blizzard of obscenity. After years of painstakingly setting up front men to hide his identity, some stupid, small-time reporter and an even more stupid police department now threatened everything he'd built since leaving the Army. Perhaps he had underestimated Tom Kingman.

CHAPTER 14

By ten, Tom had showered and found some reasonably wrinkle-free "work" clothes, defined as "non-jeans pants and shirt." He had coaxed his moody car into starting and was pulling into the *Sentinel-Leader*'s parking lot, thankful for nearly six uninterrupted hours of sleep. He marched into the *S-L* building, his body and brain running on his breakfast of strong coffee from a little coffee shop a block from his house. He navigated the sea of "Hi, Tom" and "Great story" greetings to his desk, which was directly across from Skip's. Tom landed in his chair and faced about ten pink telephone message slips. Nobody wanted to "go to voicemail" any more. Scanning them, he decided they could all wait until he had checked the news wires to see what they had done with the *S-L* stories on the shooting. He had long since checked his cellphone for messages from Hillary.

"Thanks for tweaking up the shooting story, Skip," Tom said. "You're the Van Gogh of words, but with two full earlobes. You should have thrown your byline up there, above mine."

"Sure, then *I'd* get all the calls from the crazies," Skip answered. "Bylines don't impress me. I knew you'd say it should be up there, but it's not a big deal. I'm not looking for a movie deal or a date."

"Better think about that one. I know you've already got a great woman, but the movie deals … with your looks and charisma? Get outta here. You'd be *huge*. I'm thinking seven figures per movie, cash, plus an entourage. You and Mila Kunis would be uncontrollable chemistry on film. I'll be your agent and squeeze them for every dime. I'll do it for a scant thirty percent."

"I'll pass. Sure, I've got the bod for it," Skip stretched his arms in a mock bodybuilder pose, "but I wouldn't want those paparazzi jackals chasing my kids around or trying to catch me and Leah doing the nasty."

"So write a book. You got the chops for it. I keep telling ya ...."

Skip shrugged. "I'd hate to take time away from the girls and Leah to write it. What would I write about? And besides, do you know what the odds are of getting a book published? 'Remote' is optimistic. Also, I can't stand the rejection."

After a pause in Tom's extended praise, Skip conceded: "Marx said he didn't like the second paragraph."

"There's a *shocker*," Tom said, sarcasm flowing deep. Jack Marx was the chief city news editor, a good people manager and judge of what types of news should get the best play in the paper, but also a master at second guessing everything from the brand of toilet paper in the bathroom on up.

"Marx wouldn't know a good sentence if it bit him in the dick, assuming he has one. I suppose he thinks you should mention what kind of underwear Pollard was wearing or where he went to grammar school. The guy never met a big picture he couldn't miss, or a pile of copious detail that he didn't *adore*."

By the time Tom had returned selected calls, checked his email, discussed strategy with Skip, and given Bear an update, it was nearly eleven.

+++

Downtown at police headquarters, Chief Banks pecked out the number of Woodbury County Attorney Dick Anderson's direct line. Banks had just taken his seventh call on the shooting from Greater Siouxland Chamber of Commerce members. "Siouxland" was the name for Sioux City and the surrounding area. Looking at Sioux City on a map shows it at the exact point where Iowa, South Dakota and Nebraska meet. The Missouri River formed the border between Iowa and Nebraska, and between Nebraska and South Dakota, while the Big Sioux River was the border between Iowa and South Dakota. Sioux City, Iowa, South Sioux City, Nebraska, and North Sioux City, South Dakota were continuous towns that made up Siouxland. In the mid-1990s, part of the very southeastern tip of South Dakota, once sand and silt dunes wasteland used primarily for keg parties and illicit outdoor screwing, was transformed into an upscale housing development and golf course known as Dakota Dunes. Sioux City had also rejuvenated its downtown waterfront, a landfill a century ago, into a nicely landscaped park that housed a riverboat casino.

Ironically, in 2014 the riverboat was torpedoed when a new Hard Rock Hotel and Casino maneuvered away the boat's state gaming license. Without a gaming license, the river boat had no reason to exist and finally sailed away after a brief legal scuffle. The Hard Rock was in the former "Battery Building," a historic downtown structure just blocks from where Banks placed his call.

"Dick, this is Jimmy Banks. Listen, what's the update on this shooting? I know you saw the paper this morning. Are you going to leave Hillary Reed on the case or take that over personally?"

In his office not more than a hundred yards across Douglas Street from Banks, Anderson glanced up at Hillary, who was sitting in front of his desk. She had been in the middle of updating him when the phone rang. Hillary returned his gaze steadily until Anderson diverted his eyes back to his desk.

"It's Hillary's case, Jimmy," Anderson said, glancing furtively at Hillary, who reacted with a slightly raised eyebrow. "She's the best attorney I have, better equipped to handle an investigation that calls for thoroughness than I am, that's for damn sure. Plus she's not an elected official like I am, so nobody can accuse her of looking for votes. I'm sure I'll have my hands full dealing with the public, at least the faction that believes Pollard's live-in's insane story."

"I'm sure there will be some crazy theories from the public nut jobs on why my men shot Pollard," Banks said. "Self-defense, of course, won't be one of them."

"Agreed, but ignoring that vocal minority would be a mistake since they usually find their way into the paper and on TV," Anderson countered. "It's important that we have someone to counter their wild charges. Plus we have an independent witness, a respected journalist, no less. No need to worry on this one."

"We just don't need a long, drawn-out investigation here. I've got the Chamber of Commerce so far up my butt when I pull down my pants to take a shit I see wing tip shoes hanging out my ass. If this thing drags on for weeks, people will start thinking you guys found something wrong and are trying to figure out how to cover it up. All I'm asking is that you ask Hillary to get this done ASAP."

"I already stressed that to her. She's been working on it virtually non-stop since the shooting," Anderson said, lifting his eyes to Hillary, who was studying the documents on her lap, feigning lack of interest. "We'll get back to you as soon as we have something."

"Thanks. I'll probably walk over later today and see how everything's going. If you need anything from the department, please call me directly."

"Okay. Thanks."

Anderson let the phone drop onto its cradle and looked at Hillary. She'd gotten to bed shortly after Tom left but still made it to work by eight thirty, looking her usual fresh, crisp self. Anderson knew Hillary's cool, intelligent, friendly girl-next-door persona played very well in the courtroom. Juries loved her, and Anderson hadn't been elected to a record five straight four-year terms as Woodbury County Attorney by messing with what worked, let alone what juries loved.

Four years ago Anderson had hired Hillary over more experienced applicants. He had a feeling her common sense approaches and unaffected mannerisms would be dynamite in front of a jury. He had been right, and Hillary's legal prowess had grown with each trial.

"That was Jimmy Banks," he began, trying to make himself look as tall as possible in his high-backed chair. Dick Anderson was a short, balding man, fifty-two years old with a noticeable tire around his midsection. "He wants us to wrap up this investigation as fast as we can."

"So I gathered."

"It's just that every day is another chance for our lovely group of authority haters to sober up and start spewing insane accusations like 'cover-up' and 'cold-blooded killing.'" Anderson leaned forward in his chair. "Jimmy's afraid this will get out of hand and attract wider publicity than it has."

After a few more minutes with Anderson, Hillary excused herself with "Looks like I've got a lot of work to do," and returned to her small office overlooking City Hall.

+++

Leaning back in her government-issue office chair, Hillary sighed and let her mind drift back to her meeting with Tom. He had always intrigued her, a feeling she hadn't confided to anyone. His complete lack of clumsy, overt flirting was refreshing and appealing. And she felt a hint of personal interest from him even when they talked about cases. She found Tom physically attractive—more cute than handsome—but had never gone beyond casual notice of his body. Until last night when their discussion had prompted Hillary to give Tom a once-over, hungry man style.

And what about last night? Why had the mysterious Mr.

Kingman headed right for her house after his adventures with the hooker? It could have waited until morning, surely. His inability to resist the seduction was disappointing. Still, he had been through a lot earlier that night and it sounded like this Stephanie came on to him from the opening doorbell. Even after that embarrassing near miss, Tom managed to admit it and talk to her about it in a frank, adult way. Refreshing. She returned to Exhibit A in this line of thought: his post-hooker visit to her house. Hardly the behavior of an uninterested, fight-the-power, hard-boiled reporter.

Hillary spun around in her chair, slipped off her shoes and flexed her tired feet. Encouraging Tom's interest risked getting involved with someone from the media. Her current relationship with him already put her on the outer edge of the Code of Professional Responsibility. If she allowed their personal relationship to deepen, then she'd face the unpleasant prospect of constantly answering her colleagues' assertions, spoken or unspoken, that she was colluding with the enemy. She'd be the prime suspect for any department leak that found its way into print. Soon, confidential conversations would stop when she entered the room and she'd hear "don't tell Tom, but . . ." twice a day. Even a hint of professional infidelity scared Hillary.

She acknowledged herself as an attractive woman. She was something short of beautiful under its traditional standards but knew she looked good enough that her appearance could take her places if she let it. She dedicated herself, instead, to building skill and intellect rather than letting her looks cultivate favors. Her chosen course required determination and unquestioned ethical purity.

Her focus had earned her a courtroom reputation as a clever, tough and intelligent attorney. Letting herself become romantically involved, with a reporter no less, might blur that focus and harm the reputation. Plus, the scar of a past relationship-gone-wrong was still pretty fresh.

Still, Hillary had felt surprising flashes of excitement when she realized she had to make a deal with the talented and intriguing Tom Kingman. It was a bit like the way she felt when she was paired with the handsome popular boy for a science project. Only she doubted Tom would just let her do all the work. She knew the arrangement would lead to seeing more of him and she liked the prospect, despite her best efforts not to. The scent of Tom's personal interest, which she detected at the police station and again at her house, gave their covert alliance the electricity of a tacit affair with none of the guilt—at least not yet.

With Banks applying the pressure early, Hillary grew eager to meet Tom later that night. Despite her professional hesitations, she felt the need to conspire with her new confidant and explore these feelings. Slipping her shoes back on under her desk, Hillary subconsciously put herself in Stephanie's place, wearing revealing clothing and encouraging, if not reveling in, men's lusty gazes. She would never do it, of course, seeing it as self-inflicted violence to her professional and personal reputation. And she thought it personally demeaning. Yet she found herself fantasizing about being the object of such heated desire. With the right man, a man she knew loved the entire woman rather than just certain exterior parts, Hillary would be as brazen and kinky as her partner wanted. She prayed for such a partner every day. As she imagined it, Hillary shifted her weight in the chair and recrossed her legs.

She felt warm and looked out the window at the rooftop cooling units on City Hall, next door to the courthouse. A shimmer of heat rising off each unit distorted her view as the air conditioners struggled to compensate for the heat of another sweltering June day. She could feel that the courthouse's air conditioning was already starting to lose the day's battle with the Iowa heat, causing Hillary to appreciate her wardrobe choice for the day: a just-above-the-knee skirt that proved to be cooler than her prosecutorial uniform, the pant suit. As she stood in front of her closet that morning, her hand had stopped briefly on the shortest suit in her closet, the one Hillary wore on those very rare days when she felt daring enough to display a little thigh.

She suddenly realized this fashion-related internal monologue may have been prompted by Tom's obvious affinity for legs. She sat back and stretched out her feet in front of her, squeezing them together in a way that created definition in her naturally muscular thighs. A hint of a smile fluttered across Hillary's lips. Perhaps the short suit would have been better today after all.

CHAPTER 15

A few minutes after talking with Anderson, Banks found the *Sentinel-Leader's* number and carefully dialed. "This is Police Chief James Banks. Let me speak to Abraham Pennington," Banks said, reclining in his high-backed leather office chair.

A few seconds later, a gravelly voice replaced the hold music. "Abraham Pennington speaking."

"Abe, this is Police Chief James Banks. We need to talk about your people getting my people killed. That's if you have a minute."

"Can you hang on for a second, Chief?" Bear asked. Without waiting for an answer, Bear put the phone down, walked across his office to shut the door, and then returned to his desk.

"What's all this bullshit about my people getting cops killed?" Bear said, dispensing with polite pretenses. "You and I know that's a lot of crap, Jimmy. Why don't you people try telling the truth down there? It's been a few years since you gave that a whirl."

"What do you know about the truth?" Banks said, meeting Bear's escalation of decibel level. "You people print whatever you want and the truth be damned. No thought to how this screws things up for us, how your little stories might mean some child rapist or murderer goes free. Just as long as you sell papers."

The Bear was chuckling now, an ironic sign that he was truly enraged. "You've been watching too many police dramas on TV.

You should have used the time instead to train cops on how to take proper care of investigations so the bad guys don't go free."

"What the hell would you know about conducting an investigation?"

"Enough to know you do it right the first time or you're screwed," Bear responded. "How many times does a beer-gutted sergeant have to screw up a case for you by refusing to get off his ass and read the suspect his rights before you'll get the clue? It's happened twice since you've been chief. We report on it and suddenly it's our fault that you can't do your job. And don't you dare talk to me about putting out a newspaper. I was doing it when your daddy was stealing wallets in New Jersey."

"Abe, let me just get your name and number down so we can tell the widows of the dead officers who to call to ask why their husbands were killed by gang members. I'll just send the grieving families to you. How much good will your precious First Amendment do you then?"

Bear hated to be called Abe—which Banks was repeating simply to irritate him—and he hated the derisive phrase "precious First Amendment" even more. "Here's the flaw in your argument. The names of those officers rippled through the gangs in a city this size twice before our paper came out. The bad guys always know more than the paper knows. It's the good guys, the citizens of this community who provide the authority and money for your escapades down there, that you want to keep ignorant. As long as I own the *Sentinel-Leader*, and that's going to be a long, long time, my staff and I are not putting up with that bullshit at all."

"Well, your staff, especially your boy Tom Kingman, is giving me a headache the size of Nebraska. All I ask is that you show some restraint. I don't think the story benefits much from having the weepy relatives plastered all over the front page screaming about police brutality."

"I forget, Chief, do you or I run this paper? Because if you run this paper, that means I must be the police chief, in which case we have a scoop because I'm the first police chief since Ed Majors who doesn't have a big glob of dog shit where his brain should be."

The Bear was now standing behind his desk, roaring into the phone with enough intensity to draw a crowd in front of his office. "And by the way, if you piss around with any of my reporters like you pissed around with Tom right after the shooting, I'm coming down there in person to stick my entire foot up your ass. You're very fortunate that Tom agreed to the interview and that you didn't do something stupid like arrest him. If that had happened, I would have made it my personal crusade to get a team of six reporters from the *New York Times*—and I know the managing editor personally—into Sioux City for a week. Hell, I'd even pay their hotel bills, including bar tabs. You think we're a pain in your ass? Think about getting ambushed by *60 Minutes* going to your car after work every day. Am I making myself clear here, Chief, or am I using too many big words?"

"Look, you old sack of shit,"—it was Banks's turn to stand up—"nobody talks to me like that. You won't get jack shit out of this department as long as I am police chief. Tom may be tight with Hillary Reed, but he's not getting the time of day from me or any of my men. And, if he ever happens to need police assistance at his house, who knows how long it may take to get there? I've tried to be reasonable, Abe, but you've pushed me too far this time."

"Well, please accept my invitation to rot in hell then," Bear roared, his face bright pink. "And if anything happens to Tom Kingman because you people stopped at a donut shop on your way to his house, I'll consider it a duty of holy proportions to see your badge implanted firmly in your ass. Good day, Chief Banks."

Bear slammed down the phone, stalked out of his office and into the newsroom, scattering the crowd that had assembled around his door.

"I have an announcement," he said to the news staff, most of whom tried to cover their eavesdropping by pretending to search through a stack of old papers outside Bear's office. "The police chief has just called me and offered his kind advice on how I should run this paper, which has been in my family for all 148 years of its existence. I thanked him and called him a dipshit with a badge, in no uncertain terms. He responded with a thinly veiled threat to me and Mr. Kingman, which I found only slightly more amusing than pathetic. So please do not expect a kind reception from the SCPD during your next encounter with them. I'm proud of you all, and we are now going to proceed with giving Jimmy Banks a public prostate exam. Keep up the good work."

With that Bear strode back into his office, replaced his reading glasses and returned to budget projections. Skip shook his head and chuckled softly. He wrote "dipshit with a badge" down to share with Tom.

Skip and Tom's relationship had grown beyond professional to personal, a rarity for Tom. He enjoyed Skip's young daughters, Ashley and Tracy, and kept up with their academic, sporting and social milestones. Skip had been touched by the lavish presents from Tom after the birth of each child, the way he remembered their birthdays and his occasional attendance at the girls' school events.

Skip had removed his sweater, which was required in June due to the *Sentinel-Leader* building maintaining a constant temperature of sixty-five degrees, even when it was forty degrees hotter outside. He sat in a T-shirt emblazoned with Carbon Leaf.

"Carbon Leaf. A band?" Tom asked.

"A great band," Skip said without looking up from his research. "In my top five for sure."

Skip was a connoisseur of bands big enough to tour regionally and play smaller venues but not big enough to be "co-opted by the heartless music profit machine," as he put it. He had a collection of concert Ts famous throughout the newsroom. Tom's musical taste trended toward 80s rock.

"Would you say they are more hippy-dippy, or kumbaya?" Tom asked, smiling.

Skip turned from his desk and gave Tom a remorseful head shake. "You are such a music philistine."

Tom let out a loud laugh and flopped into his chair.

Skip returned to his work and said without looking up, "Leah was wondering if you were busy on the twenty-eighth …"

Skip's wife, Leah, was on a mission to find Tom a mate. Leah had set Tom up on some dates, but so far nothing that amounted to any kind of relationship. Skip knew that at least one or two of the arranged dates had led to sex, but the relationships never lasted. Tom just didn't have the attention span required for a traditional courtship so he didn't talk much about the encounters.

In contrast to Leah's zeal, Tom seemed almost ambivalent about finding a partner, using work to shelter himself from starting any relationships. And, Tom obviously enjoyed his nomadic lifestyle. Skip's phone jangled to life, sparing Tom from having to respond to the relayed query from Leah about the twenty-eighth.

"*Sentinel-Leader*, this is Geoffrey Ensley," Skip answered in his best CEO voice. It was someone complaining about home delivery. Skip sighed. "I'll transfer you, sir." A series of pushed buttons sent the caller to the circulation department. Skip turned back to his desk, wondering what the hell was up with the story, if he would be able to make a Red Wanting Blue concert in Omaha later that month, and what Leah and the girls had on the docket for tonight.

Tom took the opportunity to ghost out of the newsroom. Skip knew he was gone without even looking.

+++

It was just before noon when Barry Garrett's day went into a hammerhead stall, about the same time Donna Zimmerman, the

Chief Financial Officer for Blade-Garrett Worldwide, entered his huge office for her noon appointment. After a polite "no-thank-you" to an assistant's offer of coffee or some lunch, Zimmerman and Garrett were finally alone.

Zimmerman handled her five-foot-four-inch body with the confidence of a gymnast. She arranged her professionally colored platinum-blonde hair in styles that took more than an hour to create each morning. She had a formidable makeup supply in her desk to properly maintain her look throughout the day. And Garrett could already smell her perfume across the room.

Zimmerman's smile dissolved as Garrett's assistant closed the office door.

"We've lost two more people," she said, moving to a chair in front of Garrett's massive desk. "Drewing and Sanchez. They didn't report as usual this morning and my people hear they've been hanging around the River Inn."

"Dammit. Don't these assholes read the papers? Don't they understand what happened to Pollard?"

"Either it was too subtle for them or they're running scared," Zimmerman said. "Either way, they ran right to the River Inn."

"And right into Donny Maxfield's room, no doubt," Garrett said, leaning forward. "I'm going to kill that little greasy Texas puke. Maxfield thinks he can come up here, bitch about how dull this town is and take over my empire in his spare time. Well, fuck him. I'll blow up the whole fucking hotel."

Zimmerman shrugged. "All this changing teams, on top of the shooting, is bound to stir up talk, Barry. The police in this town aren't bright, but they're a step above stupid. If this keeps up, they're bound to figure it out."

The defections made the Omaha-based meth supplier Maxfield stronger as he led the invasion into Sioux City. They figured podunk Sioux City would be an easy mark, easier than Des Moines for sure. These new meth dealers' tentacles also stretched to Sioux Falls, the largest city in South Dakota, just ninety minutes up the interstate from Sioux City.

For years, Garrett had run things in his Sioux City organization through two lieutenants, who in turn operated through several key people. No one knew anyone in the organization more than one layer above them, and only Zimmerman and Stephanie knew about Garrett's relationship with Van Grunner. Garrett thought the extra secrecy vital in a town as small as Sioux City, where a rumor can ripple around very quickly. Years of vigilance and some luck had made the system work. So far Garrett's top two people had remained loyal. As a precaution, he'd increased their percentage of the profits and given them both bonuses. Protecting his identity required tedious procedures like secret code names, encrypted and coded email and other seemingly ridiculous precautions, but it had paid off in Garrett's struggle to repel the rival organization. It seemed clear to Garrett that he was now losing the war on rival druggies.

"Donna, what the hell do you think we should do about this? I'm not worried about you, but we need to think about Stan. Is he going to hold up for us? After all, we've got a nice thing going here. Blade-Garrett doesn't pull down near the margins we make on meth, even with your home-cooked accounting. Five hundred million sheltered as of last year, give or take a few million. Not bad. But having the owner and CEO get arrested for drug trafficking does tend to screw up a business, I think you'll agree."

"Do you think we could just shut your organization down and actually rely on the trucking business?" Zimmerman said, letting her already short skirt ride up her leg a bit more. She saw Garrett's eyes eagerly snap to the offered flesh.

"I suppose we could, but we'd have to get rid of the few people who know you. I love Stan, but it's becoming evident that someone may have to go down for this. Better him than me."

Zimmerman shifted position in her chair, causing her breasts to strain her blouse buttons. "We've got some serious penetration in our security." She glanced at Garrett. "Banks said Pollard had been under investigation and that's the first any of us had heard of it. I thought you paid that idiot Van Grunner to prevent these kinds of surprises."

"I never did like that stupid redneck bastard." Garrett sat back in his chair and stared at the ceiling for a few seconds. "I doubt he would hold out on me. He likes my money too much. Just the cash from the job the other night alone will keep him in beer, rubbers, and broads for the rest of his life. That leaves the state cops."

"They might believe the local police are in on it, or just Van Grunner," Zimmerman said, watching Garrett's eyes search for any sign of her nipples under her thin bra and blouse.

"Don't even fucking say that," Garrett said, dropping the tenth anniversary paperweight he'd been spinning around his finger. "If that's true, then we might as well bail out now. I know that the state cops and the local yokels hate each other. Ever since the state accused a local cop of skimming drug evidence and then selling it back onto the street."

"Your friend Tom Kingman had a ball with that one," Zimmerman said, giving her skirt another casual hike. "No one ever filed formal charges against the local but he did get canned, largely on what Kingman published, despite all the yelling from police headquarters."

"Don't worry about Tom Kingman. He'll either back off or end up covering his own shooting."

Garrett got up from his desk, took off his suit coat and walked around to Zimmerman's chair. She smiled with satisfaction that her show had been effective.

"Barry," she purred, "I think it's time we think of ourselves and do what's best for us. I like Stan White, don't get me wrong, but we're the team that's made this thing happen for all these years. You made the money, and I laundered it clean as Iowa snow. Those state and federal auditors didn't have a clue. Stan, Van Grunner and I are the only three who know you. Only two people below us in the organization know me, and then only as an encrypted email name. One shot—maybe two—and we're out of this. Maybe we could even think about taking an extended vacation. We could be in Jamaica by morning."

Zimmerman reached up and undid one button of her blouse, letting the top of her lacy bra peek out.

"Maybe," Garrett said, his eyes sweeping the overall display.

Zimmerman undid another button and another, until her blouse hung open. She tightened her abdominal muscles and played her hand across her breasts. Garrett stood in front of his desk, mesmerized.

"We've been through a lot and been very close lately. I really enjoy our quality time together," he said.

"Besides," Zimmerman said, unhooking the front clasp of her bra and letting the cups slide off her breasts, the edge of one cup catching briefly on an erect nipple, "Stan White can't offer what I do."

"No, he can't," Garrett said, his eyes fixed on her breasts.

"He isn't nearly as versatile," Zimmerman said as she raised one leg and hooked the back of her knee over the arm of her chair while she slid her other hand down her artificially tan torso. Garrett already had his belt unbuckled and his pants unsnapped. "I think I see your point."

Donna Zimmerman had always delivered great sex, but today was more epic than usual. After some oral preliminaries, Garrett had bent her over the chair and pounded away for a few minutes that seemed to him like an hour. Zimmerman's sexual frenzy rose with the ferocity of Garrett's thrusts until she finally muffled her orgasmic screams against the back of the chair. After they had recovered their normal breathing and color, Zimmerman buttoned up and checked her hair.

It was obvious to Zimmerman that Garrett was a sex addict,

virtually insatiable and always ready. Zimmerman thought Garrett could easily sustain a regimen of twice-daily sex well into his eighties. But, as with all addictions, Garrett's was also his weakness, and her ticket to a lot of money. She had already successfully tucked away five hundred thousand in cash over the years that not even Garrett knew about and had easy access to three million more that Garrett also did not know about. She wanted even more. And if letting Garrett bone her morning and evening did the trick, that was no problem.

Since she had discovered Garrett's addiction about five years earlier, Zimmerman had let her suit skirts get shorter and her undergarments become more erotic. By now, there probably wasn't a room at Blade-Garrett where the two hadn't copulated. It didn't take much to get Garrett to jump her, wherever they happened to be. Zimmerman played him like a fine musical instrument. She also knew there were other women besides Garrett's wife. It wasn't surprising that it took a team of vaginas to keep Barry satisfied. Her strategy was to deliver the added benefit of office kinkiness that set her apart.

Zimmerman inspected her suit for any damage or staining. Finding everything in order, she kissed Garrett lightly and said, "Maybe tonight."

"Maybe," Garrett said, buckling his belt, trying to remember if he was seeing Stephanie tonight. If he was, perhaps he could cancel—or maybe do both. "But I think we just agreed on what we should do."

"It's the only way. And that was much better than a handshake."

Garrett just nodded slightly. Zimmerman turned, spritzed herself with the perfume she kept in her suit pocket and recreated her business smile.

"I'll let you know how those figures come out, Barry," she said a bit too loudly as she opened the door. "I appreciate your input."

"My pleasure," Garrett said. "I'm always available, Donna."

CHAPTER 16

Garrett spent the rest of the day mapping strategy. Donna Zimmerman's accounting talents surpassed even her sexual skills. She was so talented, in fact, that Garrett now needed her to locate the millions squirreled away in banks around the globe. He'd been careful to build in safeguards that meant Donna also needed him to get access to that fortune. He didn't kid himself that she wouldn't take off with some young stud if she knew how to get to the big money. Instead it was Garrett who would jet off into the sunset with Zimmerman if things got bad enough to go to the backup plan. They could hop around the globe for years, living off their secret bank deposits and screwing like rabbits. The local talent could always be relied upon to supplement Garrett's sexual needs, as long as he could pay.

He considered the prospects of having Donna Zimmerman at his sexual bidding. She could make a porn star whimper in bed. He found himself getting hard again and, for a second, considered scheduling an emergency afternoon budget conference in her office. Despite her physical and accounting talents, Garrett wasn't ready to chuck it all and run away with Donna quite yet. He had to explore a few other business options first. It was still possible for him to hold his empire together, if he got a couple of breaks, cleaned up a few things and didn't panic. He could always bang

Zimmerman. She seemed to like it as much as he did, if not more. As the day wore on, Garrett found himself thinking less about Zimmerman's familiar talents and more about the unfamiliar Tom Kingman, specifically what he knew and what he would write. By the end of the day, Garrett had convinced himself that Tom was his main threat in the short term. If Garrett couldn't deflect the attention, Stan White could soon face a crime-world version of downsizing. He reprimanded himself for not knowing more about Kingman before now. Since the shooting, Garrett's network had produced Tom's home phone, address and cellphone number and a fairly detailed report on the man, including a warning not to underestimate him.

The state police were a long-term hazard. Garrett could control the dim-witted, self-important police chief Banks with flattery and the occasional orchestrated loss on the golf course. Stephanie's seductive powers were his ace in the hole. A good old boy like Banks would have trouble saying no to Stephanie. One video camera hidden behind the bedroom air vent and Banks would be well under control. But blackmail was messy, so Garrett held that option as his emergency trump card. There were plenty of other smart people in the Sioux City Police Department, though, and he reminded himself not to judge the force by the chief.

Kingman was a much tougher problem. And Hillary Reed. Banks had hinted that those two had cut some kind of deal. Garrett now wondered if they held "budget meetings" of their own. He could see himself having a meeting with Hillary Reed. Kingman and Reed also had enough integrity to bother Garrett. Kingman would never fall for the ego stroking that controlled Banks. And he might even say no to Stephanie, especially if Kingman and Reed were doing the nasty. "Committed, monogamous relationship" and all that bullshit. Tom had shown his balls on that state police vs. local cops scandal by somehow getting cops to talk dirty about each other. Reed was an Ice Princess. Give Garrett ten Hillary

Reeds—minus the moral virtue—and he would rule the world. Garrett didn't need business planning software to know the combination of Tom's digging with Reed's official power to shape the investigation led to trouble.

Garrett put the ideas of Van Grunner talking or Kingman and Reed finding a link back to him on the table for consideration. The level of detail in the morning paper convinced Garrett that it was only a matter of time before Kingman called for comment on the big story of Garrett leading the drug ring. The headline "TRUCKING BOSS RUNS DRUGS" scrolled through Garrett's mind, chased by an image of him being led away in handcuffs from the Blade-Garrett Worldwide building, his employees, including Donna Zimmerman, gawking innocently at the crush of reporters outside, every step taking him farther and farther from that retirement opulence he'd worked so long for.

Garrett shook off the images. The prospect of these events threatening his empire was virtually unthinkable. He hadn't built his business from a single truck running on borrowed fuel money into the transport behemoth of today without attacking when needed. If necessary, Garrett would console himself with a few years of Donna Zimmerman's sex therapy. But it hadn't come to that yet.

What he needed was to send another message, this time addressed to Tom Kingman and Hillary Reed. The embryonic plan Garrett had conceived at breakfast sprang freshly into his mind. As the day wore on, Garrett did an increasingly poor job of feigning interest in his routine business reports and forecasts. He instead fixated on the plan, developing a two-stage strategy.

Garrett wanted to write it down, make a nice flow chart of all the variables, but he feared that seeing such an outrageous plan on paper would convince him that it was too wild, too brazen. He even thought of telling Zimmerman but then decided she already knew enough that could be used against him. She was smart and cunning, but for now she didn't seem to be a threat. Zimmerman did know that Garrett had more value for her free than behind bars. And Garrett didn't kid himself that Donna wanted him just for his erection. She could easily get sex from most any man including those much younger than him. Garrett figured it was his combination of cash, charisma, and crotch that turned Donna on.

Garrett's plan would require Van Grunner to do a riskier job. One that, if bungled, could actually draw more attention to the case. But, if he succeeded, he might come out of this unscathed. He put the odds at fifty-fifty, sixty-forty at best.

By about 4 p.m. Garrett was committed to his new vision. He sat back in his leather desk chair, looking around his large office. Garrett's gaze bounced over photographs of himself with successful clients and an old photo of him and Missy sitting in their first truck. Missy looked fresh from the trailer park, plump and barefoot in cutoff shorts and braless in a black tank top. Back then, he and Missy were glad to have anything, let alone the title to a huge semi-trailer truck and the ability to call themselves real business owners. Garrett's eyes hopped from the trailer-park Missy across several other pictures to a photo of him in a golf foursome. Second from the left was James Banks, grinning ridiculously. If things came to pass as Garrett hoped, he'd be playing Banks like a cheap fiddle for at least a year.

Garrett picked up his private line and dialed a number he knew by heart.

"Hello?" Bryan Van Grunner sounded groggy.

"It's me," Garrett said, knowing Van Grunner would recognize his voice. "I've got a job for you."

+++

Tom Kingman sat just a block away from the police department at the Clerk of Court's Office in the Woodbury County Law Enforcement Center. Tom's online search hadn't netted much. Not knowing what else to do, he had come downtown to "look at the paper" even though, in theory, everything from way back in the paper era was now available either online or in a digital database somewhere. He had hiked this trail a thousand times before, so often that the clerks automatically released the electronic lock and allowed him behind the counter to access the public files unsupervised.

Another big benefit of coming downtown to look at the paper, even though there was a dwindling amount of it, was that Tom had built relationships and trust with the clerks, who knew the less documented details of what went on in the court system.

That's why Tom took time to talk to clerks about their kids and husbands, or maybe compliment their outfits, just to remind them that he cared. It wasn't an act. He did care … about the clerks *and* the cases they handled.

For the better part of two hours, Tom sifted through the dozen or so old paper files he could find documenting Chuck Pollard's criminal exploits. Mostly small-time stuff, except for the one possession of methamphetamine charge five years ago. That eventually got Pollard sent to the state pen in Anamosa. Tom vaguely remembered the case. It was one of a few things that had turned up during his earlier computer search of the *Sentinel-Leader* clipping library.

In Iowa, prison sentences are almost always "an indeterminate term not to exceed" a certain amount, in this case ten years. The exact length of each sentence was almost always less than half the maximum, and usually they ended up about a quarter of the "not to exceed" time. The state parole board determined sentence length based on how each convict behaved in prison. So while the sentence sounded like ten years the average prisoner was out in a little less than three, thanks to time off for good behavior, working and participating in programs while inside prison. Judges argued that the system gave prisoners incentive—points toward early release—to behave and participate in rehabilitation programs. Critics called it soft.

The only exceptions in Iowa were penalties for "Class A felonies"—first-degree murder, first-degree kidnapping and first-degree sexual assault involving life-threatening injury—all of which carried mandatory sentences of life in prison with no chance for parole, ever. A lifer could hope that some governor would commute the life sentence to a period of years, making him or her eligible for parole. It did happen, maybe once every five years. Tom agreed with the state's penalty for first-degree murder. Calls for the death penalty filled the Iowa Legislature each year but so far hadn't made it into law. Iowa's penalty for murder was already death, albeit a very slow one from old age rather than lethal injection.

Two fruitless hours had drained Tom's enthusiasm. Pollard gave Chicago as place of birth, so visiting the hometown was barely an option. Finding a real local address on a booking sheet was as likely as hitting the lottery. Online information services available to journalists had been a dramatic leap forward in finding real addresses, but Pollard was still proving to be an elusive target. Skip and others had already talked to the neighbors on West Jarred. No one admitted knowing anything about Chuck Pollard even though he had lived there for two years, a relative lifetime given Pollard's nomadic history.

Even the landlord had little to say beyond "he paid his rent on time." That, after all, was the main attribute he was looking for in a tenant.

So much for civic duty out there in the 'hood.

Pollard's "occupation" line on the old booking reports usually showed "none," ruling out former employers as a possible source. No big loss. Controversy-shy businesses in Sioux City would probably not talk anyway. With such a small customer pool, they saw even a minimal chance of angering anyone as bad business. Grabbing employees as they left work and trying to get something out of them before the boss got wind of it was also pretty pointless. Tom gathered all this worthless information in his small notebook. Driver's license number, mother's name, height, weight, and eye and hair color. All of it. Why? Tom had no idea. Maybe once planted in his notebook, the info seeds would eventually germinate into something beautiful just waiting to be harvested later. Sometimes innocuous bits of information like height or eye color did trigger mental lightning bolts.

So far no lightning in the Pollard case. Tom rocked back in his chair, rubbed his eyes, and tossed his pen onto the desk. He stretched his arms, watching the clerks buzz around the records area. They kept track of criminal files ranging from public urination to murder, while serving a steady flow of people, mainly attorneys, at the front counter. He had yet to find a clerk who wasn't blessed with a sense of humor or willingness to help despite the blizzard of bad news clerks waded through every day.

The clerk's office was led by a subdued man named Douglas Graves. The real power was with the second-in-command, Vera Norsma, a thirty-eight-year veteran of the clerk's office. Vera usually wore modest-length dresses and pumps with heels just a bit too high by mid-2010s office standards. She completed the throwback look with the occasional strand of pearls. Vera was an island of the 1960s amid the swirling, pants-and-flats casualness of her twenty-first century coworkers.

"Tommy, dear," she called across the room, as Tom continued his stretch. Her high heels chased the greeting over to Tom. "Loved your story today. Must have been quite a thing to actually see a shooting. I'm certain I would have wanted a stout whiskey afterwards, had it been me." Vera punctuated her joke with unrestrained laughter that stirred smiles around the room. "I bet Mr. Pollard flew backwards like Superman stunt flying when those bullets hit him." More laughter, although a bit more subdued.

"Don't believe everything you read in the papers, Vera," Tom said, "and, yes, Mr. Pollard did experience the stopping power, or should I say throwing power, of two police-issue nine millimeter hollow-point rounds in the center mass."

"Well, Chuck Pollard is all over our computer system like a virus," Vera said. "I thought my computer was stuck on the same screen this morning when I looked him up. It went on for twelve entries. Mostly small stuff like assault and carrying dangerous weapons. He did go to prison for a few years on a methamphetamine charge."

"I only found these six in the big index book," Tom said, gesturing weakly toward the files strewn over the desk.

"Six? You won't find much in those missing older ones. No background to speak of. Although my cousin Morey mentioned this morning that he drove trucks with a Charles Pollard years ago."

"Your cousin knew Pollard?" Tom said, marveling at how small a place Sioux City really was. "What company would that have been?"

"The big one in town here. You know, what's-its-name . . . Blair-Parrott or something like that," Vera said, straightening her dress slightly, surveying her working minions with satisfaction and then glancing at the counter to make sure everyone was being helped.

"Blade-Garrett?" Tom corrected.

"That's the one," she answered, her face looking as if she had just discovered the last piece to a complex puzzle. Tom knew better. She was making him work for it. A mind like Vera's could probably tell you the date that Blade-Garrett was incorporated and give you the file number for the articles of incorporation at the state Capitol.

"Morey said Mr. Pollard was there for a few years and then suddenly left. The official story was that he got a better offer and went to a similar company somewhere around here. But Morey knows all the drivers at the other companies and none of them ever heard of Charles Pollard."

Light bulb.

"And isn't it a coincidence that Morey also worked with Bryan Van Grunner at Blain-Parrot?" Vera said so casually that Tom imagined the sentence fluttering to the desktop and disappearing into the wood grain.

Lightning flash.

Tom sat up so fast his knee rammed into the underside of the desk.

"Van Grunner worked at Blade-Garrett too?" Tom tried to grimace away the pain. "Morey knew him there? When was this?"

"Right before Van Grunner joined the police force. The story was he quit trucking to be a cop. Guess he traded the truck stop for the donut shop." More laughter from Vera.

Vera was saying something about how trucking was no life for a family man and Morey had given it up when he met his wife, Bertha, or whatever her name was. Tom didn't hear it all. He was too busy thinking of Barry Garrett's smiling photo from the paper's archives. Certainly fit Stephanie's description of a mover and shaker, a chamber luminary, but so did fifty others in town. When Vera finally finished, Tom wanted to kiss her. "Can you show me those other files?"

CHAPTER 17

Back in his office, Garrett heard Van Grunner yawning on the other end of the phone call. "What job?" Van Grunner said, starting to understand both who was calling him and the nature of the proposed work.

"I want you to take care of a loose end that you left dangling on West Jarred Street. It was supposed to be a clean shooting, Bryan, but somehow you managed to get a reporter involved. Why didn't you just film the whole thing for the evening news, while you were at it?"

"What did I do? Kingman must have gotten there just after we did," Van Grunner responded. "They got scanners down at the paper. Usually reporters don't show up at domestics. Total fluke he was there. We had just capped Pollard when the stupid shit fell off a lawnmower outside the window. Hot shit reporter standing on a lawnmower to witness the crime. He didn't put that in his little story, did he? Besides, he just backs up my claims that the shooting was justified."

Garrett exhaled strongly. "Yeah, but what he's putting in the paper will have me shitting toothpicks for a month. It's a shame your bullet didn't go through Chuck and get Kingman too. A two-for-one deal. What about that other cop, Powers? He's a rookie. Is he under control?"

"He has no clue," Van Grunner said. "He was freaked out about it all. Powers actually helped our cause by shooting at the same time I did, so we both hit him. If I would have known Kingman was at the window, maybe I would have shot wide. But I didn't see him and it was a genuine bang-bang situation. Like I told you on the phone right afterward, nobody, including that dickhead Kingman, suspects a thing."

Garrett was not reassured. He always found Van Grunner's assessment of someone else's mental capabilities more amusing than reassuring. "So where did Tom get everything he put in today's paper?" Garrett already knew where Tom got it, but he was testing the cop.

This time Van Grunner snorted. "I think he's screwing Hillary Reed. They must have worked out some kind of deal."

"A deal? Hmmmm. Perhaps we should make an offer of our own."

+++

Tom hustled Vera Norsma to the records archive as politely as possible. "You want to see them all? I suppose you're going to put these all back, too."

"Sure, I'll put them back," Tom offered.

"No, you will not. The last thing we need around here is some reporter putting files back God knows where. We'd never find them again."

With Tom close behind, Vera walked briskly between the shelves. Her right hand quickly skimmed over the files, deftly plucking out the appropriate numbers and handing them to Tom without wasting time confirming the contents before immediately scanning for the next file. When she finished, Tom had six more files in his arms, making an even dozen.

All of the files were too old to be in the computer system. A computer record check would show the crime, disposition and case number, of course, but not the details. When Woodbury County switched to paperless records, they didn't go to the time and expense of scanning everything from old cases into the system. For the details of those cases, you had to hit "the stacks."

Tom thanked her and tried to keep from running back to the desk. Fifteen minutes' work confirmed what Vera had told him— Pollard had listed Blade-Garrett as "employer" for some five years.

"Booking sheets are wonderful things," Tom said to the amused smile of a clerk nearby. In particular, Tom silently thanked whoever thought to include the questions "occupation," "employer," and "time on job" on booking sheets. A decade-old file answered those questions with "truck driver," "Blade-Garrett," and "five years."

Seeing anything but "unemployed" or "laborer" on a booking sheet was rare enough. Usually "time on job" was a number followed by "months" or even "weeks" rather than years, so seeing "five years" in that space was like seeing winking neon on the page. If you had a job, however, it was good to make sure it was on record because that could help you make bond. Tom made photocopies of the booking sheets, paid the clerk for the copies and got a receipt for his expense report. He then stacked the files in order, and set them on the edge of the desk. He made a special trip to Vera's desk and waited until she got off the phone to thank her.

"Any time, Tommy," she said. "You're so cute when you find what you're looking for. Your ears turn red."

"Vera," Tom said, "I'd like to call your cousin Morey just to confirm he worked with Pollard."

Vera looked at him for five seconds without talking. "That would be up to him, wouldn't it? Let me get him on the line." She snatched up the nearest receiver and dialed the number from memory, paused and then said a few sentences into the phone while motioning at Tom.

She stepped closer and held out the receiver. "He said he'd answer a few questions."

Big of him.

Tom took the phone, confirmed with Morey that Van Grunner had worked there, gave Morey his name and number so he could write it down, and hung up. He thanked Vera again and took his rosy ears out of the courthouse just before it closed at four thirty. He headed for Blade-Garrett's headquarters on Interstate 29. The headquarters would close promptly at five. Tom got there at 4:57 and ran from his car to the main entrance just as a security guard was approaching to lock it. By the time he pushed the door open, the guard was within three feet.

"Hi," Tom greeted the unsmiling guard. "My name is Tom Kingman from the *Sentinel-Leader.* Can I get a word with Mr. Garrett?"

The guard sneered. "Sorry. We don't take press inquiries down here. You'll have to call our public relations people in the morning."

"The morning will be a little late for me, officer. Can't you just make a call or two and see if anyone —"

The guard suddenly had a hold of Tom's left arm, squeezing it like a steroidal kindergarten teacher controlling a recalcitrant student. Tom winced and flashed back to his lawnmower dive.

"Sorry, sir, but you'll have to leave now."

Tom pulled his arm away, stifling another grimace. "And your name is?"

"My name is 'Officer' and your name is 'Leaving.' "

"Fine. I just wanted to let Mr. Garrett know who to call when he reads the story tomorrow and wonders why I didn't ask him for comment."

"Leave now or I'll call the police," the guard said, pulling a cell-phone like he was drawing a gun.

Surprised he hasn't tried to tase me yet … bro.

"Maybe I should go, officer"—Tom leaned close to get a look

at the security man's corporate identity tag—"Mike Larkin." Tom pulled out his notebook from his back pocket and in one fluid motion he plucked the pen from his breast pocket. He wrote the name on the pad, making sure Larkin could see. "I appreciate all your help. You wouldn't have the number for your friends in PR would you?"

"The general number is 266-1000. The operator can direct you."

"PR 266-1000" went into the notebook under "Mike Larkin." Tom flipped the pad shut with a quick flick of the wrist and then reholstered it in his back pocket with a nod. Larkin held eye contact with Tom as he stepped back, shut the door and locked it.

"Have a nice day," Larkin said through the glass as the lock bolt popped home.

What a warm guy.

Tom walked back to his car in the nearly empty visitor lot. The corporate types must leave early, Tom thought. The cars of the employees—presumably those out on the road driving trucks—were in a fenced-in lot behind the building. Tom could see another uniformed guard back there.

So much for that idea.

Tom came in the *Sentinel-Leader's* employee entrance at about five thirty with customary urgency, to enjoy the embrace of the icy *Sentinel-Leader* air. The night shift was just an hour and a half into their day while the day shift blazed away at their keyboards, trying to finish stories so they could leave. Skip Ensley sat among them. His daughter had a soccer game that night, and he typed at a rate that showed his determination to see it. Tom exchanged waves and hellos on the way to his desk.

"Skip," Tom said as he got to his desk. "Blade-Garrett."

Skip looked up from his typing, mildly annoyed at being interrupted at all, let alone with such a cryptic message.

"God, you found something," Skip said, the light slowly coming on in his eyes. "I can always tell because you look like a bird flew up your butt and your ears get red."

"Found it, babe. Got the goods. Brought home the bacon. Hauled the mail . . ."

Skip leaned back in his chair and shut his eyes. "Okay, okay, are you just going to tell me this time or do we play that fun game, 'Guess what Tom knows'?"

"If I just came out and told you, would you truly appreciate my brilliance, my cunning investigative skills, my journalistic prowess?"

"It would be a serious shame if I couldn't appreciate all those things and more," Skip said, resigning himself to investing five precious minutes in this conversation. He mentally calculated whether he could still get there in time to catch Ashley's first kick. This called for a preemptive strike.

"Blade-Garrett?" Skip said out loud. "Everybody knows Blade-Garrett. Big trucking company. Barry Garrett's empire. Correctionville's favorite son. Goes way back. Employs a lot of people. Chuck Pollard used to work there."

Tom's jaw dropped for a second and then he gave an exaggerated shrug. "You know, you used to be fun to play this game with, but now that you're so damn smart, I'm going to have to play with Marx."

"Marx?" Skip scoffed. "You'd be playing your game for hours before he even had a clue that you were talking to him."

"Okay, smart guy," Tom said, emptying his pockets of his keys, cellphone, notebook and a small digital recorder he sometimes carried. "You figured out that Pollard worked for Blade-Garrett, but do you know who else worked for him?"

Skip looked up at the ceiling, feigning concentration.

"Bryan Van Grunner."

Tom's smugness leapt from his face to Skip's.

"You little punk," Tom said, his grin returning. "You've been power sifting again, haven't you? I've warned you about all that worldwide web stuff. Spend a lot of time in cyberspace and you'll lose touch with reality. And the porn sites. Look out! One day I'll come in here and you'll just hold up your network card and expect me to plug myself into it so we can chat."

"Right. Like any computer could handle talking directly to you. You'd blow its processor inside of a minute."

"So Vera at the courthouse told me that Van Grunner and Pollard used to work together and you found it out from a machine. At least I had some human contact."

"The bios page on the Sioux City Police Department's website showed that Van Grunner worked for Blade-Garrett before he joined the force. They posted the bios to try and humanize the police force. No photos though. They're not that human. I didn't know that Pollard worked there too or that they worked together. Just took a shot."

"Devious," Tom said. "You can't imagine how proud I am of you right now."

Skip chuckled as he returned to his story, more intent on finishing and getting to Ashley's game than exchanging banter with Tom.

"So, they both worked for the same person a while ago. I'll put it in my second-day story, along with bio information on Powers, Van Grunner and Pollard," Skip said over the muted click of his typing.

"Damn straight you will."

"Are Vera's files a good enough source that Pollard worked there?" Skip asked.

Tom pulled the folded copy of Pollard's arrest sheet out of his front pocket and threw it across Skip's desk. "I got the documentation."

"Five years, geez," Skip said as his eyes finally reached the magic line.

"If you do the math, Skip, you'll see that the two worked at Blade-Garrett at the same time," Tom said over the clicking of Skip's keyboard. "I'm not saying they were best friends or shared a sleeper cab or anything, just that they worked at the same place at the same time."

"Did you call Van Grunner?" Skip asked. "We should call Van Grunner to see what he has to say."

"I'd give him a call, but good luck to me getting him on the phone," Tom said. "Got his home number? I don't. He's unlisted. *Shocker.* Maybe you could call the station and leave a message."

"Me? This is your big discovery, Tom. I've been here grinding out this story all day while you were down sipping cappuccino and exchanging Margarita recipes with the court clerks. I'll work this 'both employed by Blade-Garrett' bit into my story while you call."

"For the record, it was instant decaf, not cappuccino," Tom said. "I have *cappuccino* with the court administrator." Tom looked at Skip for several seconds.

Tough newsroom.

Tom scooped up the phone and dialed the police chief's office from memory. "Bryan Van Grunner, please," Tom said, making a cheery voice come out of his grimacing face. "This is Tom Kingman of the *Sentinel-Leader.*"

There was a pause. Tom's gaze circled his desk as he listened.

"He's not in?" Tom asked, his grimace contorting into mock surprise. "Could you give him a message for me? Please tell him I'm working on a story about him and Chuck Pollard working for Blade-Garrett at the same time." Tom waited while the secretary repeated it all back to him.

"That's right. Please ask him to give me a call. It's Tom. K-i-n-g-m-a-n"—he gave his office number—"Thanks."

"He's 'out on patrol,' " Tom said, hanging up. "He'll 'get right back to me.' So much for that whole 'administrative leave' after gunning someone down, I guess."

"And monkeys will fly out of my butt," Skip said while continuing to type. "Speaking of monkeys and butts, while you were napping at the courthouse, Banks phoned Bear. Bear called him a 'dipshit with a badge.' I wrote that one down especially for you. He came out of his office afterwards and said we shouldn't expect any cooperation for quite some time."

"Dipshit with a badge? Outstanding. Sorry I missed it. Somebody should have grabbed video for me. You can't swing a dead cat without hitting someone taking video with their cellphone these days. Nobody got video of that? You call yourselves reporters?"

"You've got to call Blade-Garrett," Skip said. "They'll be mentioned in the story. You have to give them a chance to respond."

"I just came from there, Skip. They've got a real fun guy named Mike Larkin on security in the lobby who threw me out. His helpful suggestion was that I call their PR department."

"You've still got to call them," Skip said. "Leave a message. Be on record."

"Oh, I'll call them." Tom snatched up the phone. "You better believe I'll call them. This is me, calling them. Not sure when you became such a journalistic stickler, Skip. It kind of turns me on. Just gotta be honest with you."

"I'm just one of the little people working here while you talk gibberish," Skip said.

After a few seconds of silence, Tom got the expected voice mail for Blade-Garrett public relations. "Hello. This is Tom Kingman of the *Sentinel-Leader*. I'd like to talk to someone about the fact that a man who was shot last night, Chuck Pollard, once worked at your business with the man who shot him, Officer Bryan Van Grunner. It's five forty-three right now. We're writing a story about this for tomorrow's paper. I was at your business at four fifty-five p.m. today, but a conscientious security officer named Mike Larkin directed me to call this number. Please give me a call as soon as you can"—he again gave his office phone number—"Thank you."

"I called. I left a message. I'm sure they'll get right back to me. Better keep this line clear."

"You called," Skip agreed. "And now they can't claim you didn't. While you were calling, I wrote it into the story with a few 'could not be reached for comments.' It's called *journalism.*"

Tom called the story up on his computer and read through it. It was straightforward and simply written. Vintage Ensley. Besides the Blade-Garrett connection, the story gave an update on the investigation from official sources and some more claims of brutality from unofficial sources. A national group had issued a statement claiming all cops were sadistic bastards, but so far the potential protesters seemed to be placated by the level of information Hillary and her crew were dishing out. Skip prepared to leave as Tom edited in a few words to clarify a point within the story.

"You need me to stay?" Skip asked, rather feebly.

"Ashley's scoring goals tonight, right?" Tom said, not looking up from his work.

"Yeah. Her team plays at Floyd Park at seven."

Tom glanced at his watch. "Well, why are ya standing around here blabbing, man?" Tom said, tossing a brief smile at Skip. "Story looks great and you're the greatest. I'll go through it and hang out until the copy editors are done ruining it. Tell the family hi for me."

"You're coming to the game tonight, right, Tom? Ashley has been talking about it for a week. For some reason Ashley and Tracy both think you're funny."

"Because they're bright, intelligent, perceptive girls who take after their mother," Tom said. "Of course I'm coming. I'll be there as soon as I get the okay on this story from the hacks."

"I'll tell her. See ya soon," Skip said, fast walking toward the door.

CHAPTER 18

Tom started through the story for a second time, his mind drifting from Ashley Ensley's soccer game to his meeting later with Hillary Reed. He figured the game would be over by eight, giving him an hour to get home and make sure the place was cool and clean before she got there. By six forty-five, Tom stood by his car, rummaging his pocket for the keys. He had left them on his desk. Nope, found them camouflaged by a wad of quarters in his left front pocket.

As he turned from the *Sentinel-Leader* parking lot toward the soccer fields, he told himself his haste had more to do with a seven-year-old girl than it had to do with a late-twenties woman. Glancing in his rearview mirror, Tom saw his own eyes and laughed.

+++

Word of Tom's visit to Blade-Garrett headquarters reached Garrett's inner sanctum quickly. Garrett spun around in his luxurious office chair and leaned forward, putting both elbows on his desk and pressing the phone to his ear.

"Mr. Kingman has become very annoying," Garrett growled. "He was just out here asking about you and Pollard working for me at the same time. Security sent him away, but PR just told me they got a voice mail from him. I expect something in the paper tomorrow. We've severely underestimated him. It appears that, contrary to your assurances, he *does* have a clue and may be getting more all the time. It's time we make him an offer."

"An offer," Van Grunner's voice rattled in the phone earpiece. "Like he's going to consider any offer we might have. He'd probably just put it in the paper."

"Don't be such an idiot." Garrett leaned back in his chair and rubbed his forehead. "Of course we're not going to say, 'Hello, this is Barry Garrett, head of the local methamphetamine distribution network, would you consider not putting any more details about the shooting in the paper?' We've got to make it clear on a more personal level that we are not happy with Mr. Kingman's work."

"So, what are you saying? I smack him around some? I'd be fine with that," Van Grunner said.

"That would be fine if I decided against doing the smart thing," Garrett said. "We're taking enough risks without also risking Tom identifying you. No, something less physical to start with. Perhaps drive by and pump a few rounds into the side of his house, just to let him know we know where he lives. Besides, everyone will blame it on gangs or Mexicans."

"So you want me to pop off a few rounds into some reporter's house?" Van Grunner asked. "Sounds kind of reckless."

"Exactly, Bryan." Garrett grew tired of always having to spell things out for everyone. "Reckless enough to make him wonder what the hell he's gotten himself into. He works for the *Sioux City Sentinel-Leader* not the *New York Times*, for christsakes. A reporter for that tiny rag is going to risk his life for a story? I don't think so."

"Look, Barry, this is all getting kind of heavy, you know? I did Chuck for ya and we got pretty lucky on that deal, what with Powers shooting that dickhead too. Maybe we should lay low and hope things blow over."

"Blow over? And what if it blows over by me going to jail,

Bryan? Think I'm going alone? Two more members of our organization headed for Omaha to work for the competition today. That's got me in a bad mood. They're reading this shit in the paper and deciding that I'm damaged goods. That has to stop."

"So why don't we just kill him? Bury his body in the middle of nowhere. It'll be years before they find him, if ever."

"Regrettably, a couple of things are keeping Tom alive," Garrett said. "First, he witnessed your shooting Pollard, which gives us both stay-out-of-jail-free cards for that job. Second, if we kill him, the idiot police might start thinking the Pollard shooting wasn't so innocent. Third, I know the *Sentinel-Leader* publisher—that pompous bastard —would launch a crusade to find whoever killed Tom, even if it took years and he had to import every reporter he ever met to get the job done. We'd like to avoid that kind of attention if we can."

Garrett sighed. "So, we can't kill him, at least not now. I'm as disappointed about that as you are, Bryan, but we can test Mr. Kingman's devotion to his profession. Does he think his job is worth his life? I'd like to find out."

"If this is such a good idea, why don't you do it?" Van Grunner said.

Garrett bounced to his feet behind his enormous desk. "Look, you son of a bitch. I scooped you out of the trailer park ten years ago and gave you a great job driving a truck. Then, when you showed promise, I let you handle special cargo from our raw material supplier down south. You never blinked when I gave you your cut—equal to about six months of your cop salary—for just one special shipment. I didn't hear you complaining when you bought your cars and spent money on your bimbos. Now I pay you for information and the occasional odd job like this. Your ass is as exposed as mine. You did the shooting, Bryan. You know the penalty for murder in this state. They put you in prison and you never come out. And you know how fond they are of convicted cops at the state pen. You've got as much to lose as I do."

"Okay, okay, when should I do it?" Van Grunner asked.

"Tonight. Go by his house and make sure he gets the message. I want to hear about holes in his siding by morning. I hope he gets the message that next time it will be him, not his house, that needs exterior repairs."

"You're the boss. I know a car I can spring for a couple of hours without anyone noticing. I'll email you copies of the police report after the fact so we can decide if Mr. Kingman is rattled enough by the whole thing."

"Excellent. With any luck, Tom will decide that this story isn't worth the trouble."

"At least his stuff in the paper today confirmed my story to the letter," Van Grunner said.

"Well, he's done us that service, now he can just rest a while. Make sure he gets the message."

"I'm on it, Barry," Van Grunner said. "The little shit won't know what hit him."

+++

Tom scanned the sea of minivans as he turned into the Floyd Park parking lot five minutes before Ashley's game would start.

"Field six," Tom reminded himself out loud as his car bounced over the rutted gravel lot. He found a parking spot on the far end, kicked open his door almost before he had the car in park and took off running toward field six. The opening whistle had just sent the seven-year-olds into action as Tom jogged up to the Ensley family. Skip had managed to make it home from the *Sentinel-Leader* in time to change into shorts, a fresh The Mowgli's band T-shirt, unlaced low-top sneakers and an old-school Gateway computers cap. He followed the action with a video camera.

"Hey, Skip," Tom said as he stopped, feeling his skin sprout sweat from his brief run in the June heat.

"Tom," Skip said without looking from the viewfinder. "You showed up. Wow. The stars must be aligned."

"Glad I didn't miss the kickoff. Where's Leah?"

"Off chasing Tracy, I think."

Tracy had just turned three. Tom called her "Dart Vader" because she was always darting off to wreak havoc, sending one of her parents scurrying after her. He turned to the field and easily spotted Ashley Ensley. She had her father's lack of height and her mother's flowing, sandy hair. Ashley's jaw was set in concentration as she joined the scrum of players kicking wildly at the ball.

Seven-year-olds in Sioux City's Youth League played a three-on-three form of soccer. There was no goalkeeper, but the goal net was much smaller and the field one-fourth regulation size. Organizers thought correctly that three-on-three would give each player more chances to touch the ball. When an errant kick sent the ball out of bounds, Tom let out a yell that made Skip jerk his head around from his camera in surprise.

"Ashley!" Tom yelled, waving both arms until he had her attention. Tom gyrated his hips while dancing around in a mock cheer. "Go Ashley, go Ashley, go Ashley."

Ashley laughed, covering her mouth and then waved back, just a bit too cool to verbally return his greeting.

"Score one for Uncle Tom, Ashley!" Tom yelled back, a split second later making a shocked face and mouthing "Uncle Tom" to himself in disbelief. Tom turned to Skip, beaming, who now trained the video camera on Tom. The glowing red light on its front told Tom the camera was recording.

"Show me that move again, Tom," Skip said, chuckling.

Tom recreated his gyration for the camera and chanted in a much lower voice, "Go Ashley, go Ashley, go Ashley."

"Dom!" came a small voice from behind him, seconds before the owner of the voice slapped Tom on the butt. He spun around and feigned surprise when he saw Tracy standing behind him, ready to take another swing, her knees smeared with mud. She smiled wildly up at Tom towering overhead.

"Who are you? A bad guy? A silly pants? A three-year-old appliance destroyer?"

"Tacee," she said, pointing to herself.

"Tracy? I know a Tracy, and she likes to be tickled on the stomach." Tom scooped up the small girl and tickled her around the belly button. Tracy shrieked with laughter, slapping playfully at Tom's face. "Hi, Tracy," Tom said, just before Tracy connected with a slap to the forehead. "Hey! Nice punch. Now give me a kiss or I'll toss you into that ditch," Tom said as he turned her toward a slope at the back of the park.

"She'd love that," Leah Ensley said, walking up behind him. "That's where we just came from." Tom accepted Tracy's peck on his cheek before setting her gently back on her feet. Tracy ran off to play with the three-year-old sister of one of Ashley's teammates. "Tracy, no mud," Leah called after the girl, then turned again to Tom.

In many ways, Leah was the opposite of her husband. She was almost an inch taller than Skip and very thin. Whereas Skip had a rounded face, Leah had the fine facial bones of a child. At some angles she looked birdlike with her quick eyes and longer-than-average nose.

"Mrs. Ensley," Tom said with exaggerated formality.

Leah responded by hugging Tom.

Tom looked shocked for a second. "What's with the women in this family, Skip?" he said after Leah released him. "They hug everybody or what?"

"You're tough to resist, Tom," said Skip, who had returned to recording the game. "I'd hug you myself, but I'd hate to miss Ashley's goal." Almost on cue, Ashley found herself with the ball at midfield, nothing but open green between her and the goal.

"Go, Ashley!" Leah yelled as she grabbed Tom's arm. The Blade-Garrett security guy would have been impressed with her iron grip, Tom thought, thankful that Leah had a hold of his non-damaged arm. Ashley gave the ball a boot and turned on a jet of speed, her little cleated feet skimming over the lush, well-watered grass as she caught up to the ball as it rolled near the goal before calmly tapping it in.

"Yeahhhhh," Tom cheered. "Way to go, Ashley!" A few seconds after the goal, Ashley and her two teammates ran off the field, replaced by the three other members of her team. Ashley leaped into Leah's arms for a hug and then dove onto Tom, who had squatted to make it easy for her. Tom tumbled onto his back with the seven-year-old on top of him. "Way to go, Ashley," Tom said, enjoying the feeling of Ashley's unabashed hug.

"Thanks for coming, *Uncle* Tom," Ashley said, giggling at Tom's self-imposed title and then taking a swig of water from a bottle offered by her dad. "I didn't think you were going to make it."

"It was close. Sorry I missed those other games," Tom said. "Looks like I got here just in time to see the Ensley Scoring Machine net another goal. Beautiful."

Ashley rolled her eyes and then laughed. "Thanks. I've got to go over and stand with the other girls. Are you coming to our house after the game?"

"Can't do it, Goalzilla," Tom said. "I'm having someone over for dinner tonight."

"A girl?" Ashley asked, her eyes widening as Leah's head whipped around in surprise.

"Maybe." Tom parodied Ashley with his own widened eyes.

"Tommy's got a girlfriend, Tommy's got a girlfriend," Ashley sang as she headed back to stand by her coach and teammates.

"A girlfriend?" Leah shot a questioning look at Skip, who just shook his head in innocence.

Oh geez. Should have just said I was busy.

"No, not a girlfriend," Tom said. "Get 'hold of your estrogen, Leah. It's a woman I'm working with. She's a friend, but not a 'girlfriend.'"

"Ah, a girl who's a friend. I see," Leah said. "You know, that little girl with the ball out there right now?" Tom looked up and saw a small blonde girl erratically dribbling the ball down the field. "Her mom has a cute sister about your age. A biologist. Maybe you could have *her* over sometime for dinner."

"Are you a justice of the peace or something?" Tom asked. "Do you get paid a commission based on the number of bachelors you find brides for? Is that it?"

"I think you'd make a good husband and father," Leah said. "God knows why. The only thing you're missing in your life is a woman to share it with, Tom. Can I help it if I want you to be as happy as possible? You're great with kids. Ashley and Tracy are crazy about you."

"That's because I'm the fun guy. You and Skip take all the tough duty like telling them 'no' and I show up for the fun stuff like acting like a lunatic at their soccer games or taking them to drive go-karts. I don't know if I could handle the entire parenthood package." Tom looked at Skip, who was pretending to watch the game, his video camera lowered until Ashley returned to the field, and then back to Leah. "Besides, I suck at getting home by six and I'm not so hot at vacuuming."

"You act like there's some kind of college course you can take to prepare you for parenthood," Leah said. "There's not. You do it like Geoff and I did it—just plunge in."

"Really, Leah, I don't think I want to hear about plunging in. There are children around."

"I see through your act," Leah said, her tone so serious that Tom worried for a second that he had offended her.

"Act?"

"Yeah, your act," Leah said, moving closer to Tom. "You make your jokes and change the subject whenever we talk about women. I think you use all that funny stuff and talk about being a bad husband and father just to keep yourself from realizing you really *do* want a long-term relationship. And that scares you because you think it would mean putting something—*love*—in front of career. So if a woman starts to get too close, you've got these deflector shields that pop up and push her away. Big stud reporter finds it easier to just avoid the entire question."

Tom felt a flash of irritation. He couldn't tell if it came from Leah lancing him with the truth or from her incessant marriage evangelism and amateur psychology. Deep down he feared having anything in front of career would dull his professional edge and mess up his ordered chaos of a life. His six-month relationship with his last girlfriend, Joan, confirmed a lot of Tom's fears in that area.

He did his best quick-draw move with his notebook from his back pocket, spun it around, plucked the pen from his breast pocket and extended both toward Leah.

"Maybe *you* should take this," he said.

"There you go again, funny guy," Leah said.

I got your point, Leah, let it go …

As if reading Tom's mind she closed her eyes briefly and nodded an apology. Tom just smiled and rubbed her lightly on the shoulder. "I really do appreciate your concern. Honestly." Leah smiled, returned Tom's shoulder touch before leaving to check on Tracy, who was throwing dirt clods against a shed down by the ditch.

"She can be dogged," Tom said to Skip. "She'd be City Hall's worst nightmare if we ever got her on the beat."

"Sorry about that."

"Hey, it's okay," Tom said. "You guys have such a great thing going here—your temperaments fit together well, you share the same priorities, and above all you love each other more than anything. And you're doing a great job raising two amazing girls. I appreciate being a small part of it, and I get why Leah wants everyone to have the same thing."

"Our pleasure," Skip said. "Leah's right, the kids do love you. I think things like this with the kids get Leah's estrogen bubbling or something." Tom laughed as he watched Ashley trot onto the field for more playing time.

"Go Ashley!" Tom yelled after her. He turned to Skip, who was fiddling with his video camera, about to resume filming. "In a lot of ways I envy what you have, Skip," Tom said, looking down at the ground, stopping Skip mid camera adjustment. "Wife and family, it's hard to beat that. But I don't know if I'm ready for the sacrifices that kind of life requires."

"If this is sacrificing, I wish I had started sacrificing years before I did," Skip said, glancing at Tom and then training his camera on the field with exaggerated deliberateness. "Come on, Ashley!"

Ashley scored another goal but her team lost six to five. While Ashley swilled down water, took possession of her post-game snack, and said goodbye to her teammates for the season, Tom chatted with a few other people he knew in the crowd.

"Great job tonight, Ashley," Tom said as he walked with the Ensley family toward their van. "Two goals were great, but doing your best and having fun are always the main things."

Ashley's untucked youth soccer jersey and loosened shin guard straps made her look like a jock fresh from athletic battle. "Who's the girl you're going to see?" Ashley said, her shin guards flapping with each step.

"A woman who's helping me with a story."

"Is she pretty?"

"Prit-tee?" Tracy echoed.

Tom raised his hands in surrender. "You're both related to your mother, aren't you?" Ashley just shrugged. Tracy hit Tom dead center with a scrunched-nosed smile that almost made him forget what he was going to say. "Yes, she's pretty. But we're just friends. That's it."

Ashley shrugged again. "Uncle Dave brought a girl to our house for Thanksgiving last year who he said was a 'friend' and now she's got a baby growing inside her tummy."

"Dave was friendlier with his friend than I am with mine," Tom said. Ashley looked at him blankly. "There's no baby going to be growing," Tom explained.

"What's her name?" Ashley said as they reached the van.

"I can't tell you," Tom said. "It's a reporter secret."

It really is this time.

"Please, I won't tell. Pleeeeeease."

"Sorry," Tom said, casually glancing at his watch. Eight twenty. Tom's heart accelerated from normal to panic in one click of the second hand. "Wow, eight twenty. I really have to go," Tom said, turning to Leah and Skip and then back to Tracy and Ashley. "Ah, great game, Ashley. I'll come over this weekend and maybe we can go to the pool, or something. I, ah, I've got to go. See you all later." Tom turned and trotted off toward his car.

"Oh yeah," Leah said, opening the van door for Tracy. "She's just a *friend*."

"Dom funny," Tracy said, as she dove into the back of the van.

CHAPTER 13

Tom got back home at eight thirty, about five minutes sooner than it would have taken if he traveled the same distance at legal speeds.

He scrutinized his house as he turned into the driveway. It looked pretty good, although some of the paint in the front could use some work. Tom noticed for the first time some peeling trim near the roof peak. Where did that come from? No one would confuse Tom's neighborhood for Hillary's. Her part of town, Metling Drive, was a very solidly middle class area where everyone took great care of their property and a basketball hoop crowned every other driveway. In contrast, a few of Tom's neighbors didn't have to worry about mowing because they had dirt front yards. And in the height of the summer, nobody, including Tom, mowed much since even watering the grass was an economic luxury. Plenty of neighbor kids spent the day barefoot and dirty running around the block, apparently unsupervised.

Bud Caldwell sat on his back porch next door and waved as Tom got out of the car. Chester bounced up from lying next to Bud and raced to the fence between their houses to meet Tom. Bud sat in his favorite patio rocking chair, watching two birds battle for the last bit of old bread he'd thrown out.

"Hey, Tom," he called, raising a wrinkled arm. "Why don't you come over for a sandwich and a beer tonight? Chester could use one of your famous belly scratchings."

"I'd love to, Bud, but I've got company coming and I'm really in a hurry right now."

"I bet she's pretty," Bud said with a chuckle as Tom quickly leaned over the chain link fence to pet Chester, who licked Tom's hand before racing off. He made a huge arc in Bud's yard and came back to the fence for more attention.

"How did you know it's a she?" Tom asked, a bit flushed as he turned for his back door.

"I didn't," he said, chuckling. "Guess I've picked up a few of your tricks."

"Remind me never to show you my really good stuff. Besides, it's business. She probably doesn't even like hockey or NASCAR or drinking beer."

"Well, give her a chance," Bud said, returning to his rhythmic rocking. The small radio on Bud's porch table played music too soft for Tom to identify. "You've got plenty to offer a young lady. I remember when I first started courting Bess. I thought she was the princess and I was the frog. Turns out she had a thing for frogs and we made it fifty-nine years. You never know."

Bess's death three years ago had plunged Bud into depression. It took a year just for him to learn to shop for groceries and run the dishwasher. At first, Bud lived on microwave meals. But Tom, Chester, and lots of other friends helped him become more independent, more willing to take the time to prepare good meals for himself. Despite the more than fifty years difference in age, Tom and Bud had grown close. The two men had shared a meal at least once a week ever since.

"I sure miss Bess," Tom said, suspending his hurry in order to acknowledge Bud's loss.

"She's with Jesus now. She was a special lady and she sure liked you. Life's just not complete without someone to share it with. I was lucky; I had all those years with Bess. Now it's just old Chester and me."

"I'll come over for that sandwich sometime soon. Right now I have to clean up so the pretty girl who's coming over doesn't think I'm a total slob."

"Okay. Have fun," Bud said, again raising an arm as Tom disappeared into his back porch.

Once inside, Tom checked the refrigerator. The pre-made deli side dishes were ready to go. All he had to do was grill the marinating steaks and everything would be set. Tom decided he should wait until Hillary arrived to start the grilling. No need to rush her right to the dinner table the second she got to his house. He wanted time to put her at ease, give her an excuse to relax out of her prosecutor shell.

He shuddered. Maybe turning the thermostat down to the mid-sixties that morning wasn't such a good idea. The place was nearly cold enough that he could see his breath. He cranked the temperature control back to seventy-three degrees and glanced again at his watch. She'd be here in twenty minutes and he still had to change clothes. The way she talked, Hillary would be coming right from work, which meant a business ensemble. Tom, however, wanted badly to get out of his rumpled, sweaty-collared work clothes. But what should he wear? Shorts? Too casual. Tom's limited wardrobe rotated through his mind.

Casual, yet virile.

He dressed in tan twill pants and a short-sleeved cotton shirt.

The house temperature, food, and occupant were all ready for Hillary by 8:55 p.m. Tom sat stiffly on his couch, compulsively surfing the internet on his laptop. He checked the headlines at a world news site and then surfed to a site he used to monitor his few stocks. The doorbell rang. Tom bounced to his feet, almost dropping his laptop. A flush of sweat coated his normally arid underarms. He hadn't heard Hillary's Camaro pull up.

Get a grip on yourself, man. Don't go sprinting to the door. Have some dignity. You're ugly and your house is a mess. This woman isn't

*interested in you and you really don't want her to be. It's important
to admit that and move on.*

He set down the computer on his coffee table and walked
to the door with an ersatz casualness and pulled it open. Hillary
responded by opening the screen door.

All Tom could notice was the June breeze rippling through her
auburn hair haloed by the orange sun about to touch the horizon
over her shoulder. He greeted her with an unrestrained grin.

My God. I'm acting like a high schooler.

"Hi, Hillary," Tom said, suddenly concerned that his effort to
tamp down his Lifetime Channel moment may be making him
nervous, insincere, or just a dork. "Come on in. Did you find me
okay?"

"Sure," Hillary said, stepping through the doorway and into
the living room. Tom saw her gaze sweep the room. She kept smiling. Good sign. "I didn't realize you lived so close to downtown."

Shit. She hates the neighborhood. Well, I could always move.

"Yeah, welcome to the 'hood. It looks rougher than it is. I've
been here for six years. I got a good deal on the place and I like the
neighbors. Really honest, hard-working people."

"Like the guy next door? When I drove up his dog came racing around the front of his house. A little old man was just sitting
on the front steps smiling at me. He told his dog to 'leave Tom's
friend alone' and the dog ran right by me and loped up to sit with
the man. Then they both just stared at me. I swear the dog was
smiling."

"That was Bud and his dog, Chester. We talked over the fence
for a couple of minutes when I got home. I mentioned I had a
friend coming over." Tom glanced at the carpet.

The 'friend' thing just slipped out.

"Love your house," Hillary said. Tom took advantage of the
move to look at Hillary as she turned. A slim black skirt that
reached the knee, bare legs and sleeveless white top. Tom noticed

some definition in her arms. A small cross sparkled from a gold chain around her neck.

"I see you've brought some work," Tom said, nodding at the jumbo attorney-style briefcase Hillary carried.

"Yes, I did, and there are some very interesting things in here. I think you'll be very intrigued."

Tom found himself breathing shallowly. "Great. I suppose I ought to get the food going first. Is steak okay? I usually grill most of the time during the summer."

"Sounds fabulous," Hillary said, setting her briefcase gently on the coffee table. She breathed in deeply, shedding stress with her exhale.

Tom jolted himself out of a stare and hurried to the refrigerator. The grill out back had been heating for about ten minutes. "Got these from Corman's Meat Shop over on Twelfth. Packing-plant fresh. I'll just pop out and get these started," he called to Hillary, who was circling the living room, inspecting the decor.

"I'll come with you," Hillary called back, replacing a small antique typesetter's tool she had picked up from the mantel. "It's cooling down pretty fast out there. Could turn out to be a lovely night."

"Can I get you anything?" Tom said. "I've got soda, some wine, whiskey . . ."

"Beer?" Hillary said.

"Of course. An American bachelor pad without cold beer? I'd be deported. It's in the fridge. Help yourself."

"Beer it is then." Hillary opened the refrigerator, selecting some Red Stripe, always a good choice in the heat. Once out the back door, Tom saw Bud had returned to his backyard seat. Chester lay gnawing on a toy at Bud's feet. They both raised their heads to look at Tom as he came out the back door.

The Iowa summer humidity had stayed below its usual suffocating level during the day—which would be heralded by a

Sentinel-Leader "relief from the heat" story tomorrow—giving way to a very pleasant dusk. The slight breeze fluttered through Hillary's blouse.

"Hello, Tom!" Bud called, raising his arm again. "Who's your friend?"

Bud. Give us a break here. You're about as subtle as a kick in the crotch.

"My neighbor, Bud. You met him and Chester on your way in," Tom said quietly to Hillary, who responded with a wave. Chester scrambled to his feet, bodysurfed down Bud's back steps and raced over to the fence. "Do you mind?" he murmured to Hillary, reaching for the gate in Bud's fence.

"Not at all," Hillary said, stepping through the gate and crouching down to talk to Chester.

"Hello, boy," she said, scratching him behind the ears. "You're a pretty boy, aren't you? What a good boy you are." Chester sat in rapture and responded to her stroking with a lick to the cheek, drawing a laugh from Hillary. "Thank you! Good boy." Hillary stood up again and strode confidently toward Bud's deck.

"Lucky bastard," Tom whispered to Chester as he bent briefly to pet the dog. Chester responded with a lick to Tom's nose. It took Tom couple of fast strides to catch up with Hillary, who smiled brightly as she reached the Bud's deck steps. Bud was already standing as Chester bounded up the steps ahead of them and reclaimed his spot next to his master.

"Bud Caldwell, this is Hillary Reed. She works at the courthouse," Tom said as the two shook hands. Tom tried to avoid introducing prosecutors as prosecutors, knowing that sometimes they preferred to avoid the litany of questions that often came with revelation of their actual jobs.

"I'm a prosecutor," Hillary said, surprising Tom with her candor.

"Tom told me he had company coming over tonight, but he

didn't tell me it would be such a beautiful young lady," Bud said. "I would have dressed up a little bit if I had known."

"Well, thank you, Bud," Hillary said, kneeling to vigorously rub Chester's belly which the dog gleefully offered. "And please call me Hillary. A charming man like you must be married."

"I was married for fifty-nine years. My Bess died just a few years ago."

Hillary's smile vanished. "I'm sorry to hear that. It must have been wonderful to have someone to share your life with for all that time."

"It was a blessing. Bess and I were made for each other. A wonderful woman and I miss her. I keep telling Tom he ought to find himself a good woman and quit running all over creation. Settle down and have some kids. I've got six of them, all moved away with their own families. Now and then they all come back here and see their grandpa. What a wonderful time that is. Chester and I sleep for a week straight after the grandkids have been over." Laughter splashed out of Bud and Hillary. Tom stood behind Hillary.

Leah Ensley has nothing on Bud in the marriage promotion department.

"It was nice to meet you, Bud. And you too, Chester," Hillary said, clamping a hand on either side of Chester's head causing the dog to stop panting suddenly and hit her with the full power of his brown eyes.

"The pleasure was all ours," Bud said, as Chester got back to his feet. "You two have fun. Enjoy those steaks. Tom's quite a good cook."

"Thanks, Bud," Tom said, turning away from Hillary and making an exasperated face at Bud. Both man and dog seemed to shrug.

Tom followed Hillary through the fence gate and back to the grill. He put the steaks on the grill as he saw Bud say a few words to Chester, who responded by bounding to the back door, nearly smacking it with his nose. Bud slowly stood up, stretched and shuffled into the house.

At least the audience is gone.

He tended to the steaks for a minute and then turned to Hillary, who reclined in a patio chair, legs crossed, the naked heel of one foot peeking out of her dangling shoe. She accepted an opener for her beer but waved off the offer of a glass. Tom sat opposite her, poured his Red Stripe into the glass and raised it. "Here's to the end of a long day," Tom said.

"A long day," Hillary echoed, tinking her bottle against Tom's glass and then taking a deep drink.

"Should we stay out here or go in?" Tom said.

"Let's stay out here for a while. The breeze is nice and the mosquitoes haven't shown up, yet."

"So, our friend Pollard used to work for Blade-Garrett," Tom said, taking another sip of his beer.

Hillary stopped in mid-drink. "That's right, but how did you know that?"

"Journalism!" he said with exaggerated flair. "I was at the courthouse today and took a look at a few records, just to get an idea of who we were dealing with."

"Didn't you think I would tell you what I found?" Hillary said, her features hardening.

"Ah, sure. I knew you'd bring over the files. I just decided to take a look at the paper files at the courthouse. You know how some stuff on paper doesn't get into the digital record. So I just grabbed a few files and noticed that Pollard listed Blade-Garrett as an employer on an arrest sheet or two. I figured we'd share information tonight."

She sipped her beer and let her face relax. She closed her eyes again, enjoying the swirl of alcohol, warm air and gentle winds. Tom moved to the grill to tend the steaks, grateful to put some space between them for a moment.

"Well, that matches what I found." The County Attorney's

office had duplicate paper files with all their notes and some other information not in the public files. Tom checked the grill burner level and then sat down again across from Hillary.

"I also called Pollard's probation officer. Seems Mr. Pollard was a good employee of Blade-Garrett and suddenly resigned. The probation officer didn't know much because it happened after Pollard had finished probation. Pollard said he was going to work for the competition but somehow never started the new job. About then his minor brushes with the law started."

Hillary drank from her squatty Red Stripe bottle, now more than half empty, and leaned forward in her chair. The move brought her to within a foot or so of Tom. It was close enough for him to smell her perfume and see the texture of her lips. For several seconds, they looked at each other. He could see her eyes moving around his face.

Whoa, what's happening here?

After a few seconds, he leaned back. Small talk suddenly started coming out of Tom's mouth, much to his surprise. He asked her how long she had lived in her current house, where she lived before that—all the first level of personal information most people were willing to share.

A few minutes before the steaks were done, they decided to stay outside to eat. Together they got the rest of the food out of the refrigerator and took it out back. She seemed in no hurry to talk business.

"You said last night you were from Counciltucky, right?"

"Council *Bluffs*, yes." Tom nodded. "For someone who lives in *Sewer City*, you seem quick with the pejorative nickname."

Sioux City had attracted the nickname "Sewer City" decades ago when the city was a rough, not-so-well-kept packing plant town. All the large packing plants were long gone from Sioux City, taking their smell and mess with them, but, like Council Bluffs, Sioux City still labored to shake the unflattering moniker.

"Why does a kid from Council *Bluffs* become a reporter, of all things?" Hillary said as she cut into her steak. "That's almost as bad as being a prosecutor."

"The pay is about the same," Tom answered. "I looked it up."

"Oh the joys of having your salary be public information," Hillary said. "So we know neither of us does what we do for the money. Why did you become a reporter?"

"I'm not sure. I like to write, but I really love to solve puzzles. When I was a kid I was always working on some ten thousand-piece jigsaw puzzle and any three-dimensional puzzle, like the Rubik's Cube, right up through high school. And I was killer in math."

"How about now?"

"Now I work on puzzles for a living."

"That's it, puzzles?"

"Journalism, at its core, is public service, like prosecuting criminals," Tom said, trying not to sound preachy or like he was giving his standard reporter speech to a sixth grade class. He looked at Hillary with his "I know this sounds hokey" expression and hoped for understanding. "I'm not Mother Teresa or anything, but it really is about giving people the information they need to be members of society. Everyone seems to think I'm in it because I like to see my name in print. But I really just love writing, getting paid to snoop around, solving puzzles and telling stories that help people."

"But you *do* like seeing your name in print, right?" Hillary finished her last bite of steak.

"Yeah, it's okay. My mom sure likes it. A lot of people still think being in the paper is a big deal, so I sometimes get treated pretty well. At least the same number of people, though—and many of your colleagues—think we're all vultures who get paid based on how many lives we ruin."

Go ahead, go there. Let her in. Tell her. She's different.

"But I really do it for that moment when I know I've got something big, and I'm the only one who knows how big it is. That's such an electric feeling I can't describe it. I just have to get to my keyboard and write it all down. It's almost an obsession. That feeling is worth spending twelve hours at the courthouse or a couple weeks with homeless bums. I just *have* to get the story. Maybe it's like you sending a rapist away or something."

Tom stopped himself abruptly and looked down at his plate. It had been a flash of professional passion he shared with very few people.

"Have you got that electric feeling now?"

Yes, although it may have nothing to do with a story.

"Not yet," he answered. That was true, at least regarding the story. "Some vague twinges based on what I've seen so far, though. So how about you? Why law?"

"It's a lot like your puzzle fetish, I guess. The law fascinates me," Hillary said. She leaned forward. Tom noticed the light from the sinking sun splashing across her hair, bathing her cheek in a golden glow. "The law helps bring some order to chaos. Being an attorney is really about thinking, looking things up, developing and executing strategy and being persuasive. Being a prosecutor also involves a bit of puzzle-solving skill as well, and the ability to work well with a team that includes everyone from police to pathologists. I love the courtroom experience. It's one-on-one in there. My job is not only to argue better than the other attorney, but to orchestrate my witnesses and exhibits in a way that builds and builds until there is no reasonable doubt."

"It seems to me—at least sometimes—like you're stalking your prey more than 'orchestrating' something."

"Is that your image of me?"

Uh-oh. If we were in court, Hillary could claim I 'opened the door to this line of questioning.'

He glanced up to find Hillary's gaze pinning him to his chair.

"Actually, law was second on my list of career possibilities." Tom paused to savor Hillary's arched-eyebrow reaction before continuing. "Law just seemed too book intensive for me, I guess, and required all those extra years of school. I think I'd like building a strategy of how to use evidence in a trial."

"You might make a great lawyer," Hillary said, letting the subject drop. It was her turn to inspect her empty plate.

Tom looked at her for several seconds.

What the hell? I've come this far. Might as well go for it.

CHAPTER 20

Tom inhaled, filling himself with resolve as well as oxygen. This was the second encounter with Hillary that he'd found himself heading into a deep discussion topic.

"I think you *are* a great lawyer, Hillary," Tom said, haltingly. A bolt of internal electricity shot through him. "I'm glad you were on call Tuesday. I was glad to see you at the police station that night. I have to admit, I like our little arrangement, in part because it gives me a chance to get to know you better."

Hillary glanced up with a quick smile before looking back down at the table.

I can't believe it. I'm knee-deep in the hurt locker with this woman.

"You're one of the best prosecutors I've seen," he continued, emboldened by Hillary's smile. "A methodical machine in court. A legal predator with a more gentle edge than the hard-core sharks. You've got a great sense of humor. You don't overestimate yourself or have pretensions. And juries always look like they want to hug you."

I sound like a ninth grader trying to get a date.

He couldn't hold back. "And, I appreciate your willingness to talk to me and not treat me like the town gossip who wants to put everyone's bra size in the paper." Tom's gaze came to rest on Hillary's breasts.

Smooth, Tom. Real smooth.

Hillary looked down at her chest with raised eyebrows. "It's 36B," she replied with a subtle smile. Tom's cheeks hemorrhaged into crimson, and Hillary let out something very close to a giggle.

"Well," he said. "Since I don't have my notebook on me, I guess we'll just keep your size out of the paper for now." This time they both laughed. He felt her shoe brush his pant leg just as his cell-phone chirped to life, jolting him out of his Hillary intoxication. She checked her phone as Tom dug for his own.

"I think it's me. Sorry," he said.

"Trust me, I know how it is."

"Yeah," Tom said into the phone.

"Tom, this is Carol at the paper. I have a question on the story you and Skip did for tomorrow."

"Sure," Tom glanced at Hillary and held up one finger. He wanted her to know this would be short.

"Your story says 'a review of court records Thursday showed Van Grunner and Pollard worked together' but Thursday is tomorrow. Didn't you look at them today, Wednesday?"

"Yeah. Thanks for catching that. It should say 'a review of court records Wednesday showed Pollard and Van Grunner worked together.' It's a pretty stupid mistake. Sorry."

"No problem. That's it. Nice story."

"Thanks. Has Van Grunner called me back?"

"Not that I know of."

"I'm shocked. Give me a call if you hear from him or you need me for anything else." Tom disconnected. He got the day wrong. *The day!* What a goddamn rookie mistake. He looked at Hillary.

Distractions make you lose your edge.

"You're putting that in the paper?" Hillary quickly sat up. "Is that a good idea?"

"Shooter and shootee used to work together? I think that equals news. Besides, my colleague Skip figured it out as well. It's just part of a larger story on the backgrounds of everyone involved in the shooting."

"I understand," Hillary said, "but anything other than straight cop-shoots-druggie-in-self-defense makes people with anti-police axes to grind come out of the woodwork. And, remember, I don't want Van Grunner looking dirty or his friends inside and out of the department will head for the interstate."

Tom sat back and took a big drink of beer. "I appreciate that," Tom said, "but it's coming off as a coincidence. Besides, you got me—star witness—that says Van Grunner shot in self-defense. Who's putting the heat on you guys to hustle it through? Seems a little strange that Banks is so antsy to have this finished. Is someone pressuring him?"

"I don't know for sure," Hillary said. "If someone is, so far they've just called Banks and then he calls Anderson. Maybe Anderson will get some direct calls after your story runs. So far nobody's called me."

"Are you okay with this story I'm doing?" Tom heard himself say. He had never asked a lawyer that question in his life. Ever. He was shocked by the question now, as if someone else had said it using his voice.

"I'd rather not see it in print," Hillary said, looking at him, "but you found it on your own, so I don't see how I can insist you not print it. Besides, we've got you—the star witness."

Whew. No idea what I would have done if she said "no."

Tom nodded his understanding and flopped back in his chair.

"Tom," a voice called over the fence. Tom knew that voice and the sound of jangling dog tags coming toward the fence.

"I know now is not the best time," Bud continued, "but could you come over and take my trash out to the curb when you're done over there? It's pretty full and Chester seems to think there is something for him in it. I caught him snout deep in the trash a couple of times. It will only take a second and I'd appreciate it."

"Take out your trash?" Tom said, glancing at Hillary, who stifled a small laugh. "Ah .. sure I'll get it out there in a second." To Hillary: "I take it down to the curb for him. He's not so steady on his feet any more …"

"Thanks," Bud said. "Let's go in, Chester, it's time to get ready for bed." Chester went from the ground to the top of the deck stairs in two bounds and disappeared into the house in front of Bud, who gave one final wave. Dusk had long passed, and the Iowa mosquitoes were starting to feed.

"Do you mind? Only take a second," Tom said, feeling a mosquito impale his back. "I better do it now or he'll keep bugging us … er … me."

"Of course not. He's a charming man. Seems to like you quite a bit. It's great of you to help him out."

"Oh, he's a great guy, but he tends to get a little too tense about stuff that shouldn't make you tense, if you know what I mean. Like this garbage thing. I guess when you get older, sticking to routines becomes more important."

"I'll take the dishes into the house and get my files out."

"Thanks. This will only take a second. We can use the kitchen table or the coffee table in the front room, whichever you'd like."

Hillary nodded as she rose and started stacking the dishes. Tom shot a look at her chest as she bent over to get the plates. "Still 36B," Hillary said, calmly continuing to pick up the plates without looking at Tom.

Busted … again. She doesn't seem pissed about it, though.

"Ah, let me just get that trash."

Tom swung open the gate in the fence that connected his yard with Bud's and walked briskly toward Bud's backyard, "36B" still rolling through his mind. He heard Chester bark inside the house.

"It's just me, Chester," Tom yelled. The barking stopped and Tom saw Chester pop up at the side window, his head tilted slightly to the side. He waved at the dog and then maneuvered the wheeled, plastic trash can from beside the deck down the driveway toward the curb. It was only about half full. The deck was in the back of the house and the curb about twenty feet beyond the front door. The lawn needs mowing, Tom thought, and he ran through his Saturday schedule, wondering if he would have time to help Bud with it.

Chester barked again. And again and again.

Chester. Chill. It's just me.

Chester sat in the front window now, looking past Tom's house, toward the corner. Barking more urgently. Tom turned, following the dog's gaze up the street, still holding the garbage can. A small black car was coming down the street. One of those wannabe sports cars.

"Turn your lights on," Tom said, half disgusted that someone would be so careless to drive without headlights at nearly 10:00 p.m.

Get a grip, Chester. It's a car. You've seen cars before.

Tom resumed course for the curb when he saw the streetlight reflection on the passenger's side door shimmer and roll. Car slowing, power window rolling down.

Maybe the guy's lost and needs to ask directions.

Tom shrugged. He was almost at the curb where he decided to pause, making himself available to give directions. Iowans are helpful like that. Two steps later, he heard the approaching car's engine hesitate and then leap up an octave as it went into full acceleration. The noise whipped Tom's head around just as the car's lights came to life. Blinded, Tom stood stunned near the curb, momentarily holding Bud's trash can until he recovered enough to release it.

Shit. Now what?

He scanned a mental picture of Bud's front yard for possible refuge: bushes, trees, front steps? Back toward the house was better than into the street. Tom started to turn for the run back toward Bud's house when he saw it—the first flash from inside the car. A dull pop immediately followed the flash, like thunder follows the lightning in a thunderstorm. Two more flashes and pops from the middle of the front seat.

What the fuck? A gun? Shit, a gun.

Suddenly, Tom's legs abandoned their post. The grass rushed toward his face and he landed, blades from living and dead grass protruding against his cheek and into his mouth.

Oh shit. Am I shot?

Two more pops. The car would be on top of him in a second. Tom's brain went into a sidespin as it acknowledged that someone was firing a gun from inside a car.

Who? Why? What a way to die. On Bud's front lawn, shot while taking out the goddamn trash. Who gets shot taking out the trash?

The roaring car was less than a second away now. Tom tried to look at it but Bud's trash can a foot in front of his face blocked his view.

The trash can! It wasn't much, but something. Tom threw himself forward, landing on a patch of parched dirt behind the can. He rolled onto his side, trying again to see the car. There was one last pop followed almost simultaneously by a "thunk" and a sharp pain on Tom's forehead.

And then everything went dark.

CHAPTER 21

Hillary had just reached the couch and grabbed her briefcase's handle when the shooting started. At first she didn't recognize the sound. Tom's windows and doors were shut and the central air conditioner had just cycled off, but it sounded like someone had hit the house with a stick or maybe a rock.

The appearance of a hole in the front window framed by radiating cracks provided her gunfire epiphany and motivated her dive in front of the couch. Section 708.6 of the Code of Iowa, of all things, flashed through her mind: "Firing into an occupied house with the intent to injure or provoke fear or anger in another is 'terrorism,' a 'Class C' felony. The maximum penalty for terrorism is ten years in prison or a fine of $10,000, or both such fine and imprisonment."

And then—almost as surprising to Hillary as her instant legal reference recollection—she screamed.

+++

For a few seconds, Tom assumed he was dead or would be soon.

Lying in a pool of my own blood covered in Bud's garbage was not how I imagined going out.

He had hoped for something heroic, something worthy of a large, well-attended funeral. Like saving a toddler from a runaway car or giving his life to expose Erin Brockovich-level polluters who caused mutated babies or something. Or maybe dying after he capped some punk attacking an old woman.

Anything but on a dead lawn covered with the neighbor's trash.

Tom's brain played a montage of his parents' crying faces, banner headlines and a huge church full of reporters who had gathered like police officers to honor one of their own killed in the line of duty.

What if there is a God?

The images faded and Tom's eyes fluttered open. He hadn't passed out. Instead something was covering his eyes. He could feel some warm liquid running down his face, passing along his nose inside his right eye and headed for his mouth. His brain must be oozing out of his forehead. When the ooze reached his mouth, Tom discovered his brain tasted like ranch dressing.

Tom raked the trash off his face and dabbed a finger into the ooze, holding his hand in front of his eyes. White, greasy and cool, not red, sticky, warm with a copper smell. Good signs. He gingerly probed the source of pain on his head. No blood and no hole, just a tender spot near his hairline.

Thank God.

Tom felt the skin tightening as the swelling rose. He flopped over flat on his back, setting off another avalanche of trash over his head. His first sight after returning from near-death was the letters T-E-R-T-A-I. He pulled the object off his face and held it at arm's length. A garbage-smudged edition of *Entertainment Weekly* featuring a serious actor with a gun.

"Where were you when I needed you?" Tom asked the fictional cop and then flipped the magazine away from the mound of trash covering his upper body.

"You've gotta be shitting me," Tom croaked.

Footsteps. Someone running toward him. But the car had gone around the corner. Most likely the driver wasn't coming back to finish the job. Still, Tom struggled to sit upright. His brain posed the question:

Run?

It crackled and buzzed like a shorting television.

"Tom!" he heard. And then again, closer. "Tom!"

He slumped back down as he recognized the voice and Hillary's face appeared in his field of vision. Tom reflexively reached up and touched her upper arm as he regained visual focus.

"He's gone," she gasped. "Are you okay? Tom? Tom?"

"Yeah, I think so," he rasped as he noticed his touch had smeared mustard on her arm. He was about to sit up from the garbage pile when his face was covered again, this time by a giant set of nostrils and a large pink tongue. "Chester," Tom said, trying to push the 85-pound rescue effort away while avoiding getting licked on the mouth as he spoke. "I'm okay, Chester. Really. I'm fine. Come on, Chester. Chester. Yeah, I love you too, Chester."

Tom managed to clear the mental static and sit up, despite Chester's attention.

"Are you hurt, Tom?" Bud called, halfway down the driveway.

"No, Bud, I'm fine. No holes. Just got smacked in the head with your garbage can."

"I'll call the police," he said, heading for his house.

Tom grabbed the dog by both cheeks and brought his face up to Chester's eyes. "You go with Bud."

Chester hesitated, looking from Tom to Bud and back again, let out a slight whimper of confusion and looked again at Tom. "Go on, boy," Tom whispered. Chester gave Tom one last lick and then bounded after Bud.

"I feel so trashy," Tom said to Hillary, who had her eyes closed. Her lips moved slightly as if she were saying something before reopening those stunning green eyes. "Are you praying?" he asked.

Hillary looked at him for a second and nodded. "Seemed like a good idea," she said as she held out her hand to help him up.

"Well, amen to that," Tom said, a bit taken aback by her religious reaction. A cascade of garbage fell off him as he got to his feet. Standing set off a new round of dizziness. Hillary helped steady his sudden lurch, impressing Tom with her physical strength.

"Are *you* okay?" Tom said, suddenly remembering that Hillary had probably been inside the house.

"Yes. Your house has some holes in it, though."

"I guess I'll get that new siding sooner than I expected," he said, feeling elation at her safety wash over him.

Hillary's concerned look caused Tom to continue. "I'm fine, really." He turned and roughly pushed the garbage can behind him. "My head feels like someone smacked it with a hammer. Any extra holes?" Hillary examined his wound closely, then shook her head no.

Tom reached down and picked up the toppled can. It was about four feet tall and made of industrial grade, thick plastic with one set of wheels on the bottom. There was a bullet hole about three inches down from the top rim and a large dent on the inside, about halfway down. "Hello there," Tom said, his eyes widening. "Small caliber, probably a twenty-two." He gingerly felt his face and hair. "I bet I look really stunning right now."

Hillary leaned forward, craning her head around Tom's to inspect him. "Totally hawt," she said, and then kissed him lightly on the lips. Before Tom could react, Hillary pulled back a few inches, her eyes scanning Tom's face.

To hell with restraint.

He grabbed Hillary and kissed her firmly. His body flushed as he felt Hillary return his kiss, wrap her arms around his back and squeeze her 36Bs into his chest. Hard.

"You must be feeling all right," Bud said from his front steps. The sound of his voice separated Tom and Hillary.

"I'll be fine, Bud," Tom said without looking at the man, then added more softly, "Maybe I should get shot at more often."

Hillary tossed Tom a glance and licked her lips. "Ranch dressing?" she said, scrunching up her nose.

"The police are on their way," Bud said. "Did you get a look at the guy?"

"No," Tom said, brushing the last of the trash off himself. "I saw the car pretty well. Late-model Nissan. Black. No front plates. Smoked windows. I only saw signs of one guy inside and he seemed pissed off at my house and your trash can."

"Hillary," Tom said, "we need to get inside. Bud, can you and Chester stay here and make sure nobody messes with this can? It probably has a bullet inside it that the police will want."

"Chester and I will keep an eye out for the police. Better go take care of that head."

"Thanks." Tom and Hillary hurried back to his house, glancing at the splintered holes in his siding as they passed. Once inside, he picked up her briefcase and held it out for her. "You should go, Hillary," Tom said, taking the new liberty of caressing her shoulder.

"Leave the scene of a crime?" she responded.

"Yes. Leave the scene of a crime. I know it's probably some kind of violation of the lawyer's oath or something, but my friends with the TV cameras are on their way right now, you can bet on that. When they see your car in the driveway, they'll figure it out. Neither of us needs to be on TV right now." Tom touched his hair again and resolved to wash up before the police arrived. "I may not have much choice, but you do."

"Good point. I hadn't anticipated that the shots-fired call would likely attract media. You'll need to tell the officers I was here and that I said publicity would compromise an ongoing investigation. Tell them to contact me for a statement. I didn't see the car or the shooting, or anything material to the crime."

Tom handed her the briefcase. "I'm sure they'll get around to coming to see you, or you can walk across the street to the station tomorrow. I don't think it matters where they talk to you, just that they do talk to you."

"But the neighbors. They probably saw me, us, out front. And what about Bud."

"Doubtful TV will stick around to ask, especially if I talk to them, and I'll have a word with whoever shows up from the paper. Don't worry about Bud. I'll talk to him and he'll be happy to avoid the media. You should go. Now." Tom was almost pushing Hillary out the door.

"So what's next?" she asked.

"Somebody just shot at me, and way worse, they could've hurt you," he said. "That pisses me off and makes this a helluva lot more than a news story for me. Oh, I'm going to find out who it was. Make no mistake. But I'm going to need your help."

Hillary looked down at the floor.

"Both professionally and personally," Tom added, almost involuntarily.

She reached out her hand, running her fingers lightly over Tom's cheek, around the back of his head and pulled him toward her, kissing him again. Tom was starting to get used to this.

"Things may be different from now on," he said. "I'm relieved you're okay and I want to see you again, soon, so we can talk about everything that happened tonight. But we'll need to be more careful."

"Call me," she said, and then vanished out the door. A few seconds later Tom heard her car roar to life and retreat down the driveway. Hillary had just gone through the intersection when the first police car came around the corner at the opposite end of the block, lights flashing and sirens blaring. Tom turned for the bathroom.

I'm not going to face the Sioux City Police Department with a face full of ranch dressing. They'll find enough humor in this as it is.

He started the hot water and looked in the mirror, a bit scared of what he might see. His forehead had a scrape where the trash can had hit him. Tom thought he could almost see the knot rising. Chester had done a pretty good job cleaning the ranch dressing off his face, but there was a glob of something in his hair above his right eye and something greasy near his left eye.

I must have looked tough giving Hillary my speech about being pissed off with smears of garbage on my face.

Tom grabbed the nearest washcloth and sluiced it under the warming water. After a couple rinsings, he wrung out the washcloth and went to his refrigerator for some ice for his throbbing head.

CHAPTER 22

The whole trip home, Hillary argued with herself over what she was doing. Leaving the scene of a shooting? Questionable at best. A prosecutor should know better. But something kept her driving until she got home. She found her own arguments convincing: she hadn't seen anything at all, so she had nothing to offer to help with the immediate apprehension of the shooter. Therefore where and when she gave her information didn't matter much in this instance. Plus general knowledge of her being there really might endanger an ongoing investigation. Those arguments, combined with her desire to continue her exciting arrangement with Tom, smoothed the rough ethics of the situation.

Her feelings for Tom weren't just physical urges, although she felt growing physical attraction to him. The sudden onset and depth of her feelings had taken her by surprise. She couldn't define the source or exact nature of those feelings just yet. Hillary sensed that Tom shared her feelings. She could tell by the way his kiss was full of warm tenderness rather than lusty heat.

Hillary wasn't really happy being single, but she hadn't fully recovered from a catastrophically bad relationship years ago. She also found the process of dating and searching for a mate taxing. She'd been praying for God to bring her someone; could Tom be answered prayer? Hillary had to protect her relationship with Tom until she could answer that question, and figure out what had come over her.

Hillary liked the way Tom looked at her when she talked. It was a look of appreciation and genuine interest in what she said, not just bullshit and come-on lines to get her in the sack. Maybe that's what made him so attractive, all the non-verbal communication that affirmed her as an intelligent person. Sure, he looked at her body now and then and seemed to like what he saw, but he also seemed to like what he heard and felt from her as well.

Hillary would call her boss, Dick Anderson, as soon as she could and tell him everything, including her decision to leave the scene. Tom had urged her to leave, but she had made the decision. If there were consequences she was ready for them. Anderson, however, didn't need to know about her growing attraction to Tom.

+++

Four hours after the shooting, Tom sat on his couch. He looked as if someone had propped up his unconscious body, arranging his limbs in positions that might appear natural but really weren't. The house was dark and locked. Tom had nailed some old plywood from the garage over the broken window. It would keep everything secure and the elements out until he could fix the window. God knew when that would be.

"Just you and me tonight, buddy," Tom said to Chester. Bud had insisted that Chester spend the night with him as a sort of early warning system. Chester lacked the macho, protective air of a Doberman, German Shepherd or Rottweiler, but nobody would get into the house or probably even approach it without Chester raising hell.

Right now Tom was trying unsuccessfully—despite the aid of generous portions of his favorite single malt scotch—to untangle his nerves and decompress. Even though he sat on the couch, motionless, his brain buzzed with replays of random seconds from the shooting. Slow motion, fast motion, freeze frames. The sounds of the shots stuck in a repeating loop inside his head. The pain of something hitting his head and the brief-but-wild fear of dying. The sight of Hillary praying and feel of her first soft, warm kiss.

Suddenly Tom's pants started ringing. He took his time getting the phone out of his pocket, half hoping the caller would get tired of waiting and hang up, until he saw the caller ID. "Hillary?" he said into the phone. The light from the touch-screen reflected on his cheek.

"Hi. I was just thinking about you. Sorry I didn't call earlier. I figured you'd probably be asleep by now. Did I wake you?"

"No. I'm sitting on the couch with the lights off with my friend Glen, looking at the lovely new hole in my front window, glad there aren't any bloodstains on the carpet."

"Glen? Glen who?"

"Glenlivet. He's only twelve years old, but he's a great listener and has a very calming effect on me."

"Ah. Glenlivet scotch. Glen *is* very calming. I'm more of a bourbon girl. How were the police?"

Tom's shoulders sagged. "Cordial," he said. "Some even showed concern. Very touching, really, in a heavily armed sort of way."

"How's the head?" Hillary said, her voice soft.

"It's fine. They acted like they wanted to call an ambulance and maybe a medical helicopter but I managed to talk them down. Glen and four ibuprofen are helping, plus I put so much ice on my head that it's either much better or numb. Either way works for me right now. Don't tell anybody, but I have some hydrocodone left over from a broken arm a few years ago that I can dip into if needed. Don't worry, it was prescribed to me, counselor. That's a last resort, though, and probably a bad idea with alcohol. I can't feel my lips when I take it. I assume the officers have been to see you already."

"Yeah. Lieutenant Benning himself came over. Nice guy. Needs to floss more, though. I managed to put up with his 'I told you so' innuendo bullshit."

Tom surprised himself with a guffaw of laughter, then winced and touched the bump on his head with just his fingertips. "Unfortunately I know exactly what you mean ... wait, did you just say 'bullshit?' ... have I corrupted a member of law enforcement?"

"I get like this when someone shoots at me," Hillary said.

"We have that in common, then. Too bad it takes something so extreme to bring it out, because I like the tough chick edge you've got going here. It's very—sexy." Tom waited for Hillary's reaction to the s-word.

"Calm down. I think you're letting your friend Glen do the talking for you."

Tom struggled to his feet, looking out into the street. The police had taken the can, garbage and all, from Bud's front lawn.

"Are you going to be on TV tomorrow?" Hillary continued.

"Yeah. You'll be glad to know I washed off the ranch dressing first. I told them the truth: I was taking out my neighbor's trash when some guy started popping off rounds. First at my house and then at me. Then I lied and said I didn't know why."

"What about the paper?" Hillary asked.

"Skip was here. I gave him more details, but he's not going to write what I really think is behind this. I went off the record with a newspaper reporter. That was totally a first for me. You'd have been proud. Skip will focus on my brush with death, how it felt, what I thought, that kind of stuff. I told the cops you were here, of course, but your name never came up in my media interviews. You'd have been proud of me answering only what was asked, volunteering no information. I'd be a star witness in court. Nobody asked me if anyone else was here so I didn't lie. Not saying I wouldn't have lied if they asked me, but at least I didn't have to."

Tom heard Hillary yawn. "Benning said they were treating

me like a witness, and they don't release names of witnesses, even though I only witnessed the aftermath, ranch dressing and all."

Tom felt strange benefiting from a standard ploy police used to dam up information.

"I told my bosses at the newspaper the truth," Tom said, rubbing one hand across the fabric of his sofa cushions, "that we were having dinner at my house, that you weren't injured and that you went home. We're going to leave all of it out of our story, though. Nobody's real comfortable about it, but we're hoping it will protect our later scoop. I also left out the kissing part." Tom took a big breath. "God, my head is starting to pound."

"You sure you're okay?"

"Yeah," Tom said, swirling the amber scotch around his glass. A once-full bottle was now at half mast. He had impressed himself earlier by not just drinking right from the bottle. But drinking single malt from the bottle was an abomination, even in moments of extreme stress such as this. "I'll be fine. No extra holes, remember? A lot of it is stress related, I'm sure, which will be better in the morning. Oh, and Benning also popped by here, I guess before he came to see you, full of questions. Talk about role reversal. He asked me why someone was shooting at me, besides it being open season on news buzzards. He's a funny guy. Should take his act to the Hard Rock downtown."

"What did you tell him?"

"I said, 'A drive-by shooting? Someone must have been *really* pissed I put that their kid was arrested in the paper?' Mainly I said I don't know. Like you said, we're kind of close to downtown, so maybe it was just some gang bangers trying to scare the shit out of people. That fits into Benning's view that Sioux City is little Fallujah. He'll figure it out someday. I think we both suspect this is connected to the Pollard thing. You think there's a leak and they know you're sniffing around?"

"Possible, but doubtful," Hillary replied. "We've kept it pretty buckled up. More likely they know *you're* fishing around."

Tom yawned. "The only thing I'm not sure of is if this was a warning or an attempted murder."

"A warning," Hillary said immediately. "Otherwise, why shoot up your house with such a small-caliber gun? If he were really shooting to kill, he would have used a nine millimeter or a for-ty-five, maybe even a shotgun, not a tiny twenty-two or twenty-five caliber which would never penetrate your exterior walls. And why only take one shot at you if he's out to kill? The driver had to see you on the lawn with no cover long before he started shooting and he could have easily slowed down and used the whole magazine. Do the job right."

"Thanks for that fun scenario," Tom said. "Hold on a second while I go throw up."

"Sorry," Hillary said. "I'm just saying that if the motive was murder, he could have done a much better job. He hit the house to send a message and added the exclamation point by shooting the trash can."

"His exclamation point almost became my involuntary bowel movement," Tom said. "It was nice shooting, though. I have to give him that. Especially that last shot into the trash can. He hit it from a moving car at a range of ten or fifteen feet. That's either a great shot or a lot of luck. I'd bet on great shot. Hitting that shot without trying would be an incredible fluke."

"Me too. So somebody who knows how to shoot."

"That narrows it down to about a million in this state. Ever since the concealed weapon permit became a lot easier to come by, it seems every third person is packing heat in Iowa. I'm glad to be alive, don't get me wrong, but why not just shoot me and have it over with?" Tom said.

"It's one thing to shoot at someone to scare them," Hillary said, "but you jump into a real tough neighborhood of the Iowa Code if you murder someone. Even for someone with no moral qualms about killing, they're looking at maybe three years in prison for shooting at your house, if they do any time at all, and life without parole for shooting *you*. And, maybe they're giving you a chance to get the hint before taking it to the next level, so to speak."

"Yeah, well, I'm horrible at getting hints," Tom said, touching his injured head again. "Just promise me if bad things happen you'll prosecute them 'to the fullest extent of the law.'"

"*That* I can guarantee," Hillary said. "I'll wear my ass-kicking pumps to court. You seem to know a lot about law. Maybe you *should* have been a lawyer."

"And pass up the huge earning potential and international prestige of being a journalist? No way. The only thing more foolish than giving up the glamorous life of a reporter would be wasting a law degree by becoming an underpaid prosecutor."

Tom let the sound of Hillary's chuckle wash over him. His head instantly felt better. "Could be worse. I could be a public defender," she said.

"Thanks for calling, Hillary, but I really need to get some rest," Tom said. The scotch and fatigue were starting to converge.

"One more question. Are you safe there?" Hillary said and then paused. "You could stay over here."

Don't tempt me.

"Yeah, I'm okay. They won't be back tonight. I appreciate the offer. Maybe some other time."

It's not that Tom didn't want to spend the night with Hillary, but staying at her house would just put her more at risk. Plus, he would be in that uncomfortable position of not knowing if it was an invitation to sleep in the spare room or an *invitation* of another sort. The relationship was pretty new for the second *invitation*, Tom thought, and he didn't want to give himself any opportunity for Mr. Happy to start doing the thinking and ruin what might have been. He would, however, put that rain check in his pocket for later.

Tom continued: "Tomorrow night I want to see Stephanie and pump her—er—question her. She knows a lot more than she was saying Wednesday morning."

"I'd better come with you," Hillary added, too quickly for her casual tone.

"Do you think that's a good idea?" Tom asked. "What if the presence of another woman shuts Stephanie up?"

Before Hillary could respond, an idea flashed across Tom's head as he switched the phone to his left hand and sat forward on the couch. Maybe he could turn Hillary's presence into an asset.

"Should I pick you up somewhere?" Hillary asked, ignoring Tom's objection.

Tom stretched his back and ran his hand through his hair. "I'll come get you," he said. "I'm going to find out when Stephanie is in town. If it's tomorrow night, we'll go back to the Regal and try to figure out what room. I'll call your cell. I've already got your number saved in my phone. Hope that doesn't scare you."

"Not at all. See you then. Good night."

"Good night. I'm sorry you were here during the shooting, but I'm glad you were here after, if that makes any sense."

"I understand," Hillary said, her voice soft. "I'm glad I was there too. I'll say a little prayer for you tonight. See you in the morning."

CHAPTER 23

Tom replayed the end of his phone conversation with Hillary, landing on her mention of prayer.

Not something you hear every day.

Is Hillary some kind of Jesus freak? It struck Tom as odd that someone so self-reliant would go in for all the religious stuff. He hadn't been to church in years. It all just seemed like a lot of mumbo-jumbo. Father, Son and Holy Spirit. Which was it? There just wasn't enough hard evidence to convince Tom that God was real, not that he had spent a lot of time looking for evidence. But Hillary seemed to believe.

Tom pocketed his cellphone and walked into his bedroom, untucking his shirt as he went. He stopped briefly at a bookshelf. Holy Bible. Yep, he had one. Tom pulled it down and fanned the dusty pages. That's a lot of copy. "In the beginning …"

Isn't a very catchy lead paragraph.

He replaced the book and continued into his bedroom, attaching the charger cord to his phone. Chester followed him into the room. Tom stripped off his rumpled shirt and sat topless on the edge of his bed. He took off his shoes, socks and pants and stood in front of a large dresser mirror, wearing only his briefs. Scrapes on his elbow and head from the mower fall were sore but healing. Left fingers bruised during his Regal hotel escapades were lavender-yellow. The fresh knot high on his forehead from the garbage can was already turning dark. He looked like a football wide receiver who had run too many crossing routes in linebacker land.

He quickly exchanged his briefs for some old shorts and walked to the laundry chute. Chester, now stretched out on his side in doggy exhaustion on some pillows Tom had put down for him in the corner of the room, raised his head to see where Tom was going, but lowered it when Tom stopped just a few yards away and within the dog's view. The laundry chute was behind a small door at the base of a hall closet only ten feet from the bedroom. The small door revealed not a chute but a compartment about six inches deep created when the laundry chute was sealed off during downstairs remodeling by a previous owner.

Tom knelt, reached into the compartment, pulled up a nearly invisible back panel that formed a false bottom in the compartment and retrieved a black case with an embossed "S-W" logo on its top. He studied the case for a few seconds and then stood, spun the lock dials to the appropriate sequence and flipped the lid open. The hallway light glinted off the Smith & Wesson's satin stainless finish, as if the pistol was blinking itself awake after a long nap. He hesitated, then removed the gun and one of the two loaded magazines from the case.

Setting the magazine on a closet shelf, Tom grabbed his car keys, found the smallest key on the ring and quickly opened a silver trigger lock. He dropped the lock back into the case, which also contained his earplugs, shooting glasses, a half-empty box of bullets and the gun's second loaded magazine, then returned the case to the amputated laundry chute.

With the pistol in one hand and the magazine in the other, Tom returned to the bedroom and sat on the side of the bed. He held the gun firmly by the grip, rotating his wrist to reintroduce it to the pistol's pound-and-a-half heft. It had been nearly a year since he had last visited the practice range. Tom's gun ownership started two years before that, fathered by the shock of his first death threat. He had gone to the sheriff's office on impulse to fill out a gun permit application, only to find a former co-worker, Linda, working as the clerk who took applications.

Tom sheepishly asked for a permit form, watching a glimmer of surprise flutter across Linda's face. He couldn't decide if he should offer some false justification for applying for the permit—"I'm taking up sport shooting"—or keep silent. He kept silent, partly because he didn't want to encourage discussion and partly because he didn't want to lie. His legal right to a permit was justification enough. Still, he imagined Linda gossiping to her family and friends, "Tom Kingman got a gun permit today," in the same tone she'd use if he'd been convicted of a crime or filed for bankruptcy. For some reason the application process made Tom feel dirty, as if he had carried a pornographic magazine to a store cash register only to find a female acquaintance on duty as the cashier. He was on solid legal ground, but ethically and morally there were acres of room for argument.

Tom returned to the sheriff's office nearly two weeks later, more than a week beyond the mandatory five-day wait. Linda just watched as Tom signed the permit, paid ten dollars and walked out carrying his yellow slip titled *Iowa Annual Permit to Acquire Pistols or Revolvers.*

Permit number WP4-392A12R allowed Tom to purchase as many guns as he wanted for a year. After that he had to renew the permit. The unassuming slip of paper made him feel like a human with the safety off. He could now walk into any gun shop in Iowa, pick out a gun and a box of fifty hollow points, throw down his cash or credit card and permit and walk out packing heat. No safety courses. No training. Just him and the pistol, or pistols, of his choice.

Tom had agonized for another week after getting the permit, trying to decide whether to actually buy a gun. He carried the permit in his wallet like a teenager carries a condom (just in case) making four or five inspection trips to Sioux City's two most popular gun shops. There he fondled each weapon, trying to convince himself that he was ready and that everyone was doing it. One more handgun in circulation didn't matter in a country that already had about sixty-five million of them.

Tom remembered the seductive feel of the two-pound, one-eyed steel beings nesting in his hand while gun shop employees talked their enthusiastic, macho gun sales talk. Stopping power, accuracy, range, recoil, easy to clean, blah blah blah.

An emotional cocktail formed by equal parts terror and excitement fueled Tom's many swings from gun fascination to repulsion. Rationally, he knew the chances of needing the gun for self-defense *or* a break-in while he was home were extremely remote. Emotionally, he admitted to taking some comfort in the weapon. Sitting on the bed, he wondered how Hillary felt about guns. She probably saw enough people seduced by the dark side of guns to make her wish they didn't exist.

Tom's purchase agony finally came down to this: taking a life with a pistol scared him, but going down without a fight scared him even more. The threats gave him mental probable cause to get a gun. So he used permit number WP4-392A12R to buy a compact Smith & Wesson nine millimeter semi-automatic, pretty low on the macho meter, as guns go. He couldn't remember the exact date, but he remembered it was a Thursday when he threw his credit card and permit to acquire on the counter of Jones Gun Works.

Too bad I couldn't write it off on my taxes as a business expense.

At less than two pounds loaded and just seven inches long, it was light and easily concealed. Its ten rounds were about half the capacity of larger, heavier models. Given such extremely long odds that Tom would ever fire the gun in self-defense, worrying about if he had ten or twenty rounds in the magazine seemed silly. So he chose the compact size over high capacity, telling himself that size really didn't matter—at least with a gun that he'd very likely never use outside of the firing range.

Tom looked at Chester, scooped up the magazine and smacked it into the pistol's butt, allowing himself a little dramatic flair.

Go ahead … make my day.

He pulled the slide back and slowly let the spring carry it forward again, watching the first round penetrate the barrel opening and move into firing position. He checked the safety was on. Twice. "Guns don't kill people," he said to Chester, setting the gun on the night stand. "Bullets do."

Chester looked up from his spot in the corner.

"Just let me know if they're coming, boy," Tom said as the dog tilted his head as if trying to understand. "So we can both run. If not, just hope I don't drop this thing on my foot and kill us both." Tom snapped off his bedside light and pulled up the sheet. He thought of Hillary, considered praying but decided to consider it further and drifted off to sleep.

+++

"Did you do it?" Barry Garrett said into his cellphone.

"I did it," Van Grunner answered.

"And?"

"I think he got the message. He was on his neighbor's front lawn holding the goddamn trash can when I did it."

Garrett chuckled into his bourbon and water. "Did he see you?"

"He couldn't see my face. The skinny shit looked like he might have pissed his pants, though. I even shot the top of the trash can while he was trying to crawl under the grass behind it. It was a hell of a shot. I used a little twenty-two so I wouldn't accidentally kill anyone in the house. The gun's history. I threw it into the Missouri River."

Garrett took a drink. The bourbon was expensive, the ice made from imported water. "Good. We'll see how it looks in the paper. I wonder how Scoop will like being the subject of the story for once. Well done. Just make sure they can't trace the car to you and we'll be fine. I'll call again soon."

+++

The shrill chirping sound made Tom sit straight up in bed and started Chester barking. Another chirping provoked more barks from Chester. Tom blinked his brain back online and recognized that his cellphone was ringing, and that somehow his gun had leaped into his right hand. Chester let out two more woofs.

"Chester," Tom said. "Come on. It's the phone."

Chester sat up in the corner and looked from Tom to the chirping phone.

Tom set the gun back on the nightstand. He rubbed his eyes back to life, squinting to focus on the nightstand clock.

God, 2:32 a.m.

Tom unplugged the charger cord. "Unavailable" on the caller ID. "Hello?" he croaked into the phone, surprised at his own voice.

"Good morning, Mr. Kingman," a male voice crackled through the phone. Tom was suddenly wide awake.

"Morning," Tom said, trying to drive the quaver out of his voice. "What can I do for you?"

"You can stop putting my business in the paper," the voice said.

"What business would that be? And who is this?" Tom's voice had grown firm enough to get Chester on all fours. Tom held out a hand to try to prevent the dog from barking. Chester barked anyway.

"Sleeping with dogs tonight, Tom?" the voice said.

"One of my bad habits," Tom said.

"I know how much that dog means to you, Mr. Kingman. But,

you know, there are sick people out there. A little antifreeze in the water bowl. Who knows?"

Tom looked at the gun in his hand.

I may need you after all.

"Look, tell me who you are, or I'm hanging up."

"Why don't you come out in your backyard, Tom," the voice said. "It's lovely out here and I'd rather talk in person. I've got some information that might help you in your story."

"How did you get this number?" Tom said.

"Let's just say I'm resourceful. Now get out here and don't call the police. Don't make me come back another night. I might mistake your house for, oh, Mr. Caldwell's next door or maybe Ms. Reed's house on Metling Drive and, well, tragic accidents happen." The man abruptly hung up.

A bead of sweat tumbled down Tom's cheek as he turned off his nightstand light.

I sooooo should have been a lawyer. Or an auto mechanic. How many mechanics get their houses shot at?

He shut his eyes, trying to slow his racing thoughts.

Call the police? No.

Tom couldn't risk that his caller wouldn't act on his threat to break into Bud's or Hillary's house some night. The thought of a shadowy figure in his backyard, even now watching the house, made Tom's head pound. Was this just a ploy to get him in the backyard and shoot him? But why? Why not just break in and do the job if that was the whole purpose? And why shoot him now after sparing him on the front lawn hours ago? Was this a follow-up to the trash can shooting?

This whole story is just fucked up.

He had to go outside, face this guy. Tom wanted to hear what he had to say. He most of all wanted to regain control by figuring out who was shooting at him. A major clue had just invited Tom into his own backyard. Plus, Tom was starting to get really pissed off.

He flipped his gun's safety off. He was going outside, but he wasn't going alone. He pulled off his shorts and put on his pants from the day before and tightened the belt enough to hold his lethal companion in the back waistband. He stepped into a pair of still-laced sneakers from the shoe collection near the end of his bed.

"Chester, stay," Tom ordered, as he closed the dog in the bedroom. Chester whimpered in protest. The last thing he needed was Chester crashing through the back door and getting them both shot. Tom eased his way through the kitchen to his back door. He looked through the kitchen windows but saw no one. The corner streetlight cast its pale light diagonally across half of the yard, leaving the rest in shadows.

Tom eased the back door open, struggling to control his breathing and rising pulse. The bravado of the bedroom ebbed away with each step. Waiting a moment to make sure his eyes had fully adjusted to the dark, Tom crept down the back steps, taking care not to let the door slam. He didn't know if he should expect a greeting or gunshot. He stood in silence for several seconds, straining for any suggestion of movement, rustle of grass or whiff of tobacco that would give away his intruder.

"Thank you for coming out, Tom," a disembodied voice said, pulling Tom's gaze to behind his detached garage to his right. The man picked a perfect hiding spot, Tom thought, with easy escape routes either down the alley to Tom's right or straight back, between two houses to the other side of the block. Trees and the moonless night shrouded both escape routes. Tom cursed himself for not anticipating the positioning.

He took a step in the direction of the voice. His mind raced.

Is the guy armed? About to cut me down? Should I go for my gun? Do one of those drop- and-roll TV police tricks?

"That's close enough." Tom saw the short barrel of a shotgun protruding just into the section of the yard lit by the corner streetlight. Tom's right hand made a slight, involuntary move for the gun in his waistband.

"Don't do that, Tom," the voice said quickly, as the shotgun muzzle rose up to aiming level. "We wouldn't want to wake the neighbors."

Tom extended his hands out from his body. "No, we wouldn't. I just had an itch. Mosquitoes are terrible out here."

"And you without your shirt. Pity." The shotgun slowly returned to waist level.

"What's this about?" Tom said, lowering his hands a little but still keeping them wide at his side. Tom heard a rumbling in the distance.

Thunderstorm coming.

"It's about you giving up your little First Amendment crusade before someone gets hurt," the voice said as the wind started picking up. "You were fortunate earlier tonight. These *random*, drive-by shootings can easily turn tragic. But, it may not even be you, Tom. What about those cute kids? Ashley and Tracy. That Ashley sure is a great little soccer player. She's got a bright future. And Tracy? What a zest for life. But, I'm sure they'll be fine. Healthy young girls and all. Still, there are a lot of perverts out there, even in a town as small as Sioux City. Some of them with a sick fondness for little girls, too. Children kidnapped and sold into the sex trade. Tragic. Turns my stomach, to be honest. Well, you've heard the horror stories."

A cold fist gripped Tom's spine, sending a shaft of ice up his back.

"Actually, I guess you've actually *written* the horror stories for the rest of us to read, haven't you?" The voice paused to let out an icy chuckle. "Why don't you go back to writing real news like those stories and forget all about Chuck Pollard? He's just another dead, wife-beating, drug dealer. Who cares how he died? Better yet, why don't you take some time off? Maybe go somewhere with

Ms. Reed. She's a very intelligent and attractive woman."

"Why don't I?" Tom said. His mind barely managed those three words. The storm added a punctuating slash of lightning. Tom looked up to see a network of lightning bolts fan across the underside of the storm cloud like veins branching across the back of an old person's hand. The thunder came a second later.

Rain soon.

"What a great idea," the voice said. "There isn't always going to be a trash can handy when you need one, is there? I'm looking forward to reading your stories."

Tom stared at the gaping, thumb-diameter hole at the end of the shotgun barrel. His life was one trigger pull from ending. He couldn't breathe. His brain said "inhale," but his lungs ignored the order. Ashley, Tracy, Hillary, Bud, his cellphone number, the shooting, even Chester. Shotgun Man knew it all. Tom felt the suffocating grip of real fear.

Tom saw the jagged bolt of lightning streak across the sky a split second before the boom of thunder. The storm was upon them, rolling overhead like a massive alien vessel.

Like in the movie Independence Day.

"You better get in out of this storm," the voice said. "Just go back inside. If you come back out and I'm still here, well, that would be unfortunate."

Tom nodded and backed up a step, reaching without turning for his back door. He had just touched the back door knob when a ribbon of lightning connected with a transformer on a power pole along the edge of Tom's yard. The transformer exploded in unison with a boom of thunder and rained sparks onto the street below. Every streetlight in the block winked off, plunging Tom into blackness.

In one motion, Tom threw himself toward the front of the garage and pulled out his pistol. The expected shotgun blast didn't come. Tom edged to the far side of the garage and peered around, just as rain started pouring. He could hear Chester barking inside the house, but he couldn't see six inches ahead in the pitch black. But then again neither could Shotgun Man.

Tom suddenly had home yard advantage. And another thing: the clap of thunder seemed to blow the door open on Tom's rage.

Hold onto that shotgun, because I want them to find it in your hand, along with my ten rounds in your fucking chest.

Another bolt of lightning lit the powerless neighborhood like a huge strobe light. Tom saw a figure in a large, dark raincoat trotting down the alley. Shotgun Man had run behind Tom's garage, up a slope into an unused alley, a pool of light from a flashlight bounding out in front of him. The alley was about seven feet above the backyards in the block, tapering down to nothing in back of Tom's garage. A retaining wall ran along the alley and the yards below, making the alley a sort of plateau overlooking the yards.

Tom aimed his pistol at the retreating figure, now about fifty feet away, as his brain ran through the pre-fire checklist.

Safety: off.

Weapon: cocked.

Round: in firing position.

Finger: in firing position. Confirm contact with trigger.

Target: acquired and tracking.

But as soon as the lightning stopped flickering, the figure vanished into the darkness, leaving only the weak glow from his flashlight. Tom considered firing at the flashlight's bobbing dot of light. One of his ten rounds would likely find the target.

But what if that light isn't Mr. Shotgun? What if it's Mr. Chigliac from three doors down looking for his dog?

Tom jerked his gun down and trotted after the man, using his knowledge of the terrain like night vision and the wall for both guidance and protection from the fleeing figure. His brain rummaged for a memory of what was along the wall in his neighbors' backyards. He remembered the Nguyens' swing set just in time to swerve around it. He leaped over what he thought was a plastic sandbox in the shape of a turtle in the Hendersons' backyard.

The rain had soaked Tom in the first minute of his run. Now his nervous sweat mixed with the driving rain sheeting off his torso. Another lightning flash had just given Tom a snapshot of the figure when something grabbed and held his right ankle, sending him sprawling into the retaining wall. He felt his gun and then his chest hit the jagged surface of the wall as Tom bounced to the ground. He managed to hold onto his gun as he groped his ankle with his left hand. A dog chain.

You gotta be shitting me.

Tom struggled to unwrap the chain, thankful that it wasn't connected to a dog. With only seconds until the man reached the street and his escape, there was no way he could untangle the chain in time without light. Tom hopped on his free leg as far as the chain would let him and then jumped up, flinging his elbows over the top of the retaining wall and onto the shoulder of the narrow alley plateau above. He looked like an outfielder stuck on the wall after trying to make a home run-robbing catch. Tom hung there, his armpits over the top of the wall, his free foot scratching for a toe hold, and struggled to clear his vision.

Another lightning strike, followed in a second by the thunder. The lightning was already moving away, even as the rain continued its frenzy. Tom looked down the vacant alley, hoping to get a glimpse of something, anything, that would help confirm his suspicions of Shotgun Man's identity. The man jogged into view from behind some trees about twenty-five yards away and ran to a car parked facing the wrong way along the curb, allowing him easy access to the passenger-side door. The sky went black again, robbing Tom of his light source just as he had almost glimpsed the car. He leaned across the wall as far as he could. He grabbed some large weeds at the top of the wall with his left hand and pulled himself up farther. His gun hand landed in a puddle, sending up a plume of muddy water.

"Come on," Tom said to the sky, his voice gurgling through the rain. "Just one more."

Please God, let me kill this filthy piece of shit.

In that instant, another lightning bolt branched through the sky. Just as the weeds came loose, Tom saw it. A red BMW. The next thing he knew he was falling off the wall, still clutching the weeds and his gun. He landed flat on his back in the sodden grass at the base of the wall and closed his eyes, even as his thumb moved to engage the safety of his gun.

CHAPTER 24

Ten minutes later, Tom burst back into his house, dripping down the hallway and into his bathroom, calming Chester as he went. He set his muddy gun on the vanity near the sink and grabbed a towel. Before he could start wiping himself off, he leaned over the toilet and threw up. Chester stood by, tilting his head to try to understand.

+++

The lightning bolt knocked the power out for about an hour. After recovering his composure, Tom lit an oil-burning lamp—which, like his gun, he kept for unlikely emergencies—and sat dripping on the toilet for a few minutes before taking a thirty-minute nearly scalding shower. His mind replayed the lightning's illumination of the BMW over and over, interrupted with the faces of Ashley and Tracy.

For an hour after the lights came back on, he sat at the kitchen table and disassembled his gun, which he had rinsed in the shower, cleaned, dried, oiled and reassembled it. It had been a long time since he had learned to break it down, but the muddy mess forced him to recall the lesson.

The gun reassembled, Tom reached for the freshly cleaned

magazine and thought about Hillary, Ashley and Tracy.

Not ... going ...

He slapped the magazine into the butt of the gun.

to fucking ... happen ...

He pulled the slide back and chambered a round.

you sick son of a bitch.

By 7 a.m., Tom was on his second pot of coffee and riding a wave of rage. The bright sun and birds chirping in the morning coolness did little to quiet his mental storm. By the time the devastating afternoon heat rolled in, the birds would suffer in silence along with the humans.

"I am getting *really* tired of this shit," Tom said out loud, "and it's gonna stop."

He pulled on a clean shirt and took Chester outside, leaving his gun on the kitchen counter, just inside the back door. After thanking the dog with a kiss on the forehead, he opened the gate and sent Chester bounding back to Bud's house. Before Chester even reached it, the back door came open and the dog trotted inside. Tom waved, shouted thanks to Bud for his concern and for sending Chester over ... and lied that everything was fine.

After checking the street, Tom retrieved the paper from the front steps and flopped down on the couch, his gun standing guard on the end table. The story about the trash can shooting had made the back page, the second most prominent spot in the paper. Skip had done a nice job with it. An hour later Tom had shaved and unearthed a sport coat from his closet to go with his casual pants. He didn't normally wear sport coats, especially in June, so it would attract attention from those who knew him. But after last night, he thought he should get in the habit. He carried this one to his car in a way that helped conceal the gun in his hand. For now, Tom draped the coat over the back of the passenger side seat and stowed his gun in the glove box. He was pretty sure he was breaking a law, but he really didn't give a shit.

The storm had been intense but brief and left only damp spots along the curb as evidence it had happened at all. Tom didn't even remember turning the steering wheel, working the brakes and accelerator or doing any of the other things he must have done to drive to work. He jarred himself out of the trance to find himself at his desk, pawing through a pile of pink phone message slips, the blinking voice mail button signaling a dozen more recorded messages.

He mostly made calls during the morning and answered internal and external email, trying to divert his mind from the night before. A survey of his voice mail showed most calls were from other papers, including the daily in Des Moines, which had apparently roused itself enough to figure out that Sioux City was, in fact, in Iowa. Tom spent some time returning the calls. Do unto others and all that. He answered the reporters' questions warily, trying to be honest but casual. He volunteered only enough to convince his interviewers of his openness and sincerity. Tom went for the "just bad luck, I guess," tone, offering thanks to Hillary's God that the reporters weren't yet interested enough to go to the extreme step of traveling to Sioux City.

It's not that he feared competition—bring it on—but his life and job would be simpler if the satellite trucks and *New York Times* hacks just stayed the hell out of his town. People would be less tense. Nobody would fawn over the big-city news boys and girls. He could generally get information faster and easier. Sources didn't get testy because thirty reporters called during a day. Plus, Tom needed room to go on the offense and maneuver. He was really, really tired of this shit.

"You did a nice job with the story today," Tom said to Skip, who was just getting to the office after starting his day at an interview.

"Thanks. Sorry about what happened. I would have been shitting. Leah gave me hell all night for not forcing you to come stay with us."

"I hope you told her I refused your offer and that I'm a stubborn asshole. Besides, if someone is stalking me, the last thing I want to do is bring them over to your house and put Leah and the girls in danger." Tom smiled bravely, trying to preserve his secret until he could get Skip alone.

"You know that if we can ever help you out, just call," Skip said. "You can hang at our place any time. If you're concerned, Leah and the girls can stay with her mom and dad for a while."

"I appreciate it. If it ever comes to that, I'll let you know. Hey, let's get some lunch. We never do lunch anymore," Tom said.

"It's only 11:10," Skip said, looking at his watch. "Kind of early for lunch, isn't it?"

"I missed breakfast. I didn't have much of an appetite."

That, at least, was true.

"All right. I've got nothing going on. Let me just tell Marx we're going out for an hour."

They took Skip's car and decided to go a Chinese restaurant downtown.

"So what do you want to tell me?" Skip said as he fastened his seat belt and started the car, turning the air conditioner on high.

Tom tried to look innocent.

"Look, you're not the only reporter on the planet," Skip said. "You've never eaten lunch before one o'clock in your life and I know when you've got something on your mind—you stop being a smart ass. So what is it?"

"I had company early this morning," Tom said.

"I take it you're not talking about Ms. Reed," Skip said.

I wish.

During the twenty-minute ride to the restaurant, Tom recited his backyard dialog, nearly verbatim, and then described his run through his neighbors' yards, including getting snared on the dog chain and seeing the red BMW.

"Shit. Do you think Leah and the girls are in danger?"

"If I thought that, I would have been at your back door last night with my own shotgun and an attack helicopter. No. I don't believe they are in danger. I think the guy was trying to push my buttons, which he did, make me think he's a big tough guy. We need to stay cool, as hard as that is, and play this thing out."

"We're talking about my kids here. No story is worth their lives."

"This is *me* you're talking to. I love Ashley, Tracy and Leah like family. If I thought that quitting this story would keep them safe into old age, I'd have been gone long ago. The truth is, I'm fucking pissed off, and I'm going to nail this ass clown to the ground and piss on him myself."

"Just don't do anything stupid, okay?" Skip said. "What's this story all about, anyway?"

"It's a meth ring. It has to be. A thousand percent between us, Skip, but Hillary thinks Van Grunner is dirty. He certainly fits the description so far. On the night of the shooting, I saw Van Grunner threaten the victim's live-in. Hillary asked me not to report seeing any of that stuff. I told this all to Bear. She thinks she's close to getting enough on Van Grunner to nail him for being part of some methamphetamine ring, but the state cops want more time to see if it goes farther in the department. Hillary said if I printed all the spooky stuff he did after the shooting, it could screw up her work."

"How do you know that wasn't just a line to keep a lid on the story?" Skip asked.

"I don't *know*," Tom said. "I just *feel* on this one. And, no, I'm not thinking with Mr. Happy. I agreed to keep it out of print, but I wanted in early and deep when they nail Van Grunner and whoever else turns up dirty. I know I'm gambling on Hillary, here, Skip. But after last night, I'm pretty sure she's onto something. If it was just Van Grunner helping himself to a few ounces in the evidence bin here and there, they'd just bust him and call it good. This has to be about kilos, not grams."

Skip turned a corner without signaling. "Then we're talking about enough motivation to blow a hole in your chest with that shotgun. Why not just walk away and let Hillary and the state police move in?"

"No offense to the state boys, but what if they just nail Van Grunner? I think that means it leaves Mr. Shotgun still out there. It wasn't Van Grunner's voice. I'm almost sure of that. Besides, it has to go higher than Van Grunner. He doesn't pack the gear to mastermind a multi-state meth ring. He's always going to be somebody's grunt. In three or four months, after the Pollard shooting is long past and maybe they've made the case on just Van Grunner or maybe not, I become the one who knows too much. You'll find me at the bottom of the city reservoir tanks up in Grandview Park, if you ever find me at all. And I'm not going to have some guy out there with a sniper's sight on Ashley and Tracy for the rest of their lives because of my story. That shit is *not* going to happen. Look, I'm going to make my move in the next couple of days. If it doesn't turn out, I'll forget I ever heard of Chuck Pollard and Bryan Van Grunner and leave it to the police."

"I'm glad he didn't, Tom, but what kept the guy from just killing you last night?"

"The same thing that kept the shooter from killing me in the drive-by. I must be worth more to them alive than dead, or killing me would cause more trouble than it solves. Or some of each. I'm mad at myself for not anticipating the return visit last night. I left myself wide open but Shotgun Man still only wanted to talk. I think I have an idea why, but I'm not sure."

Skip pulled into a space in the restaurant parking lot, but left the car—and more importantly, the air conditioner—running.

"Are you going to tell Bear?" Skip asked.

"No way," Tom said. "Bear would arm the entire newsroom, issue Kevlar body armor and start calling everyone he knows in the news business to launch some huge investigation. This situation requires more stealth. Bear is the nuclear option."

"What are you going to do then?" Skip said.

"I think I know who the big boss is and I have a plan." Tom unbuckled his seat belt and opened his door to get out.

Skip looked at him. "Mind telling me? Off the record, of course."

CHAPTER 25

Tom thought Skip had done a pretty good job feigning an appetite at the restaurant. After they agreed someone might be watching, Skip maintained appearances by eating half of his shrimp and snow peas. Tom suspected it all might come back up later after Skip had time to think about what they discussed in the car and the plan Tom outlined inside the nearly empty restaurant. That plan included Leah and the girls taking a trip to Leah's parents' farm outside Lee's Summit, Missouri, for a week or two. Leah had vacation time coming and the girls loved grandma's. Skip would stay and help Tom.

After returning to the paper, Tom walked from Skip's car to his own and drove to Tiffany's, a dive bar downtown. He left his sport coat and gun in the car and walked into a small, dingy establishment typical of the yet-to-be-gentrified part of downtown. Tom had heard the owner chose the name in the late-1990s to inject some style into the place. He failed. It ended up instead as a sort of alcoholic oxymoron. If the bar were a girl, she'd be from a seedy tenement rather than a posh penthouse. The decor was early American rundown: a schizophrenic blend of sports gear, highway construction signs, cheap prints of semi-famous paintings and portraits called "wine bottle with fruit." Tabletop ads, some handwritten, surrounded small vases holding a single faded silk rose.

Classy.

Tom took a second to let his eyes adjust from the bright daylight to the dim room. He navigated to the bar and ordered two bottles of Sam Adams Boston Lager, the only beer he could find that wasn't in his "mass-market swill" category. He declined the offered glasses, not trusting the dishwashing practices in a place like this. Tom and his beers made their way over to a dark booth about halfway toward the back of the bar.

"Thanks for meeting me," he said as he slid into the booth, glad he could keep his back to the drunks huddled at the bar.

"Yeah. Let's just keep it short. You're a pretty hot property right now, what with your witnessing the shooting and then getting shot at yourself. Nice goose egg you got on your forehead there. From last night?"

Tom nodded. "I almost got knocked out by a garbage can."

Neal Powers smiled.

Neal hadn't shaved that morning. A muscular man with wide shoulders, Neal wore his hair shaved to fine stubble. Slightly yellowed eyes looked out through small oval frames. The hip glasses contrasted with his old work shirt worn untucked. Quite a different look than Officer Powers had sported when Tom last saw him at 219 West Jarred.

Tom slid a fresh beer in front of Neal.

"Thanks," Neal said.

Tom couldn't tell if the bar had air conditioning or the June heat just hadn't seeped in through the windowless walls yet. The empty beer bottle on the table, along with the nearly drained bottle in Neal's hand, announced that he had been here awhile, and it was barely past noon. No visible signs of drunkenness. But Neal hadn't talked much yet. Tom noticed a smudge of grease on Neal's right inside forearm and his hands looked rough and scarred, the hands of a mechanic. Maybe the shirt was from a former professional life.

"Yeah," Neal said, pulling Tom's beer into line with the other two bottles, "I heard all about that garbage can shooting. Even read the story in this morning's paper."

Neal's message had been on Tom's voice mail when he got to the paper that morning. He said only that he was returning Tom's call for comment on an earlier story and gave a number. Tom had returned the call and found it was Neal's cellphone. Tom was surprised to have a cop's cellphone and even more surprised when Neal agreed to meet at Tiffany's, a place that minimized the chance of either of them being recognized.

"You undercover here or what?" Tom said, his voice theatrically low.

Neal chuckled. "Nah. I'm on vacation for a couple days. *Paid administrative leave* to be precise." Neal stopped suddenly and took a big drink of beer. Tom reciprocated with a smaller drink.

Neal continued: "But I went in yesterday just to see everyone and let them know I'm not going insane or anything. That's when I got your message."

I'm surprised my message actually survived long enough for you to see it.

"Thanks for calling back, although I have to admit I was surprised to hear from you," Tom said, leaning back. "Look, I don't want to seem ungrateful, but why did you call back? I would think every cop in the county wants to stay at least a hundred miles from the press about now."

"You called me, so the right thing to do is to call you back. Besides, I've got some bad feelings about this shooting."

I like this guy more and more.

Tom produced his notebook from his back pocket in one fluid movement. Neal's eyes followed it onto the table. "Bad feelings? What about?"

Neal raised both eyebrows. "For one thing, I've got bad feelings about being quoted in the paper right now. I don't see any upside in it for me. I'd just get labeled as the Media's Boy and people would stop talking when I came into the room."

"I know the feeling," Tom said.

"Maybe, after this is all over, we can talk for a story," Neal continued, "but right now we have to be off the record. We can talk and maybe it's in my interest to help you, but it's got to be very off the record. 'We didn't meet' kind of off the record. Okay?"

Tom retracted his notebook to his pocket as smoothly as he had pulled it out.

It was worth a shot. Glad I didn't spook him.

"I'm already forgetting who you are," Tom said. "But in a month, when the smoke clears, just remember who was your buddy today."

"Fair enough. For some reason, I'm trusting you on this one. Maybe it's because you didn't hype the original shooting story too much and didn't take any cheap shots. Although I'm not sure why you let Van Grunner's rib kick and threats to the woman go. Maybe post-shooting stress has affected my thinking. I just want you to know the stakes for me before we talk here."

Tom checked for any flicker of deception in Neal's eyes. Nothing. Still, he would add a dash of skepticism to anything Neal said. He wouldn't be the first cop to try to manipulate the media to make himself or the department look good.

Journalism 102: Sources don't always have to know what you know.

"Who's investigating the Pollard shooting?" Tom said, leaning back and sliding one of the small table signs into reading range. Onion rings for $1.79.

"Just the county attorney's office and our own internal affairs people."

"No state cops, Department of Criminal Investigation?"

"Are you kidding? After that pissing match you helped set off between the department and the state guys? The DCI is in no hurry to come all the way up here from Des Moines to investigate an open-and-shut justified-shooting case. They've said they'll review the county attorney's findings and videotaped statements to decide if they want to investigate it. But you were there. It was justified all the way. You said as much in your newspaper stories."

Yep. I've replayed it a hundred times and it still comes back self-defense.

Powers had just told Tom that his eyewitness story had kept the state authorities from caring too much about the news that Pollard and Van Grunner worked together way back when. Tom had made it easy to write that off as a coincidence. Sioux City was a small town. The two had similar, lower-income family backgrounds. A lot of people have worked for the same company, especially one as big as Blade-Garrett. Not that big a deal. The DCI had way bigger fish to fry without bothering themselves to come all the way out to Sioux City for a no-brainer. They'd let the DCI agent assigned to Western Iowa handle it.

Tom reached for his beer. "So what do *you* think we should talk about?"

Neal bowed his head and rubbed a hand over his scalp stubble. "It's Van Grunner," he said, looking down at the table's edge. "He's been acting strange lately. Look, most all the cops in the department are normal guys. Committed, honest, all of that. It's a good group, ninety-eight percent. But Van Grunner is definitely in the two percent. He's always been strange, from what I can tell. A real bad-boy-turned-cop. But lately he's been stranger than usual. He's always been a borderline racist. Saying something just barely over the line and trying to play it off as a joke. But these days he's talking to me about the shooting like we're best buddies. For anyone else, I wouldn't be so suspicious. Band of brothers and all that. But for Van Grunner to thank me for anything less than giving him a thousand dollars makes me nervous. He's acting like I dragged him out of a fire fight in Afghanistan or something. Just a feeling I have, really."

"A feeling?" Tom said, taking another drink and hoping for more proof than a feeling. "Did you talk to the chief or someone else in the department about it?"

"No. I don't have anything more than just a hunch, and rookies can't run around accusing veterans of acting weird on a hunch. Plus everyone is so racially sensitive. I don't want to bring up race unless it's really bad and I have some proof. Besides, some people I know in the state drug task force tell me they've heard —" Neal paused. If it was for effect, it worked. "That there might be something happening inside the department."

"A bad cop?"

Neal shrugged. "You said it, not me. Hell, I'm just a rookie patrol cop. I just wanted to let you know, maybe I can help you. Just don't get the wrong idea. I'm not a huge fan of the press, but I'm a black man in an incredibly white department. It would be easy for them to let me take the fall for anything strange, if you know what I mean."

"I understand. Any thoughts on who shot my trash can last night?"

"Nope. But I'd be careful if I were you," Neal said, finishing the beer Tom bought. "If some of this stuff running around is true, you should lock your doors at night."

No shit.

"One of my windows has a hole in it already," Tom said, sitting back. "But I'm sure Lieutenant Benning is on the job, giving it top priority, seconds away from an arrest. In the meantime, I'll lock up. Don't worry about that." Tom thought of the small silver and black gun he'd had breakfast with that morning and that was now chilling out in his glove box, unlocked and loaded. "Tell me, before you guys busted in and shot Chuck, what was Van Grunner saying?"

"Just that we had to be ready to fire, the guy could have a gun, stuff like that. It sounded like he was worried I wouldn't pull the trigger. And, to tell the truth, it was all reflex. I saw Pollard's gun swinging toward me and I shot him. Simple as that."

"Was Van Grunner on duty last night?" Tom said, keeping his eyes on his beer bottle's label.

"No. We're both on paid administrative leave for now. Standard procedure, they tell me. I might get cleared to work tonight. We're shorthanded and there's no doubt it was a justified shooting. I have to call in around two this afternoon to find out. The lieutenant tells me there will be another couple of reviews by the state and feds later, but we may come back to work pending all that. The taxpayers get real edgy when cops get paid to sit home."

"Any concern about being cleared?" Tom threw the question out more to test Neal's ability to remain calm than anything else. Van Grunner would have pistol-whipped him in response to a similar question.

"I have no concern about my actions, no. The guy had a gun, he turned it on us, so we shot him. I expected him to fire at us and he did, so we took him down. You saw it."

"I did, and thanks for not sending any rounds through the wall of the house. How did you get in on that call? Was that your patrol district that night? If I remember the radio traffic, you were in D-10, District Ten, but West Jarred is District One or Two if I recall right. So technically you were out of your district."

"I was on my way back from dinner at home, if you can believe that. I live just a little north of Pollard's house. I heard the call and decided to back up the district car on my way back to my patrol area. Dispatch called off the cover car, car fifty-nine I think, since I was there. Great timing, huh? It was lucky too, because the cover car would have never got there in time."

Tom banged his tender elbow against the back of the booth seat and winced. "About as good as my decision to stand on a lawn mower," Tom said.

Neal's laugh broke the tension.

"You looked funny as hell when you fell off that thing," Neal said. "I caught sight of your arms flapping as you went over. I mean, standing on a lawn mower? Who stands on lawn mowers?"

Tom smiled.

"I figured it was too dark to mow his grass, and I was too short to see you guys in action without standing on something and it was the only thing I could find. You always want to keep your weight centered on those things. I found that out quickly." Tom rubbed the back of his head, emphasizing the painful lesson. The fingers smashed in the hotel stairway door were yellow, but not nearly as painful. Tom saw Neal glance at his hand.

"What do you know about Van Grunner?" Tom asked.

"Not much," Neal said. "He's certainly got a short fuse. When he started kicking you at the crime scene, I had no idea what was going to go down, and less of an idea what I would do about it if he didn't stop. I was glad Benning showed up when he did. Hey, why didn't you put that stuff in the paper? It's not like a reporter to let that kind of stuff slide."

"Let's just say I sometimes let stuff slide, for a while, to see if it grows into bigger stuff later. And thanks for getting between us. I saw that and appreciated it."

"Yeah, I couldn't just let him beat on you," Neal grunted. "I'll look forward to reading about your 'bigger stuff.' "

Tom smiled. "Officer Powers . . ."

"Call me Neal."

"Neal." Tom paused to let the first-name familiarity settle on them both for a second. "Do you know anything about a high-class prostitute from Omaha named Stephanie or Brenda? Works out of the Regal?"

CHAPTER 26

Neal leaned forward. "Brenda? Stephanie? Let's see…. Short brown hair, killer legs?"

"That's her," Tom said.

"Stephanie Lansing," Neal said. "At least that's the most recent name she's used, which is definitely not her real name. She's from Omaha. We suspect she's got some regulars up here but we don't have any proof. The vice boys have taken a couple of runs at her, but she doesn't take any new clients without a personal recommendation from someone she trusts, and that's a pretty short list. She charges seven hundred and fifty a night. I've heard she's worth it. Pretty expensive for around here, considering you can get a blow job for twenty bucks down on Lincoln Avenue."

Tom grimaced.

Most of the girls on Lincoln would have to pay me money. They should offer a free HIV test with every transaction.

"If you pass Stephanie's background check—and that's a big if—she'll meet you anywhere," Neal said, "but it's got to be classy. No Eastside Motel for her. The Regal is her first choice, sometimes the Hard Rock hotel."

"Any idea when she comes to town?" Tom asked.

"Why, you looking for some action? I would think that would be a little pricey for a reporter," Neal said, smiling.

"Maybe I have expensive tastes. Maybe she's my wayward sister. Maybe I'm looking to sell her newspaper advertising. You never know."

"You better take your advertising rate card to the Regal tonight, because we got a tip she'll be there. Not that we can do much about it except stake the place out and see which doctors and executives show up. And that's problematic because it's not against the law to meet a woman at a motel for sex. It's very hard to catch money exchanging hands. It's all cash, so she just puts it in her bag and if we bust her she says it's hers and we can't prove otherwise. So it's *hard*—if you'll excuse the expression—to prove it's more than consensual sex, which still isn't illegal, thank God. It would be nice to mail some photos to a few wives, though, but that would probably only get the department sued."

"Thanks, Neal," Tom said, glancing at his watch. "I better go. Give me a call if you want to talk more." Tom took out one of his cards, wrote his cell number on the back even though Neal had already called him on it, and dropped it onto the table. Neal whisked it into his pocket without a look.

"I may find some things out that I need your confirmation on or help with," Tom continued. "Whatever you can do I'll appreciate."

"Give me another card and your pen," Neal said. Tom obliged. Neal flipped the card over, wrote two lines and gave both card and pen back. "That's my cell, which you already have I guess, and private email address. See ya again sometime, Tom," Neal said as Tom rose. "And don't do anything illegal tonight."

Tom nodded and headed for the exit. There were no sex crimes on the docket for tonight, but beyond that he couldn't promise. Squinting as he hit the early afternoon sunshine, Tom scanned the vehicles parked along the street as he walked back to his car. No red BMW. The cars he could see were nondescript and empty. The humid afternoon quickly enveloped Tom, sending a sheet of sweat down his back. He pulled out his phone and dialed Hillary's direct office number. She answered as Tom slumped into his hot car, hurrying to get it started and crank up the air conditioning hoping it worked today.

"This is Tom. Sorry to call you at the office, but tonight's the night. I'll pick you up at your house around seven. I figure Stephanie's 'shift,' if that's what we want to call it, won't have started that early."

"Okay. Seven."

"I'll see ya then," he said, ending the call.

Tom drove back to the paper. He parked and bailed out of his hissing, ten-year-old Taurus. The air conditioner had let him down again and the hissing sounded a lot like an automotive death rattle to Tom. He'd been saving for a new car for five years and was just waiting for it to go "tits up" as his auto-mechanic father would say before making the move on a new Mustang. Tom hurried for the frigid relief of the *Sentinel-Leader* building. He navigated the employees-only security door and swerved through the newsroom crowd to his desk, savoring the room's chill. Ironically, the *Sentinel-Leader's* highly suspect HVAC system reacted strangely to Iowa's climatic extremes. The hotter it got outside, the colder it got inside. During these days of 100-plus degrees, the news room hovered at about sixty-five. When the sub-zero winters came, temperatures inside the *Sentinel-Lea*der would climb to about seventy-five. It took a while for Tom to adjust to seeing copy editors wrapped in sweaters when it was 101 degrees outside and wearing t-shirts in the minus-ten-degree winters.

Despite the meatlocker conditions, Skip sat at his desk, his tie askew and his open collar sporting a sweat ring. He'd been outside a lot today. There were three empty foam coffee cups and a half-eaten bag of tortilla chips on his desk.

"Hi, Tom," Skip murmured, barely glancing up as Tom threw his keys on his desk.

"As a friend, Skip, I just want you to know you look like shit."

"Thanks."

"You know I'm always going to be there for you when you need to hear the truth," Tom said, sitting down.

"Have you looked in the mirror at all in, say, the last forty-eight hours?" Skip replied without looking up. "You look like something my dog deuced out this morning."

"And I feel even worse, but thanks for the concern."

Skip coughed out what Tom took for a chuckle and then resumed his typing at full speed.

"Leah and the kids?"

"Leaving this afternoon. The kids are thrilled. They love cows and pigs. Leah's doing okay. Luckily her boss is a saint and it's a slow time at work."

Tom gave Skip a nod, hoping Skip knew how much he regretted even minor involvement of his family. Skip's family was his weak link, Tom thought, something anyone who wanted to play rough could take advantage of. Look what just an oblique threat to his wife and kids had done. Tom wondered how much of a muckraking, story-breaking journalist he himself would be with a wife and kids of his own. He bought a gun the first time his own welfare was believably threatened. What would he do if he had kids? A cruise missile? Shoulder-launched Stinger?

Tom slowly turned to his computer and found the contact file he was looking for, noted the number, and punched it out on his office phone. The phone rang three times before a female voice answered.

"Hi, Jodi? Tom Kingman."

"Tom Kingman. I haven't seen you in months. How have you been?"

Jodi was a friend of a former coworker. They had dated a few times but found there wasn't much between them beyond casual friendship and parted on good terms.

"Fine. Listen, I'm in a rush, do you still work at the Regal?"

"Yeah. Why?"

"I need some help finding someone who's staying there."

"Just call the front desk and I'm sure they can help you," Jodi said.

"That's a problem since I don't know her real name. And I'd rather not have anyone know I'm looking for her."

"Is this for a story?" Jodi said, her voice suddenly becoming low and hushed. "Am I going to be one of your unnamed sources? This is *so* cool."

"Yeah. You're my deep throat." *Did that sound bad?* "Sorry we're not meeting in a downtown parking ramp. I just need you to help me find this woman. She's tall, brunette, great dresser, killer legs, high class, expensive clothes. I think she comes from Omaha, a regular at the Regal."

"You've always had a thing for legs, Tom," Jodi said playfully. "When I wore my short skirts, I knew you'd do anything I wanted."

Guilty as charged.

"Do you know her?"

"I know her. Hard to miss someone like that. Some kind of consultant or something. Always pays in cash. Every male who works at the Regal hangs around the lobby when she's staying with us, hoping to see her walk down the stairs. She never takes the elevator to the lobby; she comes down the grand staircase from the second floor. Likes to make an entrance. I personally don't think she's *that* hot."

"That sounds like her," Tom said. "Is she there tonight?"

"Let me call Darlene, she's working the desk right now. I'll call you back."

"Just don't tell Darlene it's for me, okay?" Tom rattled off his phone number, hung up and pretended to work on something on his computer. When the phone rang again in ten minutes, Tom pounced on it. He forced himself to pause to smile and shrug at a startled Skip.

"Kingman."

"Tom," Jodi said, sounding like she had just discovered the missing tapes that screwed Nixon for good. "She's *there*. Right now. Just got here twenty minutes ago. Darlene saw her talking to the maid outside room 1191 after she delivered a toothbrush to a guy on the same floor. She didn't even have to violate rules by checking the computer. Pretty sure it's room 1191. Hey, don't tell me you have a thing going with her ..."

Not a thing-thing, but possibly a thing.

"No, Jodi. Not a thing. Thanks. I owe you big time ... and keep this to yourself for now, okay?"

"Anytime, Tom. I do feel like Deep Throat ... don't take that the wrong way."

"You've got much better legs than Hal Holbrook," Tom said, hoping Jodi would catch the movie reference. He hung up and checked his voicemail. There were fourteen messages waiting.

One by one he listened to at least a few words of each message and then pushed "#" to skip it. Anything but sources could wait until next week or next month. Tom's finger was poised over the pound sign again when the second-to-last message came through the phone earpiece. "This is Todd Walters in Des Moines. Give me a call." Tom punched the pound sign, dismissed the last call and turned back to his computer.

He typed "Todd Walters" in and searched his contact list. In a blink the entry appeared at the top of the screen. He scooped up his office phone and dialed. Todd Walters answered on the fourth ring. "Motor vehicles, Todd speaking."

"Todd. Tom Kingman. Thanks for calling me back. What do you have?"

"I've got the plate you called about yesterday. Sorry it took so long. Our computers just came back up this morning. Boy, is the state patrol ever pissed off. They couldn't run anyone last night."

Tom rolled his eyes.

Government low-bidder computer system. Walters has always been chatty, even when we were in college together.

"I bet," Tom said. "What did you find out?" Walters read off the owner of the plate Tom had called in. Tom let the pencil fall out of his fingers as he finished the last letter of the name Walters dictated.

Yep.

"Hey, does this have anything to do with you getting shot at the other day?" Tom heard Walters saying. "I read about that in the paper down here this morning. Did you shit your pants? I would have. I was surprised to see it. Usually when the Des Moines paper has something about Sioux City, it's a meth bust or something."

"Let's just say that was nothing I'd want to do again. Now I know how deer and pheasants feel. No, this is another deal. I can count on your discretion, right Todd?"

"Oh sure," Todd said. "How can I tell anyone without admitting I ran a plate for you on the sly? We both know how well that would go over."

"I appreciate it, Todd. Let me know if you ever get back to Sioux City. Coming for the class reunion next year?" They had both graduated from Morningside College across town.

"Yeah, I might come up. I hear we got a good football team this year. Thank God for the internet. I get squat about the Mustangs in the rag here."

"Great, let me know. You can stay at my place, if you don't mind being shot at. Thanks again," Tom's voice trailed off as he hung up the phone. He wasn't even sure if Walters had finished talking.

CHAPTER 27

Tom pulled into Hillary's driveway at 6:55 p.m. He had been circling her block, staring at his car's digital clock for the last ten minutes. He had considered sneaking across the block to the back door in case he had a tail but dismissed the idea. Shotgun Man already knew about Hillary and nothing attracted attention like a man walking between houses.

Hillary came to the door in skinny black pants, bare feet and a dark blue blouse.

"Hi, Hillary," Tom said, accepting her gestured invitation to step into her foyer. He didn't know if she expected him to kiss her. He supposed she didn't—he wasn't sure *why* not, however—and decided to let Hillary make the first move. She immediately leaned forward onto one foot and kissed him lightly on the lips.

"Hillary, we have to talk about us, you know, you and me and what's going on with us," Tom said.

"Is there a *you and me*, Tom?" Hillary asked as she padded barefoot across her living room to a pair of flats, Tom focusing on her feet.

"We keep kissing each other, so that's my first tip," Tom said, his eyes lingering on the arch of Hillary's foot. "I am a paid observer, you know."

"Good, let's just say there is an 'us' and leave it at that, kind of undefined for now," she said as she quickly tucked her feet into her shoes. "What can I say? I like your lips. It's been a while since I met any I wanted to kiss. If we start overthinking this, I might convince myself that it's a mistake."

Let's underthink it, then.

"You really know how to turn a guy on, Hillary," Tom said as he sat down on the couch. He had learned long ago that the vacuum of silence was usually preferable to what people said just to fill it.

"Put yourself in my position," Hillary said. "Getting involved with a newspaper reporter. I'm a prosecutor. It's not the most career-prudent move, you know. People might start to question my loyalties and stop talking when I come into the room."

Welcome to my world, where people not only stop talking when I come into a room, they can't wait to leave it.

He decided to let her statement go for now. Tom, after all, had his own questions about how involvement with Hillary would change *his* professional and single, nomadic personal lifestyle.

"Hillary," Tom said slowly, "something happened last night."

"You mean after the shooting?" Hillary asked as she plopped her house keys into a small purse and started rummaging for something more.

"I had a visitor at two thirty in the morning."

"Someone broke into your house?" Hillary said, her voice climbing.

"No, no. Someone called my cellphone and invited me into my own backyard for a chat."

"And you immediately called the police, I hope."

Tom gingerly felt the bruise above his eye and then pulled his fingers back far enough to inspect them for blood. "No, I didn't call the police," he said, satisfied for the seventeenth time today that he was *not* bleeding or oozing pus. "The guy said if I did that, he'd just disappear for now and maybe give you, Skip Ensley's family, or Bud a surprise visit later."

Hillary dropped into the chair near her couch, still holding her open purse. "Really?" She looked around her house. "He knows where I live?" She plucked a small phone out of her purse. "I'm going to call my contact at the state police . . ."

"And tell him what?"

"That you got a threatening call last night."

"I got the call," Tom said, "and then I went out into my backyard and talked to him."

"You did *what*? He was in your backyard? He could have shot you right there," Hillary said, her finger still poised over the phone's touchscreen.

"If I hadn't gone, I thought he'd just come back and shoot me or you later. Besides, it would be silly to waste such a good shot at me earlier in the evening just to come back and kill me later at night. I didn't think he wanted to kill me given all the better chances he'd already had."

"What if it had been another person, not the one who shot at you earlier that night?"

Tom shrugged. "I didn't think of that. All I could think about was this guy breaking into your house and spending the night."

Hillary nodded slightly, lowering the phone. "I'm with you on wanting to avoid that if we can."

"So I went out and found this guy with a shotgun behind my garage. I couldn't see his face, just the end of the gun. I got a good look at that. He basically said, 'Back off this Pollard story or I'll kill you or your friends,' but in much more clever and indirect words."

"Then he left?" Hillary asked.

"That big thunderstorm hit as we were finishing our talk. Lightning fried a transformer in back of my house and knocked out power to the block for about an hour. He got away down the vacant alley behind my house. I chased him but couldn't get a better look at him."

"You *chased* him?"

"It was pitch dark, and I knew the terrain, so I chased him. I wanted to get a look at him or his car."

"God must have been with you," Hillary said.

"I don't know about the Almighty, but my nine millimeter was with me," Tom said.

"Did you see anything?" Hillary asked.

"Not much," Tom said, flopping back on the couch. He flexed the lightly yellow fingers he'd smashed in the Regal stairwell door. "I got snagged in a damn dog chain in Mr. Ortega's backyard. I did manage to see Shotgun Man get into a red BMW."

"Red BMW," Hillary said, reclining in her chair and pulling one foot almost all the way out of her shoe.

"That doesn't narrow it down too much. Everybody trying to convince themselves they're big stuff has a BMW these days."

"In Sioux City at least that's a little more limited number than elsewhere. I'm keeping my eyes open for red BMWs anyway," Tom said. "And I might have my DMV friend tell me how many red BMWs are even registered in Sioux City. Or maybe the whole county. Can't be that big a list."

"You're running plates now?" Hillary asked.

"Off the record?" Tom smiled.

Turnabout is fair play.

Hillary nodded and Tom continued: "Yep. Ran one the other day that you may be interested in." Hillary tilted her head in curiosity. "I saw a spotless red BMW in the parking lot the night of my close encounter with Stephanie. Almost on a whim I wrote down the license plate and had my friend run it."

"Let me guess," Hillary said. "Chief Jimmy Banks."

"I wish," Tom said with a slight chuckle. "How about Barry Garrett?"

"Garrett? Wow."

"It was registered to Blade-Garrett Worldwide, which means company car."

"And who else at Blade-Garrett would have a BMW for a company car?" Hillary asked.

"Certainly not their chief mechanic."

"This is getting pretty crazy. Let me call my state people."

"Remember how you said you needed time to wrap up your investigation?" Tom said. "Well, now *I* need time. You call the state cops. They come. Shotgun Man finds out and comes back to see us both one night, maybe a month from now. Please, just give me a couple days. It's got to be Garrett. We confront Stephanie tonight, see what we get, regroup, and then you can call the cavalry if you want to."

Hillary paused, then returned her phone to her purse. She crossed over to sit beside Tom and abruptly hugged him, hard, and then gave him a lingering kiss. "You should stay here tonight. We'll be safer if we're together."

"I'd love to stay, but let's see how things go with Stephanie and then we can make plans, including who stays where." He rubbed the top of Hillary's leg gently. He was slowly becoming more at ease with touching her. Just two days ago they had barely ever even shaken hands.

Hillary reciprocated by putting her hand on Tom's upper thigh as well. Tom subdued—with some effort—his urge to pull her hand higher. "So," he began, sliding his hand off Hillary's leg to try to defuse the growing physical distraction, "how do you think we should approach this?"

Hillary sat up and ran the hand that had been on Tom's leg through her hair. "You've dealt with her before. What do you suggest?"

"She was all over me last time we met, so it's good you're coming with me, unless she's into the number three, in which case we may be screwed, literally," Tom said, pausing for a reaction from Hillary but getting none. "I know it *could have been* my rakish good looks and machismo that turned her on last time, but, then again, monkeys may fly out of my ass any second now. It could *possibly* have been she was setting me up for something."

"I thought she wanted to tip you off and was all damp to be your anonymous source," Hillary said.

All damp?

"So did I. But anonymous sources are a lot like over-eager witnesses: they almost always have ulterior motives. Once in a while you come across one that's motivated out of love for the inner workings of democracy, but more often there's something in it for them."

Hillary agreed with a slow nod.

"We both think Mr. Shoulder Holster was Barry Garrett. He matches the description from the rear, anyway. You'll probably never see a photo lineup of the feature I saw from the side, and definitely not in the condition I saw it." Tom grimaced. "Not sure I could or would want to identify that. But, let me just say here as a male-to-male courtesy that Barry has nothing to be ashamed of in that area. But they all look the same anyway."

"No, they don't."

Tom reacted to Hillary's statement with an exaggerated eye flare and then continued. He wondered what Hillary's faith had to say about her apparent *biblical* knowledge of penises. "Besides all that, his red BMW being there at the same time is either a wild coincidence or a huge tip. Pretty careless of him to park it where someone could see it."

"So Garrett is her client."

"Yeah," Tom said, examining a small figurine of a girl on a horse that had been sitting on the end table. "I think Garrett was with Stephanie when the Pollard shooting happened. While I was stuck in her bathroom, I heard him say he had 'come back' early. I bet he got a call about the shooting, found out it was going to be front page, and had to leave to take care of some business."

"So Stephanie called you," Hillary said.

"For some reason, which Garrett didn't see coming. So that's why he drove the company car back down to the Regal to hook up with Steph again. No reason to hide since he had no idea I was on the scene. But before he got there, Stephanie gave me the white-hot treatment, for whatever reason." Tom put the figurine down carefully and then turned it to an angle he liked. "At least I'm pretty sure that Garrett didn't know."

"Why would Garrett put her up to it?" Hillary said.

"To find out what I know. Give me some false tip to lead me off into Neverland. Hard to say. Maybe she was going to tell me someone else did it, like the mayor or, knowing Garrett, one of his competitors. She could hardly tell those stories to you official people, but a reporter overcome by her body might let himself be influenced to write wild, anonymous-sourced stories and really screw up the official investigation or put his competitor in the shitter, just to get more num-nums from Stephanie."

"An *unethical* reporter, sure."

"I've met a few," Tom said, "and I bet you've run across one or more who would have accepted Stephanie's offer then hidden behind the First Amendment when it turned out to be total bullshit."

"But then when Garrett came back, why didn't Stephanie tell him you were there?"

"That's the fly in the ointment. If she was doing all this for Garrett, no way he comes back. She uses her professional skills to take possession of my manhood, sends me on my way to do her bidding, then calls Garrett to report. *Then* maybe he comes over and they do the naked pretzel. On the other hand, I can see Stephanie leaving me in the can and giving Barry one hell of a distraction so I can get away if they're not in it together," Tom said. "If she's fronting for Barry, that's screwed up if he finds me in the can. Besides, a married, virtuous, church-going Chamber luminary CEO making the beast with two backs with a prostitute could almost become a bigger story to said unethical journalist. Couple cellphone pictures, some video and you'd have something worth a nice monthly *stipend*, if you get my drift. So it's pretty safe she doesn't want a good client knowing she's giving him a hummer in front of a reporter. Bad for business."

Hillary turned toward Tom, causing her right knee to touch his left. "So now we go back and see her, and then what?"

"We make her an offer," Tom said, doing his best Brando Godfather and relaxing his knee into Hillary's. "We show her an exit. Maybe she wants to talk to you before this blows up and Garrett burns her as a hooker. Look, she didn't give me up in the hotel so there's probably no way she told Garrett that I was there. That makes me think she's trying to take Barry down. Stephanie struck me as a sophisticated, intelligent woman. I think her weakness is that she's not as confident of her brain as she is of her body. Who knows? Maybe we can convince Stephanie that her brain can be as powerful as her body. And we got you, Hillary Reed, Assistant Woodbury County Attorney, who takes down pukes like Barry Garrett for breakfast."

"I don't know what I can offer her," Hillary said. "Just maybe go off the record tonight and try to get her to come in and talk—with her lawyer, I'm sure—about a deal tomorrow. You think that will be enough?"

Tom stood up. "Let's go see."

Hillary stood up as well. "You drive."

Tom glanced at his sport jacket in the back seat as they climbed into his car, suddenly self-conscious about the only semi-clean interior. He had one more delicate subject to talk to Hillary about when they got to the hotel. The drive to the Regal would take about fifteen minutes.

CHAPTER 28

"I met with our friend Neal Powers this afternoon," Tom said as he cleared Hillary's driveway and turned down a loud hip-hop song throbbing through his radio.

"Wow, you've been busy … full of surprises. What did Neal tell you?" she asked.

"Are we off the record?" Tom grinned. "I can't believe how much fun that is for me to say. And I wouldn't want Neal to get in trouble for talking to the media."

"We've been off the record ever since you were covered with garbage," Hillary said. He gave her a five-minute recap of the interview. "Interesting," Hillary said, relaxing back in her seat. "Van Grunner looks dirtier and dirtier, doesn't he?"

"Oh, he's dirty, but he's also a good shot. I'm just glad he hit the trash can and not me."

"You think Van Grunner shot at you?"

"Pretty sure. Who else? In this town? Random drive-bys? Somebody pissed at me for a story? Sure, people get pissed, but enough to fire rounds into my house? No way. Despite what Benning thinks, this ain't gangland and I don't work for the *LA Times*. Gotta be someone connected to the story, and so far that narrows it down to Van Grunner, Joyce, Neal and we think Garrett. If Neal is in on it, why would he meet with me? And popping rounds into a house is below a drug kingpin. Garrett would send a grunt to do that. Joyce is probably already shacked up with a new squeeze. She got over it the minute she figured out her 'brutality' suit was for shit."

Hillary turned abruptly to Tom. "Garrett and Van Grunner?"

"They used to work together. We're guessing Steph was telling me Garrett is the man behind everything. It's not a big stretch. We're just not sure *why*. And of all big six—who, what, when, where, how and *why*—why is always the most elusive."

"Maybe Neal met you to see what you know, throw you off," Hillary said.

"Maybe. He was hammering the beer at twelve thirty in the afternoon and looked pretty fried to me, though. If he's messing with me, he should be an actor not a cop." Tom turned a corner slowly, vowing for the fifteenth time that month to get a car with more reliable air conditioning, soon. At least Hillary had the courtesy not to mention it.

Tom continued: "Van Grunner sure is acting the part of dirty cop, though. Besides, you said you already thought he was dirty, remember? 'Don't print this, Tom, or you'll screw up our Van Grunner investigation.' What *do* you have on him, anyway?"

"Reports that he's abusive, unprofessional, maybe on the take. He disappears on patrol, claiming to be checking something or having radio trouble. His radio always checks out fine and where he said he went never quite rings true. He always seems too interested in what the drug guys have going on, down to the fine detail, which he says is because he's interested in working in the unit. So far we haven't gotten much we can take to court, but there's been a lot of shadowy corroboration, enough at least to dig deeper. What we've found makes me think we can nail him. Maybe set him up with some fake info and get him to screw himself."

Tom gave her his best "go on" look.

"I can't tell you much more, Tom. Even if there continues to be a 'you and me,' there will always be some things about work I can't tell you. Not that I don't trust you; I have to be able to say truthfully that I haven't spoken to *any* reporters about some things. But I can tell you, if this all turns out to be true, you won't see me crying at his trial."

"I know Van Grunner is a caveman," Tom said without taking his eyes off the road, "but do you two have some history? Just that there's been some talk …" As soon as the question was out, Tom feared the answer.

"No. He *wanted* to have some history with me when I first got this job, but I turned him down. I can't prove it, but 'the talk' you mentioned probably started with him as revenge for turning him down. I don't know if I was angrier at the come-on in general or that he used some line that only the most codependent bar slut would fall for. He's physically attractive, if you like the muscular type. I am sure he's the kind of man who would get himself off and be out the door … wham, bam thank you ma'am."

Hillary paused, looking out her window for a second.

"Besides, he's the opposite of everything I appreciate in a person, things like intellect …

Check.

"Humor . . ."

Check.

"Depth …"

Check.

"Sensitivity, compassion and kindness …"

Check, check and check.

She gave Tom an 'about to confess something' look he'd seen on hundreds of interviewees, "and faith."

A basketball end-of-game buzzer filled Tom's brain.

Five-for-six on that list. Usually pretty good. Deal-breaker?

He managed to take his eyes off the road long enough to give Hillary a long look.

Tom parked along the curb at the back of the Regal Hotel. Before Hillary could open her door, he grabbed her arm and reached back for his sport coat. "Dressing up, Tom?" Hillary said, glancing at the coat.

"Time for show and tell."

"Right here?"

Tom smirked. "Maybe later." He had his coat in his lap by now. "Right now I wanted you to know about this, unofficially." He reached into the glove box and pulled out the Smith & Wesson. He made sure she got a good look at the gun before quickly placing it into his coat pocket. He awaited the reaction.

"A gun? That's great. You'll get us killed with your own gun. Do you really think you need that?"

"Twenty-four hours ago I was lying on Bud's lawn with what I thought was my brain running down my face. Eighteen hours ago some guy was pointing a shotgun at my chest in my own backyard. Last time I saw Stephanie she was going down like the Titanic on a guy with a shoulder holster. I'm sleeping with this thing."

"I detest guns. They're little misery time bombs, waiting to go off and screw up people's lives. I see the shitty aftermath every single day. A couple years ago we prosecuted a guy who broke into a house, found a gun in the bedroom and liked it so much he shot the man and his wife in bed, just for the hell of it. You wrote about it. We're just lucky he didn't kill the kids sleeping down the hall. But he sure woke them up. Guns are so overrated."

"So is getting shot. So is showing up at a gunfight with a notebook and a copy of the Iowa Code."

"Have you ever carried a gun?" Hillary asked.

"In my hand, yes. On my body, no."

"When's the last time you fired it, if ever?"

"Last May."

"When's the last time you checked it?"

"Last night."

"Did you get it legally?"

"Yes."

"Do you have a permit to carry a concealed weapon?"

"No."

"Do you really think this is a good idea?" Hillary asked. "I'm an officer of the court, if you get caught carrying that thing, it could mean my job. We're just going to see a prostitute."

"First of all, it's a good thing you had no idea I was carrying it, right? You had no idea! You can't control a wild-ass reporter, your honor! Second, it's not the prostitute I'm worried about ... the gun's not for her, anyway. It's her armed clients that kinda make my butt pucker. Maybe getting shot at made me crazy, but ..."

"Yeah, well, I *do* know about it and I don't like it," Hillary cut him off sharply. "Just promise me you won't panic and start waving that thing around. I can't imagine a single plausible scenario in which you would have to use it, and if one does come up, we're probably both dead. Wear it if it makes you feel like a stallion. I just think guns are nothing more than lethal trusses for someone's manhood."

Tom didn't respond but blinked away the sting of Hillary's insult. It was unfair, he thought, especially after he'd been shot at and held at shotgun-point in the same night. He didn't have time or energy to recount for Hillary the personal gun debate he went through before purchasing. Maybe another time. Instead Tom just pulled a small holster out of the coat pocket, leaned forward and clipped it onto the back of his belt.

Sitting in the car, Tom cocked the weapon slowly to get a round into the chamber. He felt Hillary studying him.

"Put the safety on, please," Hillary said.

"But what if I have to draw and fire?"

"Then I guess we're dead, Wyatt Earp. You can leave a note that says, 'Hillary made me keep the safety on' in your pocket for the EMTs to find and share with your next of kin. I'll probably be lying on the next slab over, so I won't mind. You won't have to draw that thing, let alone draw and fire, so let's compromise and leave the safety on."

Tom was actually on board with leaving the safety on, but he didn't really care for Hillary's *tone*. "Did I describe that guy's shotgun earlier? It had a barrel as big around as a baseball." He saw Hillary gathering breath to respond and cut her off. "Okay, okay. We'll compromise. The safety is on. Do you know how to use one of these things?" He clicked on the safety, leaned forward and slipped the gun into the holster.

"Smith & Wesson. Nine millimeter. Looks like a compact, double-action model, satin stainless over polymer, ten in the magazine, one in the pipe."

Day-um.

"Geez. You got a Smith & Wesson tattoo someplace I can't see that not telling me about?"

"My father is a gun nut. He has one just like that, along with about twenty-three other guns. Nice use of our family's money. Other kids went on vacation with their families; we went to Billy's Gun Depot and spent seven hundred dollars on a flintlock pistol. He and my brother thought I couldn't learn anything about guns. They were wrong. As for the tattoo, maybe someday you'll find out, maybe not."

"Just tell me you like hockey," said Tom.

"Hockey? We're about to go up and see a hooker, you're packing a gun and you want to know if I like hockey?"

"Hockey is important, Hillary."

"I like hockey. Love to go watch the Musketeers," she said.

"A Junior A hockey fan! So are we a match made in heaven or what?" Tom asked.

"Jury is still out," Hillary answered, opening the car door. "Bring your phone, please. I'm leaving mine and my bag here." She fished a small ID card holder out of her bag, put it in her back pocket, put her purse under the front seat and got out.

Standing at the front of the car, Tom was very aware of the pistol, which delivered a sharp pain as it pressed against the small of his back.

Keeping the safety on will at least keep me from shooting myself in the ass.

He could see how carrying this thing around all day *would* be a pain in the ass, literally and figuratively. Hillary's stern opposition to the gun notwithstanding, Tom felt justified in carrying it given the events of the last three days. He had no idea under what circumstances his gun might see the light of day. He hoped he didn't have to worry about it and could soon return it to its hiding place in his house.

Donning the sport coat instantly triggered beads of sweat that tumbled down the center of his back, stemmed only by the press of his holster. He quickened his pace to get into the air-conditioned Regal, hoping Hillary would match his stride. Once inside, Hillary came up beside Tom as he flapped the front of his coat open and closed, enjoying the cooling sensation of the air reaching his sweaty back. He walked toward a darkened, secluded corner with Hillary in tow.

"Stand right there for a second," Tom said, slipping into the corner behind Hillary.

"This is a strange way to get a look at my ass."

"If I wanted to see your ass, I'd be adult about it and let you go up some stairs in front of me," Tom said as he tugged on the holster wedged uncomfortably in his back. He pulled it hard to the right, then discovered the leather strap that kept the gun from coming out of the holster on its own had come unsnapped. He refastened it as Hillary glanced over her shoulder.

"What's the matter, gun got you by the butt?" Hillary said.

"Hilarious. Why don't you say it louder or just hold up a sign that says 'Packing Heat' with a giant arrow to my head."

"You remind me of when men stand up to rearrange them-selves because it's on the wrong side of their trousers, as if no one will notice the self-grope."

"Can you *please* just keep your mind off my trousers?" Tom said, stepping back in front of her and adjusting his coat with an exaggerated movement. "Business before pleasure."

"I'll try to tame my raging desire, but it won't be easy. Who were you hiding from? There's nobody here but us."

Tom turned to find the room empty except for the desk clerks who were around the corner, out of sight and hearing.

"Maybe I *did* just want to look at your ass. Nothing in the *Iowa Code* against that," Tom said. Returning to business, he contin-ued: "What do you think about just going up and knocking on her door?"

"What if she has a customer?"

"How about I call her room and find out how she feels about meeting me again."

"What if she says no?" Hillary asked. "Then we're out of luck."

"She's going to say no when she has a second chance at this?" Tom said, brushing his hand through his hair, adjusting his coat and doing a quarter turn in front of Hillary, who just shook her head.

Tom smiled at his own wit. "If she says no, we go home and you call in the state police. But she won't say no, will she? Not if our theories about her are correct."

Hillary shrugged and nodded. Tom picked up the nearby house phone and dialed 1-1-9-1, flashing back to his first encoun-ter with Stephanie and already girding his loins, almost literally, against a second assault. Hillary's presence would greatly fortify his defense.

Her purring voice answered on the third ring. "Yes?"

"Hello Stephanie. Tom Kingman. Remember me? Last time we saw each other I was checking your bathroom tile and you were checking something else."

"I've been waiting for your call. I'm impressed you found me before I knew you were looking. Not surprised, but definitely impressed."

"I'd like to come up and continue our conversation," Tom said.

"I'd love to continue what we started, Tom. That would be wonderful. I have some time—enough time—before my next meeting. Come on up."

Tom hung up and turned to Hillary, again feeling the chafe of his hidden holster and hoping he didn't look too flushed.

CHAPTER 29

"Let me guess," Hillary said, raising an eyebrow, "she offered to finish the job."

"Not in those words, but that was the subtext." Tom walked beside Hillary to the elevators, his hand resting between her shoulder blades, trying to look like the casual, dashing young escort. Tom imagined they instead looked like the parents of two with a minivan right outside. Hillary, he thought, had certainly dressed the part. Tom couldn't decide if that was good or bad. But then again, look who was talking. Mr. Fashion Plate.

As they waited for the elevator, Hillary reached a hand around Tom's waist. Tom couldn't decide if she was reaching for him on her own or as part of her role. Hillary's forearm landed on top of the gun, causing both of them to jump. Hillary dropped her hand and flashed Tom a glare as the elevator doors opened.

They rode alone up to the eleventh floor and found the room. Hillary stepped out of sight of the peephole and nodded to Tom. He knocked and door popped open almost immediately. No door chain this time. Stephanie extended her jeweled hand. He instinctively took it and was nearly inside the room when he remembered Hillary. He grabbed Hillary's arm and pulled her into the room with him.

Stephanie's face went blank as she released Tom's hand and

backed into the room. "Who's this?"

"A friend of mine. She's helping me work on this story."

"*She's* helping you?"

Calm her down. Reassure her. Send signals that Hillary is no threat to her.

"Yes. She's a colleague."

Of sorts.

"But I thought this was going to be a private meeting, Tom," Stephanie said, brushing some unseen particle off her business suit lapel. Hillary stood silently against the closed door.

"Hello. I'm Hillary Reed," she said, extending her hand.

Stephanie turned and walked toward the back of a sofa that faced the fireplace in the opposite wall. The room was remarkably like the one Tom was in before. A bit smaller, but the same fireplace and expensive pseudo-antique furnishings. He could smell the fresh flowers on a small table near the door—or was it Stephanie's perfume? The painting on the wall was a very good print of an early 1900s city street scene.

Stephanie wore a tan business suit with a skirt so short it would grind any board meeting to a halt and shoes with heels a couple inches above "office appropriate." Tom didn't bother to mask his gaze as he appreciated her tanned, toned, naked legs. She turned back to her guests, walked to the back of the couch and spun around like a runway model. Stephanie perched on the back of the couch, crossing her left leg over her right with unnatural slowness. The jury was still out on underwear, but the verdict was definitely in regarding her blouse: absent.

Tom sensed Hillary moving to his left and managed to break off his stare. Stephanie was in front of him on the right, putting Tom's body between the two women. Hillary gently brushed her hand against Tom's butt.

Just letting me know she's there.

"We would like to know how you know so much about the

death of Mr. Pollard," Hillary said.

Shit. Hillary is just charging in like a skinny-pants-wearing bull. This isn't an interrogation room. The law can't compel anyone to answer here. What the hell is she doing? I'm supposed to ask the questions. This is my source.

"Stephanie," Tom interjected, trying to reverse the hardening in Stephanie's face and resume control of the conversation, "let's start with your first name. Maybe I should call you Brenda?"

"My working name is Stephanie, as I'm sure you've confirmed. Let's just leave it at that."

"Why did you call Tom?" Hillary said. Tom turned and glared at Hillary, flaring his eyes wide open for a split second to deliver a visual curse word.

Too direct. Too damn prosecutorial. You're going to spook her.

"We think you know a lot about the shooting," Tom said, tossing Hillary another 'please shut up' look, "and we'd like to talk a little more."

"Then lose Gloria Steinem here," Stephanie said.

Great. Hillary and Stephanie get all pissy, she throws us out and I end up figuratively but not literally screwed.

"Can we all just calm down for a second?" Tom kept himself between the two women. The cherry on top of this craziness would be a full-on chick fight. "We just want to talk a few minutes and then we leave, forever if you want."

"Fine," Stephanie said. "But *she* can wait in the hall."

So much for subtle and circular. Time to let the cat out of bag.

"No, *she* can't," Tom said. "Hillary is an Assistant Woodbury County Attorney, a prosecutor. We're working together on the Pollard shooting and some interesting related cases. We think you can help us."

"Prosecutor?" Stephanie asked, her face dissolving into shock. "Why didn't you just bring the cops? I thought reporters kept anonymous sources anonymous."

"People are starting to shoot at Tom," Hillary said. "We've gone way beyond getting a news story. We're talking about serious crimes. Drugs, murder, attempted murder. It's time to do the smart thing and make yourself a deal before all the deals are taken. We only have room for one cooperative witness and whoever gets there first, well, they get the best deal."

"I read about your 'accident,' Tom," Stephanie said, turning to Tom as if Hillary didn't exist. "How much do you know now?"

"Bryan Van Grunner is dirty," Tom said, emboldened by his early success in defusing Stephanie's initial hesitancy, "but he's too small-time to do this by himself."

"A-plus," Stephanie said, "and he's disappointing in bed, unless you like to have sex with a well-built jackhammer." Stephanie looked at Hillary, who replied with a raised eyebrow.

"Does this go farther in the department?" Tom asked.

"Why should I tell you with Ms. Prosecutor standing right there?"

"Because I'm the one making the deals today," Hillary responded, almost before Stephanie finished her sentence. "You tell me all about your friend, Barry—off the record for now—and I'll see what I can do about getting you a little probation and maybe some community service work pulling weeds in the highway medians. Although they would probably issue you a different outfit for that."

"I'm sure you'd have something perfect for it in your closet," Stephanie said. She moved to a round table just in back of the couch to Tom's left, casually slid open a small drawer and dipped her hand in. Tom flashed back to the shooting on West Jarred.

His right hand was on its way to his gun while his left moved toward Hillary's shoulder.

Draw, shoulder Hillary out of the way and fire. Remember the safety.

Stephanie's hand flashed in the drawer and she paused to

rummage while talking about going back to Omaha or something, Tom wasn't sure.

Here we go.

His hand slid under his sport coat and closed in on the butt of his holstered gun. He tried to remember what side the safety was on. He grabbed the gun butt, popped off the strap that kept the weapon in place and clicked off the safety.

Tom had complete control of his gun, holding his impulse to draw until he at least saw a glint of steel in Stephanie's hand.

As Stephanie took her hand out of the drawer Tom saw a glint—of cellophane, not steel. Cigarette pack cellophane. Tom exhaled and opened his hand in a spasm, allowing his gun to flop back into its holster. He left the safety off and dropped his hand back under his butt before easing it slowly around to the front of his leg, trying not to draw Stephanie's attention. He reached up and touched his jacket lapel to show Hillary that his hand was empty.

Cigarettes. Judas priest. Cigarettes.

Tom could imagine himself telling the cops, "She pulled a pack of cigs on me, man," as they hauled Stephanie away. Tom hated cigarettes, but not that much. Nothing uglied up a beautiful face faster than a lit cigarette.

"I told you before—think Chamber of Commerce," Stephanie said, punctuating her sentence with the sizzle of a match strike. The tip of her thin, dark cigarette glowed as she started it with two long drags. The mouth Tom had once wanted so badly now reminded him of an industrial chimney. He knew Hillary could cite the *Iowa Code* section she was violating by smoking in her hotel room.

Resistance is no longer futile.

"You know, Tom, we could still work something out privately," Stephanie said as the smoke rose and she moved to open the sliding glass door for ventilation. She turned to Tom and unbuttoned the top button of her blazer with her free hand, confirming Tom's earlier verdict that there was nothing underneath. It was a good bet that there wasn't anything under the skirt, either. Tom focused on the cigarette smoke, intentionally breathing it in, effectively using the resulting nausea to armor himself against Stephanie's sexual firepower.

"Get rid of your friend and let's get much more comfortable," Stephanie said, turning back toward the couch and allowing her blazer to gape open and give Tom an Academy Award red-carpet-worthy shot of to-the-waist cleavage.

"I don't think so," Hillary interjected. "Better button up and we'll all be more comfortable." Tom hoped he looked cool and uninterested to Hillary.

Bond, Tom Bond.

"Maybe you can even join us, Ms. Prosecutor. Just keep your mouth shut—I mean don't say anything—and it might be interesting. I don't mind it on special occasions. If nothing else, you could run the video camera."

An image of Stephanie and Hillary in a naked embrace barged its way into Tom's head causing an almost imperceptible nose crinkle. He looked quickly at Hillary, using her calm exterior to fortify his own cool.

"That's a very interesting offer, Stephanie," Tom said, "but first I need your help with my story. Why don't you tell us what you know and then let Hillary see what she can do for you?"

"It's over." Hillary jumped in like a hockey teammate joining Tom's attack on goal. "Your client is done. We're closing in on him."

That, Tom knew, was a lie. But Hillary's verbal blow still seemed to pack the desired punch.

"Of course you already know who the boss is. Your girlfriend here cleverly dropped his name a minute ago."

"Barry Garrett," Tom said.

Stephanie nodded, just barely.

"What's the story?" Tom asked. "Why did Garrett want Pollard dead? Garrett's got a ton of money from his trucking business."

"You know, maybe I do want to make a deal," Stephanie said. "One like that woman who blew the president back in the late nineties. What was it, 'transactional immunity?' That means immunity from prosecution not just for prostitution, but from any other things that may come up. Maybe you should come back when you have an agreement for me to sign. We could blow this town open."

"Transactional immunity?" Hillary said, crossing behind Tom to his other side, again brushing his butt with her hand as she went.

I like her new 'I'm here' signal.

"You know that means broad immunity from prosecution for anything you admit to under oath. This isn't a case with Constitutional implications, Stephanie. Let's stay realistic. You'll have to give me a sample of what you know before I can go to my boss for any kind of deal."

"How do you think Garrett got all of his money?" Stephanie said. "Delivering truckloads of TVs? Maybe. But maybe one of those TV boxes didn't have a TV in it. And maybe those trips back from the Mexican TV plant included some undocumented cargo tucked neatly out of sight. Something you could cook into a powder worth a lot of money around here. I never touch the stuff because I've got all the energy I need, but I know a good recipe."

"Methamphetamine," Tom said. More a confirmation than a revelation.

"Oh, but you knew that," Stephanie said. "The action in this town is all about crank."

"But how did they set up Pollard?" Tom asked. "I was there. It was self-defense."

Stephanie glanced at Hillary. "Are we off the record?"

Hillary didn't respond.

"Then, *hypothetically*, of course, Pollard could have been an idiot," Stephanie said softly, turning her attention back to Tom. She stepped forward and brought her lips to within a few inches of his, running her hand over his chest as she spoke. "He might have even been an idiot addicted to crank."

Stephanie finished the statement by lightly pecking Tom on the lips. Tom smelled her cigarette breath. A casual step, drag of cigarette and turn, and Stephanie was back at the couch. "Maybe someone just waited until Van Grunner was on duty, got Pollard cranked up and told him his wife was humping anyone with a cock. They might have even given him some expertly altered photos that appeared to show Joyce getting boned by some guy."

For such an elegant exterior she's sure fluent in trailer park talk.

Stephanie paused to take the final drag off of her cigarette and noisily exhale.

"You know what that stuff does to you. Makes you paranoid, freaky. They would have known he would go right home and smack her around. Then Van Grunner *hypothetically* calls someone who calls the cops on a burner phone, screams into it that someone's killing his or her neighbor, gives the address, hangs up and throws the phone in McCook Lake. Now Van Grunner would get a legitimate call from dispatch to go over there. I imagine he might even wait down the block for the call, pretend it's news to him and roll up to the door."

"Clever," Hillary said, "and difficult to prove."

"If someone actually pulled off my *hypothetical* scenario, it certainly would have been clever and difficult to prove." Stephanie narrowed her eyes. "And if Van Grunner shot a bit early, who would know? Besides, no one would believe the bitch wife. When some other cop showed up, Van Grunner might have gotten some luck. Pollard might have been so wired he took a shot at them. That's a lucky bounce. Then, if it turned out that a reporter witnessed the seemingly justified shooting, that's another bonus."

Stephanie ground out her cigarette in an ashtray on the round table. "Of course you'd want that reporter to be alive to testify that it was a legit shooting. Maybe you shoot at him or threaten him, but you wouldn't want to kill him. You're a lucky boy, Tom. Being the star witness has kept you alive these last two days."

"But why murder Pollard?" Tom said, again looking at Hillary, who glanced back at him.

Stephanie shook her head. "Who said *anyone* murdered Pollard? I was just thinking out loud how it might have happened, *hypothetically*. If you want me to talk more about it, I'm going to have to know what's in it for me."

Stephanie grabbed the open pack of cigarettes off the table and dropped them back into the still-open drawer and shut it. "You know, Tom," she said, "you and I were almost in the movies. When you first visited, I had a video camera behind the glass fireplace doors. If Barry hadn't come back so soon, we would have made art together. We could have gotten big money for it on the internet. I've been thinking about starting my own website offering photos and interesting video clips to subscribers. Lots of women are getting rich off sites like that."

"Huh. I wouldn't know about that." He glanced at Hillary. "It wasn't my best side, anyway." He looked at the smoked fireplace doors, imagining how the camera would have been set up.

"Don't worry; it's not set up tonight. But the camera's in the back if you want to make a movie later."

"Why record you and Tom?" Hillary asked.

"Barry's idea," Stephanie said, looking at Hillary. "Blackmail. Tom's not married, but everyone has a mom and dad who might not want their son to become an internet porn star. They seem especially shocked by such lurid behavior here in Podunk, Iowa. What would having something like that on the internet do for Tom's golden reputation? *Someone* would probably post it to those free porn sample sites. That's the beauty of smaller towns, everybody knows everything and it doesn't take much to make you a pariah."

Stephanie looked at Hillary from head to toe. "I don't think you'd look good on film, Ms. Prosecutor. The camera adds ten pounds, you know."

"I'll take your word for it, as an expert," Hillary said. "Too bad Garrett came back and broke up your plan."

Stephanie let out a small laugh. "It wasn't a total loss, though. I got some good video of Barry and me. It will come in handy if he ever forgets who kept him warm at night while his bulimic wife was puking up dinner. The video wasn't as good as you and I would have been, Tom. I would have enjoyed that much more, and that always comes through in the film."

So, she's an artist *at heart I guess.*

"So why help Tom get away?" Hillary asked. Tom moved over to the back of the couch, letting his right butt cheek touch it.

"Barry thought I was going to invite Tom up the following night. He had no idea you were here." She turned to Hillary. "Once Barry crashed our party, I decided to give Tom a show, which he seemed to enjoy very much. Some guys love to watch."

Tom looked down, avoiding eye contact with Hillary.

"And I got my insurance video in case Barry decided to cut me off. A businessman like him wouldn't want a video like that playing around town. And Barry likes to talk after sex, so let's just say I know more than what position Barry Garrett prefers."

Hillary pulled her shoulders back and clasped her hands at the small of her back. "Very interesting. Now why don't you just button up and we can all go down to my office and make our own video?" Hillary said, raising her voice. "One where we all keep our clothes on and you talk about everything you know, including Mr. Garrett's favorite positions, if you think that's pertinent. Then I'll see what we can offer for your testimony."

Stephanie put her hands on the back of a chair next to the round table, her gaze circling up to the ceiling. She curved her shoulders forward, her blazer again gapped, giving Tom a clear view of most of her breasts.

They heard a noisy group walk past in the corridor.

"It's tempting," Stephanie said finally. She stood and plucked the matches off the table with her right hand, and then transferred them to her left hand. "But, it's not going to work. Because by the time we get downtown, Garrett will be somewhere over Kansas, about to make a hard left for Jamaica."

"How do you know that?" Hillary said.

"It's quite a story," Stephanie said, rubbing the matchbook cover with her thumb, "one that Tom would do justice to in print, I would think. Seems that Barry has been humping Donna, his company's Chief Financial Officer, and now the two of them figure it's time to relocate their business."

Hillary moved next to Tom so that they were both directly in front of Stephanie and perpendicular to the back of the couch. She gave Stephanie a quizzical look.

"As Mr. Kingman would say, 'I've got my sources,'" Stephanie said. Tom let the small of his back press against the back of a couch, just to reassure himself that his gun was still there.

"I found out today that Barry and Donna are running off. With the combination of this Pollard thing getting ugly and some rival drug dealers carving up his territory, Barry decided it was time to jump on a plane to nowhere with his slut accountant. I'm sure they have a few million squirreled away."

"What, did they call you up to say goodbye or something?"

If we circle around this thing anymore we'll wear a path in the carpet.

"No. As I said, I have my sources."

Tom looked at Hillary, knitting his eyebrows. Hillary gave a tiny shrug.

Stephanie opened the matchbook and then slid out the cigarette drawer. Tom looked at the floor, his brain racing through possible next moves while bracing for another onslaught of cigarette smoke. "I don't suppose you'd care for a cigarette," she said, pausing to look at Hillary, who faced the table drawer about three feet from Stephanie.

"No, thank you," Hillary said. "I don't smoke."

"I hope you don't mind if I . . . "

Tom was too shocked to even extend his arms as he tumbled. By the time his shoulder sank into the seat cushions of the couch, he realized someone had pushed him over. He was still trying to sort out who and why as he cartwheeled over and smacked his ass smartly onto the floor.

What the fuck?

CHAPTER 30

When Tom scrambled to his knees he saw Hillary and Stephanie struggling on the other side of the couch, in front of the round table. "Hillary," Tom blurted in her general direction. "What the hell are you doing?"

Hillary and Stephanie tumbled to the ground, their bodies entwined in a heap. Stephanie's skirt exposed her left buttock with Hillary pinned underneath. They both grunted as Hillary's left hand maintained its white-knuckle grip on Stephanie's right wrist. Stephanie's wrist writhed violently like an angry snake with a black steel head.

Gun. Where the hell did that come from?

Tom lurched to his feet, reached for his gun and found nothing but empty holster.

Shit.

He groped the holster as if he expected the gun to magically reappear then looked at his feet, frantically scanning the floor for the weapon. He checked underneath the couch and then started pulling couch cushions off as Hillary and Stephanie continued to wrestle on the floor, legs and free arms flailing in blurs of motion.

He pulled off the seat cushions one at a time.

Shit.

Where.

Is.

That.

Gun?

Tom threw the couch's center back cushion against the wall hard enough to send two framed pictures crashing to the floor. His gun was wedged in the back of the couch, butt up. Stephanie and Hillary struggled back to their feet, bobbing up on the other side of the couch like swimmers breaking the water's surface simultaneously less than two feet from Tom. They faced each other— Stephanie to Tom's right and Hillary to his left. Hillary clung to Stephanie's wrist as Stephanie punched at her with her free hand.

Stephanie landed a hard left to Hillary's temple and ripped her gun hand free. Tom could tell Stephanie planned to sweep her arm around as if throwing an underhand softball pitch and shoot Hillary in the abdomen.

Too late to grab his own gun, Tom lunged across the couch and punched Stephanie just behind her left eye. Stephanie gave an involuntary grunt and fell away from Tom and Hillary, sending her gun skittering across the carpet. Tom brutally yanked Hillary across to his side of the couch and grabbed for his gun only to realize Hillary had already grabbed it and, in a split second, was on her feet in a regulation police firing stance with Tom's gun aimed at Stephanie's chest.

Pretty hot.

"That's enough, Stephanie," Hillary said in a calm but loud voice.

Stephanie froze sitting halfway up on the floor, her gun nowhere in sight. Tom could hear Hillary and Stephanie's labored breathing as Stephanie slowly sat up fully, then stood up and backed away, blood oozing from a cut near the corner of her mouth onto her left breast. Tom got to his feet, making sure to stay out of Hillary's line of fire.

Stephanie, now without shoes, seemed much shorter. Hillary

squeezed Tom's gun—finger on the trigger—keeping it aimed between Stephanie's fully exposed breasts. "We all need to calm down," Hillary said as she regained her normal breathing. Tom stripped off his own rumpled jacket and let it drop over the back of the couch.

"Jesus, does everyone I meet in this town pack heat or what?" Tom panted. Stephanie looked past the gun and into Hillary's eyes, managing to look cold and predatory even in her exposed condition.

"I think we've chatted enough," Hillary said. "Now I've got assault with a deadly weapon and maybe attempted murder. So we're going downtown, and you can either do the time, or you can give us what we need for search warrants for Garrett's house, car, and company. At least we'll take down the meth ring, if not the ring leader."

Stephanie shook her head and continued as if Hillary hadn't even spoken.

"I was going to kill you with your pants down tonight, Tom, with a big knife that's in the end table. I'm not sure why, to be honest. Maybe just my way of showing Barry how a real Alpha takes care of business. But when you went and invited the Prosecutor here to our party, well I was disappointed and intrigued. I thought it would be fun to have you act your parts. The intrepid reporter. The prosecutor so tough half her coworkers think she's a dyke."

News to me.

"You should really take her down and fuck her, Tom. I think she could use it. You both disappointed me with your cliché offers of protection and deals for me turning on Barry. So unimaginative."

Tom got to his feet and glanced at Hillary. Stephanie didn't seem to realize that Hillary was armed and dangerous and Stephanie was not.

Hillary barely suppressed a smile.

"Tom, call 9-1-1, please," Hillary said.

Tom patted his pants pockets and checked his coat, which was still draped on the couch. No phone.

"Lost my phone," Tom said, going to one knee to again look under the couch. He spotted the room phone, smashed on the floor during Stephanie and Hillary's brawl.

"There's a phone in the bedroom," Hillary said. "We'll use it to call my friends who have a nice place for you to spend the night. They're going to love you at the women's prison in Mitchellville."

"No, you don't, honey," Stephanie said, slowly moving to block the path to the bedroom.

"Stephanie," Hillary said. "Come on. Don't do something irrational. Mitchellville is better than the morgue."

"No, it's not." Stephanie leaned against a chair to move it two feet, revealing her gun on the floor.

Of course she finds her own gun before we do. This day just keeps getting weirder.

"Stephanie," Tom said slowly, moving a step toward her while taking care to stay out of Hillary's line of fire. "We can still have that talk. You can still be the one who takes down Blade-Garrett. I'll make you famous for that."

Stephanie's jacket draped back over her breasts as she moved her weight from leg to leg.

"We *could* have been a team, Tom," she said as calm returned to her voice. "I fuck information out of whoever you want me to and you write all about it. There's no man alive who can keep things from me, including you, if Barry hadn't shown up when he did."

Stephanie reached down and picked up her gun, slowly raising herself back up to full height with the gun at her side.

Fucking shoot her!

Hillary glanced back at Tom, her eyes flashing uncertainty. Tom sensed tension run up Hillary's upper torso as Stephanie slowly stood up. Tom felt like what he was, an unarmed bystander.

"Now I have to kill you both and then go to the airport and

kill those two," Stephanie said. "I'll just drive back to Omaha and fade out of sight for a few years. I love L.A. This town is a shithole anyway. I got him off for four years, and he's just going to jet off with that bitch accountant of his and bone her senseless in Aruba or somewhere? 'Thanks for the fuck, Stephanie. Have a nice life.'"

Stephanie took another step toward Tom. He felt Hillary step back slightly.

"Well, fuck you, Barry," Stephanie accented her points with wild hand gestures, seemingly forgetting that one of her hands held a gun.

"Enough talk," Hillary said. "Drop the gun, *now*, or I'll kill you where you stand."

Dirty Hillary. Make my day.

Stephanie turned her head to Tom. "We would have been great together. Why did you ruin that by bringing the prosecutor? I trusted you and now you've forced me to do this. I'll be seeing you in your dreams."

Then Stephanie turned to Hillary and raised her gun.

"Stephanie!" Tom yelled just as Hillary fired. Twice.

The shock of the gunshot made Tom recoil and grab both ears, trying to press the pain from them.

"Jesus," Tom said, not sure if he was praying or swearing.

Stephanie lurched back as the nine millimeter slugs hit, her arms and legs flailing in impossible directions until she landed with a thud, still holding her gun.

"Dammit," Hillary blurted, lowered her gun.

Tom thought he might start hyperventilating as the lingering smell of gunpowder swept over him and his ears slowly came back to life. They both inched toward the couch, trying to improve their view of Stephanie on the other side, Hillary keeping Tom's gun ready.

Stephanie sprawled on the floor, her right hand out to the side and left one folded over her chest. Her eyes and mouth were open, and her expression was blank. A pool of blood rapidly formed under her upper back where Hillary's shots exited. Tom scanned the far wall until he found the divot left by a slug.

The next thing he knew, Tom was on his knees, heart racing. He flashed back to Pollard sliding down the screen in front of him back on West Jarred. "I think I'm going to be sick," he said with a cough.

Hillary's breathing grew more and more relaxed with each passing second as she moved resolutely over to Tom. She reset the gun's safety and forcefully lodged the weapon back in Tom's holster.

"You're entitled to one 'I told you so,'" Hillary said, kissing him lightly on the cheek.

This woman has steel ovaries.

Hillary walked to Stephanie's body and checked for a pulse. It was a formality.

Pretty good shooting for someone who doesn't like guns.

Hillary knelt and then sat back, her feet tucked under her butt. She closed her eyes and her face went blank for five seconds, before her eyes fluttered open again.

Amen.

Hillary went to Tom, now back on his feet, and put her hand on his sweat-soaked back just above the newly holstered weapon.

"She was going to kill us both," Hillary said, speaking slowly, her head a foot from Tom's. "What choice did we ... I ... have?"

"*We* didn't have a choice," Tom said. "I would have shot her when she went for her gun. What were you thinking?"

"I was praying."

This woman prays more than the Pope.

"Praying? Jesus Chri —" Tom shot a glance at Hillary and cut himself off.

"That's how I usually start," Hillary said. "Look, she went for it slowly. I figured she wasn't coming up firing. I thought we could still talk her out of using it. Maybe I gambled with both our lives, but I just couldn't shoot her when I didn't feel threatened."

"Yeah, well, she wouldn't be oozing blood all over the floor if we hadn't come here. That's something for us all to pray about for the next year," Tom said turning to Hillary. "You heard her. I left her no choice."

"She had lots of choices," Hillary said. "You didn't make her do anything. You didn't make her pull out that gun. You didn't make her want to kill us. She said she was going to kill you with a knife, remember? She could have cut her losses by coming downtown with us."

"What about you, Hillary? You just shot someone. Self-defense, sure, but . . ."

Hillary hugged herself briefly and took a big breath. "Speaking of things to pray about."

Tom replaced Hillary's self-embrace with one of his own.

"Yeah, well, speaking as the one unarmed person at this party, I appreciate your marksmanship," Tom said as they came back to arms' length after a ten-second hug. "Pretty sure self-defense will be an easy sell. You're hardly some gangster attorney who goes around killing women. The gun we claim she pulled is right there beside her, complete with her finger prints and not ours. And besides, what choice did you have?"

Hillary nodded, her business face returning. "I better go call the police to make sure they're on their way. Then it sounds like we should get to the airport."

"I think you can skip the ambulance," Tom said.

Too much?

"I think you're right."

Whew.

Hillary walked around the end of the couch, glancing again at Stephanie's body. It lay like the main course on the elegant white carpet plate, garnished with a growing cranberry-colored blood pool. Hillary headed for the phone in the bedroom. Just as she reached the phone, the hotel room door burst open, causing Tom to spin around involuntarily.

A big man moved through the doorway, holding a large, dark semiautomatic pistol aimed at Tom.

CHAPTER 31

"Well, if it isn't the media," Bryan Van Grunner sneered as he made sure the door closed, scanned the room and advanced gun-first toward Tom. Van Grunner's eyes darted twice to Stephanie's body. "I see you've met Stephanie, and that you've put away the pen and pulled out the sword. Let's see it, fuckhead."

"See what?"

"Your dick. What do you think? Don't make me shoot you in the face and check the body for it later. The gun. Let me see it. Two fingers. Very, very slow."

Without taking his eyes off Van Grunner, Tom tried to sense where Hillary was in the bedroom. She wasn't by the phone. He could see it still on its hook in the bedroom.

Tom looked down and reached back to unholster his gun. As he looked back toward Van Grunner, Tom let his eyes arc through the bedroom door. He saw a flash of what could have been Hillary's head, peering around the threshold. Tom hesitated, searching for a plan.

"Why did you do it, Bryan?" Tom slowly produced the gun. "Why hook up with someone like Barry Garrett?"

"Because I wanted to help my fellow man," Van Grunner said. "You try dealing with the filth of life for forty thousand a year, especially when you can give them what they want and make five or ten times that. They'd get it anyway. I figured I might as well get a piece of the action. Plus the badge means I get to smack faggots and minorities around legally. Now give me the gun before I shoot you, press this gun into poor Stephanie's hand, put your gun back in your dead hand and then go have a beer."

"But why kill Pollard?"

"Because he shot at me. You were there. I had to kill him."

My being there has been the gift that keeps on giving during this whole adventure. Stephanie told us the truth about that much. If you are as stupid as I think you are, you'll tell me.

"That's not what Stephanie said," Tom said. "She said you went out there to kill him and just got lucky that Neal and I were there and that Pollard was stupid enough to take a shot at you. Having witnesses was like hitting the Alibi Lotto. Barry wanted him dead, for some reason, and since you're Barry's boy, you scurried out and took care of it."

"Is that what Stephanie imagined?" Van Grunner said pressing his lips into a theatrical frown. "Stephanie," Van Grunner said, mock disappointment dripping from his voice as he turned to the corpse, "after all we've meant to each other."

He tapped Stephanie's leg with his foot. "Come on. Wake up and tell the nice reporter that you were kidding." Van Grunner kicked Stephanie's leg hard. "Get up, Steph, and tell him you were kidding."

You really are a fuck.

Van Grunner held an exaggerated shrug for a second. "I guess she's not in the mood to talk right now." He looked again at Tom. "I know how this all played out. You two had a lovers' spat. Or maybe you did business and she started to blackmail you."

Van Grunner shrugged again. "So you shot her. And, you know what? I'm not going to shoot you. I'm going to take you in for it and laugh every time I see stories about it in your own paper. Good thing there *happened* to be an off-duty police officer in the hotel who heard the shots. Now, I'm afraid I'm going to have to place you under arrest. You have the right to remain silent. Anything you say can and will be used against you in a court of law. But I'm sure you studied these rights when you were a college boy. Or maybe Hillary Reed filled you in. Or vice versa. So let's just go downtown and get you fitted for an orange jumpsuit and some waist chains. But first, I'll take that gun. *Now.*"

About twenty feet behind Van Grunner, Tom saw a brief wink of a red LED. It was gone again in less than a second. Van Grunner pulled his pistol's hammer back with an enormous thumb. Tom held up one hand like a traffic cop and presented his gun.

"Now that *is* disappointing," Van Grunner said. "We've got chicks on the force who have bigger guns than that."

"Let's ask Stephanie if it's big enough." Tom regretted saying it even as it left his mouth.

"Maybe I'll just shoot you in the crotch with it and then I'll ask you," Van Grunner said. "Throw it over there, smart ass." Tom made a feeble throw. The gun landed about two feet to Van Grunner's right.

"You pack a chick's gun and you throw like a girl," Van Grunner said. "Now, turn around, because I have to cuff you and take you downtown. I hear they're running short of bitches at the penitentiary in Fort Madison. Your smooth, narrow ass will be a big hit in the shower. Oh, and I wouldn't count on Stephanie's gun being around when the other boys in blue arrive."

Tom saw the red pinpoint in the back of the room again.

"Well done, officer." Hillary's voice knifed through the darkness, clear and confident. Van Grunner spun around. For a second Tom feared Van Grunner would fire blindly.

Tom collapsed on his gun, scurried around the end of the couch and took aim at Van Grunner between the back couch cushions.

"Who the fuck is back there?" Van Grunner said, swinging his gun in wide arcs from Tom to the source of Hillary's voice while backing toward the door.

"Assistant Woodbury County Attorney Hillary Reed, officer," the voice said. Tom could see the outline of Hillary's body in the shadows as she took a step forward, one Cyclops red pinpoint eye in the middle of her head.

"Hillary Reed, I should have known you were back there," Van Grunner said, his smirk returning. "You were probably just getting your clothes back on from boinking Scoop here. Maybe Stephanie didn't like it, or vice versa. A threesome gone bad. Is that why you killed her, Tom?"

"Tom didn't kill anyone, officer. We came to talk to Stephanie about the death of Mr. Pollard; she produced a gun and attempted to kill me. In the ensuing struggle, I shot Stephanie with Mr. Kingman's pistol."

Pretty formal language, especially toward someone who's swinging a cocked gun around.

Hillary suddenly stepped out from the shadows, revealing the red LED dot on the front of a small video camera she held out in front of her. Van Grunner straightened up when he saw the video camera, lowering his gun slightly.

"What is this, home movie night?" Van Grunner asked, his smirk fading.

"I found this in the back while you and Mr. Kingman were discussing this case. Apparently Stephanie liked to document some of her activities. I can see how you would suspect Mr. Kingman of murdering Stephanie, at least preliminarily, until you've had a chance to interview all the witnesses and examine that gun near Stephanie's body. I've been videotaping your police work here for the last few minutes and also took the liberty of calling for backup. But I think you can put your weapon away now and we'll all just wait for other officers to arrive."

"And why should I do that?"

"Because you're going to be smart this time, officer." Hillary spoke without looking away from the video camera view panel. "You're going to allow me to present investigators with this recording, wherein you describe how you shot and killed Chuck Pollard in self-defense and pursuant to your duties as a police officer. Of course there is the matter of selling drugs for Mr. Garrett, but I'm sure the court will take into account your cooperation in bringing Mr. Garrett and his associates to justice. That is, of course, if we manage to arrest him before he flees."

Van Grunner looked down at the floor for a few seconds, his gun semi-lowered.

"You didn't call the police," Van Grunner said.

With the camera in her right hand, Hillary held up her left hand, turning a cellphone toward Van Grunner so he and Tom could see the "911" across the screen.

"I found this next to the camera," Hillary said, holding up the phone. "Now we're on tape at police headquarters as well."

"This is Assistant County Attorney Hillary Reed," Hillary said loud enough for the speakerphone feature to pick it up. "I need police at the Regal Hotel, room 1191."

Hillary lowered the phone, ignoring the dispatcher's series of questions, and addressed Van Grunner: "Officer Van Grunner, it's time to be smart. It's over. There's probably a crowd outside right now. You can't fire a shot inside a hotel in downtown Sioux City without drawing a crowd fast. Quit now and you've got a chance to beat murder. Otherwise, you're going down for drug dealing *and* first-degree murder."

Van Grunner looked up at Hillary, then the camera and finally the phone.

"I shot Stephanie," Hillary said. "There's no gunpowder on Tom's hands. Mine must be covered with it. Her prints, not ours, are on her gun. And my prints are on Tom's gun. Your plan won't work. I'm offering you a chance."

Van Grunner looked toward Tom, who ducked lower behind the cushions, keeping Van Grunner's chest in his sights, and then he turned back to Hillary and her camera.

"You think Barry Garrett cares what happens to you?" Hillary asked from behind the viewfinder. "We believe he's at the airport right now, getting ready to run. You can help us catch him and save yourself or you can let him get away and sip cocktails in Belize while you do time at Anamosa."

Van Grunner lowered his gun, flipped it over so he was holding it by the barrel and thrust it at Hillary. "I would like to surrender myself to your custody," Van Grunner mumbled.

Tom got to his feet, his own gun trained on Van Grunner from about ten feet away. He moved around the end of the couch, still aiming, bringing himself closer to Hillary and in front of Van Grunner, who didn't seem to notice.

"Give it to me," Tom said, in a voice that nearly came out as a snarl.

"Shut up, newsboy," Van Grunner snarled back. "Sorry to tell you this, but you still look like a skinny punk with his mom's gun." Van Grunner slapped the gun roughly into Tom's hand, the force momentarily bending his straight arm.

Hillary stopped her video camera, lowered it, and stepped back beside Tom, who had lowered his gun and handed Van Grunner's to her.

"Thank you," Hillary said.

"And my mom's gun was a forty-five," Tom said as he spotted his phone peeking out from under a chair and stooped down to retrieve it. "You can quote me."

Three bangs at the door startled Tom, Hillary, and Van Grunner. "Police, open up."

"Where have I heard that before?" Tom said, holstering his gun and moving to the hotel room door as Hillary punched "end" to disconnect the 9-1-1 call.

Van Grunner slumped into a chair. For a split second, Tom thought he detected a weary sadness on his face. By the time Tom opened the door, Van Grunner's look was back to "defiant."

"Officers," Tom greeted them as they stormed into the room, weapons drawn.

CHAPTER 32

Tom held his hands away from his sides and slumped back against the wall as the police marched past. He was too tired to raise his hands any higher. Three police officers entered the room all at once. One of them crossed immediately to Stephanie's body and knelt to check the pulse, being careful to stay out of the blood.

The other two stood between Hillary, Tom, and Van Grunner, who sat in a chair staring at the floor. They lowered their guns after Hillary set Van Grunner's gun on a table and backed away.

"What the hell is going on here, Bryan?" the tallest, thinnest cop of the group asked Van Grunner.

"Officer," Hillary cut in, "I'm Hillary Reed, Assistant Woodbury County Attorney. Please place Officer Van Grunner under arrest."

She gestured toward the gun on the table. "He has surrendered his weapon to me."

"Yeah, right," the thin cop coughed, taking the gun. "And I'm Chief Banks."

"You're working late, Chief," Tom said, drawing a scowl from the cop. Hillary pulled her driver's license and county attorney ID card holder out of her back pocket and handed them to the cop.

"This video camera contains evidence," Hillary said, holding up the camera as the cop studied her ID. "I would like you to secure it and make sure it gets delivered to police headquarters."

The thin cop glanced at the video camera in Hillary's hand and then returned to studying her identification. He abruptly turned to Tom. "How about you?"

"I've never been much into video," Tom said.

"Funny guy. How about some identification?"

Tom pulled out his wallet and handed over his driver's license and *Sentinel-Leader* ID card. "A reporter?" the thin cop said.

"A reporter," Tom repeated. "And just so everyone doesn't freak out, I want you to know I have a gun on me." Tom turned so the thin cop could see the holster clipped to the back of his belt, being sure to hold his hands away from his body.

A familiar voice came through the doorway. "I'll take that." Neal Powers entered and took Tom's gun out of its holster with a latex-gloved hand. He checked the safety and tucked it into the front of his black, woven leather police gun belt.

"I don't suppose you have a permit to carry a concealed weapon," Neal said.

"I don't suppose I do."

Neal turned to Hillary. "I heard you say we're arresting Officer Van Grunner today. Why is that, Ms. Reed?"

"Hey," the thin cop said, "who died and made you captain, rookie?"

Hillary jumped in. "An eighteen-month investigation has shown Officer Van Grunner is involved with Barry Garrett of Blade-Garrett trucking in trafficking methamphetamine in and around Sioux City. He's admitted as much to Mr. Kingman and me and, by surrendering, indicated his willingness to help us bring Mr. Garrett to justice."

Well, there goes the scoop.

"Come on, Bryan. They've got to be full of shit, right?" the thin cop said.

"Shut up, Leon," Van Grunner said. "I think I better talk to my union rep and a lawyer."

"Wait a minute. Who shot her?" Neal asked, stabbing a finger at Stephanie.

"I did," Hillary said, "with Tom's gun."

"Why?" Neal asked, making sure Tom's gun was still secure in his belt.

"Because she was trying to kill us. She was about to shoot us with that gun on the floor beside her, so I fired in self-defense," Hillary answered. "Stephanie said that Garrett plans to escape in his private jet taking off from the Sioux City airport tonight. Please send someone out there to make sure that does not happen."

"Nobody's doing anything until I call the lieutenant," Leon said.

"Call the lieutenant?" Tom said. "Hillary just said that Garrett is probably gassing up right now. You guys have to send someone to the airport."

"We don't *have to* do anything. And neither of you is calling the shots here," Leon said as he activated his walkie-talkie, still looking at Tom.

"D-7 to L-4," Leon said into the microphone.

"L-4," a voice acknowledged.

Awesome. L-4 is Benning.

Leon walked into the back of the room where Tom heard sporadic words. The cops in the front of the room had their radios turned too low for Tom to hear what Leon was saying. They stood resolutely between Tom and the door.

No exit.

"Neal," Tom said in a very low voice. "Stephanie said Garrett is jetting out of the country. We've got to stop him."

"Who's going to believe you?" Neal replied in an equally hushed tone. "Come on. Barry Garrett? He's huge in this town. A regular philanthropist. We'll have to hear it from Van Grunner before we move on him, and he's going to lawyer up."

"I hope your jurisdiction extends to Trinidad because that's where he'll probably be by tomorrow."

Leon walked back to the group, turning down the volume on his radio as he approached. "The lieutenant said Bryan, Mr. Kingman and Ms. Reed need to take a ride downtown."

"I'll take them," Neal said, glancing quickly at Hillary and Tom.

Leon looked puzzled and then, as if realizing how he looked, tried to compensate with an exaggerated authoritative voice. "You guys can stay here and secure the scene and wait for the meat wagon and the crime scene techs," he said, turning to the other cops in the room. "I'll take Van Grunner. Neal, put reporter boy here in an interview room. Dick Anderson is coming in from home and he'll meet Ms. Reed in the squad room."

"Okay, let's go," Neal said, motioning to the door. Tom crossed the room, picked up his jacket and returned to the group.

"Why do I get the sterile interview room and you get the squad room?" Tom asked Hillary as they walked out. "I bet there are couches, a pop machine, TV, everything in the squad room. I get the plastic chairs and white walls, again."

"I guess it's who you know," Hillary responded with a shrug. To nobody's surprise, there were people in the hall, primarily hotel guests and a few staff members.

Once Tom, Hillary and Neal were alone in the elevator and the doors closed, Tom turned to Neal: "Come on. The bad guy is going to get away, and I know how much you cops hate that. Let's take some initiative. Just drive us to the police station ... by way of the airport ... to make sure they don't have any corporate jets departing for the Dominican Republic right now. What do ya say?"

"I say that I'd like to keep my job," Neal said, without looking at Tom.

"What if you heard it from Van Grunner or even Stephanie? Then would you take a little detour?"

"Van Grunner is with Leon and Stephanie is dead, so I'm not sure how that would be possible."

Tom turned his sport coat over in his arms and reached into the pocket.

He pulled out a small, silver digital audio recorder, still running. "Digital technology is a gift from God, right Hillary?"

"You recorded it?" Hillary said, grabbing Tom's shoulder.

"In high-definition audio."

"You didn't tell me you were recording it," Hillary said, eyes glued to the recorder.

"You'll find I'm full of mystery and unpredictability."

"I'm not sure if I can use that in court."

"I *know* I can use it in print. It's also a nice gesture for us to let our new best friend, Neal, listen to it as he drives us slowly toward police headquarters, keeping in mind all the possible detours to the airport."

The elevator doors cleared to a lobby with more curious guests in it. They maneuvered out the door and Tom spotted a TV news van pulling in. Close call.

Once in the car, Tom said "I'll sit up front so I can play this for you." Without waiting for a reaction, he opened the front door and got in. Neal shrugged, opened the rear door for Hillary, then got into the driver's seat.

Tom was holding the fast-replay button and then pressing the player to his ear to listen for a few seconds. Neal had just cleared the parking lot when Tom gave a satisfied grunt.

"Here it is. Listen." He turned up the volume. The car was an old, out-of-service cruiser primarily used for transporting lieutenants and captains wherever they needed to go around town. Since it never carried prisoners, there was no need for a protective barrier. That allowed Hillary to sit forward so she could hear as well. Tom held up the recorder.

He pushed *play*. The voice was clear but not very loud, and there was a lot of background noise. Still, they could all hear Stephanie incriminate Garrett and talk about his exit plan. Tom clicked off the recorder and looked at Neal.

"So Stephanie, a prostitute, implicated Garrett and Van Grunner before you guys killed her," Neal said, still not looking away from the road. "We're going to need that recording, by the way. Now you want me to drive to the airport to make sure Garrett's not making a run for it? How do you know he won't just drive somewhere?"

"Because he's Barry Garrett, and you can't drive to Jamaica. He'd be spotted right away if he drove somewhere. He might head for Omaha, but he'd be snagged on I-29 in no time. Why would he even do that if he could just jump in his Lear and fly away? Let's hope he takes time to stock the mini-bar before taking off."

Tom glanced at Neal, whose expression hadn't changed.

"Look," Tom said, growing exasperated. "I'm going to call a guy I know at the private flight service at the airport to see if he knows if any small planes are getting ready to leave. Just one call."

"Call him."

Neal wants more sources and confirmation than even the most anal newspaper editor.

Tom fished his phone out of his pocket, found the charter flight service number in a few taps and called.

"Juan? Tom Kingman," Tom said, turning back to the front of the car as he talked. "I know you're at work. Sorry, buddy, but this is the *big* one. I need a huge favor from you and I don't have time to explain. I just need to know if any corporate jets are preparing to depart." Tom paused again, this time looking out the window. They were only a few blocks from the police station.

"Nope, that's not it. Nope. *Jets,* not Joe Farmer's one-seat Piper Cub." There was a pause. "You just got a plan from a corporate jet? Hang on."

Tom put his phone on speaker and said. "Can you repeat what you just said, Juan?"

"I said, we got a corporate jet preparing for a flight to Miami right now."

"Is that Barry Garrett's jet by any chance?" Tom didn't take his eyes off Powers.

"Yep. Like I said, headed for Miami."

And I'm the governor of Iowa.

"Thanks, Juan. I'll call back and explain what this is all about later."

Tom hung up. "Happy?" he said to Neal. "Barry Garrett is topping off fuel right now. You've got probable cause: the recording. Hillary and I reported to you that he's dirty. She's a goddamn prosecutor, for God's sake. What more do you want?"

Neal hit the brakes and turned violently to the left, headed for the interstate on-ramp. "We're going to the airport. Just buckle up and shut up."

Tom stretched the shoulder belt across his torso as Hillary also got belted in the back. "Hallelujah. Let's see what this thing can do." Neal flipped a switch and Tom heard the light bar on the roof start to whir. They weren't in traffic, so Neal held off on the siren. They raced through downtown Sioux City and onto the interstate for the ten-mile drive to the airport, quickly accelerating past eighty-five miles per hour.

Tom leaned over far enough to see the speedometer.

"Does this thing go any faster?" Hillary said from the back seat, just as Tom opened his mouth to ask the same thing. Tom glanced back at Hillary with a mock look of surprise. Neal just tilted his head toward Tom, raised his eyebrows and punched the gas. The police car quickly topped one hundred miles per hour.

"We'll be there in about three minutes," Neal said as he flipped a switch, activating the car's siren to accompany the lights.

"What about radioing airport security or Sergeant Bluff police?" Hillary yelled over the siren.

"If I do that, I know Benning will order me to stop," Neal said. "Let's see if there's anything out there before I announce that I'm disobeying orders."

CHAPTER 33

Barry Garrett was many things, but unprepared wasn't one of them. A few weeks ago he had readied a bag with $75,000 cash, his passport, two changes of clothes, some vital papers, his laptop computer loaded with encrypted files, and two extra magazines and a couple of boxes of ammunition for the forty-five caliber pistol he always carried. He'd stowed another quarter of a million cash onboard his plane last week and made sure it was serviced and ready to fly at a moment's notice.

When Donna Zimmerman called with news of a shooting at the Regal, Garrett instantly had a bad feeling. Stephanie was at the Regal, and Garrett was supposed to meet with her and Van Gunner there later to talk about how to handle Kingman and Reed. Garrett gave Missy an excuse and rushed from his house, the prepared bag already in the trunk of his BMW. He had headed to the Regal, planning to look the scene over from a distance, maybe spot some cars in the parking lot. But halfway there he got another call from Zimmerman, who apparently had someone on the inside at the hotel. Stephanie had been shot and was probably dead. Tom Kingman was in her room. Van Grunner had surely arrived for their meeting by then.

That and the sight of police cars at the Regal were enough for Garrett. He veered off for the interstate and told Zimmerman to meet him at the airport. She answered simply, "I'll be there in twenty minutes," and hung up. When Garrett got to the airport, he almost expected the police to be waiting for him. When they weren't there, and everything seemed like a normal early evening at the tiny, two-gate Midwestern airport, Garrett hurried through the charter customer service center and out onto the tarmac just as his plane was being pushed from its private hangar. He had just gotten aboard and was on his second scotch when Zimmerman pranced toward the plane wearing an impossibly short, tight, red skirt and carrying two bags. Zimmerman took her time climbing the steps to the plane, enjoying watching the flight crew pretend not to look up her skirt.

She dropped her luggage in the back and sat down next to Garrett, running her hand up his inseam to within an inch of the bull's-eye. "Stephanie is dead. I think Tom shot her. I don't know why, but that's what I hear. A woman was with Tom, probably Hillary Reed. I think Van Grunner was also there, but I'm not sure what he's up to. My source is a cleaning woman at the Regal I've helped out financially off and on."

"You've been keeping track of me," Garrett said, enjoying the relaxation induced by five ounces of scotch.

"Keeping track of my investment," Zimmerman said, running her hand lightly across Garrett's attentive crotch. She leaned close enough to whisper into his ear.

"I know you screwed Stephanie twice a week for three years. I don't blame you. She was a very sexy woman. I just wanted to make sure you didn't get into anything that would endanger our operation." She leaned over and kissed Garrett lightly on the lips, enjoying the sharp single-malt tang. Garrett's only response was a look of exhaustion. The crumbling of his empire made Garrett look older than his forty-four years. His normally stylish business attire had become an ill-fitting costume on an under-rehearsed actor. He was set for life, on his way to a tropical paradise, but angry that a stupid shit of a reporter had brought him down. It was a personal affront that had drained him of swagger and would take a lot of time to get over, even in paradise.

"Where should we go?" Garrett said, trying to force to himself to be upbeat.

"Bermuda?" Zimmerman said. "Some little tropical island with young, dark studs in thongs who will bring me drinks ... and a difficult extradition policy."

The phone to Garrett's left buzzed. He answered and heard the pilot say, "We're cleared to take off, Mr. Garrett."

"Where does our flight plan say we're going?"

"Miami."

"Right, get us into the air and head for Miami. I'll call you when I want to divert to that private air strip in Birmingham."

"Birmingham?" Zimmerman said. "Why Birmingham?"

"I've got a buddy down there with an air strip and a big tank of fuel just waiting," Garrett said. He hung up the phone and took off his coat, throwing it across an adjacent seat as the plane started to taxi.

"That thing is sexy," Zimmerman said, running her hand over the butt of Garrett's gun in his shoulder holster, "but why do you wear it?"

"Lately it's because I think people will want to kill me, rob me or both," Garrett said. "Don't worry, Jimmy Banks gave me a permit." Zimmerman laughed and swirled a chilling bottle of champagne in its ice bucket. Once they were airborne, she would help Garrett forget about what he was leaving behind. But first, they'd toast to the one million in bearer bonds she had taken from the Blade-Garrett vault on the way out the door.

+++

Neal topped out at one hundred and six miles per hour before turning off the interstate and onto the road that led to the airport just as his hand moved over to the police radio and turned up the volume. "Seventy-seven?" the female dispatcher said. "Seventy-seven, what's your position, please? Seventy-seven?"

"I'm car seventy-seven," Neal said to Tom. "Benning is probably freaking out because we're not at the station right now. He probably figures you shot me and took off with the car." He picked up the radio microphone and pressed the button.

"Seventy-seven. Ogden Avenue approaching the airport. I'm in pursuit of a suspect. Request cover at Sioux Gateway Airport." Sioux City's airport had the unfortunate FAA designation of "SUX." Local residents had decided to embrace and have fun with it, even creating a "Fly SUX" line of apparel to promote flying from Sioux Gateway rather than the much larger Omaha airport.

"Seventy-seven? L-4." It was Benning. "Powers, where the hell are you?"

"I'm at the airport, Lieutenant, acting on information from a witness."

"What witness? Get your ass back in to the station or you're through in this department, do you hear that, officer?"

"Seventy-seven. Requesting cover at the airport," Neal repeated.

"Just stay there. I'm on my way," Benning hissed.

Neal clipped the microphone to its holder on the middle console. "I hear pensions are overrated anyway," he said.

Neal's replacing the microphone caused Tom to notice that this old-school police car was complete with a sawed-off shotgun held vertically in a bracket by the radio. Neal braked hard to a stop in front of the charter service and killed the engine. Tom bounced out of the car, realized Hillary couldn't open her door from the inside and quickly freed her from the back seat.

"Does Garrett have a white jet with a green stripe?" Neal said, looking across the roof of the car, past Tom.

"Yeah. Green and white," Tom said as Hillary stepped out of the car. "You know anyone else in Sioux City who can support a corporate *jet*?"

"Shit," Neal spat as he ducked back into the car like he was taking sniper fire. Neal was starting the car as Tom and Hillary looked at each other and then caught sight of the taxiing jet headed for the main runway about a hundred yards away.

Tom's butt had barely hit his seat when Neal sent blue smoke rolling off the spinning back tires. The car flashed through an open gate leading to the tarmac in front of the charter service's garages.

"I'm in such deep shit now, I might as well get fired *and* sued," Neal said as he flipped on the patrol car's siren while they pursued the plane, which was turning into takeoff position about seventy-five yards in front of them.

Hope this old pig of a car can make it that far.

"You're sure that's Garrett's plane, Tom?" Hillary yelled. Tom was glad to know she had made it back into the car before Neal floored it.

"It's Garrett's. I was inside it once when we did a feature on him. Took his photo in there. I remember the tail—Bravo Gulf Whisky—Blade Garrett Worldwide—and the big green stripe. I thought 'dollar green' at the time."

Neal's car was about fifty yards behind the plane as it paused before starting its final takeoff roll. Tom knew they had about 500 feet to stop the plane before it got airborne. He turned to Neal. "Give me my gun."

"Are you nuts?" Neal said.

"I'm stopping that plane if I have to jump in between the wheels, Neal. Now give me my gun." Neal had just started his responding protest when two small holes appeared in the windshield and one in Hillary's window.

"Watch out," Hillary yelled from the back, slumping down in the seat.

"What the fuck?" Tom yelled as he popped his seat belt and slid down, trying to use the dash for cover. Tom saw Garrett hanging out the open door of the plane, waving his .45 at them. Neal swerved directly behind the plane's tail to get them out of the line of fire. He handed Tom his gun.

"Run us close and I'll go for the tires," he screamed over the rush of wind and wail of siren. Neal would have to widen his angle at the last second and tuck the hood of the car under the plane's left wing to give Tom a shot. He closed on the plane, which was picking up speed, and at the last second swerved to the left and under the wing.

Tom aimed in the general direction of the landing gear and fired three times. The gun recoil sent the second and third shots into the plane fuselage above the wheels as the spent shell casings tinkled down the runway in their wake. This was a little different than shooting paper targets at the firing range.

Almost as soon as Tom started firing, he saw muzzle flashes from the plane's open door. Garrett was going for the windshield. It suddenly struck Tom that he had only five shots left in his magazine. He took more careful aim at the wheels when another muzzle flash came from the inside of the door. Neal let out an animal scream and the car veered violently to the right, nearly hitting the plane and pulling Tom back through the window and into Neal's side.

Tom saw nothing but the blue cotton of a police uniform as he struggled to control his flailing gun hand and overcome the momentum that had hurled him into Neal. A second later, Tom recognized the scent of Hillary's hair, which for a nanosecond struck Tom as a ludicrous thing to notice given the chaos of the moment. Then he realized her body was draped over his.

Neal let out another yell as the car lurched back to the left, throwing Tom back against the passenger side door hard enough to make him worry about falling out.

When he managed to focus on the driver's seat, he saw Neal clutching his shoulder. Hillary, the front of her blouse smeared with blood, was steering the car, her abdomen balanced on the back of the car seat while her feet bobbed in the air. For a horrible second, Tom thought Hillary had been shot. But when he looked closer he saw the blood was smeared onto an undamaged blouse. No bullet hole. It was Neal's blood. The car started to slow.

"Don't you stop," Hillary screamed at Neal.

Neal stomped the accelerator again, causing the car to leap forward.

"I've got it," Neal growled. His left hand, covered with blood from his right shoulder wound, was now back on the steering wheel as blood trickled down his right arm which lay lifeless at his side. Neal picked up speed as Hillary flopped back on the back seat with a thud before reappearing just in back of Tom's head.

"Give me that *fucking* shotgun," Hillary barked.

Hillary's profanity struck Tom as if they had just hit a monster pothole. Tom looked at Neal, who was breathing hard through his nose and closing on the plane, which was already starting to nose up.

Two more shots rang out from the doorway, both thudding into the car hood with the sound of a can opener puncturing a tin can. Tom's hope—or was it a prayer?—that the bullets hadn't killed the car was answered with no sudden decrease in speed.

The door of the plane closed again. Its nose wheels would come off the ground any second.

"Give her the fucking shotgun," Neal said, matter-of-factly.

Tom laid his gun on the seat and unclamped the pump-action shotgun. "Loaded?" he asked. Neal nodded. Tom handed it butt first into the back seat and heard Hillary jack a shell into the chamber.

"After this is over, Hillary," Tom said, "we've got to talk about your language and this whole gun thing you've got going on."

"Get us up there, Neal," Hillary yelled. "Tom, put every round you have left into the engine. Watch out for my head. The wheels are mine. Neal, if we miss, you ram that *son-of-a-bitch*."

Hawt.

Hillary turned to the bullet-riddled back passenger-side window, reared back and slammed the shotgun butt into it, sending the entire window dancing down the runway behind them. Their car closed on the plane, approaching from behind so fast that Tom worried about the tail coming through the windshield. At the last possible second, Neal swerved left to give Tom and Hillary a better angle and tucked the nose of the car right under the wing.

Tom and Hillary were halfway out the window simultaneously. Tom took one second's extra care to aim and fired.

First shot.

Second shot.

First shotgun blast.

Third shot.

Fourth shot.

A second shotgun blast.

Fifth shot.

A third shotgun blast.

The slide on Tom's pistol flew back and stayed there, confirming that it was empty. At the same moment the plane veered wildly to its left and Tom and Hillary ducked back into the car just as the car and plane made contact.

The car's roof crumpled slightly as it locked together with the plane and slid one and a half revolutions, tire smoke and jet exhaust mingling. During the spiral, Tom expected burning airplane fuel to splash his face like hellish aftershave. He imagined the contents of ruptured aircraft fuel tanks flooding the car and instantly roaring into an inferno, melting car and occupants into goo.

The fire didn't come. Seconds after the plane and car finally stopped sliding, Tom heard something land heavily on the roof of the car and shatter the police light bar. From under the dash, Tom heard two quick steps on the hood and the sound of someone jumping onto the ground. It had to be Garrett.

Neal was struggling to unfasten his seatbelt by reaching over his body with his left hand. Tom reached out and stabbed the seatbelt button, freeing Neal, who managed to use his left hand to draw his from its right-handed holster.

Tom followed Neal out the door, pivoted and opened the back door. "Hillary!" She appeared, still holding the shotgun. A small cut under her ear, near the jaw line, oozed a bit of blood. "Are you okay?"

Hillary nodded and gestured toward Garrett. "He's headed for the cornfield."

Like hell he is.

Ten strides into his pursuit, Tom realized he was unarmed. His empty gun was still back on the car seat. If Garrett had a gun, he just had to stop and turn around. At this distance, with no cover, Tom was dead. He needed to overtake Garrett before he had the same epiphany.

Garrett was about forty feet from the cornfield. Tom had no idea where Hillary and Neal were. He thought of Hillary.

Please God, don't let this asshole kill me.

Tom reached deep for one last burst of speed and dove at Garrett's waist. He hit him in a glancing blow, but fell across the back of Garrett's legs, spanking Garrett's upper body to the ground and sending his .45 skittering across the tarmac until it plunked into standing water just off the runway.

I got you now, motherfucker.

Garrett lashed out at Tom with his left fist, catching him square on the side of the head. Tom rolled over, stunned by the punch and seeing flashes of black. He sensed some Garrett body part near his shoulder and grabbed on. It turned out to be Garrett's head. Garrett responded by biting Tom under the left arm.

"Stop biting me, you freaky bastard," Tom screamed and threw his knee into some section of Garrett, causing Garrett to gurgle pain from underneath Tom's arm. "I am really getting sick"—Tom landed a left—"of being shot at"—he drove a knee into some part of Garrett—"all the time."

Something hit Garrett with a thud, and Tom felt him to go limp. Tom drove another knee into Garrett and rolled away, getting himself between Garrett and the submerged gun. As Tom rolled onto his back, he saw Garrett's slumped body and torn suit five feet away.

"Uh-uh," said a female voice. "I don't think so, Mr. Garrett. This ride is all over." Hillary stood over Garrett. She had clubbed him with the butt of her shotgun and now had it pointed right at his crotch.

"You have the right to remain silent," Hillary said almost playfully. "You also have the right to lie still, or I'll exercise my right to blow your balls off."

Hillary turned her head toward Tom, held the shotgun with only her right hand, ran her left hand through her hair and smiled.

Amen.

Tom flopped back onto the tarmac and coughed out a laugh, his chest still heaving from the sprint. He heard running footsteps and sirens in the distance. A pinch from his empty holster distracted Tom just as he raised his left arm and looked at his watch, calculating the hours until deadline.

What a story.

CHAPTER 34

From a room on the fourth floor of Northwest Iowa Regional Medical Center, Tom could see the Veterans Memorial Park, its straw-colored grass writhing in a hot wind as if pleading for water. Heat shimmered off the massive spinning air conditioners on the white-pebbled roof two floors below.

Sioux City's streak of days over ninety degrees had hit eleven by noon. After the events of the last week, he would be content to do weather stories for a while. Despite the sweltering scene outside, Tom shuddered subtly in the room's chilled, disinfectant-laced air. Forty-eight hours had passed since Tom and Hillary had shot down their first enemy aircraft. Hillary's third and fourth shotgun blasts left gaping holes in the left rear landing gear tire. Tom had scored four out of five hits on the engine, which a mechanical post mortem proved were fatal wounds for the Learjet.

Neal had ordered the pilot and a disheveled Donna Zimmerman out of the plane, made them handcuff themselves to a runway marker, and then helped Hillary hold Garrett face down on the tarmac. Garrett had mumbled something into the concrete about suing for false arrest. Benning and three other police cars had arrived a minute or so later. While officers with med kits had attended to Neal's shoulder, Hillary and Tom had sat together on the tarmac, staring with a mixture of shock and fascination as

Benning had launched into a tirade about "interference with official acts," carrying a weapon without a permit, destroying Officer Neal Powers' career, exposing the city to legal liability and blah blah blah.

By the time Benning had finished, Tom was on paragraph fifteen of his mental first draft. Bear had met the cars at the station and demanded that Tom be charged or released on the spot, making it clear that charging him would bring an encampment of journalists to Sioux City by morning. Since then Tom had written his stories and given his formal statement, and now sat in front of Neal's hospital bed.

"I liked your stories," Neal said. Tom turned his head from looking out the window to focus on Neal, who was propped up in bed. "You stayed pretty straight and didn't hype it too much. The bits about me getting shot made my wife queasy, but she's okay. My sons think it's kind of cool, now that they know I'll be all right. I saw we made the network TV news last night. Maybe I should get an agent."

"Thanks. I couldn't have done it without you." Tom stretched back in his chair. He'd written a story about the chase and arrest for the morning after the shooting and then written an exhaustive story the next day about the investigation and the results of search warrants and police interviews that continued to unravel the Garrett empire. Hillary had made good on her offer of front row seats as Garrett went down.

Stephanie's body was barely cold when the regional media started showing up in Sioux City. And, since it involved the hot topic of methamphetamine, a few national media types brought their blow dryers to Iowa in order to stay a few days as well. He'd heard that at least one network anchor might even show up to host the nightly national news focused on the "American Meth Problem" live from Sioux City.

Tom lamented that his town was getting all the attention for a relatively small problem. Maybe they would at least work in a few of the many great stories about Siouxland.

Faced with statements from Hillary and Tom, Tom's audio tape and Hillary's video, Van Grunner had decided to make a deal with state and federal prosecutors. His shooting of Pollard, even though it was contrived, *had* been justified. Nobody had been able to prove Stephanie's *hypothetical* scenario of Van Grunner setting it all up. So far nothing in the investigation pointed to any other cops being involved, much to Chief Banks's relief.

"The doctors say I could get out late today or tomorrow morning," Neal said. "The wound was a little bit tricky and they just want to make sure there's no infection. They say no permanent damage."

"Well, I'm just glad you were only winged," Tom said.

"So am I," said an increasingly familiar voice from behind him. Tom turned to see Hillary in the doorway.

Casual skirt, tan legs, and that fabulous auburn hair.

After all the gunfire had died down, their various duties had kept Tom and Hillary apart much of the time. Tom had managed to see her a night later for dinner at her place. They spent a few hours talking about everything except work. There was no talk of "spending the night," whatever that might have meant. Tom was strangely relieved that he didn't have to deal with that relationship milestone at this point in his frazzled life.

For some reason, maybe because of all they had been through together, Tom now felt more relaxed with Hillary than he ever had with anyone else, male or female. There were a still few stones in the road, the Bible being one of them. Hillary swore by it. Tom swore with it. He found himself being more careful in his speech around Hillary.

The scriptures notwithstanding, Tom was interested enough to take the next few days off just to see more of Hillary. While the newsroom buzzed over his leaving a hot story, Tom let Skip and a stable of eager, young *Sentinel-Leader* talent take his place in the news feeding frenzy. For the first time ever, Tom needed a break from the hunt. Then again he'd never been on a hunt like this most recent one.

"Hi, Hillary," Tom said turning to the door, the warmth of his eyes matching hers.

"Hello, Tom," she said softly, allowing her gaze to hang on Tom for an extra second before turning to Neal.

"Good news, Neal," Hillary said. "Benning has gotten hold of himself and no longer wants to assign you to moping halls for the rest of your life. The publicity," she nodded slightly at Tom, "in this case has everyone thinking, rightly, that you're a hero for taking the initiative and acting so decisively to bring this major drug dealer to justice. You sounded great on NBC last night, by the way."

"I was really nervous," Neal confessed.

"I'm sure the fact that Mr. Garrett is turning out to be the Crank Kingpin of the upper Midwest, and the fact that this police administration had no clue about it until Officer Powers here stopped the plane, did have some bearing on Benning's attitude toward Neal," Tom said. "The department needs a few heroes and some good press right about now. There are a lot of good people down there. And give Garrett credit, he had an amazing system for covering himself that worked for years."

"We'll probably be investigating and prosecuting this for years," Hillary said, flopping into a chair next to Tom.

"We?" he said

"Well, maybe not you-and-me we. For sure not me. I told Dick that, considering I shot a woman and an airplane involved in this case, maybe I wasn't the best person to handle the prosecution."

"What kind of deal is that?" Tom sat forward. "Shoot a suspect, shoot down a plane and you think you shouldn't lead the prosecution? Who says lawyers have no ethics?"

"I'm sure he gave you no argument on resigning from this

case," Neal said. His smile shifted to a grimace when he absent-mindedly moved his shoulder.

"Sounds like at least they're not all knotted up about you shooting Stephanie," Tom said.

"No. Thank God for your recording, Tom. It's a great record of what happened and shows it was all self-defense and we gave her more than ample opportunity to surrender. I may be handling low-profile cases and misdemeanors for a while to stay out of the spotlight, but this whole thing doesn't look career ending for me. Besides, there are other areas of law. I'm not locked in to being a prosecutor my whole life."

"Even without the audio, I'm sure nobody would have thought you just busted in and capped her because you didn't like her shoes," Tom said, looking at Hillary's sandaled toes.

"They were very impractical," Hillary deadpanned. "Those shoes sacrificed comfort on the altar of good looks."

"Amen and amen," Tom said, flaring his eyes at Neal, who laughed again, this time without the grimace. Hillary walked to Neal's bedside and took his left hand. "Thank you again, Neal, for chasing that plane. I'm so sorry you got shot in the process."

"Well," Neal said, squeezing Hillary's hand, "when we drove out on the tarmac, I pretty much figured if we didn't stop them, we'd all be screwed for sure, and I'd be kicking myself for the rest of my career. Our only chance for redemption was capturing Garrett before he got airborne. But I gotta admit when I let Tom give you the shotgun, I thought we were all going to jail."

"Why *did* you let Tom give me that shotgun?"

"When you dropped the f-bomb back there, I figured we might as well *all* get crazy like the white lady in the back seat. Besides, I knew you'd come over the seat and grab it yourself if Tom didn't give it to you."

"You were right about that," Hillary said. "After all we'd been through, including the Regal shooting, I wasn't going to let Garrett just fly away."

"So, Tom, are you going to jail for carrying a gun?" Neal said, turning his head from Hillary to Tom while still holding Hillary's hand.

"I doubt it," Tom answered. "Talk about bad publicity. The worst they can get me for is carrying a concealed weapon."

"'A person who goes armed with a dangerous weapon *concealed* on or about the person, or who, within the limits of any city, goes armed with a pistol or revolver, or any loaded firearm of any kind, whether *concealed* or not, commits an aggravated misdemeanor,'" Hillary recited from memory, and then smiled.

"Do you have the whole *Iowa Code* memorized?" Tom asked. "It's a little sexy, but a lot spooky."

"I only memorized the criminal section," Hillary said. Tom couldn't tell if she was kidding.

He stood up and approached Neal's bed. "I'm shooting— sorry—*hoping* for a deferred judgment so I can do some community service or something, stay straight and have the whole deal expunged from my record. I'll be on my best behavior, your honor. Felons who carry guns don't even do time for it, so I'm not too worried. They did confiscate my gun and I may never see it again, though. A few hundred bucks down the drain. But there are plenty of other guns out there."

"Maybe you need to get a lawyer," Neal said.

"All the best legal minds are prosecutors around here," Hillary interjected, "but I can recommend a few for you."

"Well, Hillary and I have to run," Tom said. " Famous people like us have packed calendars, as you can imagine. Meeting the governor for lunch, provided he can find Sioux City. President flying in this afternoon to get our views on the anti-crime bill. Some NRA meetings. That sort of thing. You understand. And then we might go eat at the mall food court."

Neal raised his good arm. "Say no more. Tell the President

hello for me. My wife and kids should be here any second. You're famous for blowing this thing open."

Tom rolled his eyes. "Famous? For what? I got a break named Stephanie who put it all in my lap, literally. She rolled over on Garrett and I was there to hear it. There's your Ace Reporter. You two did all the work. I just came along for the show."

"Make sure your family calls if they need anything," Hillary said to Neal as she grabbed Tom's arm and towed him toward the door. "Don't get him started on being 'famous.'"

The two walked down the corridor, Tom fighting an urge to take Hillary's hand like they were some kind of high school couple. "Who do you think came to your house with the shotgun, Tom?" Hillary asked in sudden seriousness.

"I think it was Garrett. Had to be. He was just making sure his boy Van Grunner had done it right."

"But how do you know?"

"I don't know for sure. He's all lawyered up and won't say anything at all. But who else could it have been?"

"Our search warrants did turn up a few shotguns among the Garrett's handguns. But what about the red BMW? There is more than one of them around."

"My friend at the DMV ran a query on all red BMWs in the metro. There are only forty-one but they're all registered to very upstanding rich people with no apparent connection to Garrett. It may have come from outside the county or maybe I got the color wrong. It was dark and raining hard and I was connected by the ankle to a dog chain if you recall."

"Guess we'll never know for sure," Hillary said. "I do know that Garrett's being held in the county jail on a huge bond, which he won't be able to post since most of his assets are frozen, so he won't be paying anyone visits for a while." They went together through the revolving door.

"God, it's hot out here," Hillary said.

"Was that another prayer?" Tom said, a little surprised at Hillary's use of "God." Maybe she wasn't quite as Puritan as he thought. "Because we could use the Almighty on this heat wave. Another week over ninety and I'm going to pop. Take it up with him, will ya? Days in the eighties, rain at night?"

"You sure seem interested in my prayer life," Hillary said casually. "Maybe you should come with me to church."

"Whoa there, Hill," Tom said holding up one hand. "Let's not get nutty. I'm all for taking things slow. Speaking of taking things, let's take my car. We can leave yours here for the antique lovers to admire."

"Your car? With the unreliable air conditioning? Pass."

"Come on, I got it fixed."

Hillary rolled her eyes and reluctantly followed Tom through the parking lot.

"Do you think you can get anybody for killing Pollard?" Tom asked.

Hillary stopped and looked at him.

"Off the record, of course," Tom said, making exaggerated eye movements from side to side, as if looking for anyone listening or following.

Hillary sighed. "Doesn't look good. Van Grunner was smart or lucky enough not to implicate himself on my video. It didn't help our case that I cut him off when I did, but if Van Grunner had admitted that he conspired to kill Pollard he would have probably killed us both. You can only go to prison for life once, no matter how many you kill, so I stopped him soon enough to give him a reason to keep us alive—even if it did totally flush my murder prosecution."

"And Stephanie's whole *hypothetical* example on my tape isn't evidence of anything," Tom said.

"Even if we use that as a blueprint to how they did it," Hillary said, "we can't find any evidence. The 9-1-1 call was from a reloadable phone purchased at Target, with cash, farther back than store security tapes go. We can't place Pollard together with Garrett or Van Grunner before the shooting, except for way back when they both worked at Blade-Garrett. Pollard had methamphetamine in him, but we can't prove where he got it or that Garrett deliberately loaded him up with it. We just don't have anything on the shooting."

Tom suddenly veered off to the driver's side of a new black Mustang. Hillary stopped in mid-sentence and turned sharply to follow.

"Thank you for borrowing a car with a functioning AC," she said, admiring the sparkling car. Tom unlocked her door with the key fob and got in. As Hillary buckled in, inhaling the new-car smell, Tom sat back and started the engine, turning the air conditioner on high and enjoying the immediate rush of cool air.

"Whose car is this?" Hillary said.

Tom looked at her for a second and then held his thumb and forefinger about three inches apart, blocking out each word in a mid-air headline as he said it. "By Tom Kingman, New Mustang Owner."

Hillary laughed. "This is your car? When did you buy it?"

"Picked it up this morning."

"The paper must be paying more than I imagined."

"I drove that piece of crap Taurus for years saving for this … and Bear gave me a sort of signing bonus," Tom said. "He asked for my commitment to stay with the paper at least another three years. With the bonus and raise he offered, plus the money I'd saved up, I decided to buy this. I got tired of sweating my ass off and playing Car Start Roulette every day in my old car. Plus, the last week has given me a bit more incentive to enjoy life while I can. *And* this one has more room under the seat for my gun."

"Gun?"

"*Kidding*, Hillary. No guns. I'm unarmed."

"You know," Hillary said, looking around the car's interior, "this is rear-wheel drive. Not that practical in the snow."

"Like that Camaro of yours?" Tom said. "Any luck finding an eight-track for that thing?"

"I just figured you as a four-wheel-drive kind of man," Hillary said, injecting artificial bass into her voice.

"Thank you for that," Tom said. He gave the accelerator a jab with his foot, causing a throaty roar from the engine. "Two point three liter turbocharged engine, three hundred ten horsepower. I wanted something that could chase down airplanes."

Hillary raised her eyebrows and nodded steadily. "It will probably be good for that." Tom put his arm over the back of the seat, letting his fingers brush Hillary's hair, and turned so he could back the car out of its parking spot.

"So you accepted Bear's offer?" Hillary said with a suddenness that surprised Tom.

"I said, 'I'll stay for three years if Skip stays for three years.' Skip and I are sort of a team. So Bear made a contribution to Skip's daughters' college fund."

"The *Minneapolis Intelligencer* calling you twice in one week with job offers had nothing to do with Bear's offer, I'm sure," Hillary said.

"Ah, Minneapolis. I couldn't deal with that traffic. And, no, it had nothing to do with the events that led up to us sitting in this sweet ride, which has heated *and* cooled seats, by the way. I told Bear I'd stay. We didn't sign anything, of course, but I gave him my word and that's all it takes with Bear and me. I wasn't looking to leave Sioux City, *not now*, so I was going to stay anyway. But, I accepted the raise. It would have been rude to turn it down."

Tom backed out and headed for Sioux City's only shopping mall. He glanced in his rearview mirror as the car turned from the parking ramp to the street. Was that a red sports car about a block back, by the curb? Small driver. Could have been a woman. Dark hair. By the time he looked again three other cars had blocked his view.

"So looks like *we're* not moving for three years, Tom Kingman, Mustang Owner." The word *we're* chased the vision of a red car out of Tom's head.

Must have been fatigue and leftover paranoia.

"But *we* are going somewhere, right?" Hillary asked, running a hand through her hair.

Tom looked at her and smiled. "Are we off the record?"

— The End —

ACKNOWLEDGMENTS

If I relied solely on my own efforts, this book would still be a crappy blob of Word files born in 1998 and destined to remain forever imprisoned on my hard drive. I'm thankful to the many friends who have helped me transform it instead into the book you're reading. Thanks to author, friend and Morningside College class-mate, Diane McCallum, who first inspired me to dust off *Officer Involved* after more than a decade of hibernation. Thanks also to author and friend, Tammy Kaehler, whose amazing insight and advice dramatically improved my manuscript, and to friend and editing pro, Phyllis Yearick, for her exceptional skills and support.

I'm also in debt to the many other friends and family who read my manuscript and offered honest appraisals that improved it with each reading. I'm also grateful to everyone at Mill City Press, who helped me see this printed in my lifetime. And here's to the people of the Siouxland—an area that includes Sioux City, Iowa; South Sioux City, Nebraska; and North Sioux City, South Dakota where I went to college and lived for fifteen years—for the setting my characters get to explore. Some of my favorite Siouxlanders are my former colleagues at the *Sioux City Journal*, who inspired the creation of Tom Kingman, and the members of the Woodbury County Attorney's staff, who inspired the creation of Hillary Reed.

Finally, thanks to my daughters, Jena and Haley, and my wife and life partner, Rhonda, who endured my rants, long seasons of self-doubt and moments of manic excitement both in general and in connection with this book. Rhonda's love and support sustain me in all I do, including writing.

Oh, and you! The prospect that you will be even slightly entertained by this book kept me going through the nearly twenty-year odyssey of getting it into your hands. Thank you for reading my book.

Bill Zahren
June 8, 2015
West Des Moines, IA

Psalm 136:26

ABOUT THE AUTHOR

Bill Zahren is a fifth-generation Iowan born in Lake Park. He graduated from Morningside College in Sioux City, Iowa, and worked for the *Le Mars Daily Sentinel* and *Sioux City Journal* before moving to West Des Moines where he now lives with his wife, Rhonda. Bill and Rhonda have two daughters, Haley and Jena. Bill works as a full-time freelance marketing writer when not drafting the latest adventures of Tom Kingman and Hillary Reed.

Follow Bill at:
Twitter: @BillZahren
Web: www.billzahren.com
Facebook: facebook.com/billzahrenauthor

CPSIA information can be obtained
at www.ICGtesting.com
Printed in the USA
FFOW05n0928021015

9 781634 137720